I0634630

BRIDGE
of LIES

BRIDGE
of LIES

Greg Dinallo

INTEGRATED MEDIA
NEW YORK

All rights reserved, including without limitation the right to reproduce this book or any portion thereof in any form or by any means, whether electronic or mechanical, now known or hereinafter invented, without the express written permission of the publisher.

This is a work of fiction. Names, characters, places, events, and incidents either are the product of the author's imagination or are used fictitiously. Any resemblance to actual persons, living or dead, businesses, companies, events, or locales is entirely coincidental.

Copyright © 2021 by Greg Dinallo

978-1-5040-7380-6

Published in 2021 by Open Road Integrated Media, Inc.
180 Maiden Lane
New York, NY 10038
www.openroadmedia.com

For my wife Gloria, the love and center of my life for sixty-four incredible years. I miss her terribly.

BRIDGE
of LIES

Prologue

"Let's talk Vladimir Putin," the president said as he swept into the Oval Office, joining several members of his staff. He dropped his copy of the day's National Security Briefing on his desk and settled in, framed by the bulletproof windows that overlooked the wintry Rose Garden. "For years he's been covering Assad's ass and blocking resolutions condemning Syria's government for war crimes. When I slammed him at the summit for Russia's aggression in Ukraine and the Crimea, he changed the subject to Syria. Shortly thereafter he authorizes airstrikes on Syrian rebels. Why? What's his strategy?"

Chief of Staff McDonough's chiseled features were taut with frustration. "He's spoiling for a fight, sir. A top Russian think tank just released a report that states: The main goal of Putin's foreign policy is to make an enemy of the United States."

"You left out the part about him openly despising me," the president said with a wry smile.

"He's desperate," McDonough went on. "The political opposition is relentless, *The Economist* is beating him up on a weekly basis, and the price of oil's in the toilet and taking the ruble and the economy down with it. He feels frustrated, irrelevant . . ."

The president nodded in amused reflection. "I can empathize."

CIA Director Brennan smiled thinly. "Furthermore, unemployment is so high he's using pension funds to build infrastructure to create jobs, and he's pressuring the oligarchs to divest from global markets in case push comes to shove with the West—which it will, thanks to the mess in Ukraine and the Crimea. Not to mention Merkel thinks he's delusional. She really has his number." He chuckled at a thought. "Though I hear his Lab had hers the other day."

The president arched a brow. "His Lab?"

The DCI nodded. "She was scolding Vlad for the airstrikes when the animal came bounding into his office and earned its crotch-hound merit badge."

The president smiled and glanced over at the family dog curled next to his chair. "Don't think Bo's got the chops for it. So, where we going with this?"

"The key to this guy is his psychology," National Security Adviser Rice replied. "The more insecure he feels, the more he lashes out: The crackdowns on gays and intellectuals, the Pussy Riot thing, political prosecutions, taking control of the media . . ."

"Tell me about it," the DCI said. "The man has a massive ego. It's not about foreign policy, it's about him, about lost power, lost empire, lost glory. He's a Cold War warrior driven to restore the influence once wielded by the Soviet Union. That, and the fact that he despises Clinton, is what drove him to dump Medvedev and trash the reset."

"Bull's-eye," the president said decisively. "He's operating from a position of weakness. NATO makes him feel especially vulnerable. Way I see it, his support of Syria is sleight of hand, a diversion to shift our focus from Ukraine, Crimea, and the Baltics, where it should be."

The NSA nodded. Her voice took on an edgy rasp. "The pressure to act is on us, sir. I'm forced to ask, what is the appropriate response?"

"Proceed with the G20. Ratchet up economic sanctions. Cancel round two of the London talks," the president replied without missing a beat. The latter referred to meetings between the secretary of defense and his Russian counterpart to coordinate military actions in Syrian war zones. "And . . ." the president added, "I appreciate that no one uttered the phrase 'no-fly zone' preceded by the adjective 'Syrian.'"

McDonough glanced at his watch. "Putin's in Sochi. If I place the call now—"

The president's brows went up. "No. He may have made it to the top of the ladder at the UN, but we're going to keep him on a lower rung. Let John handle it," he said referring to the secretary of state. "Anything else?"

"Well, today is Terror Tuesday, sir," the DCI replied, reminding the president that on the second Tuesday of every month he decided which of the terrorists tracked down by the National Counterterrorism Center would be targeted by drone strikes. "I have the kill list here," Brennan went on, slipping a folder from his briefcase.

The president waved him off. "We'll get there." He came out from behind his desk and dropped into one of the side chairs. "State of the Union on that punch list?"

"Yes, sir. Hemingway's working on a draft," McDonough replied referring to the president's bearded speechwriter. "I'll book you some face time."

"Good. My favorite speech of the year. I really enjoyed teaching constitutional law to my students, but I love teaching it to the Supremes."

The assembled staffers broke into laughter.

"Anything else?" the president asked again, signaling he wanted to move on.

McDonough nodded. "Two items: You're proclaiming today National Pearl Harbor Remembrance Day, and one of our Joint Task Force people got a heads-up on a story by the Russian journalist Nina Grafinskaya that's running in *Novaya Gazeta* tomorrow."

"Grafinskaya. She blew the whistle on Serdyukov, didn't she?" the president said, referring to Russia's former defense minister who perpetrated a $230 million tax fraud.

"Yes, sir. She and a colleague named Katkov have exposed many cases of government corruption. She's blowing the whistle on Putin now. According to her sources, despite forcing the oligarchs to bring the bacon back home, the Kremlin is planning to invest heavily in our financial markets instead of their own."

The president's brows went up. "Assuming Ms. Grafinskaya's sources are right, do we know which sectors the Kremlin is targeting and why?"

"No sir. Our people are trying to establish an encrypted email connection with Ms. Grafinskaya before asking for more details."

"Keep me posted," the president said, shifting his look to the kill list atop the DCI's briefcase. "Okay, John, who's in the cross hairs this week?"

"A number of high-value targets, sir—one of particular interest in Yemen."

A short time later, at Villa Bocharov Ruchey in Sochi, Vladimir Putin finished the last of his twenty laps and pulled himself from the pool. His dacha, high above the Black Sea, had docking facilities, a helipad, a tennis court, and two swimming pools. He used the saltwater one daily under the watchful eyes of armed bodyguards, one of whom handed him a towel that he used to dry his Botox-smoothed face. He slipped into a robe, then noticed an aide standing at a respectful distance. "You have that look, Sergey."

Foreign Minister Lavrov nodded. A thin smile tugged at the corners of his mouth. "I've just had a call from Kerry."

"Sanctions are being tightened. The London talks are off," Putin said. It was a statement, not a question.

"Yes sir, as you predicted."

Putin allowed himself a self-satisfied smile. A short time later, showered and zipped into a Sochi Winter Olympics jogging suit, he joined Lavrov and a group of aides in the dacha's conference room. It had several large flat-screen televisions, an oval table encircled by plush armchairs, and a view of the sea "So, we're rid of the Americans, their meddling president, and his Reset button for the foreseeable future . . ."

Lavrov lit a cigarette, seeming to preen. "The conventional wisdom is his foreign policy is a total failure. Mother Russia won't be a priority for the rest of his term."

Putin's eyes flared with contempt. "That won't stop them from treating the Motherland like a second-rate power! I vowed to end her humiliation and restore her dominance, and I will. Ukraine has been destabilized, NATO is rattled, and when we start building that bridge to the Crimean Peninsula, they'll get the message."

"If I may, sir . . ." Mikhail Patrushev began in a deferential tone. The deputy chief of the FSB, which took over where the KGB left off, had thoughtful eyes and a narrow face topped by a shock of gray hair. "I understand there is a gambit in play that suggests it might be wise at this time to refrain from any further such provocations, and allow the brilliant masterstrokes you just referenced, along with our great triumphs in Sochi, to continue to enhance our global image while lulling the Americans into—"

"Lulling?!" Putin erupted. "I'm not interested in lulling, I'm interested in dominating! In stopping the Americans in their tracks. Not for a month or a year but forever!" Putin's eyes hardened in bitter reflection. "9/11 was the real Christmas gift, not Snowden. But we wasted it. We need to create another such opportunity." He glanced to an ascetic-looking man at the far end of the table. Alexie Bortnikov, chief of the FSB, was Patrushev's boss. "I don't mean to wake you Alexie, but I expect *you* to take the lead on such matters."

"I prefer to listen before I leap, sir," Bortnikov said with an amused glance at Patrushev. "I believe Nikolai Misha was about to report Directorate-S has developed a covert operation with the potential to achieve your goals. We refer to it internally as the Adamov Op."

"Your disarming tribute is much appreciated, Alexie," Putin said, acknowledging that Adamov was a cover name he'd used as a KGB agent in Berlin in the 1980s. He let Bortnikov bask in it for a moment, then erupted. "But I can be contacted via email, snail mail, cell phone, text, and courier. Have I been deleted from your distribution list?!"

"No, sir. We wanted to be sure it was viable before bringing in Yakunin to brief you," Bortnikov replied, referring to the head of the Russian railway system. "But—"

"Yakunin?" Putin interrupted, looking puzzled. "He makes the trains run on time. Are you saying this *gambit*, that will stop the Americans, is *his*?"

"Yes sir," Bortnikov replied coolly. "And it's a very good one—a time-sensitive plan—that could destabilize the American government for a very long time. Despite that debacle in 2010 when the CIA rolled up our sleepers, one highly skilled asset, embedded in their national security apparatus, eluded the dragnet and has been working on it. But at the moment, it's in danger of being compromised."

"By whom?" Putin asked in a concerned hiss.

Bortnikov slipped a printout from a folder and handed it to him. "The front-page story in tomorrow's *Novaya Gazeta*, sir."

"Grafinskaya?" Putin groaned on seeing the journalist's byline. "Again?"

The FSB chief nodded. "She claims, that despite pressuring the oligarchs to bring their wealth home, you're planning to secretly invest billions of pension assets in the United States."

"She's right," Putin said sharply. "And I'm fully committed to making it happen, but I'm tired of her accusations, her efforts to demean the Motherland, her . . . her treasonous diatribes. She's dangerous and must be stopped."

"Sir, just to be clear, are you suggesting—"

"I'm suggesting you do what's good for your country," Putin interrupted. He paused, letting his chest fill with pride. "You recall my speech on Russia Day?"

"Yes, sir. It was stirring."

"You recall what I said of the Western powers?"

"You said, 'Either we will beat them, or they will beat us.'"

Putin smiled. "You have your answer." His head cocked in thought. "You said this Adamov Op, as you call it, is time sensitive. How sensitive?"

"Within sixty days, sir," Bortnikov replied. "At which time America will be in turmoil, and Mother Russia will be garnering the international respect and acclaim she deserves. The details are highly compartmentalized. I can be more specific in private."

Putin shook his head no. "I need deniability, not details," he snapped. "Total, absolute, irrefutable deniability. Destroy, destabilize, incapacitate the United States government? Yes. Start World War Three? No. This cannot, I repeat, *cannot* be connected to the Motherland or to me in any way. If you can't guarantee it, pull the plug now. Right now."

"The cell executing the op is staffed with some of our most accomplished, skilled, and dedicated operatives, sir. They would fall on their swords to protect you and Mother Russia."

"As will you, if you're wrong." Putin burned him with a look and added. "No progress reports. We will not speak of this again. Is that clear?"

"Yes, sir. We won't disappoint you."

Putin nodded smartly. His eyes shifted and locked onto Lavrov's with a decisive glint. "We must change our strategy, Sergey. And, as Deputy Patrushev has so wisely suggested, for the next sixty days, our entire approach to the Americans must be, dare I say, *reset*. While SVR is executing the Adamov Op, we will be *enhancing* our global image—and attending to more pressing matters at home." A wolfish grin curled a corner of his mouth, then his eyes hardened and found Bortnikov's. "Grafinskaya . . ."

The FSB chief nodded, getting the message.

"And her sources," Putin added, eyeing him and the others with suspicion.

Chapter One

Nikolai Katkov had four women in his life whom he loved with selfless abandon: His mother, a caring educator, whose eighty-six years under Soviet rule had taught her that the path to hell was paved with good intentions—a painful lesson that failed to temper her son's zeal for investigative journalism. His ex-wife, Alexa, a physician, whom he met while being treated for wounds inflicted by KGB thugs at an anti-Brezhnev rally and whose career became endangered by his muckraking and radical politics, putting an end to their marriage. His girlfriend Vera, a militia dispatcher who alerted him to crackdowns on organized crime, political corruption, and the acts of violence they spawned, helping him to break such stories. And Nina Grafinskaya, his star student at his alma mater Moscow State University. Katkov recognized her writing skills, penetrating intelligence, and fearless determination to dig out a story were equal to his, and he brought her to *Novaya Gazeta* as his protégée. In contrast to his rumpled weariness, Grafinskaya was tailored and intense. Like many chic Moscow women, she lived in designer jeans, T-shirts, and Tods, and wore her hair pulled back, emphasizing her striking profile and eyes that always seemed to be in search of something.

Everything about Grafinskaya was chic, right down to the Williams-Sonoma apron she wore when tending her roof garden that was replete with vine-covered trellises and a glass-enclosed greenhouse, but she loved the feel of the soil between her slender fingers, fingers that could type 125 words per minute and shunned work gloves, presenting her manicurist with a daunting challenge. Indeed, the earth was considered sacred to Russians. Emigrants took small pots of soil with them to their adopted countries. Those who left for the cities kept them in their apartments, and the rich, black soil in Grafinskaya's planting beds had come from the family farm on the outskirts of Nizhny Novgorod 150 miles east of Moscow, where her parents had lived their entire lives and were now buried side by side.

On this morning, as she often did before leaving for work, Grafinskaya moved between the rows of planters in her climate-controlled greenhouse, cutting stems with her forged English pruners, and it wasn't long before she was clutching a bouquet of Russian sage, the luminous light-blue perennial that continues to bloom outdoors into October and well into winter indoors.

Novaya Gazeta's headquarters were at Number 3 Potapovsky Pereulok, a five-story concrete building opposite a fenced park about a mile from the Kremlin. Grafinskaya unlocked the door to her office and ran a finger over the mezuzah affixed to the jamb. Its ornate metal housing was well burnished by the ritual. She set her briefcase and flowers aside, discarded the wilting ones on her desk, and headed for the ladies' room with a vase for fresh water. She returned to find Katkov slouched in a side chair, reviewing a hard-copy draft of her story that claimed the Kremlin was secretly planning to invest billions of Russian pension funds in American financial markets. It would run the following morning, and he was playing devil's advocate as they had been doing for each other for nearly two decades.

"Is it airtight?" Katkov challenged. "You have a source you can trust?"

"*Sources*," Grafinskaya replied as she set the vase on the desk and began arranging the flowers. "One in Bortnikov's inner circle and the other someone close to Yakunin at RZD."

"Bortnikov?" Katkov said, his brows arching in tribute. "That's as airtight as it gets. But Yakunin?" he prompted, sounding puzzled. "He thinks free enterprise is voodoo economics. He's been banging Beijing's state-capitalism drum for ages."

"Tell me about it," Grafinskaya said. "But RZD just paid a billion for controlling interest in GEFCO, a French freight logistics company. What I don't get is American railroads are off-limits, right? It's national security stuff. I'm wondering what the hell the Kremlin's up to."

"Makes two of us. I think you need more before you can use the RZD angle."

"I know. I know. Two independent sources. Got one. Waiting on the other to confirm."

"Good call," Katkov grunted, scanning the pages through graying curls that tumbled onto his wire-framed glasses. "This para about shell corporations is a little thin."

Grafinskaya nodded, toying with the flowers. "I agree, but rumor has it a Canadian billionaire of French-Russian extraction is the front man."

"Grusha . . ." Katkov hissed, using an affectionate nickname for her. "If you're right about this . . ." he went on, moving closer to the electric heater. "You have hard data? Proof?"

"You should know better," Grafinskaya scolded playfully, flicking drops of water from the vase at him. She settled at her computer and, after several mouse clicks, turned the monitor so he could see it. "Email exchanges between directorates."

Katkov's eyes widened. The documents were stamped SOVERSHENNO SEKRETNO "*Top-secret* email exchanges," he said, lighting another cigarette as he came to grips with it. "Backed up? Protected?"

"Of course. You can always put your finger on them if need be," Grafinskaya replied, knowing there was no need to explain. "Vitaly thinks it's dangerous," she went on. Vitaly Yarshevsky was *Novaya Gazeta's* editor in chief. "I could leak it, I suppose. Publish anonymously. Use a pseudonym . . ."

Katkov frowned. "Your sources know it's you. An hour after we run it, so will FSB. There's no way you can hide." He exhaled a stream of smoke, studying her. "What is it, Grusha? I've never seen you like this. You're not yourself. It's as if you're . . . you're losing your edge."

Grafinskaya shrugged and gave a reflective sigh. "Michaela told me she and Sasha are planning to get married."

"Married? Hey, he's a nice kid, but Mika's barely twenty."

"Twenty-one." Grafinskaya glanced to a group of framed snapshots of Michaela at various ages in ballet costumes, encircling the vase. "Look at her," she went on with a wistful sigh. "All of a sudden I find myself thinking it might be nice to grow old kvelling over my grandchildren."

"You? Grow old? Never. You'll age gracefully and die typing furiously in midsentence." Katkov held her eyes. "You have to go with this, Grusha. You know you do."

"Who said anything about not going with it?" she challenged, her eyes coming to life. "You couldn't stop me if you tried."

The following morning, the story ran on *Novaya Gazeta*'s front page under the headline RUSSIAN PENSION FUNDS TO CREATE AMERICAN JOBS.

Grafinskaya had gotten in early, anticipating the response, and had spent several hours fielding calls and emails that were filling her inbox faster than she could open them. She was deleting those deemed unworthy when another appeared, sending a shiver up her spine. Her fingers froze

at the keyboard. Her eyes stared at the bold typography in the address bar
that said:

Sender: **United States Federal Bureau of Investigation.**
tjonesjttf@nctc.gov

Subject: **Your Pension Funds Article**

She toyed with the mouse, sending the cursor careening across the
screen, then moved it into position and opened the email. The message read:

*Would like to chat. Can secure encrypted link if you provide your
public key.*

Tom Jones, Special Agent in Charge
FBI Joint Terrorism Task Force
National Counterterrorism Center—McLean, Virginia 22102
tjonesfbijttf@nctc.gov

She didn't have to translate it because it was written in Russian. A
long moment passed before she clicked on Reply: *What is your "special"
area of investigation?*

The agent's reply came quickly: *The Russian Federation*

Grafinskaya typed: *I'll give it some thought.*

She sent it, took a deep breath, and hurried to an editorial meeting. She
wasted no time briefing Yarshevsky, Katkov, and other staff members on
her FBI email contact. Their reactions ranged from intrigue to caution, but
in the end they agreed with Grafinskaya, who insisted that the FBI agent
could be a very valuable source.

She knew Special Agent Jones had questions for her, and, on returning to her office, she typed up a list of questions for *him*, then attached
it to her reply along with her public encryption key. Her finger hovered
above the mouse. Then she clicked Send and leaned back in her chair,
staring at the bare trees in the snow-covered park across the street, her
head tilted in thought. Moments later, she was scrolling through a folder
labeled "Published Work" in search of an article that she'd written several
years ago.

Katkov had remained in Yarshevsky's office after the meeting to help
with damage control. The Kremlin's paper pushers were already rattling
their sabers over Grafinskaya's story. Some were demanding she reveal her

sources. Others were threatening to file charges against the newspaper for divulging classified information. While Yarshevsky huddled with *Novaya Gazeta*'s lawyers, Katkov was on the phone lobbying a former colleague, with strong connections and weak scruples, who was now gainfully employed in the Kremlin's media office.

Grafinskaya turned her attention to archiving the source material she had used for the story and organizing new material for a follow-up piece. When finished, she removed the flash drive—on which all her files were automatically backed up—from her computer and slipped it into her purse. She was gathering the rest of her things when Katkov stuck his head in the door.

"Hey, *Grandma*, you've got a lot to celebrate," he said with a jaunty laugh. "Come on, drinks are on me."

Grafinskaya tilted her head to one side and raised a suspicious brow.

"Oh, Grusha," Katkov groaned, getting the message. "Not to worry. I still have my Moscow Beginners card. *You* get the hard stuff. Caffeine and nicotine for me."

"A quick one," she said with a glance to her watch.

Katkov led the way from the office. The worn leather bag, hanging from his shoulder, was stuffed with the tools of the trade—laptop, cell phone, voice-activated recorder, spiral-bound notepad, several packs of Marlboros, and a dog-eared copy of *The Overstreet Comic Book Price Guide*. Grafinskaya locked the door, then swept a forefinger over the mezuzah.

A short time later, they were at a table in Café OGI. The crowded, smoky watering hole was favored by local intelligentsia and journalists—people who knew they weren't living in a democracy but acted as if they were.

"Nikasha . . . can I ask you something?" Grafinskaya said as the waiter set a glass of chilled vodka in front of her that Katkov eyed with a mixture of fear and longing. "Well, I mean, *Michaela* wanted me to ask you . . . if . . . if you'd give her away."

"Me?" Katkov mumbled, sounding surprised. "Yes, of course I would. But what about her . . . her . . ." He let it trail off, wishing he hadn't said it.

"Her father?" Grafinskaya prompted, her voice taking on an edge.

Katkov winced. "Something tells me he's still nowhere to be found."

Grafinskaya nodded. "Besides, Michaela wouldn't invite him, let alone ask him to walk her down the aisle."

"Guess that makes me the father of the bride," Katkov said with a laugh. "Is it formal? Do I get to wear a cutaway or—" He saw Grafinskaya's

13

expression change. She looked anxious now. Her eyes were wistful and moist. "What?"

"You . . . you *are* the father of the bride . . ." she said with trembling lips.

Katkov looked incredulous. He sat unmoving for a long moment trying to process it. "Grusha . . . are you serious?"

Grafinskaya lowered her eyes and nodded.

"My God. How? When? Why didn't you . . ." Katkov sighed and let it trail off.

"We . . . we had broken up. I was . . . was already living with Dmitry," Grafinskaya replied, groping for words. "We were young, sex-crazed, and . . . and careless. Just like *we* were, as you may recall. By the time I realized I was pregnant, I just assumed . . ."

"Assumed? Does that mean you're still not sure? Or . . ."

"Oh, I'm sure. I've known for years," Grafinskaya replied with unwavering certainty. "Since Mika was about two. Life was good. I was getting one scoop after another, Dmitry had been selected for the Bolshoi. It was exciting, a dream come true . . ."

"Yes," Katkov said, his mood brightening. "Those *were* exciting times. The Russian Spring, the promise of democracy, a free press . . ." He let it trail off, then, having heard it in her voice, prompted, "But? . . ."

"But Bolshoi policy requires new dancers take a physical. Some insurance thing. They do x-rays, scans, blood tests. Dmitry passed them all with flying colors—" Grafinskaya paused, eyes clouding at the memory. "All but one . . ."

"Which revealed he was impotent," Katkov said, finishing it.

Grafinskaya nodded solemnly. "I hadn't been with anyone else, so . . ."

"*I'm* it . . ." Katkov said with a mischievous twinkle.

Grafinskaya nodded and smiled, taken by his charm. "It didn't cost Dmitry his position with the company, but he was devastated and obsessed with the idea that I'd cheated on him. And that's when it began: the alcohol, the drugs, gone for days on end. I didn't know what to do. What to say, so I . . . I did nothing . . ." She sighed, letting it trail off with a helpless shrug.

Katkov lit a cigarette, exhaling through his nose and mouth. "Does Mika know?"

"No. No, she doesn't. I'm sorry. I . . ." Grafinskaya took a long swallow of vodka. "So many times I wanted to tell her, but when she was little it . . . it would have been too confusing. And as she got older, and Dmitry was off

God-knows-where with a needle in his arm . . . I was afraid she'd feel that she'd been rejected by *two* men, *two* fathers. So—"

"I wouldn't have rejected her, Grusha. I never have, and I won't now."

"Yes, Nikasha, you've been wonderful. I should have said something to her . . . to *you*. But I could never find the words, and there never seemed to be a right time, and . . . and Dmitry was out of our lives, and we were really happy, and I guess I was afraid of ruining it all . . ."

Katkov reached across the table and took her hand. "I think it's time to talk to Mika, don't you?"

Grafinskaya winced with uncertainty, then nodded. "I'm meeting her for dinner." She forced a laugh and, rolling her eyes, added, "I'm her official wedding planner. You think maybe . . . maybe you could come along?"

"Of course," Katkov replied, his eyes glistening. "I'm sure she'll understand." His expression brightened and, he added, "She might even like the idea. Uncle Nikasha. Papa Nikasha. Pain-in-the-ass Nikasha. I'm still me. I mean—" Katkov's cell phone rang. He grimaced, then slipped it from his shoulder bag. It was an obsolete Yota with a contacts directory and basic Internet capability. "I should take this. It's Vera."

Grafinskaya nodded.

Katkov thumbed the Talk button. "Not a good time. What's going on?"

"Lubov just popped-up on my radar," Vera replied into the pipe-stem mic affixed to her headset. "Hold on, it's coming in now," she added, eyeing her data-filled monitor.

Igor Lubov was a former KGB officer who had taken over Teknokrata, a graft-riddled government technology conglomerate. About a month earlier, Katkov wrote an exposé in *Novaya Gazeta* "Werewolves in Epaulets"—about corrupt former KGB generals and Kremlin officials who take over such businesses. The story forced the Kremlin to crank up its cosmetic anti-corruption campaign. Which meant the accused official would be arrested, brought to trial, and acquitted, slinking-off into retirement with his ill-gotten gains nestled in offshore bank accounts.

"Here we go," Vera resumed. "Yeah, yeah, a team's being dispatched."

"To where?" Katkov grunted with impatience.

"Lighten up. I'm waiting on the location."

Vera's workstation was in the basement Ops Center of No. 38 Petrovka, where militia headquarters was located—one of six such stations facing a computerized map of Moscow on which the locations of militia personnel and units were marked and constantly updated, along with crime sites as incidents were reported.

"Got it," Vera said. "According to the warrant, a militia unit and an RIC team are en route to 45 Tverskaya." The acronym stood for Russia Investigative Committee, the Kremlin's version of the United States FBI.

"Tverskaya . . . that's his girlfriend's place," Katkov said, relishing the thought.

Vera laughed. "Sounds like you're in for a fun evening!"

"I'll keep you posted." Katkov set the phone on the table and looked over the top of his wire frames at Grafinskaya with ambivalence. "They're taking Lubov down."

"Business is business," she said without missing a beat. "You should go."

"I know. I'm sorry," Katkov sighed. Half of him wanted to be with Grafinskaya when she broke the news to Michaela. The other half was driven to get the story and, if he was honest with himself, he was relieved to have been saved by the bell, to have been given time to come to grips with the startling news that Michaela was his daughter.

"Maybe it's for the best," Grafinskaya said, draining her glass. "It'll give me a chance to talk to her first."

Katkov nodded and paid the tab.

A cold wind lashed them with biting gusts as they left the café and paused on the sidewalk, hugging each other tightly, their fists buried in the puffy down of their parkas. "It'll be okay, Grusha," Katkov said as he leaned back, looking into her eyes that were moist with emotion. "It will," he went on, brushing a tear from her cheek. "I'll call you. Maybe I'll come over. Okay?"

Grafinskaya bit a lip and nodded.

They stood there for a moment, motionless, wordless, then hurried off in opposite directions. Neither had noticed the man in the sunglasses at a corner table in the café who slipped a baseball cap with a NASCAR logo over his shaved head and took his time folding his newspaper before following them outside. He paused to light a cigarette, then slipped the lighter into a pocket of his winter warmup suit and began walking in the same direction as Grafinskaya.

Chapter Two

JTTF, the FBI Joint Terrorism Task Force, was located in the National Counterterrorism Center in McLean, Virginia, a few miles from CIA headquarters. The X-shaped complex, known as Liberty Crossing, had the look of a suburban office park and sprawled across a hilltop bounded by the Capital Beltway, the Dulles Toll Road, and Dolly Madison Boulevard. Swooping interchanges sorted traffic onto a network of interstates, one of which ran arrow straight into downtown Washington, DC, ten miles east. Agents and analysts from more than forty law-enforcement agencies worked here. All wore NCTC badges—rather than those of their home agencies—to reinforce the concept of a single, integrated staff that shared data, intelligence, and analysis.

Special Agent Tom Jones made a left into Tysons McLean Drive and guided his BMW through the tree-lined turns that led to the JTTF staff parking area. A few vehicles were queued up ahead at the security kiosk. Weather forecasters were predicting the warmest December on record, and he didn't need to lower the window to swipe his CA card through the reader. He swiped it again in the lobby, then took the elevator to the third floor. Dozens of flat-screen monitors were suspended overhead displaying data on the world's trouble spots. The news crawl running across the one tuned to CNN read U.S. ADDS TO TRADE SANCTIONS ON RUSSIA. RUBLE LOSES HALF ITS VALUE.

Agent Jones strode beneath them at a brisk clip and negotiated the maze of office landscaping, exchanging patter with colleagues en route to his workstation. Lean and precise, with short-cropped hair, eliminating the need to decide whether to part it on the left or right, Tom wore fitted suits with the mandatory American-flag lapel pin, crisp white shirts, and boldly striped ties that he preferred to those dotted with frolicking animals. He drained his morning latte, tossed the container in the trash, and checked his emails. Several dozen bold-faced entries filled the inbox. His eyes darted to one that read:

Sender: **ngrafinskaya@novayagazeta.ru**

Subject: ***Re: Re: Your Article***

He smiled on seeing Grafinskaya had attached her public encryption key, and he used it to access her list of questions. Her exposé—that the Kremlin was planning to invest billions of Russia's pension funds in the American economy instead of its own intrigued him because it raised a simple question: Was it the makings of a scandal that might merely embarrass the Kremlin, or was it a matter of national security that might endanger the United States? Several questions on Grafinskaya's list—questions about restrictions on foreign ownership of American industries, especially railroads—had just narrowed his focus to the latter. Tom looked off in thought for a moment, then crossed to the partition that separated his workstation from the next.

Agent Ruben Diaz was staring at his monitor in a snow-blind trance, clicking through a spread sheet titled "Vory V Zakone." It listed thousands of phone calls collected in an NSA metadata sweep that he was using to build a link chart of Russian organized-crime syndicates on the East Coast. Ruben had the coal-black eyes, aquiline profile, and lithe stature of the Spanish conquistadors who were his forebears and favored softer-cut, Armani-style menswear.

"Hey, Ruben," Tom called out. "You worked with our Amtrak people on that Atlanta Yards thing last year, right?"

"They worked with *me*," Ruben replied. "*Por que?*"

"Got a reply from that Russian journalist I tweaked . . ."

"Grafin-what's-her-face?"

Tom nodded. "With a list of questions. Seems the Kremlin might be eyeing our railroads. Who's the sharpest knife in the drawer over there?"

"At Amtrak? Lana Nichols. Hands down. Smart as they come. Gives as good as she gets. Stubborn when she knows she's right . . ." Ruben paused and raised a brow in tribute, before adding, "Best ass in the building."

"*Sex and the City*, Nine Inch Nails, Ketel One cosmos?" Tom prompted.

"Vodka rocks."

"Sounds promising."

"You don't stand a chance." Ruben cocked his head, reconsidering. "On the other hand, the word is she's into fencing."

Tom raised a curious brow.

"Draw your saber and challenge her to a duel," Ruben cracked with a sly grin.

"Yes," Tom hissed with a little fist pump. "There *is* a god." He settled at his desk and googled Lana Nichols.

The search banner read: 129,000 results (0.24 seconds)

Lana Nichols's bio was interesting and impressive, and Jones wasted no time scrolling the JTTF directory for her email address. Before forwarding his exchange with Grafinskaya—which included her list of questions—he typed a note asking Nichols to review the contents and let him know if she had some time that afternoon to discuss it.

Less than fifteen minutes after Tom sent it, a shapely, self-possessed woman in her early thirties with red hair and hypnotic green eyes that peered from behind a mask of freckles, slithered between the partitions into his workstation. "Agent Jones?" she said extending a hand. "Lana Nichols. I've got ten minutes. Fifteen if it's interesting. And I've got them now."

Tom nodded. "Interesting yes. Urgent no. So, thought I'd do some homework before getting back to Ms. Grafinskaya."

"Quick question before we get into it," Lana said with a flip of her hair. "We've got at least a dozen Amtrak people working JTTF. Why me?"

"I could say MIT computer sciences major, MBA from GWU, meteoric rise through Amtrak ranks to Special Agent in Charge and assignment to JTTF—" Tom replied, rapid-fire. He paused and smiled. "But what really clinched it was when Ruben told me you have the best ass in the building."

"I do," Lana fired back. "But it's not much of a compliment coming from the *biggest* ass in the building."

"Won't take no for an answer, huh?"

"Precisely."

"That's what he said about you."

"Enough about me, Agent Jones. I've got a lot on my plate."

"Makes two of us."

"What do you need?"

"Your expertise," Tom replied, matching her cadence. "Assuming you reviewed the material, and assuming that this journalist is right, that the Russians plan to invest in American corporations, and that—having acquired a controlling interest in a French overland freight company—she suspects one of their takeover targets might be an American railroad, what are the—"

"Takeover? An American railroad?" Lana scoffed, interrupting. "Never happen. Section 232 of the Trade Expansion Act of 1962 as amended by

Section 127 of the Trade Act of 1974 and the Reorganization Plan of 1979 puts tight national security restrictions on radio, TV, all forms of coastal and inland shipping, air transportation, and all things nuclear. Furthermore, the International—"

"Furthermore," Tom interjected, continuing to enumerate, "the International Emergency Economic Powers Act grants the president authority to regulate, among other things, the import or export of securities transactions where a foreign entity is involved. I'd call the Kremlin a foreign entity, wouldn't you?"

"An *evil* entity," Lana replied pointedly. "For the sake of clarity, foreign entities *can* invest in restricted American companies, but there are percentage limitations which prohibit them from gaining a controlling interest or outright ownership."

"Touché!" Tom said, smiling at what he was about to say. "I believe your bio mentioned something about fencing? Captain of the girls' high school team, wasn't it?"

"*Women's* team, MIT," Lana corrected with a glance at her watch. "And your specific question is?"

"Could the Russians circumvent all that and take over a restricted company by, say, setting up a shell corporation with an American front man?"

"Sure. Every corrupt financier, banker, and government official on the planet knows the easiest country to set up an untraceable shell corporation is the good old U.S. of A, but it'd be complicated and illegal. Why would they even chance it?"

"Good question. Nina Grafinskaya might have the answer. If she does, we have to get it. Now, Agent Nichols"—Tom cocked his head, eyeing her with a sideways glance—"getting back to your area of expertise, any railroads on the block these days? You hearing anything interesting out there?"

"Rumors. A couple might be in play—*if* the numbers work, *if* the board gets behind it, *if* a majority of the shareholders vote for it. Takeovers are always longshots. And there are always rumors."

Tom responded to each *if* phrase with a tolerant nod, then locked his eyes onto hers and asked, "And those companies are?"

Lana shook her head. "Sorry, that's inside information. As somebody famous once said: 'If I tell you, I'll have to kill you.'"

"Choose your weapon."

"Épée."

"You're on," Tom said with a cocky grin. "My club or yours?"

"Mine."

"Soon as you tell me which railroads are sporting For Sale signs."

"I'll have to get back to you," Lana replied with a promising smile. She took a step back, spun on a stiletto heel, and slipped out of Tom's workstation.

Tom raised a brow at the rhythmic sway of her hips. "Hey, Ruben," he said in a stage whisper. "You're missing the show."

Ruben left his desk and came around the partition. "The only show I'm interested in is the one starring Kahlid Bargishev," he said, eyeing Lana as she strode past him. "Comprende?"

Tom nodded. "The offer's on the table. Next move is his."

"Maybe our friendly Chechen counterfeiter needs a poke."

"I don't know. I think I read this guy pretty good. I got a feeling the slightest pressure might spook him."

"What if we raised the ante?"

Tom waggled a hand. "Going rate's twenty cents on the dollar. No question he'd be asking himself why I'm suddenly offering more."

"Because you have another buyer!" Ruben exclaimed, taken by his own idea. "Let him think he's got competition. Jack his testosterone. These guys are all egomaniacs. He might pull the trigger if he thinks he's in a bidding war."

"Not bad," Tom said, mulling it over. "But not yet. Go with me on this. Okay?"

"Okay, we'll give this Russian egg a little more time to hatch."

Chapter Three

After leaving Café OGI with Grafinskaya, Katkov took the Metro to Tverskaya just off the Boulevard Ring. The militia routinely restricted media access to operations against high-ranking businessmen and government officials, and he wanted to get to Number 45 before they did. He bolted out the door, charged up the staircase into the network of vaulted corridors teeming with rush-hour travelers, and got on the escalator.

Moments later, he emerged into Tverskaya Square, the throbbing center of Moscow's most elite neighborhood, where the amber glow of vintage streetlamps mixed with the electric-blue haze of an immense Pepsi sign high above. The whine of sirens propelled him down the esplanade that ran south from the square. Flashers atop militia vehicles swept through the darkness and across the façades of the posh apartment buildings. Katkov saw the officers clambering from their cruisers and made a beeline for Number 45. Despite the freezing temperature his skin was slick from exertion.

"Hey, hey?!" one of the officers called out. "You can't go in there!" He and several colleagues were in pursuit of Katkov when onrushing headlights turned night into day. An armored personnel carrier sporting the letters "RIC" thundered to a stop, blocking their way. The rear doors opened, and large men in black SWAT helmets, fatigues, and body armor, brandishing AK-47s charged into the lobby of the building. Katkov was about to follow when the militia officers caught up with him.

"This is a police operation!" the sergeant with the head of an angry St. Bernard barked, filling the air with spittle. "No unauthorized personnel!"

Cujo! Stephen King's snarling killer canine! Katkov thought as they muscled him aside. "I *am* authorized, dammit!" he retorted, shoving the press pass that hung from his neck into Cujo's face. "Nikolai Katkov. *Novaya Gazeta.* I wrote the damned exposé. You wouldn't be here if it wasn't for me."

Cujo glared at him. "No, I'd be at the hockey game with my wife and kids!"

"Hockey?" Katkov scoffed, his face glistening with perspiration. "This op is the hottest ticket in town. You like Pussy Riot?"

"Pussy Riot? Those sluts should be back in Lubyanka where they belong!"

"Hey, there are Pussy Riots and there are *Pussy* Riots. You want to see one in the flesh? Follow me!" Katkov turned toward the entrance. One of the officers pinned him against the limestone façade. Cujo was binding Katkov's wrists with a zip tie when a car came down the street and parked behind the armored personnel carrier. The unmarked Lada 110 was standard RIC issue, and, as senior chief investigator, Sergei Churkin rated car and driver. He unfolded his lanky frame from the back seat, badged the officers hassling Katkov, and said, "Churkin, RIC. What the hell's going on?"

"He's a reporter, sir," Cujo replied. "He tried to breach our perimeter, and—"

"He's with *me*," Churkin retorted. Tailored and precise, he wore a black tie tight to the collar of his white shirt, a dark-gray wool suit and a double-breasted overcoat topped by a Borsalino with a speckled feather in the band. He much preferred the beige linens and Panama hats he wore decades ago as a young KGB operative in Havana. "We wouldn't be here if it wasn't for him."

Cujo groaned and rolled his eyes.

"That's what *I* told him," Katkov chimed in. "But he wouldn't—"

"*Katkov*," Churkin warned, burning him with a look. "It's monkey time, Katkov. Hear no—See no—Speak no!" he said, rapid-fire. "Got it?"

Katkov nodded, suppressing a grin.

"Cut him loose," Churkin ordered. "This is an RIC op—federal, not local. Traffic control, perimeter security, and mop-up are yours. Lubov is mine." He turned on a heel and strode into the building. Katkov followed him down a corridor to the entrance of an apartment where the RIC assault force had deployed. Churkin scanned the area, then nodded. Two RIC men stepped up to the door and drove a battering ram into the keyed latch plate. Pieces of the lock mechanism and splintered frame flew in every direction.

The assault force entered an apartment decorated with high-priced paintings and monumental pieces of sculpture, the latter draped with hastily discarded pieces of clothing, lingerie, and pantyhose. Champagne bottles littered the floors. Dunes of powdery cocaine drifted across glass-topped tables. More than a dozen naked young women and corpulent, pale-skinned men, who were engaging in sex acts like interlocking puzzle pieces, disengaged and ran in every direction. Blinding flashes from a photographer's strobe turned the bizarre scene into a staccato ballet as the RIC officers pursued the fleeing partygoers.

Churkin spotted a pulchritudinous young woman struggling with some officers who were attempting to wrap a comforter around her naked torso. "I have a few questions for Ms. Pornographskaya, here," he said as he joined them.

"It's *Portrovska*," she exclaimed, clutching the billowing down. "*Portrovska!*"

"That's what I said," Churkin joked as they directed her aside. "Where's Igor?"

"Who?"

"Igor Lubov. Your high-tech sugar daddy. The guy who owns this pleasure palace."

"*I* own it! He gave it to me for helping him run the company."

"*Rip off* the company," Churkin corrected. "To the tune of a hundred and fifty million, according to the arrest warrants. Now, where the hell is he?"

An RIC officer leaned in from an adjacent room. "Lubov's in here, sir."

"Well, cuff him and haul his ass out of there."

"Easier said than done, sir."

Katkov and the photographer followed Churkin into the room to find Lubov hanging from the ceiling in a trapeze-like harness. His body was crisscrossed with leather straps. Massive areas of flab bulged from between them like pink balloons. A dominatrix stood to one side, wrists cuffed behind her, making her breasts spill from her lacy bustier.

Katkov and Churkin exchanged smirks. "These tech-company moguls get all the perks," the CI said, unable to contain his laughter. "Lavish apartments, orgies that make Strauss-Kahn look like an altar boy, not to mention the latest in S&M paraphernalia."

Lubov glared through the eyeholes of a leather ski mask with chrome studs and Hannibal Lecter mouth buckles and growled, "Get me out of this, you bastards."

"As soon as we document the crime scene," Churkin replied with a nod to the photographer. The room had just come alive with blinding flashes when Katkov's phone rang. It was Vera.

"Someone reported finding a woman's body in an elevator," she said in a tense whisper. "According to the preliminary report, the victim was shot in the head."

"Thanks, but I can't. Not now. No way," Katkov said. "This Lubov thing it's . . . it's priceless. I'll get back to you as soon as—"

"Hold on, Niko," Vera interrupted. "What's Grusha's address?"

"Twenty-six Shchepkina. Why? What's that got to—" Katkov was struck by an unnerving thought. He cut it off and groaned, "No. No, oh no . . ."

"It's her building, Nikasha. I'm sorry."

Katkov's heart sank. His shoulders slumped. He felt as if he'd been gutted.

Churkin saw his reaction and was wondering what caused it, when *his* phone rang. "It's been a long day Zhukich. This better be good . . . What? Where?" he asked, coming to life. "Yeah—yeah—you sure? Okay, on my way . . . Yeah, he gave up without a fight," the CI replied, eyeing the leather-girdled blob who was being extricated from his harness. "Keep the militia on ice till I get there. I don't want those fucking rent-a-cops contaminating evidence." He crossed to Katkov and placed a hand on his shoulder. "There's been a shooting . . ."

"Shchepkina . . ."

Churkin nodded.

"The victim she's . . . she's been identified," Katkov prompted, his voice breaking.

Churkin waggled a hand. "Unofficial, but . . ." he let it trail off and sighed. "I'm sorry," he went on, his eyes leaving no doubt he meant it. "May I offer you a lift?" Katkov bit a lip and nodded. Churkin took the commander of the RIC force aside for a moment, then he and Katkov headed outside. "Shchepkina," he said to the driver as they got into the Lada. "The Ring will be jammed. Take the side streets."

Moscow's traffic arteries were always in a state of gridlock. It was just a matter of degree. A half hour passed before the Lada turned into a narrow street just north of the Ring Road. The area was home to dancers, choreographers, musicians, and performing arts administrators. Several militia cruisers and a medical examiner's van were parked in front of Number 26, a staid, Soviet-era building awash with light from emergency flashers. The crew of a media satellite van was setting up across the street.

"She been living here long?" Churkin asked as he and Katov got out of the Lada.

"Twenty years, give or take," Katkov replied in a morose mumble. "Got pregnant, moved in with her Bolshoi wannabe boyfriend."

"He still in the picture?" Churkin prompted.

"No. Couldn't handle the pressure, got hooked on vodka and crack, hasn't been seen since," Katkov replied, not wanting to get into it.

They badged the militia officers at the entrance and entered the lobby. Curious residents, hugging sweaters in the penetrating cold, strained
against the tape that cordoned off the crime scene. Several officers and a
woman in a medical examiner's vest were assembled in front of the elevator. A stocky young man whose girth was testing the seams of his suit was
standing nearby. "Got it figured out yet, Zhukich?" Churkin asked.

Zhukich responded with a cocky nod. "No mystery, sir. By the numbers.
Double-tap to the back of the head. Whoever whacked her was a pro."

"Witnesses? Anybody see anything?"

Zhukich shook his head. "If they did, they're not talking. I figure the
shooter was waiting over there behind that—"

"Nikasha?!" a voice called out, interrupting him. "Nikashaaa . . ."

An attractive young woman with long flowing hair—leggings tucked
into après-ski boots, a sweatshirt that proclaimed "Pussy Riot" peeking
from her quilted parka—came dashing across the lobby in the splay-footed
stride of a ballet dancer. She ran into Katkov's arms just as a lanky young
man—torn jeans, a Uniqlo vest, book bag with NYU LAW printed on
it—caught up with her. The intensity of her embrace, the anguish in her
eyes, the unspoken plea for Katkov to protect her, to make it all go away,
unleashed a torrent of feelings he had never experienced, and he hugged
Michaela in a way he had never hugged her before. His mouth opened. No
words came out.

"Oh my God, Niko, my God, what happened?" Michaela wailed,
looking up at him, her eyes glistening. "We . . . we were supposed to meet
for dinner to . . . to talk about the wedding . . ." she went on, her voice
breaking. "Mom's always running late, you know, so . . ." She shrugged
and brushed tears from her cheeks. "Finally, I . . . I called her, but . . .
but . . . Then one of her neighbors called me, and . . . and I called Sasha
and . . . and we . . ."

"I . . . I don't know what happened," Katkov replied, overcome with
emotion. "I'm sorry. I'm . . . It's . . . it's so . . . so . . ." He let it trail off,
unable to continue.

Churkin stood at a respectful distance before joining them. "I'm
very sorry for your loss," he said when Katkov introduced Michaela as
Grafinskaya's daughter. "And I'm sorry to have to ask, but we need someone to make an official identification."

Katkov nodded solemnly. "I'll take care of it." He left Michaela with
Sasha and followed Churkin to the elevator. The victim's body was inside

the cab beneath a green tarp on which MILITIA was stenciled. A rumpled shoulder bag was on the floor next to it. A woman's hand with cracked skin and chipped fingernails extended beyond the edge of the tarp, clutching a bunch of blue flowers. "It's her," Katkov said softly. He knew Churkin needed more and nodded they should proceed.

Zhukich stepped into the cab and pulled back the tarp. The victim's head was resting in a mahogany halo of blood from an exit wound that had torn away a portion of her scalp. She was wearing a black pantsuit and checkered wool topcoat. Katkov grimaced and emitted an anguished sigh. "Yes, yes, that is Nina Grafinskaya."

Zhukich replaced the tarp and stepped out of the elevator.

"Now, as you were saying," Churkin said, prompting him to resume his analysis. "By the numbers, no mystery, double-tap, a pro . . ."

"Uh-huh. Cut and dry," Zhukich replied in his cocky way. "The shooter was probably waiting behind that column, watching the entrance. The victim entered the lobby and went to the elevator, carrying flowers she picked up on the way home. The shooter popped her as she was getting in and was gone before she hit the floor."

Katkov was shaking his head. "*No.* No, we had drinks after work. Those aren't the clothes she had on, and those flowers, they're . . . they're from her roof garden. No, no, she went up to her apartment. This happened on the way out, not on the way in."

"You remember what she was wearing?" Churkin asked.

"Yeah, yeah, a . . . a turtleneck sweater. Black and gray stripes."

Churkin burned Zhukich with a look. "Neither cut nor dried, is it? *And* if Katkov's right . . ." He let it trail off, prompting Zhukich to finish it.

"The jeans and striped top should be somewhere in her apartment."

"Brilliant. Check her bag for her keys," Churkin said, sending Zhukich back into the elevator. The CI turned on a heel, strode to the staircase, and started climbing. Katkov was right behind him. They reached the third-floor landing and pushed through the door into the corridor.

"It's down here," Katkov said, heading toward an alcove that framed the entrance to Grafinskaya's apartment. Moments later, Zhukich burst through the door from the landing, gasping for breath, and hurried toward them clutching a set of keys.

"Not exactly a gym rat, is he?" Churkin cracked with a facetious sneer. He unlocked the door and led the way inside. Katkov followed, brushing a finger over the mezuzah. Unlike the one at her office, it was of modern design with a base carved from a block of olive wood. A thin ceramic tile was affixed to it. A white Star of David and a dove of peace had been hand-painted beneath the tile's blue-green glaze.

The apartment was furnished with antiques and quirky street finds. The walls were covered with anti-Soviet posters and reproductions of once-banned artwork, Degas ballet pastels among them, and lined with bookcases stuffed with Western literature and political pamphlets. File folders were piled in the rolltop desk. A door in the kitchen that led to the greenhouse and roof garden beyond was slightly open. Some cuttings and wilted flowers were on the potting table, along with a pair of clippers and a gardening apron. In the bedroom, a pair of black jeans and a black-and-gray striped sweater were tossed across a chair. A pair of Uggs that had been kicked off in haste were on the rug.

"There," Katkov said somberly.

Churkin nodded and glanced to Zhukich. "Bag those and seal the apartment."

Katkov looked puzzled. "You're sealing it? Why?"

"Because we need to catch whoever is responsible for this."

"Yeah, but she was killed in the elevator. Her apartment's got nothing to do with it. It's not a crime scene." Katkov paused, struck by a troubling thought. His eyes narrowed in suspicion. "You're looking for more than her clothes, aren't you?"

"Evidence. I'm looking for evidence," Churkin replied, sounding annoyed.

Katkov had no doubt Grafinskaya had gone up to her apartment to change clothes and cut some flowers to bring to Mika, but he knew there was another reason, a much more important one, and he wasn't about to reveal it to Churkin. "You're the chief investigator," he said with a facetious inflection.

"Come on Katkov, two shots to the back of the head. Her handbag wasn't taken; she's still wearing her watch and jewelry. The kid isn't a rocket scientist, but he's right. This is no street crime. It's contract work."

"Federal, not local," Katkov said with a sly smile.

Churkin nodded, then locked his eyes onto Katkov's. "We both know what this is about. I'd be careful if I were you."

Chapter Four

Lana Nichols's fencing club was in the athletic building on the George Washington University campus a few blocks from the White House. "I did graduate work here about ten years ago," she said when Tom met her in the common area adjacent to the locker rooms. "The club was just starting up. So, I'm a charter member." After changing into their kits—rib-cage protector on weapons-arm side, white tunic, and breeches—they entered the Fencing Hall, masks cradled in their arms, épées pointed downward at their sides. The pristine space had white walls, mirrors, and a half dozen pistes—the long narrow floor mats that define the field of combat—arranged in parallel rows. A number of bouts were in progress as they plugged their body wires into the system that sends signals to the scoring box and took their positions on their assigned piste.

After the traditional salute, Lana called out, *"En garde—Prêt—Allez!"* A series of explosive lunges and powerful thrusts ensued, accompanied by the metallic scraping of button-tipped sporting blades in fleeting contact. The action stopped each time an electronic beep signaled a hit; then, upon the fencers resetting their positions, it resumed—sometimes with aggressive engagement, other times with the strategic touching and tapping of blades followed by flurries of fast-moving attacks, parries, and retreats. Lana and Tom were well into the third and final three-minute period of a fifteen-point bout, the score tied at fourteen-all, when he executed an attack that allowed him to pass her on the run. *"Skachok strela!"* he exclaimed in Russian, as he had been doing throughout.

"Balestra flèche," Lana retorted, using the more common Italian and French terms as she whirled to engage him. She launched an explosive counter-parry that drove him back. A spirited exchange ensued, ending in an electronic beep signaling a hit.

"Ukol!" Tom exclaimed, using the Russian equivalent of touché to acknowledge it. "Your bout," he went on, making the traditional bow.

They removed their masks, unplugged their body cords, and began walking toward a lounge area at end of the hall.

"You're good, Tom. Really good," Lana said, leaving no doubt she meant it.

"Yeah, but you won."

"By a point. I got lucky. You went for the feint and blew the counterattack."

"Went for the *kombinrovannaya ataka* and blew the *kontrataka* . . ."

"Wait. Don't tell me. You had a Russian instructor when you were a kid."

"Uh-huh. He was from Yekaterinburg. Claimed to be descended from nobility. By the time I went off to college, I was fluent. Comes in handy in this job."

Lana nodded, then shook out her hair and ran her fingers through it. Her skin was flushed and aglow with moisture that gave the mask of freckles framing her eyes an alluring sheen. The exertion had intensified her natural beauty, making her all the more seductive. Tom stood there staring at her.

"What?" Lana prompted with a self-conscious grin.

A wry smile turned a corner of Tom's mouth. "Do I get a rematch?"

"Sure," Lana replied in a breathy whisper.

"Your club or mine?"

Lana raised an amused brow at his entendre. "Mine. It's nearby."

Lana lived in Foggy Bottom on the second floor in one of the brick townhouses that line Queen Anne's Lane just off Twenty-Seventh Street. The apartment was furnished with an eclectic mix, from period antiques to Art Deco to '70s retro. Fencing posters, photographs, and memorabilia were on prominent display.

Lana was at a sideboard opening a bottle of Chardonnay when Tom noticed two vintage dueling sabers in a cradle on the fireplace mantel. They were a matched pair, as was the tradition when gentlemen, who defended their honor at dawn, commissioned the manufacture of a personal combat sword. The blades of swords made to fight duels were razor-sharp and shorter than those of modern sporting weapons. Each was sheathed in a leather scabbard with leather ferrule and finial, and mounted to a decoratively engraved bell guard affixed to a wooden handle wrapped with silver and copper wire. A copy of a well-known credo hung in a simple rectangular frame on the wall above them.

Fencing is a school of humility and develops speed,

perfect control of the body, balance, beauty and strong
grace. It should be recommended to everyone wanting
to master their feelings and actions during their lifetime.
Through this art they will think clearly and act always
with style in their decisions.

—*Marcel Marceau*

Tom smiled, moved by its eloquent wisdom, then removed one of the sabers from the cradle and slowly slipped it halfway from its scabbard. The name of the manufacturer, Couleaux & Cie., Klingenthal, was engraved in the gleaming blade's forte. "It's . . . it's just exquisite," he said in quiet reverence.

"They were a gift from my parents when I won the nationals."

"*Bitva shpaga,*" Tom said, using the Russian term for combat sword. "A matched set . . ." he went on, sounding awed.

"*Sabre de combat en français. Oui?*" Lana prompted as she poured the wine.

"*Da,*" Tom said, placing it back in the cradle. "Have you ever used them?"

"Are you kidding?" Lana scoffed with a laugh. "They're made to draw first blood, to duel to the death." She tilted her head, reconsidering. "Well, I *do* let them out of their scabbards on occasion. Fundraisers, exhibition bouts in period costumes, that sort of thing. Needless to say, my opponents are highly skilled fencers I've come to trust," she went on, letting her tone and eye contact suggest that Tom just might be one of them. "Perhaps our rematch . . ."

"Perhaps?" Tom prompted, feigning he was crushed.

"À votre santé," Lana said, handing him a glass of wine.

"*Zdaróvye,*" he exclaimed with a grin as they clinked. "So, is it Lana after Lana Turner? Lana Wood? Lana, the Beach Boys, Surfin' USA? Lana Del Rey?"

"*Turner.* My mom was a big fan. And you? I mean, Tom Jones?" Lana said with a girlish giggle. "Come on. Was yours into the book or the movie?" she went on, eyeing him seductively. "I mean, just thinking about Albert Finney devouring that juicy pear makes me wet."

"Lucky me," Tom murmured with a Cheshire grin. He set down his glass and began, thumbing open the buttons of her blouse, an act that accelerated into a clothes-shedding frenzy as they stumbled toward Lana's bedroom groping each other. She charged on ahead, tossing aside bra and panties, and dove onto the billowing comforter.

Ruben was right, Tom thought as he pursued her. She had gold-medal buns, *médaille d'or derrière,* as fencers call it, the delightful result of being tightened and lifted, not by exercises designed to achieve such perfection but by the positions and movements demanded of the sport. They were engaged in a passionate tangle when Lana came out on top and straddled his thighs, letting one of her nipples graze his lips.

Later, satiated and short of breath, they lay amidst the disheveled bed covers basking in the afterglow. "You know," Tom murmured, caressing her. "You surprised me. I mean, you had a sort of—*You can bed me if you can outpoint me*—attitude."

"It has its uses," Lana said with a sly smile, burrowing in next to him.

Tom nodded, then tilted his head in thought. "Come to think of it, I doubt if my mother ever read *Tom Jones*. She might've seen the movie, but she named me after the singer. She was crazy about him."

"Oh, yeah, he was a real hunk, drove the ladies wild." Lana put her mouth close to his ear and began singing in a sexy whisper: "*It's not unusual to be loved by anyone. It's not unusual to have fun with anyone . . .*"

"His signature song. He was huge in Vegas. I grew up there."

"No kidding?"

"Yup. UNLV. Go, Runnin' Rebels!"

"I'm going to Vegas tomorrow for DefCon," Lana said, referring to the computer hacker conference held annually at the Rio Hotel & Casino. "Want to come?"

"No thanks. I'm not into cave-dwelling Asperger savants."

"They have their uses, but I'm more into cybersecurity corporations now. Most American railroads are underprotected: freight yards, scheduling, routing, switching—all computer-controlled systems. All this takeover talk . . . a blind test of Amtrak's Internet security is long overdue. I'll be soliciting bids for the contract." She pushed up on an elbow and flipped her hair back. "I thought maybe we could have some fun."

"I think we just did," Tom replied, curling a wavy lock around a finger. "Unfortunately, I'm working an op with Ruben. Chechen counterfeiting sting." His eyes narrowed in thought. "Speaking of takeovers, any news yet on who's in play?"

"I'm still working on it."

"Just for the record, I've got Top Secret clearance."

"I'll be the judge of that," Lana teased.

"I *do*," Tom protested with boyish charm.

"Yeah, well that intel's been SKIFFed." The acronym stood for sensitive compartmented information facility. Access to these parcels was on a strictly enforced need-to-know basis. "And as soon as I get confirmation that your clearance covers the key compartments, you'll have access to whatever intel they contain."

"Well . . ." Tom whispered, brushing his palm across the curve of her stomach and on to the mound of auburn down where the tip of his finger found its mark. "There is one key compartment . . . I can think of . . . that I've already been cleared to access." Indeed, it was all in the fingertips for fencers. In the nimble, agile, subtle manipulation of the thumb plate and pommel that sent tremors coursing through the blade creating its dynamic movement, and it wasn't surprising that this hypersensitive manual dexterity created similar effects on other fields of play. Lana arched her back and shuddered, emitting a lusty moan. Tom continued stimulating her until she was close, then slipped between her thighs and brought her the rest of the way.

The next morning, Lana dropped her suitcase onto the bed and went about packing for her trip to Vegas. Tom had showered and dressed and was knotting his tie when his eyes went to Lana's computer screen. The Google News headline read FOREIGN MINISTER LAVROV HINTS RUSSIA MAY SUPPORT U.S. EFFORTS TO DEFEAT ISIS IN SYRIA.

"Looks like Putin is pulling the president's chestnuts out of the fire."

"Or the Prez played his cards right and Volodya folded. I mean—"

"Hold it. Hold it," Tom interrupted, his eyes darting back to a smaller headline below, which read MOSCOW JOURNALIST GUNNED DOWN. "Holy shit, they whacked her!"

"Whacked who?"

"The journalist who wrote that story in *Novaya Gazeta*."

"The one you exchanged emails with?" Lana asked, pulling pieces of clothing from a dresser and setting them in the suitcase.

"Yeah, Grafinskaya. Shot in the lobby of her building. Double-tap to the head."

"She was assassinated? For blowing the whistle on a rumor the Kremlin wants to take over an American railroad? No way."

"No, there's got to be more to it."

"Not surprising," Lana said, packing her toiletry kit and several pairs of shoes. "Putin's declared open field day on journalists. This is number four on his watch. One was an American. Klebnikov. Editor of *Forbes Russia*."

"I worked on that. So when did Lana Nichols become special agent in charge of keeping tabs on assassinated journalists?"

"I'm a big fan of the First Amendment."

"So is Edward Snowden," Tom said pointedly.

"I'm out of here," Lana said, zipping the suitcase. "It's been fun. Just pull the door closed when you leave." She planted a quick kiss on his lips, shouldered her laptop case, and headed for the door. Tom was right behind her.

Lana took a cab to Dulles Airport.

Tom drove to National Counterterrorism Headquarters in McLean.

Ruben was waiting for him when he got to his workstation. "How'd it go?"

"Lost the bout. Took home the trophy," Tom replied, preening with machismo. "Gold-medal buns. God, oh God, oh God . . . Not to mention an exquisite pair of . . . vintage dueling sabers."

"An exquisite pair of what?" Ruben cackled, bursting into laughter.

"Dueling sabers. Swords. The kind gentlemen once used to defend their honor, to draw first blood, to duel to the death; said she uses them in charity exhibitions."

"Whatever. Time to put yours back in your pants, D'Artagnan, and get your head around this," Ruben said, leaning his elbows on the partition. "We got a text."

"Bargishev wants to do business?"

Ruben nodded. "You were right. You did good . . . *muy bueno.*"

"Thanks."

"Hey, when it comes to corrupt currency traders, you're my go-to guy."

"Guess I look the part."

Ruben paused and locked his eyes onto Tom's. "You still have to close the deal. I'm counting on an Academy Award performance."

"When's it going down?"

"Tonight. Amtrak Terminal. Baltimore Penn Station. The merchandise will be in a van. Bargishev will be in a town car. The payoff'll fit in a roll-aboard. You pull it through the parking lot like you just got off the 7:23 and drop it in the trunk. Bargishev gets out, drools over the cash, and gives you the keys to the van . . ."

"The backup team moves in, and he's toast."

"Burnt toast. You read him his rights in Russian and spend the rest of your life interrogating him until he gives up the Chechen warlord who's running him."

Chapter Five

It was nearly midnight in the Russian capital. The temperature had dropped into the teens by the time Katkov left Number 76 Shchepkina. He had waited with Mika and her fiancé until the medical examiner had finished her work and removed Grafinskaya's body from the crime scene. The devastated young couple headed for the apartment they were sharing. Katkov, still reeling from this horrific turn of events, was trudging down Durova en route to the Metro when his phone rang. The caller ID read *Novaya Gazeta*.

"Katkov . . ."

"It's me . . ." Yarshevsky, the editor in chief mumbled.

"It's about time, dammit. Where are you?"

"At the office . . ."

"I called. Left messages. Why didn't you come to Grusha's?"

"I thought it might be smart for *Novaya Gazeta* to keep a low profile for a while. Not to mention there are—"

"*Novaya Gazeta*'s got a story to publish, Vitaly," Katkov interrupted. "Stay there. I'm on my way."

"No, Niko. No!" Yarshevsky warned. "RIC is all over this place. They're seizing computers, rifling through archives and files. They sealed Grusha's office. They're trashing mine and going through yours. I wouldn't go home either."

"Shit. Bastards probably hacked our phones too."

"Yeah, I need to get out of here. Take a walk. Get some fresh air."

"Me too," Katkov said, completing the coded exchange that had served them well for decades. There was no need to say where they would meet.

Even at this hour, the Moscow Metro provided quick and reliable transport. In twenty minutes Katkov and Yarshevsky, the latter in a beaver coat and rabbit fur hat with ear flaps, were on the other side of town, south of the Kremlin, strolling through Gorky Park. Several years ago—in response to an edict from Moscow's Kremlin-appointed mayor—the once unkempt and crime-ridden landscape had been turned into an urban oasis of lawns and lakes amidst stands of lush trees. At night, its meandering walkways were illuminated by frosted globes that hovered, ghostlike, just above the stone pavers and areas of ground-hugging shrubbery. Now, dusted with fresh snow and bits of crystalline ice, it sparkled like a winter wonderland.

"Grusha had a feeling," Katkov said, his voice quavering with emotion.

Yarshevsky nodded. His doughy face held a piercing gaze that came from behind his frameless eyeglass lenses. "So did I," he said, sounding shaken.

"Yeah, she told me. I shouldn't've pressured her to file it."

"Don't beat yourself up, Niko. No one could've stopped her. This isn't about what Grusha wrote. It's about what she *didn't* write. Bastards must've intercepted the FBI email and freaked out."

"That's why Churkin sealed her apartment," Katkov said, seething with frustration. "He claims he did it to preserve evidence, to find her killer."

"That's bullshit and you know it."

"Grusha talk to you about anything"—Katkov waggled a hand—"delicate?"

Yarshevsky cocked his head. "No. If it's in her notes, her files, her computer, her email, they have it now, and we never will. She mention anything to you?"

"Yeah, she said she had two sources, one in Bortnikov's inner circle and—"

"Bortnikov?" Yarshevsky interrupted. "That's news to me. Scary."

"Tell me about it. The other was in RZD. The rumor was the Kremlin might be scheming to use pension funds to take over an American railroad via a shell corporation. Looks like the front man is a French Canadian billionaire."

"No shit? She never mentioned that either. That's one hot potato."

Katkov nodded. "Got to be the guy inside FSB who tipped her to that," he said, glancing over his shoulder at a woman walking a dog. "But one of the tips is unsubstantiated and she didn't use them."

"Then it's got to be something else."

"Either that or one of her sources felt threatened and burned her to cover his ass."

"Whatever. She's dead. Doesn't really matter who—"

Katkov's cell phone rang, interrupting him. "Katkov—No, no, I can't talk to you now. Mrs. Parfenov—Mrs. Parfenov, please, I don't have time for . . . Are you sure? . . . No, no don't worry. I won't . . . Thanks. It's been a horrible day. I'm sorry I was so short with you." He pocketed the phone

36

and peered over his glasses at Yarshevsky. "My landlady. You were right. FSB agents are taking my place apart."

"FSB?" Yarshevsky grunted, taken aback. "They had FSB credentials?"

Katkov nodded. "Yeah, she was positive. Churkin sold out. I knew he was a snake," he said with another look back over his shoulder.

"Only one person in all of Russia can say no to the FSB—our dear friend Volodya," Yarshevsky said with a sarcastic sneer.

Katkov stopped walking to light a cigarette. He cupped the match, covering his mouth, and said, "We're being followed."

"The woman walking the dog, and the two leg-breakers in warmup suits at the food kiosk," Yarshevsky said under his breath.

Katkov nodded. Neither noticed the man in the winter warmup suit with a NASCAR cap who was concealed in the grotesque shadows of a darkened carousel.

"Just like the old days: USSR/Russian Federation—Brezhnev/Putin—KGB/FSB," Yarshevsky said. "Nothing's changed except the names."

"And their bank balances. Then they were communists: powerful, unscrupulous, and broke. Now they are capitalists: powerful, unscrupulous, and rich!"

"Werewolves in epaulets!"

They walked a short distance in silence when Katkov's eyes widened at an unnerving thought. "Our phones, Vitaly. It's our phones."

"GPS," Yarshevsky hissed. "I hate all this fucking technology . . ."

"Yeah, just like the old days, only worse."

Yarshevsky nodded grimly. "We need to protect ourselves, Niko. Hard to do when we don't know from what." He forced a smile and began angling toward an adjoining walkway. "Better rack your brain, my friend."

"I am, but it keeps coming up empty," Katkov said, lying through his teeth. He didn't know what Grafinskaya had, but it occurred to him in the course of his conversation with Yarshevsky that if she had a lethal piece of information, something that so threatened the Kremlin they had her terminated, he knew where to find it. He quickened his step, reflecting on what Grafinskaya had said when he asked if her data was backed up: *You can always put your finger on them . . .*

Chapter Six

US Airways 478 from Washington National arrived in Las Vegas at 11:15 a.m. Lana Nichols left the terminal and tossed her suitcase into the trunk of a waiting cab. "Hi, I'm going to the Rio," she said brightly.

"You look more like a hooker than a hacker to me, honey," the driver cracked.

"Thanks, I'll take that as a compliment. So, who's the better tipper?"

"You kidding? Hookers, hands down."

"Well, this isn't your lucky day . . ."

The Las Vegas Freeway cut arrow-straight from the airport to the city and beyond. Its strategically placed off-ramps guided traffic to all the major hotels—the Bellagio, Caesars Palace, the Venetian, Flamingo, and the Rio Hotel & Casino just off the Dean Martin Drive exit. A garish sign above the entrance spelled out *The Rio* in fanciful yellow script. A pair of gigantic maracas sent electronic bursts of fuchsia, purple, and chartreuse fireworks soaring across the hotel's façade. Beneath this extravaganza, a panorama of signs were shrieking: *Penn and Teller! The Rat Pack! Chippendale's! Rocks Topless Revue!* Above them an illuminated banner exclaimed: *Welcome DefCon Hackers!*

During DefCon, the Rio was the most virus-infested Internet hot spot on Earth. Even the hackers feared being hacked, and their inborn paranoia and obsession for anonymity were on high alert. Most of the fifteen thousand attendees paid cash for their rooms and checked in under Internet handles like Phiber Optik, Mind Taser, Black Hole, and Free Radical. Many left their laptops at home to prevent them from being infected—and with good reason. Seminars on hacking Google, PayPal, and Apple were sold out. Those on picking locks, disabling car alarms, and escaping prisons were equally popular.

Not all those who attended DefCon had malicious intent. Some came with an eye toward making the Internet safer. Many were lawyers, journalists, and computer security professionals. Others, like Lana Nichols, were government employees.

A wall of frigid air greeted Lana as she ran the gauntlet of slot machines in the lobby. After checking in, she slipped into a desert-appropriate linen pantsuit and headed down to the convention center. A galaxy of monitors and dazzling data displays floated in the darkness beneath the vaulted ceiling of the Pavilion Ballroom, which had been gridded into streets lined with exhibitor booths. Some were little more than a card table, two folding chairs, and a computer; others were professionally designed with animated graphics and state-of-the-art computer equipment on display: Mandiant, Hewlett Packard, FireEye, Fortinet, and Checkpoint among them.

Lana had a list of companies she intended on vetting. Her DefCon guest packet made it easy to locate them. "Hi, Lana Nichols," she said, presenting her business card to the reps manning the various booths. "I'm JTTF's cybersecurity SAC for Amtrak."

"FBI?" many prompted warily, seeing the distinctive logo on the card.

"Hey, I'm not here to bust anyone. I need your help," Lana replied with disarming candor. "I have concerns about Amtrak's Internet security, and I'll get into details if there's a chance we can get into business." She spent the afternoon narrowing the candidates. Cyber-Borgen Security had an esprit de corps and an interpersonal chemistry that seemed to click with Lana. The fact that CEO Axel Carlsen had a degree in computer science from MIT, her alma mater, was the clincher.

"Wow, you guys are in the Flatiron Building?" Lana exclaimed when he gave her his business card. "I'm impressed."

"We set up shop in Silicon Alley when the Flatiron had gas lamps," Carlsen said with a laugh. "It cost a fortune to upgrade the services to the twenty-first century, but I love the place." A tall man in his mid-forties, he had a long, craggy face and attentive, startling blue eyes. "Sure, we can assess the threat landscape," he went on after Lana had briefed him. "Attack Amtrak's operating systems to detect weaknesses, determine if they're vulnerable to external threats . . ."

"What if I told you we suspect the Russian government may be planning a clandestine takeover of one of our railroads, and I'm concerned that—"

"That Amtrak's cybersecurity systems won't be able to detect, identify, and repel attacks by top Russian hackers," Carlsen interrupted smartly.

Lana nodded. "Couldn't have said it better myself."

"They're the best. It's in their genes. No cybersecurity system is foolproof, but I'll say this: If *we* can't hack you, chances are pretty damned good nobody else can."

"Oh yeah. All it takes is a laptop and a wifi connection and you're hacking into cellphones and PC's; activating cameras, capturing passwords and intercepting Skype transmissions. And you can do it all from a park bench. As I'm sure you know, even high-level government officials have had their accounts spear phished."

"What about zero-day exploits?"

"Depends on the hacker who detected it. Some use them. Many sell them. A well-heeled few buy them. We've been up against organizations that pay hundreds of thousands of dollars for such information. It comes down to the malware they use."

"Which brings me to rootkit," Lana declared.

"Time to meet my anti-malware team," Carlsen said, introducing Lana to Caitlin Roarke, an elfin woman with a quick mind who wore her short black hair in spikes. A safety pin pierced her left eyebrow. A line of phrases—*click to delete, anti-malware, free wifi*—were tattooed above her breastbone in a gentle catenary like a necklace. "If anyone can assure you we can handle this, it's Caitlin."

Caitlin's eyes widened in a mischievous twinkle. "He has to say that because I've an offer from Google, Dublin," she said in a lilting brogue. "But I'd have to go back home, so . . ." She let it trail off with an ambivalent shrug and got down to business. "We kick ass when it comes to this stuff. And Pashwan is the ass kicker in chief around here," she went on, introducing Lana to Pashwan Al-Attas, a slight fellow in his twenties with dark eyes that seemed alive with ideas. "Pashwan's an expert in detecting malware, identifying the bug, and writing a program to counter it."

"Call me Pash," he said with a mild British accent as he shook Lana's hand. "Yes, rootkit is a nasty one, isn't it? Bloody damn near impossible to get rid of."

"Tell me about it. If your laptop gets infected, you can trash it and buy a new one for five hundred bucks. Multimillion-dollar installations like Amtrak's, not so easy."

"Well . . ." Pash said, his eyes alive with mischief, "no need to get your knickers in a knot, just make an appointment for a root canal. I'm Cyber-Borgen's *nushprafh detrush*. That's Arabic for 'painless dentist.'"

"No one seems to be feeling any pain in this booth," Lana said with a laugh. "What are you guys on, anyway?"

"My family's coming! This weekend!" Pash replied excitedly.

"They're immigrating," Caitlin said, equally enthused. "Pash's been working on this for over a year. We all have. His wife's back there helping them get ready."

"I rented them an apartment in my building," Pash added with an uncertain smile. "There's a Yemeni restaurant just down the street and a halal butcher nearby, but Brooklyn isn't Sana'a. I hope it's to their liking."

Lana smiled supportively. "Oh, I'm sure they'll get used to it."

"We're having a Skype party tonight," Carlsen said. "You should come."

"Sure, I'll be there," Lana replied with a little fist pump. "But before we break"—she went on holding them with her tone—"it's important you know that though I'm an FBI special agent in charge at JTTF, I'm an Amtrak cybercop first. That means when it comes to cybersecurity nothing is more important than the three Right-Of-Way computer programs that monitor and operate the network of tracks that crisscross the nation and ensure the safety of passengers, cargo, and communities. I'm preparing a mission statement that will outline them and other key objectives in detail. So, I'll just shorthand them, for now: One, ESR, the Electronic Switching and Routing system that directs rolling stock to destinations across the country. Two, PTC, the Positive Train Control system that GPS-monitors and controls the speed of travel to ensure trains are operating within mandated limits. Three, RCRM, the Rail Corridor Risk Management system that oversees the makeup of rolling stock and what cargo—lumber, fuel, hogs, diapers, whatever—is going where, and determines the safest routing. To recap: The ESR, PTC, and RCRM programs are my three key cybersecurity concerns. They're what keeps Amtrak's chief of computer ops up half the night and gets him out of bed every morning. His name's Grabowski, Andy Grabowski. He's smart, he's tough, and he'll be at our next meeting. So, burn them into your brains."

Several hours later, Lana joined Carlsen, Caitlin, Pash, and other Cyber-Borgen staffers who were gathered around the large monitor in Carlsen's suite atop the hotel. An image of the living room of the Al-Attas family's modest apartment filled the screen. It was in the University District of Sana'a just off the Ring Road that goes east to the U.S. embassy and the Old Quarter, where the Ottoman Gate opens onto a maze of narrow alleys and medieval stone houses. Pashwan's father, a pharmacologist, taught at the Health Sciences School of the Sana'a University Hospital, where his mother worked as a nurse. Pashwan had been a star student at the affiliated Computer and Information Technology College. His parents, siblings, relatives, and friends of the Al-Attas family were mugging for the webcam lens atop their computer. Pash's wife, Safia, waved and called out, "I love you, Pash!

I miss you! See you soon!" She picked up his niece and held the wide-eyed child in front of the lens. "Blow Uncle Pashwan a kiss!"

"Amazing," Lana said, clearly moved. "The Internet doing what it does best."

"The global village," Carlsen said with a little fist pump. "Time for a refill?"

"Sure, why not? So, Cyber-*Borgen* Security? How'd you come up with that?"

"My family's from Copenhagen. Borgen means 'castle' in Danish."

Lana's eyes widened with insight. "Basic cybersecurity theory: Surround the king and crown jewels with impenetrable walls and a moat to deter and repel the invaders."

Carlsen nodded, then splayed his hands. "Soon to become obsolete theory. We'll probably have to change the name of the company."

"To . . . Cyber-*Alcatraz* Security," Lana suggested with a fetching giggle.

"Hey, not bad. That's the new paradigm: Let them in, toss their asses in solitary, throw away the key, and waterboard them 24/7 if they act up."

"An extraordinary rendition program for computer hackers."

"Precisely," Carlsen said, his eyes finding hers. "We'll be losing the satellite soon. They'll all go back to their cybercaves, and . . ."

"Well, I'm in no rush to get back to mine," Lana said in a seductive whisper.

"You like sushi?"

"Love it . . ."

"Great. The sushi chef's a genius. We'll call down, get some shiro maguro, a little hamachi, a creamy, yeast-infused Dom . . . talk shop . . . get to know each other better . . ."

Lana glanced to the windows and the dazzling light show below that stretched to the horizon in the darkness. "I mean, a view of the Strip, gourmet sushi, vintage bubbly . . . never happen on Uncle Sam's dime."

"A little outside JTTF travel guidelines?" Carlsen teased, raising his glass.

"Hey, everything has its price," Lana replied as they clinked.

A few moments passed before they sensed the revelry behind them was abating, as had the Skype-transmitted revelry in the Al-Attas family's apartment on the monitor.

"Sounds like they're losing the satellite sooner than I expected," Carlsen said with a wolfish grin as he and Lana joined the Cyber-Borgen staffers who were staring at the screen in puzzled silence. The Yemenis had stopped dancing. Their laughter and bubbly conversation had ceased. Their body language had become rigid and tense, as if alerted to a threat. Their heads were tilted in concern, their ears attuned to a piercing whine rising in the distance. Concern turned to terror as it drowned out their shouts and exclamations of alarm. Soon, it had become loud enough for those in the hotel suite to hear it—and to be puzzled by it. The Yemeni partygoers weren't puzzled. They had heard it before. They knew its source. They had seen them flying over the desert like vultures in search of prey, had seen them peeling off in sharp angles of attack upon acquiring their targets, had recognized the bulbous nose, downward pointing tail, and ear-splitting screech of their 750 horsepower engines as they moved in for the kill— they knew an MQ-1 Predator drone when they heard one.

They may not have known, nor at this moment would they have cared, that the airstrike had been planned and was now being carried out and con- trolled in real time by personnel in drone ops centers in Langley, Virginia; Sana'a, Yemen; and Las Vegas, Nevada. In a control room just a few miles down the road from the Rio, the center operator, the intel coordinator, and the drone pilot were hunched over their consoles in their desert camo, guiding the Predator's approach to the target and running their safety, target-acquisition, and collateral-damage checklists.

"We're signed-off on the CDI," the center operator reported.

"Okay, we're greened-up," the pilot said evenly. "Missile status: ready."

"Left selected for single fire," the operator advised. "Point of impact is targeted."

The intel operator scanned her monitors. "You are cleared to engage the target."

"The weapon is armed. Rifle! Rifle! Rifle! Weapon away!" the pilot announced as he launched one of the GBU-12 Paveway missiles that hung beneath the Predator's wings.

An instant later, Carlsen, Lana, Caitlin, Pashwan, and the other members of the Cyber-Borgen staff watched in gut-wrenching horror as a massive explosion erupted across the screen, watched as the frantic, terror-stricken partygoers ran screaming amidst the flames and smoke, watched in utter disbelief as the brick-and-mortar structure collapsed, burying Pash's family and friends in the raging inferno, watched until the screen went black and the screaming stopped.

Chapter Seven

The dog walker had drifted after Katkov as he hurried from Gorky Park. He had little trouble losing her in the knot of streets and alleys, and he took the Metro back to Mira Prospekt in Grafinskaya's neighborhood. Churkin's car, the militia cruisers, the medical examiner's van, and media satellite vans had long departed. No officers were posted at the entrance to Number 26, or in the lobby, and the neighbors were in for the night. Stanchions strung with crime-scene tape cordoned off the elevator. Seals that proclaimed CRIME SCENE DO NOT ENTER were plastered across it.

Katkov climbed the stairs to the third floor and peered out the door that opened into the corridor. No militia personnel were posted there either. He made his way to Grafinskaya's apartment and ducked beneath the tape strung across the alcove. A crime-scene seal covered the keyhole and latch plate, and several more extended across the edge of the door onto the jamb. They would have to be broken to gain entry, but what Katkov wanted wasn't inside the apartment. He brushed a finger across the mezuzah as he would prior to entering. The block of olive wood—to which the hand-painted tile was affixed—was approximately six inches long, one and a half inches wide, and three-eighths of an inch thick. Katkov slipped it from the metal channel that held it in place. The back of the wooden block had been hollowed out, but instead of the traditional verse from the Torah inscribed on a piece of folded parchment, the cavity contained a computer flash drive. He removed it, slipped the empty mezuzah back into its bracket, and headed for the staircase. "Katkov?" a familiar voice called when he reached the lobby. It was Churkin, still natty in his Borsalino and topcoat despite the hour and exhausting day. "What the hell are you doing here?!"

"Covering a story about a courageous journalist who was killed for writing the truth!" Katkov retorted, matching his tone. "And you?!"

"Trying to catch her killers!"

"Sure," Katkov grunted with a sarcastic snarl. "They got to you. Didn't they?"

"Who?"

"The *siloviki*," Katkov replied, meaning the powerful faction of neo-Bolsheviks in the Kremlin hierarchy. "The KGB!"

"Come on, Katkov. They've been out of business for twenty-five years."

"That's bullshit and you know it!" Katkov retorted. "This country is owned and run by ex-KGB generals. They just changed the name of the company to FSB."

Churkin held Katkov's look for a moment, then averted his eyes in concession. "The only person in Russia who can say no to the FSB is Vladimir Putin—and you know it," he said, purposely repeating Katkov's rejoinder.

"That's what my editor said."

"Sounds like a very smart guy."

Katkov grunted in disgust and trudged out the door walking south on Shchepkina, the strap of his shoulder bag digging into his parka. His first thought was to go to his apartment and try to stop the FSB's search-and-destroy mission, but the only thing there that he really cared about was personal. It had nothing to do with Grafinskaya, *Novaya Gazeta*, classified documents, the names of sources, the identity of sleeper agents in America, or their clandestine operations. The FSB wouldn't find it of interest. Besides, Yarshevsky and Churkin were right. Only one man in all of Russia could blow off the FSB, and his name wasn't Katkov. The smart move would be to keep as far away from them as possible. Which meant he needed to find a place to spend the night.

Katkov stared at his phone with uncertainty, his thumb poised over the keypad. He knew Churkin hadn't returned to Grafinskaya's building in search of evidence but because he'd been informed Katkov was there. He also knew the dog walker couldn't have tipped him off, because he'd given her the slip. No, as Katkov realized in Gorky Park it was because they were tracking his phone. He was on the verge of smashing it against the pavement, but he literally lived on it. Its vast contacts directory was an investigative journalist's lifeblood. The thought of losing it was unnerving. He resisted the temptation to destroy the phone and thumbed the keypad. "Hi, it's me," he said when Vera answered.

"Oh, Niko, I've been thinking about you and . . . and Grusha. It's so horrible."

"I know," he said in a weary mumble. "Sorry, to call so late . . ."

"It's okay. I've been up. Who could sleep? Are . . . are you all right?"

"I'm miserable. I . . . I can't go home. Are you alone?"

"Nikasha, I'm always alone when I'm not with you . . ."

Katkov had brightened at the sound of her voice. Its soothing Slavic purr was a welcome contrast to her dispatcher's staccato cadence and commanding tone. He really needed to be with her now, needed to be with someone who cared about him, someone loyal who he could trust, and he sighed with relief at her tenderness. "I'm on my way. Twenty minutes. If you behave yourself, I'll let you take the arrow out of my heart."

Katkov took the Metro to the Presnensky District, a working-class area in central Moscow where the city zoo was located. Vera's apartment was a short walk from the Metro stop. He trudged up the icy steps, thumbed the buzzer, and fell into her arms when she opened the door. They stood in the foyer hugging, grief-stricken over Grafinskaya's murder. Like the soothing timbre of Vera's off-duty voice, her apartment was a welcome respite from her high-tech, tension-filled work environment. Cozy and neatly kept, it was furnished with upholstered armchairs and a large sofa covered in muted fabric with fluffy pillows in which the sitter seemed to almost disappear.

"I can't believe they killed Grusha because what she wrote might embarrass them," Vera said, her eyes glistening. "There's got to be more to it than that."

"There is," Katkov said, taking the flash drive from a pocket. "I don't know what, but there's a damn good chance it's on here."

"Her work files, her notes?" Vera surmised.

Katkov nodded, his eyes brightening with anticipation. "Got any Red Bull? Coffee'll do if you don't," he said, pulling his laptop from his bag. He set it on a side table in the living room, shut off the Wi-Fi, and plugged in the flash drive—the flash drive on which all her documents, downloads, folders, and emails had been automatically backed up. The drive was named "The Front Page." Katkov clicked on Rename in the drop-down menu. His eyes went to the winking cursor in the title box. After a long pause, he smiled and typed "Wonder Woman," after the comic-book heroine. The code name not only served as a fitting tribute to Grusha but also disguised the file's contents. Furthermore, he already used a subdirectory labeled "Comic Books" to keep track of his collection. Its folders were organized by publisher and concealed among the hundreds of Wonder Woman files in the DC Comics folder, the renamed file would go unnoticed. He was about to click on Save when it suddenly dawned on him that if the FSB confiscated, or hacked into, his laptop, a global search of his files for certain words, phrases, or names would have no trouble finding *that* Wonder Woman file among the many in the DC folder, and he removed Grusha's flash drive from the UBS port, inserted one of his own, and saved it there instead.

The table had a drawer that spanned the kneehole. Katkov emptied the contents and, as he thought, its front, sides and back had been grooved to hold its bottom, forming a shallow recess below. He slipped the original flash drive into an envelope and secured it to the underside of the drawer with packing tape, then slid the drawer back into place. Driven to satisfy his burning curiosity about Grafinskaya's exchange with the FBI agent, he opened the Wonder Woman file on the duplicate flash drive, scrolled down the directory to Email, and opened the Sent file. The emails were arranged by date, with the most recent at the top of the list. His eyes darted to an address bar that read United States Federal Bureau of Investigation. It was Grafinskaya's reply to FBI agent Tom Jones. Despite the Kremlin's table pounding, the email didn't contain any information that could be considered classified. Nor was there any mention of a French-Canadian billionaire fronting a shell corporation. On the other hand, her questions about foreign takeover of American railroads *did* give Agent Jones information that wasn't in her *Novaya Gazeta* article. Even if it had been intercepted by the FSB, the email didn't contain anything that would have prompted the Kremlin to have her killed.

Katkov drained the Red Bull Vera had given him and slouched in his chair with exhaustion. He was about to call it a night when he came across the emails from government directorates—the ones labeled "Top Secret"—on which Grafinskaya had been blind-copied by her sources at the FSB and RZD. This was the raw material on which she had based her exposé of the Kremlin's plan to invest Russia's pension funds in America. Several dealt with the rumor about taking over a railroad. Of even greater interest were the names of her sources. Katkov had just jotted them down when Vera came from the bedroom and wrapped her arms around his shoulders from behind. "You should get some rest, Nikasha. Come on. Come to bed . . ."

"Yeah, I'm brain dead," Katkov grunted as he pulled himself from the chair and followed her. "I thought you were asleep."

"I was . . . for a while . . . I think . . ." Vera said, slipping beneath the rumpled comforter. "I'm covering for the shift supervisor tomorrow. I have to be in by six."

Katkov groaned at the thought of it. "Don't wake me," he said as he snuggled in next to her. "Leave my coffee on the night table and don't slam the door."

Vera squirmed, trying to get comfortable, then pushed up on an elbow. "You know what I don't understand?"

"What?" Katkov mumbled into his pillow.

"Investing our pension money in the American economy instead of ours is a no-brainer. I mean, it's safer, has more predictable growth, and isn't as corrupt."

Katkov sighed and rolled over to face her. "Not *as* corrupt. I like that."

"Regardless, I'd sleep easier knowing my nest egg was invested there. I mean, *you've* got Batman and Robin to fall back on. All *I've* got is Putin and Putin."

"That's two Putins too many," Katov said in a sleepy growl. "Actually, *I've* got two assets to fall back on: my comic-book collection . . . and you."

"Well, maybe it's time you sold one and spent more time with the other."

"Maybe . . ." Katkov whispered, on the verge of nodding off. "Sounds like . . . you're thinking of . . . of taking your pension . . ."

"Yeah, what's wrong with that? I mean, this promotion isn't all it's cracked up to be. These double shifts are more than I bargained for. Like I said, you should give it some thought too. We could travel: Venice, Paris, Rome . . . eat wonderful food, drink fine wine. Maybe we could rent a little house in the south of France, drive through Provence and the Dordogne. It would be so romantic, wouldn't it, Niko? Nikasha? Nikasha?"

Katkov didn't move. Didn't make a sound. Vera sighed, wrapped an arm around his thickening midsection, and lay there listening to his rhythmic breathing.

After a few hours of fitful sleep, Katkov awakened to discover Vera had already left. The coffee on the nightstand was cold. He lit a cigarette and staggered into the bathroom, then went to his laptop and opened the Wonder Woman file to resume his review of Grafinskaya's files. It wasn't long before he realized he had already found whatever pertinent data there was to be found. Not to mention the story of Grafinskaya's murder had to be written and filed at *Novaya Gazeta* before the paper was put to bed. He was about to open his writing program when his eyes drifted to a list of folders on the left side of the screen. From top to bottom it read: Inbox, Sent, Drafts, Spam Detector, Trash. The numeral 1 was next to the word

"Drafts." The address box for that one email read "United States Federal Bureau of Investigation." The subject line read "Sleeper Agents."

Katkov's back stiffened. His eyes snapped open. His mind raced. The implications were staggering. Grafinskaya had written a second reply to the FBI agent. The time stamp indicated she had drafted it shortly after the first but chose to save, not send it. His hand was shaking above the touchpad as he opened the draft. To his relief, it turned out to be a story she had written for *Novaya Gazeta* in 2010 about covert FSB operatives living as Americans in the United States—sleepers who had already been captured and deported. The story had been released to the media by the U.S. government. It was global news, not a Grafinskaya exposé, not something that could have gotten her killed. His heart rate had just returned to normal when he noticed the attachment. It soared when he opened it. The date stamp revealed it was written more than a year after the original story had been published. It was new information. Unpublished information. Threatening information. Information that Katkov had no doubt was highly classified!

Grusha, oh Grusha, he thought, staring in amazement at what she had come within a mouse-click of revealing to an American FBI agent. Did she have second thoughts? Did she feel threatened? Did she just want to live with it for a while? Would she have sent it eventually? He had no doubt that had Grafinskaya shared *this* with the FBI agent—had the FSB intercepted *this* email—the Kremlin would have had no trouble issuing her death warrant. But she *hadn't* sent it, *hadn't* shared it, *hadn't* revealed the information to anyone. Whatever threat she had posed to the Kremlin, whatever had caused them to act against Nina Grafinskaya, this unsent email wasn't it.

Katkov sighed with frustration, then lit another cigarette from the one he'd been smoking and kicked back in the chair, watching the smoke curl to the ceiling. The morning light was streaming through the curtains, sending delicate shadows across the yellowed paint. He was staring at them, gathering his thoughts, when it dawned on him that being the custodian of this information presented him with an unnerving dilemma.

Chapter Eight

That same day in Baltimore, dusk had fallen, and Penn Station's Amtrak Terminal was its usual rush-hour mix of gridlocked traffic and short-tempered commuters. The clock over the entrance read 7:25. The colonnaded façade glowed with incandescent warmth. Beaux-Arts light poles marched along the parking islands.

As forecast, the temperature was an unseasonable sixty-four degrees.

Agent Tom Jones was sitting on one of the high-backed wooden benches in the Main Hall reading a newspaper. His corrupt-currency-trader attire consisted of black sport coat, dress shirt open at the neck, blue jeans, loafers, and tinted glasses. A black ballistic nylon roll-aboard was parked next to him. "Anything going on out there?" he said, speaking above the throb of powerful engines that came from the gates beyond.

"Nada," came Ruben's scratchy reply. He was slouched behind the wheel of a surveillance van in a parking area with a view of the entrance. "Don't give your cojones a coronary. The freeway's a disaster. The North Charles off-ramp is backed up. They're probably just—*Espere! Espere!* Wait!" Ruben said as a black town car with New York plates turned into the parking area, followed by a maroon van with a windowless cargo section. "We have lift-off, people," he went on as the vehicles approached and pulled into adjacent parking spaces. "Nobody move until it goes down. Wait for my signal. Copy?"

"Copy that," the backup team leader replied. "Targets have been acquired," he went on, alerting his units that had been strategically deployed.

"Ready one—Ready two—Ready three," came the acknowledgments rapid-fire.

"Okay, Tommy boy, its show time," Ruben's voice crackled in Tom's earpiece. "Black town car. New York plates. Maroon van right next to it. On your left beyond the taxi line and the approach road as you exit."

"Copy that." Tom set the newspaper aside and strolled toward the exit, pulling the roll-aboard. Once outside, he crossed the taxi line, negotiated the oncoming traffic and started across the parking area. The town car was parked in a row that fronted the perimeter road. Its headlights flashed as

Tom approached. The trunk popped open. Tom put the roll-aboard inside and unzipped it, then stepped over to the maroon van in the adjacent space and knocked twice on the side door. It rolled open, revealing dozens of cardboard file boxes stacked in the cargo bay. The man crouching next to them placed one in the doorway and removed the top. The knuckles on both his hands were tattooed with a pattern of black dots. The box was filled with packets of counterfeit currency that Tom had negotiated to buy at twenty cents on the dollar. He removed one of the bills and examined it: The paper felt thin and crisp despite its apparent age. When marked with a felt-tip detector pen, the ink turned yellow, indicating the paper was of made from cotton and linen fibers—not wood pulp, which contains starch that turns the ink black. And when illuminated by an LED flashlight, red and blue fibers appeared embedded throughout. Furthermore, the color, tone, and detail of the portrait, seals, and border had been reproduced with remarkable fidelity, as had the watermark. The raised texture of intaglio printing was missing, but this was common in aged bills. "Fine work. Some of the best I've seen," Tom said in Russian, sounding impressed, which he was.

The Russian in the van thumbed a button on his phone.

Bargishev slipped out of the back seat of the town car, leaving the door open, and circled to the trunk. His angular features set between wide cheekbones were hallmarks of the Russian Caucasus, his all-black wardrobe of the Vory v Zakone. He smiled at the banded stacks of hundreds in the roll-aboard and nodded to Tom.

Tom held out a hand, palm up. "Your turn," he said in Russian.

Bargishev plunged a knuckle-dotted fist into a pocket and removed a set of keys. He was about to drop them into Tom's palm when his phone rang. His brow furrowed in puzzlement. He let it ring several times, then glanced at the screen, His eyes widened in alarm. "Take that out of there," he said sharply in Russian.

Tom's eyes narrowed in confusion. "What?" he said in Russian.

"You fucking deaf? That's not my bag. Get it out of there."

"What the hell is this? Do we have a deal or don't we?"

"Deal? I don't know what the fuck you're talking about."

"Work him, Tom, work him," Ruben's voice crackled in his earpiece. "If he doesn't take the cash and give you the keys, we can't touch him."

"What's your problem?" Tom challenged, trying to keep Bargishev engaged. "This is no time to renegotiate. I mean, if you—"

"Take the fucking bag and go!"

"I don't know what you're smoking, but no way you'll get a better deal than—"

"Fuck you!" Bargishev growled. He yanked the roll-aboard from the trunk and threw it on the ground in front of Tom.

"*Mierda!*" Ruben's voice crackled. "It's over, Tom It's over. Dammit!"

Bargishev slammed the trunk and began shouting at the driver as he got into the car. The door was still closing as it drove off at high speed. The maroon van pulled away slowly and drove off in the opposite direction. "Scramble your guys and track that van," Ruben barked at the backup team leader.

"Copy that. We're on him."

Ruben got out of the surveillance van and leaned back against it, arms folded, glaring at Tom who was approaching with the roll-aboard. "What the fuck happened?!"

"He got a text. Like he'd been tipped off or something. Really spooked him."

"Your cover must've gotten blown."

Tom nodded dispiritedly, then put the roll-aboard inside the surveillance van and climbed into the passenger seat.

Ruben was bristling with frustration as he got behind the wheel and slammed the door. "We were this close. This fucking close."

"I'm really sorry," Tom muttered as they drove out of the parking area in the direction of an overhead sign that read I-395 South—McLean.

"Hey, it happens," Ruben said, his tone softening. "You'll get over it."

"Did I just hear you say been there, done that?"

Ruben nodded. "Bogotá. Ten years ago. DEA was on a roll. There was a hit man for the Medellín Cartel. Scary guy they called Popeye. Very close to Escobar."

"Yeah, yeah, he was a legend. Took out Pedro's competition on a regular basis."

"By the hundreds."

"Got busted ages ago, no?"

"Uh-huh. Refused to cooperate. Turned down a plea bargain. Sly little *cabron*. He's talking about selling his story to Hollywood when he gets out. Anyway, by the time I got into it, he was halfway into a ten/twenty. Word was his self-esteem had cratered and we figured, a fan, a Popeye worshiper, might be able to gain his confidence, get him to open up. So I went undercover."

"You were his cellmate? Jeez . . ."

"Tell me about it. Maximum security. Minimum amenities. I played him, got the mentor/protégé thing going. Then, just as I started to reel him in, this dealer I'd busted when I was working the street ended up in the same cell block, and made me. What are the odds, huh? DEA decided I'd done my bit and transferred me back here."

An hour later, Ruben dropped Tom at JTTF headquarters and headed home, calling his wife en route. "Hey, babe, it's me. ETA twenty minutes."

"Half a day, huh," Julie joked. "That's great. Kids are still up—which reminds me, I'm making rounds for the book drive tomorrow. I'll need the Jeep."

"No problemo. Heat up the leftovers. I'm starving."

Tom had gotten a coffee from the JTTF lounge and went to his workstation to lick his wounds and make contemporaneous notes for the report. It was nearly midnight by the time he dropped into his chair, crushed by the disappointment. He was staring at his computer screen, trying to collect his thoughts, when an email appeared in his inbox:

Sender: **ngrafinskaya@novayagazeta.ru**

Subject: **Sleeper Agents**

Tom recognized Grafinskaya's email address and brightened, then his brow furrowed in confusion: *But she's dead. Murdered. Assassinated.* Indeed, because she had saved the email instead of sending it, when Katkov resolved his dilemma and sent it, the email looked as if Grafinskaya had sent it. Despite the dissonance, Tom was stunned by the subject line and wasted no time opening it.

In an introductory paragraph, written in Russian, Katkov explained that he was Grafinskaya's mentor and longtime colleague at *Novaya Gazeta* and had just discovered that shortly after she'd replied to Agent Jones's email, she had written another one but, apparently, decided to live with it for a while and saved it in a draft file. Katkov's last sentence read "In light of the recent tragic events, I think she would want you to have it now."

Grafinskaya's email followed, and, in keeping with their previous email exchanges, was also written in Russian:

> *Dear Agent Jones,*
>
> *In October of 2010, in my capacity as a journalist for Novaya Gazeta, I covered the story about Russian sleeper agents who had been arrested in the United States and deported. As I'm sure you recall, the incident caused much embarrassment and hand-wringing in the Kremlin at the time. I have subsequently learned from a reliable source that not all the sleeper agents were captured. Of those who escaped detection, one is a highly skilled asset that my source has told me is deeply embedded in a U.S. government national security agency. Unfortunately, I don't know the name of the agency, nor can I tell you the sleeper agent's real or cover names, but I have been informed that this agent operates under the code name Pochtalska.*
>
> *Yours truly,*
> *Nina Grafinskaya*
> Investigative correspondent, Novaya Gazeta

Tom's eyes were wide in astonishment. A chill ran up his spine. He felt hollow and vulnerable. In his twelve years at the bureau and JTTF, he had never come face-to-face with a danger as clear and present as this one.

Chapter Nine

After forwarding Grafinskaya's unsent email to Agent Jones. Katkov deleted it from his Sent folder and spent the rest of the morning in Vera's apartment writing *Novaya Gazeta*'s front-page story about his colleague's assassination. When finished, he emailed it to Editorial, printed out a hard copy, and took the Metro to the office.

Media satellite vans, their dishes telescoped skyward, were crowded into the parking area in front of the building. The horde of print and TV reporters, bundled against the cold, recognized Katkov and encircled him, shoving microphones, recorders, and cameras into his face as he strode toward the entrance. Many wore sunglasses. Some wore baseball caps with station call letters. The one wearing the cap with the NASCAR logo had neither microphone, recorder, nor camera. The questions came rapid-fire as Katkov pushed past them all, tight-lipped, clutching the strap of his shoulder bag.

"Can you confirm that she revealed classified information?"

"Is it true her death warrant was signed in Putin's office?"

"Is it illegal to invest Russian pension funds in American financial markets?"

"Was it a contract hit?"

Emerging from the scrum, Katkov took one last drag of his cigarette, tossed the butt in a planter, and flashed his ID to the uniformed militia personnel at the entrance.

Moments later, he blew out of the elevator into the newsroom, where staffers were dealing with the aftermath of the RIC search-and-destroy mission. Crime-scene seals were plastered across the door to Grafinskaya's office. Katkov's office wasn't sealed, but it had gotten the full treatment and everything had been displaced. The six superhero posters—Wonder Woman among them—that hung in a row on one wall were perfectly level and aligned but weren't in the right order. He had no doubt the RIC agents had removed them in search of documents, computer discs, or flash drives that might be concealed behind them. It wouldn't have surprised him if they had taken the metal frames apart in search of items concealed between the posters and the backings and *then* reassembled and rehung them. It would have been like them to do that.

The door to the editor in chief's office was open. Yarshevsky was on the phone.

Katkov tossed a sheaf of typewritten pages on the desk.

The story was titled "Crusading Journalist Nina Grafinskaya Assassinated."

The opening paragraph read "Last night, in a brutal attempt to intimidate political opponents, to silence voices that ask pointed questions of government officials, questions asked of the Kremlin on behalf of the Russian people who have every right to answers, *Novaya Gazeta*'s highly acclaimed investigative journalist Nina Grafinskaya was gunned down at point-blank range in the lobby of her Shchepkina Street residence."

"I emailed it to Editorial," Katkov said. "Thought you might want hard copy."

Yarshevsky grunted and ended the call. "It's a war zone down there, huh?" he said, scanning the pages as Katkov dropped into a chair. "Nothing compared to the trouble Churkin's ferrets stirred up here last night." He pushed his glasses up onto his forehead and studied Katkov, who was fidgeting in the chair. "You're buzzing with nervous energy like you do when you have something big."

"*Grusha* had something big—big enough to have gotten her killed if she had used it—but she didn't."

"How big?"

Katkov closed the office door, lighting a cigarette as he returned to his seat. "The Kremlin has a sleeper agent in the U.S. national security apparatus."

"Christ," Yarshevsky exclaimed, throwing up his hands. "That's it. They whacked Grusha to make sure she didn't blow the sleeper's cover."

"I said, she *didn't* use it. The point is, they killed her without knowing she had it."

"How the hell do you know that?" Yarshevsky challenged. "They could have hacked her computer. Could have been monitoring it for months, for years."

"Come on, Vitaly," Katkov groaned. "You're smarter than that. Why confiscate her computer if they had hacked it? Why seize her files? Why seal her office? These people are like bats. They shun the light. Hide in the shadows. Why turn it into a media circus? As somebody famous just said, 'It's a war zone down there.'"

"To send a fucking signal."

"Two bullets to the back of the head is a pretty strong fucking signal. No, no they're frantic, terrified. Not by what they know but by what they *don't* know."

"What if Grusha told that FBI agent about the sleeper?" Yarshevsky fired back. "There's no way FSB's computer nerds didn't intercept their emails."

"Yeah, but I know for a fact she didn't tell him," Katkov retorted. "I also know she *wrote* him a second email in which she *did* mention it—but never sent it."

"Ah! They killed her to *stop* her from sending it. Thank you. I rest my case."

Katov shook his head. "No, no, no way. They killed her *before* they confiscated her computer—*before* they could've known she'd written it." He took a deep drag of his cigarette, then exhaled slowly and said, "*I* sent it . . . a couple of hours ago."

"Chrissakes!" Yarshevsky exclaimed, bolting upright in his chair. "You should've cleared that with me first! What were you thinking?!"

"I was thinking she'd want the FBI guy to have it now."

"It doesn't sound like she was as sure of that as you are."

"I knew Grusha well enough to make that call."

"So where the does that leave us?"

"Grusha's story. I keep coming back to her story."

"Come on, we've already covered this ground. It may have been embarrassing to the Kremlin, but we both know—"

"I know. I know," Katkov said, rapid-fire. "It's not about being embarrassed. It's about being *threatened*. Exposing the Kremlin's investment scheme threatened them—threatened *something*. Grusha had no idea what she endangered."

"Nor do *we*," Yarshevsky retorted, "But the fact that she *could've* exposed a sleeper agent would've scared the living shit out of—"

"Wait, wait," Katkov interrupted, his eyes coming to life behind his thick lenses. "If you're right, the sleeper agent is *part* of it but not *all* of it. It's bigger. Much bigger. More like . . . like an operation the sleeper is working on."

Yarshevsky raised a brow in tribute. "And whatever *that* is, they killed Grusha to protect it."

"Works for me."

Yarshevsky shrugged and splayed his hands. "Still, back to square one."

"Not exactly," Katkov said with a Cheshire smile. "I have the names of her sources."

"No shit. Both of them?" Yarshevsky exclaimed and, concerned Katkov might reveal them, quickly, added, "Don't tell me. You know how they work. The Kremlin'll cook up some sham investigation, put on a show trial to muzzle the newspaper. I'll be forced to testify, and the less I know, the better."

Katkov managed a distracted nod and stubbed out his cigarette.

"What are you thinking?"

"Other than a night's sleep, a shower, and change of clothes?" Katkov replied with a wry grin. "Put the screws to her sources. See what else they know about sleeper agents and railroads. Trouble is, since FSB has Grusha's computer, *they* know who they are too."

"Then they're both either dead, in hiding, or out of the country. They'll find them, Niko. They'll find them, and they'll kill them—and then they'll kill you."

"Well, *you'll* get to write that story, Vitaly."

"Nikasha, please, don't do this. Losing Grusha is more than I can bear. I can't sleep, I can't eat. I feel sick and hollow like my insides have been torn out."

"Welcome to the club," Katkov said, his voice trembling. He let out a long breath and got to his feet. "You know, we've been dealing with this shit, with fear, intimidation, and death threats all our lives. I don't know about you, but I'm not frightened anymore. What was it our esteemed president said on Russia Day? 'Either they will beat us or we will beat them.' Well, for a while there we were winning, and they were losing: Navalny was released and reignited political opposition. The G-20 Conference was a sham. The economy was a disaster. Unemployment was at record levels and the ruble was plunging along with Putin's approval rating, but our Kremlin control freak has produced a hatful of rabbits and is turning it around: He's destabilized Ukraine. Has NATO shaking in its boots. Is building a bridge to Crimea. And is kicking Obama's ass on Syria—all of which has sent his approval rating soaring," Katkov declared in fiery summation. "No way I'm throwing in the towel now, Vitaly. No fucking way!"

Yarshevsky nodded with growing resolve, then came around the desk and gave Katkov a bear hug. "Thanks, I needed that. Go get the bastards."

"For Grusha," Katkov said softly, embracing his boss. He stepped back, then hurried from the office, his mind racing.

Of Grafinskaya's two sources, Katkov knew the one inside the FSB—in Bortnikov's inner circle—would be at the top of their hit list. He had to get to him before they did. A computer search of *Novaya Gazeta* archives produced an address and a photograph of a man in his thirties with a narrow face, shock of dark hair, and alert eyes that had a distinctive sparkle. The name of the source Katkov had typed in the search window was Mikhail Patrushev, FSB Chief Bortnikov's deputy chief of staff.

Chapter Ten

The Capitol Grille in Tysons Corner, just down Route 123 from the National Counterterrorism Center, was one of several watering holes in the area frequented by JTTF personnel. Wood paneling, leather club chairs, and a row of time-zone clocks gave it the feeling of a posh men's club. Leaded-glass ceiling fixtures gave off a warm glow. Early American portraits and seascapes of schooners with billowing sails enhanced the period ambiance. The décor extended to the cocktail lounge, where Tom and Lana, who had flown in from Vegas that afternoon, were settling into a corner booth.

"Johnnie Walker Black, neat," the waitress prompted, recognizing Tom.

"That's me . . . vodka rocks for the lady."

"Ketel One cosmo," Lana corrected.

"Ruben lied," Tom said as the waitress hurried off.

"He always does."

"Well, not always," Tom said with a wry grin, "Couple of things I can think of that he told the truth about."

Lana got the inference and laughed.

"So how'd you make out in Sin City?"

"The good news is I hired a crack cybersecurity team to test Amtrak's systems. The bad news is . . ." Lana let it trail off and nodded toward a TV above the bar where a graphic proclaimed U.S. DRONE STRIKE IN YEMEN KILLS NOTORIOUS TERRORIST. A grim-faced newsreader was intoning, "Just moments ago, the White House confirmed that master bomb-maker Sabbah al-Mesud has been killed in a drone strike. The long-sought terrorist was a key member of al-Qaeda in the Arabian Peninsula. Though pleased at the news, the president was clearly shaken on learning that entire families residing in the building where al-Mesud was in hiding lost their lives. The issue of collateral damage is making the already controversial drone program all the more controversial."

Tom nodded, his jaw taut with frustration. "Bastards hide among innocent civilians. Something about a family coming here to live with their son as I recall . . ."

Lana nodded sadly. "Yeah, he works for the company I just hired. We had a Skype party going between his family's apartment in Sana'a and the CEO's hotel suite. Half the company was there. The family's watching us, we're watching them . . ."

Tom's eyes widened in horror. "You saw it happen?"

"We all did. The poor guy's wife and parents were blown to bits in front of his eyes. He's devastated. Saved every penny to bring them over. Got them visas, an apartment. The whole staff got involved . . ."

Tom let out a long breath as the waitress set their cocktails on the table next to their cell phones. They sat staring at them in silence for a long moment.

"Cheers," Lana said, pushing past it. "So, how'd you and Ruben make out?"

"We *struck* out," Tom replied with a disgusted groan.

"Oh dear," Lana sighed. "Well, so much for changing the subject . . ."

"Yeah," Tom grunted with an ironic laugh. "I mean, all the pieces are in place. I'm face-to-face with the guy. All of a sudden—" He bit it off and groaned. "I'll spare you the ugly details. Bottom line: my cover got blown."

"Bummer . . ."

"Tell me about it," Tom said, taking a long swallow from his glass. "The upside is, the van was tracked to a warehouse on the Baltimore waterfront. We're running a rotating stakeout. See if anybody from the top of the Chechen food chain shows up to claim their merchandise. Ruben's got the four to twelve. I pulled the midnight to eight."

"You sure they were Chechens?"

"Positive," Tom replied, making a fist. "Knuckle dots. They had knuckle dots."

Lana looked puzzled. "Knuckle dots?"

"Tattoos. Each dot represents a year spent in prison. Chechen gangsters have this tattoo code they use to advertise their exploits: A spider denotes high rank. A dagger a hit man; each drop of blood on the blade is a kill. A guy sporting a tiger is a cop killer . . ."

"Yeah, I hear they're nasty customers. Lucky they didn't slash your throat."

"They do have a way with box cutters, don't they?" Tom said sardonically. "The good news is, I know why that Russian journalist was killed."

He lowered his voice and told her about Grafinskaya's second email—written, saved but not sent, forwarded by Katkov—that stated she had reason to believe a Russian sleeper agent was embedded somewhere in the U.S. national security apparatus.

"Jeez. That's got serious flap potential. You run it past Ruben?"

"No. I didn't want it in the air or on the net. We'll have some face time later."

"Good call," Lana said, her head tilting in reflection. "It's kind of weird, you know? I mean, I thought we rolled all their sleepers up a couple of years ago. The hottie housewife in New Jersey. The guy with the degree from Harvard's Kennedy School . . ."

Tom nodded. "All but one," he said in a grave whisper. "Put that together with the Kremlin's plan to take over one of our railroads . . . I'd be worried if I were you."

"Me?" Lana scoffed. "If anyone here might be the target of a mole hunt, it's you."

Tom's eyes narrowed. He looked incredulous and amused at the same time. "What? A *mole* hunt? I'm talking about Amtrak's computer systems getting hacked."

"No shit, Sherlock," Lana said. "Come on. Lighten up. It was a joke."

"Sorry. Didn't mean to take your head off. I'm really bummed over blowing that sting. We were working it for months. Really pisses me off."

"Hey, it happens," Lana said, smiling at a thought. "It is kind of funny, though. I mean, a special agent on the Russian desk, who speaks Russian fluently and has access to top-secret national security matters, gets his cover blown just as the sting is going down."

"Hey, it happens," Tom said pointedly. "You see *No Way Out*?"

"Yeah, Kevin Costner played the sleeper. Naval intelligence officer, embedded in the NSA, spoke fluent Russian. I rest my case."

"He ran with the Beltway set. *I* don't."

"*I* do!" Lana said with a laugh. "Speaking of which, it's time for that rematch. You can burn off some of that angst. What do you say?"

"Sure. I've got some time. Mine or yours?"

"Neither. I have privileges at a private club in Bethesda. Very exclusive. International clientele. World-class fencers. I think you'll like it."

"Lead the way."

"I should call," Lana said, taking her phone from the table. "Yes, hi, it's Lana Nichols . . . Ah, Julian, thought I recognized your voice. How *are* you? . . . Tell me about it. If I'm not up against an *attaque au fer*, I'm deflecting a *septime haute*! Anyway, I know it's short notice, but I'd like to come by this evening—Yes, with a guest, a special one. Can you accommodate us? . . . Uh-huh . . . uh huh, that's right . . . Perfect. See you then."

"Sounds like we're on."

Lana nodded. "It's a quiet night. Julian's quite a character. A bit of a dandy. Right out of the French Revolution." She slipped the phone into her handbag and got up. "I need to pop into the little girls' first. Don't go away . . ."

Tom watched Lana slither between the bustling hook-up action at the bar, reflecting on how she had reacted to the news of a Russian sleeper and the Kremlin scheming to take over a railroad. It was raw intelligence—a red flag that something in her area of responsibility might be endangered. Did she really think he was accusing her of being the sleeper? Did she feel threatened? Had she launched a counterattack to cover it, or was it a joke as she claimed when he challenged her? Having been trained to trust no one and suspect everyone, he had long ago learned to be his own devil's advocate, and he had little choice but to admit that Lana didn't seem at all rattled and laughed it off. Furthermore, she was an accomplished agent with impeccable credentials, and, as he had just acknowledged, the blown sting was fueling his professional paranoia and making him overreact. He concluded it was him, not her, then winced with lingering uncertainty and drained his glass, his eyes drifting after a leggy blond who slinked past him and joined several men at the bar. The one who wasted no time hitting on her was a clean-cut, Land's End type in his mid-thirties who Tom thought bore a remarkable resemblance to a married, family-values congressman from Louisiana. The news crawl on the TV over the bar now read REPUBLICAN FIELD NARROWED TO SEVEN FOR NEXT WEEK'S PRESIDENTIAL PRIMARY DEBATE. CRUZ, TRUMP, RUBIO, KASICH LEAD IN POLLS.

Chapter Eleven

Dusk was falling by the time Katkov left *Novaya Gazeta*'s offices and took the Number 1 Metro to the Zastavy District northeast of the city center. Mikhail Patrushev lived in a weathered tenement on Boyevsk Ulitsa. An all-wheel drive Lada Niva was parked out front beneath a streetlight. The back seat had been folded flat, expanding the cargo area that was filled with cardboard cartons, file boxes, and an old trunk. A man in a worn barn coat loaded several suitcases in behind them, then shut the hatch and hurried into the building. Katkov followed him down the hallway to an apartment. The number on the door read 4A. The man had just unlocked it when Katkov caught up with him.

"Excuse me? Excuse me, Mr. Patrushev?"

The man looked back and shook his head no. He resembled the photo Katkov had downloaded to his phone but appeared twenty years older. His narrow face was topped by short-cropped graying hair. Crows' feet radiated from the corners of his eyes. "He doesn't live here anymore." He entered the apartment and locked the door.

Katkov had no doubt it was Patrushev and knocked on the door. Then knocked again. "Mr. Patrushev? Mr. Patrushev, please? I'm a reporter from *Novaya Gazeta*. Nina Grafinskaya was my protégée. We were close friends. I need to talk with you."

The latch retracted, the door cracked open. "Grusha . . . you were her mentor?"

"Yes, she was my student and colleague at—"

"And your name is?"

"Katkov, Nikolai Katkov." He held up his press pass. "I'm with *Novaya Gazeta*."

Patrushev nodded and opened the door. "Yes, Grusha spoke of you. I'm familiar with your work. A secret admirer, so to speak," he said with a wry smile, dragging deeply on a cigarette. "I'm sorry. I can't be too careful. You understand." He looked anxiously into the hallway, then locked the door behind them.

The apartment was dark and musty. Something out of the Brezhnev era. Heavy drapery, massive pieces of mahogany furniture, a table with clumsy legs and scratched veneer, a lamp with a tasseled shade that gave off a dim glow.

"I can't give you much time," Patrushev said, fetching a satchel that he put on the table. He was about to put some keepsakes and mementos into it when his eyes glistened and his shoulders sagged. "I knew this was going to happen. I . . . I wanted to . . ."

"So did Grusha. She had a premonition. But—"

"No, no, you don't understand," Patrushev interrupted. "The day before her story ran, I was in Sochi with Putin, Bortnikov, Lavrov . . . the whole lot of them. I was there when Putin signed her death warrant and ordered a witch-hunt for her sources."

"You're saying they had an advance copy of the story."

Patrushev nodded. "They know what you're going to publish before you publish it," he said with an ironic sigh. "They also knew she had a source in the Directorate and were monitoring emails and phones. I wanted to warn her, but I was afraid. I returned to Moscow immediately and told my wife to start packing."

"It wouldn't have made a difference." Katkov said, his voice breaking.

Patrushev nodded grimly and began putting the items into the satchel. "My wife has family in Helsinki. I put her on the train yesterday. I'm hoping to join her."

"I just have a few questions," Katkov said, his voice taut with urgency. "The information you gave Grusha was very valuable. Can you recall anything else about the pension investment scheme, or American railroads?"

"No, I gave Grusha all the intel I had on that."

"I have information that suggests the Kremlin has a sleeper in the American national security apparatus . . ." Katkov prompted, gauging his reaction.

Patrushev raised a brow and nodded.

"Do you know the sleeper's identity? A man, a woman? A cover name? Which agency he/she has infiltrated?"

"No, as I said, I gave Grusha everything."

"Do you know if that agent has a specific mission?" Katkov pressed on.

Patrushev shot him an angry glare. "I just told you that I—" He cut it off and took an impatient drag of his cigarette. "There was talk of it in Sochi. Nothing *specific*. The *general* objective is to destabilize the American government."

Katkov shrugged. "What else is new? The Kremlin's been working on that since Hitler took to his bunker. They rev it up whenever they need to rally the troops."

Patrushev smiled thinly and nodded. "Whatever they're up to, it's a foreign intelligence matter that's being run out of SVR. Directorate S."

"Spetsnaz," Katkov said, referring to the elite group that executes special operations abroad. "So how did *you* hear about it?"

"I've been the FSB/SVR liaison for years. All the operational details are tightly compartmented. Bortnikov's the only one who has access." Patrushev stubbed out the cigarette and resumed putting the items into the satchel. "You know, years ago I used to take my niece for lessons at a ballet school. Grusha was there every week with her daughter. One day, we got to talking, and well . . ." He paused, his eyes pleading with Katkov for understanding. "Not everyone in the FSB is a Bolshevik thug. For decades, some of us have been trying to humanize the Directorate. To make it work for the people instead of against them. That's why I confided in Grusha. She was special. She wanted to . . . to make Russia a better place."

Katkov sighed, overwhelmed with sadness. "She *did* make it a better place. She broke a lot of big stories that really made a difference . . ."

"And I helped her," Patrushev said with evident pride. He closed the satchel, then took it from the table and shut off the light. "We should go." He was heading toward the foyer when his eyes came alive with a thought. "Wait, wait—the sleeper—a few days ago, an SVR memo crossed my desk. I'd seen it before and had passed it to Grusha, but . . . but that one was redacted. This one wasn't. For what it's worth, the sleeper agent was born there. In America. He's not a Russian."

Katkov's eyes widened with intrigue. "You said *he*."

"No, just a figure of speech. He/she, I've no idea. I wish I could—" Patrushev paused, distracted by a scratching sound that came from the foyer. "Lock picks."

"What?"

"Someone's picking the lock," Patrushev replied. "I was pretty good in my day." The dead bolt retracted with a soft metallic click. The door began opening slowly. "The fire escape," he said in a tense whisper, leading the way to an adjacent room.

The foyer door cracked open. A man wearing sunglasses and a NASCAR cap slipped into the darkened apartment. He held an automatic pistol with a silencer in his fist. His eyes darted to the wisps of smoke rising from the ashtray, then he whirled at the sound of a window sash being raised and ran toward the adjacent room.

Patrushev was climbing out the window onto the icy fire escape. Katkov was right behind him. NASCAR Cap stopped in the doorway and fired. The pistol emitted a barely audible *pffft*. The round splintered the window frame next to Patrushev, who took off down the fire escape. Katkov had one leg over the sill when NASCAR Cap fired again. Two more rapid-fire *pfffts*. The first round whizzed past Katkov's head. The second tore through his parka into his right shoulder. He yelped at the searing pain and tumbled onto the fire escape. NASCAR Cap lunged out the window with the pistol and spotted Patrushev below clambering down the steps. He didn't see Katkov, who had been forced to reverse direction, pressed against the brick façade to the left of the window, clutching his shoulder. Before NASCAR Cap could get off a shot, Katkov grasped the window sash with his good hand and slammed it shut with bone-crushing force onto his head. In the darkness below, Patrushev came off the fire escape into an alley, then ran to the street where the Lada was parked. Katkov stumbled down the fire escape and hurried after him. Patrushev was getting behind the wheel when Katkov caught up. Blood that had soaked through his shirt and parka was seeping between his fingers.

"Come on! Get in!" Patrushev shouted, stabbing the key into the ignition.

Katkov clambered in next to him and slammed the door.

"There's an emergency room just the other side of—"

"No!" Katkov exclaimed as the Lada took off at high speed. "No emergency room. No hospital. I'll tell you where. It's not far."

Chapter Twelve

By the time Lana returned, Tom had paid the tab and they headed to their cars in the Capitol Grille parking lot. The weather was almost balmy as he transferred his fencing bag from his BMW to Lana's Prius and got in next to her, his mind drifting to a conversation they'd had the morning after he'd spent the night at her apartment. He was dressing and watching Google News on her computer. She was packing for her trip to Vegas and used a word—a Russian word—in response to a comment he made about Vladimir Putin. It coincided with the staggering news of Grafinskaya's murder, and it went right past him. Even now, he couldn't be sure she had said it.

"So you still think the prez outsmarted Volodya on Syria?" he prompted in as offhanded a tone as he could muster.

"Outsmarted *who*?"

"Volodya. It's an affectionate form of Vladimir. You used it to refer to Putin the other morning."

"I did?" Lana said with a laugh. "That'll teach me to sleep with a guy who speaks Russian."

"That guy taught you a few other things as well, as I recall."

"That guy has an eager student . . ." Lana said with a seductive purr, "who's looking forward to her next lesson." The Burning Tree off-ramp led to a side road and a tree-lined drive that ended at a rambling country manse with stables and several outbuildings opposite a vaulted barnlike structure. A crest with crossed sabers and a banner that proclaimed SENTIMENT DU FER— the feeling of the blade—hung above the entrance. Lana parked out front and popped the hatch. Tom was tugging their fencing bags from the cargo space when she reached in and removed the pair of vintage dueling swords.

"Guess that means I qualify," Tom prompted, eyeing them.

"Told you, you were good. I meant it."

The club's interior was of post-and-beam construction with a peaked roof like the barns on French country estates—one that had been converted into a cathedral in which the art of fencing was the religious ritual. A bar and lounge area were at one end, locker rooms and a pro shop at the other. Rows of pistes covered the expanse of floor between them. Two bouts were in progress when Lana and Tom entered.

An impeccably attired man in his early sixties with flowing hair and European savoir faire greeted Lana with open arms. "Ah, Mademoiselle Nichols, *bienvenue!*" he exclaimed as they air kissed on both cheeks. "You look more ravishing each time I see you!"

"And you, Julian, are living proof that you can take the man out of Versailles, but you can't take Versailles out of the man!" Lana enthused, introducing him to Tom as Julian Levenger, venture capitalist, fencing master, and citizen of the world.

"You left out *cavalier et connoisseur de vin*," Julian scolded, his palm to his chest. *"J'ai le coeur brisé."*

Tom and Lana wasted no time heading to their respective locker rooms to change into their fencing kits. Tom dropped onto the bench in front of a row of lockers, unable to get Lana's use of "Volodya" and their brief encounter over cocktails out of his mind. True, she had handled his challenges with convincing and lighthearted equanimity, but it still bothered him. He logged into the JTTF mainframe on his phone and stared at the search window with troubling uncertainty.

A short time later, he and Lana emerged from the locker room, masks under their arms, razor-sharp dueling sabers still in their scabbards at their sides. The other fencers had suspended their bouts and were on the sidelines with Julian, who had noticed the vintage dueling weapons, and spread the word that a rare event was in the offing.

"Better make it a five-pointer," Tom said as they slipped the blades from their scabbards.

"I was thinking fifteen," Lana replied with a jaunty bounce in her step.

"With these?"

"You want to get Mr. Knuckle Dots out of your system or not?" Lana taunted. *"En garde—Prêt—Allez!"* she called out, opening with a *coupe de taille*.

Tom parried and counterattacked, the shorter dueling blades drawing them into close contact. An exchange of lunges and thrusts followed. It ended with their blades locked at the hilts, bringing them face-to-face. "The Russian agent's code name is Pochtalska," he said in Russian, glaring at her. "It means 'Postman.'"

"Robert Redford. *Three Days of the Condor*," Lana fired back as they disengaged. "The shooter who took out the CIA station was disguised as a postman."

"The Postman Always Rings Twice!" Tom called out, their blade tips circling in search of an opening. "Lana Turner!"

"My mom's favorite actress."

"It's short for *Svetlana*!" Tom retorted. "It means 'light.'"

"I know . . ." Lana lowered her saber, removed her mask, and bowed as if acknowledging the victor of a bout, then she straightened, raised her chin, and said, "It also means 'woman with a zest for life.'"

"Suits you," Tom said, removing his mask. "By the way, I ran a search when I was in the locker room: Nichols was once Nikolshevskiy. Wasn't it?"

"My name is Nichols," Lana replied, her tone sharpening. "It always has been. I was born in this country. I'm an American citizen."

"Come on, Lana, its right here," Tom said, pointing to his saber's bell guard. "Worked into the decorative engraving. I noticed it at your place. It didn't mean anything then, but it sure as hell does now."

She held his look for a long moment, then broke it off, and sighed in concession. "It was my grandfather's."

Tom nodded like a prosecutor who had just caught a witness lying on the stand. "Russian Olympic fencing team. Bronze medal. Foil. London 1948. Your mother, Katia Nikolshevskaya, USSR Olympic fencing team, Montreal 1976. Didn't compete. Slipped out of the Olympic Village. Asked for political asylum. At least, that was her cover story."

Lana nodded, her eyes aglow. "She was something. A true believer. Proud of her tradecraft. Taught me a lot. Speaking of covert ops, your SCI clearance was confirmed."

"It was never in question, was it, Lana? It was just a stall."

Lana nodded and smiled.

"And?"

"CSX is the railroad targeted for a takeover by the Kremlin."

"Your handlers would be pissed if they knew you told me that."

"They sure as hell would!" Lana exclaimed as she suddenly launched an attack that caught Tom off guard. He parried and tried to counter it, but Lana deflected his lunge and, in several lightning-fast moves, disarmed him, backing him off the piste into a corner as his saber skittered aside. Tom looked stunned. His hands raised defensively on either side of her blade. His eyes widening at the razor-sharp steel pressed against his throat. A thin line of perspiration glistened in the crease of his neck and began turning crimson. A tiny drop of blood formed on the edge of the blade, then burst and rolled across it. He forced a nervous laugh as his eyes darted anxiously to Julian and the other club members who were advancing toward them.

"Pretty good, huh?" Lana taunted. "In case you're wondering, the first move was a *Vtoroe Nameerenie*; the second was a *Kontrotvet*," she went on as Julian and the four fencers encircled them. One was a striking woman in her early sixties who bore a remarkable resemblance to Lana. She stood with athletic presence, her sporting foil at her side, and held Tom's eyes with cool detachment. "*I eto moy obrabotchik, Julian, I moya mat', Katia, i eti chleny ikh kleti*," Lana went on in Russian, which Tom knew meant "And this is my handler, Julian, and my mother, Katia, and members of their cell."

"This is ridiculous," Tom said, his tone a mixture of terror and disbelief.

"I know," she said with a remorseful sigh. "I made a little slip, there, over cocktails, and you caught it, didn't you?"

Tom nodded. "Caught 'Volodya' too . . ."

"Yes, I'll have to be more careful in the future. Won't I?"

Tom stared at her in icy silence.

"You're good, Tom. Really good . . ." Lana went on matter-of-factly. "And I like you a lot, but you got too close, too fast. I'm sorry."

"Don't," he pleaded as Lana increased the pressure on the blade.

"I warned you, remember?" she prompted, her eyes taking on a vacant glaze. "I *said*, 'If I tell you, I'll have to kill you.'"

"You don't have to do this, Lana."

Lana's eyes darted to Julian's. They held hers and hardened as he nodded. "Yes, I do," she said in a detached whisper.

"It's that big an op," Tom said, sensing the inevitability of the moment.

Lana nodded. "As big as they get."

Tom's hands were at shoulder height, bracketing the blade. He was on the verge of making a palm-slicing attempt to grasp it when, with an imperceptible twitch of her thumb and index finger followed by a nimble flick of her wrist, Lana cut his throat.

Tom's eyes widened in a mixture of horror and disbelief. His hands went to his neck. He staggered a few steps, blood from the wound flowing down across his white tunic, then gasped and collapsed at her feet.

Lana stepped back as Julian and the others moved in. Katia swept her eyes across the fallen agent, then shook her head in dismay. "I don't like solving a problem by creating an even bigger one."

"Nor do I," Julian said grimly. "But . . . but *c'était la seule décision*."

"Yeah, it was the right call," Lana said, and, with an insouciant shrug, added, "Nothing a box cutter wouldn't fix."

Chapter Thirteen

The air was crisp and cold and the sky above the dormered rooftops in the Old Arbat was dotted with stars. The streets in the elite neighborhood west of the Kremlin were lined with brick townhouses and mature trees that arched overhead in bare-leafed canopies. nineteenth-century-style streetlamps with onion-shaped globes washed the snow-dotted cobble-stones with warm light. A black Mercedes 770 sedan, its running lights on and engine purring, was parked in front of Number 36. A driver in a black topcoat, dark suit, white shirt, and black necktie was standing next to it.

The door to the townhouse opened and an elegantly dressed couple swept down the staircase to the street. The fine-boned woman was in her mid-forties and wore a mink coat over a black cashmere sheath that went to her ankles. A strand of pearls swayed from her neck. Bracelets that sparkled in the darkness circled her wrists. The gentleman wore a designer tuxedo that was shaped to his runner's physique. His lightly moussed hair was graying at the temples. The driver opened the back door of the Mercedes. The woman was about to get in when her eyes darted to something on the other side of the street. She hesitated and took a step back.

"What is it?" her escort wondered.

"Nothing. Go. I'll catch up."

"Why? What's going on? You okay?"

"I'm fine. *He* isn't," the woman replied, nodding in the direction of a figure standing in the shadows across the street. He was clutching his shoulder where bright-red blood had soaked through his parka. "It's Nikolai . . ."

"Katkov? What's *he* doing here?"

"It's obvious he's in some kind of trouble . . ."

"This is an important night for me, Alexa . . ."

"I know. I won't be long. Go. I'll take a cab."

"I'll send the car back for you," the man said as he slid into the back seat.

Katkov emerged from the shadows as the Mercedes drove off.

"Look at you, Niko," Alexa said. "It's been how long? I mean, the only time you come to see me is when someone's been shot."

"This time it's me," Katkov grunted, his breath visible in the frigid air.

"I can see that," Alexa said, looking about anxiously. "Come on, let's get off the street." She helped him up the stairs into the townhouse. It had high, coved ceilings, arched doorways that were articulated by ornate plaster moldings, sculpted marble fireplaces, and elegant antique furnishings set about an archipelago of Persian rugs.

"Looks like Slava does very well," Katkov prompted, matter-of-factly.

"We both do," Alexa said with evident pride. Then, self-conscious about her wealthy trappings, she added, "We didn't inherit all this. We're both dedicated and work long hours. We earned it." She led the way through the entry hall to a medical examining room. In contrast to the textured opulence of the other spaces, it was precise and antiseptic, without personal touches or furniture other than an examining table, a wall of white cabinets with racks of shallow drawers, and a stainless-steel cart on which medical instruments were arranged. "I see most of my patients in my office at GMS," Alexa said, referring to Moscow's most modern private health clinic, but"—she slipped a lab coat over her evening clothes—"I have a few for whom privacy is paramount and prefer they not be seen visiting a doctor."

"You mean if it got out that a corrupt government minister, corporate robber baron, or thieving Internet billionaire had come down with a head cold or popped a hemorrhoid their image of invincibility would be destroyed," Katkov said with a mischievous laugh.

"Precisely," Alexa replied with an amused grin. "Every time Angela Merkel sneezes, the euro crashes. Imagine if it got out she had a yeast infection!"

Katkov's laughter was cut short by searing pain as Alexa helped him out of his parka and onto the examining table. She slipped on a pair of surgical gloves and began cutting away Katkov's shirt with a pair of scissors. "I've seen worse," she mused, peeling the bloody fabric away from the wound. "You're lucky it's the right shoulder . . . away from the heart and major blood vessels."

"Not to mention, as you may recall, I'm left-handed."

"A *lefty* in every way," Alexa said with an affectionate smile.

"As you knew when you promised to love, honor, and obey . . ."

"I lied," Alexa said with a laugh. "So, how did this happen?"

"You know what's been going on . . ."

"This has to do with Grusha?" she said as she went about cleansing the wound, revealing a tiny circular puncture amidst the bits of tissue and clotting blood.

Katkov nodded and winced at her ministrations. "I'm pretty sure her killer is the same guy who shot me."

"My God, Niko . . ."

"Tell me about it. I think I killed him."

Alexa gasped and rolled her eyes. "You killed a Kremlin hit man?!"

Katkov tried to shrug and grimaced in pain. "I wasn't the target."

"Wrong place at the wrong time, huh?"

"*Right* place at the wrong time. Sorry, I didn't mean to ruin your evening."

"It's fine. Really. Slava's getting an award. Advertising Stud of the Year or something. He's got dozens of them. I'll get there when I get there. He'll be fine."

"I'm sure. He's just one of those guys with a knack for selling things to people they don't need," Katkov said. "I believe they're called snake-oil salesmen."

Alexa smiled, then peeled the wrapper from a syringe and filled it with fluid from a vial. "I'm going to give you a local. With a little luck, we'll get that nasty thing out of there. Actually, Slava's very good at what he does . . ."

"I'll bet. After all, he conned you into this—" Katkov groaned as she popped him with the needle and depressed the plunger.

"He is in the advertising business. *You* should be in a hospital."

"I can't. If they know I've been shot, there'll be an investigation and they won't let me leave the country. Not to mention, a bullet concealed in one's anatomy has a way of setting off the metal detectors in airports."

"I'd have thought they'd be glad to be rid of you," Alexa teased, donning a pair of illuminated magnifiers. She inserted a pair of narrow forceps into the bloody cavity in Katkov's shoulder. "Feel that?"

"A little," Katkov replied through clenched teeth as she gently twisted the forceps this way and that. "A lot, dammit!"

"As I said, with a little luck . . ." Alexa said, working the forceps. Katkov bit a lip as she spread the handles slightly, then locked and retracted them. "See," she said, holding up the bloody slug. "No need to worry about metal detectors." She dropped it in a tray. "When were you planning to go?"

"Soon. This isn't going to stop me."

"I'll be the judge of that," Alexa retorted, irrigating the wound and studying it through the magnifiers. "Don't seem to be any bone fragments lurking about, but you're grounded for at least a couple of weeks. Through the holidays for sure."

Katkov emitted a dismayed groan.

"Where you headed?"

"Washington—DC."

"Why? What's that got to do with what happened to Grusha?"

"The people who took out the contract are here. But their motive—*the story*—is there." Katkov didn't dare reveal that the Kremlin had an agent embedded in America's national security apparatus and, that he believed Grafinskaya had been killed to protect that agent's mission—whatever that mission was.

"That's what you said the last time you headed west," Alexa teased.

"Yeah, and I got the same feeling in my gut now. I guess it's in my DNA."

"I'm not sure the self-destructive gene has been identified yet."

"How about the search-for-the-truth gene?"

"The jury's still out."

"Is it still out on the one that turns human beings into greedy, vicious thugs?"

"Is that what drives you, Nikasha?" Alexa asked, dressing the wound with gauze pads. "A burning desire to rid the planet of the ugly side of human nature?"

"I don't know. I'm not sure I *want* to know. I mean . . . it makes me feel whole. Complete. Gives me a reason to get out of bed in the morning."

"I always thought it was the comic books."

"You mean all that subversive literature that ignited my anti-dictator gene and got me kicked out of the Young Communists League?"

"Well, Truth, Justice, and the American Way doesn't exactly ring with Bolshevik ardor, does it?" The chatter of adhesive tape being unrolled punctuated her statement. "Whose slogan was that anyway? Batman and Robin?"

"Superman. From the radio serial after the War . . . 1948, '49 . . . somewhere in there."

"Before my time," Alexa said, securing the gauze pads with adhesive tape.

"Mine too."

"So, back in the '60s and '70s when everyone was fighting to get their hands on copies of *Playboy* and *Deep Throat*, you were into samizdat comic books . . . ."

"Hey, my collection's worth a small fortune. Vera's talking about retiring on her pension—assuming Volodya doesn't blow it on Wall Street. I don't have to depend on the Kremlin kleptos for mine. My childhood superheroes will be covering my ass."

"Well, they didn't cover it tonight, did they? Looks like one of those nasty evildoers laced your Marlboros with kryptonite dust."

"Yeah, bullets don't seem to bounce off like they used to."

"Well, maybe Vera's right. Maybe it's time you . . . you know . . . eased up a little."

"Maybe," Katkov said, entertaining the idea. "But not just yet."

After securing his arm in a sling, Alexa gave him a tetanus shot, then took two blister packs from a drawer, popped a pill from each, and had him take them. "These are painkillers. Don't take them if you don't need them. These are a powerful antibiotic. It's really important you take them. Instructions are on the back."

Katkov nodded and slipped off the table. His shirt was in bloody tatters.

"Don't go away . . ." Alexa removed the surgical gloves and lab coat, then hurried from the room. Moments later, she returned with a man's shirt.

"Ralph Lauren?" Katkov prompted, feigning disapproval as she helped him into it. "I would've thought nothing but Gucci or Dolce & Gabbana for Slava."

"It's an old shirt," Alexa said with a grin. She helped him into his parka, picked up his shoulder bag, and led the way from the examining room.

The Mercedes was at the curb. The driver opened the back door as they came down the steps from the townhouse. "In you go," Alexa said, gesturing Katkov to get in.

"Me?"

Alexa nodded and tossed his bag onto the seat. "Just tell him where you want to go. I'll catch a cab in the Square. Oh, one last thing," she said. "That dressing will have to be changed. I'll come by your place in the morning and take care of it. See how you're doing. Call me if you have severe pain. Call me anyway."

"Thanks, I can't tell you how much . . ."

Alexa put a fingertip to his lips, silencing him. "You're my hero . . . my *superhero*." She closed the door and hurried off in the direction of Arbatskaya, where green lights atop available taxis were plentiful.

As the Mercedes drove off, Katkov spotted two men in winter warmup suits slouched in a sedan parked down the street. How could they have known where he was? Like all contract killers, NASCAR Cap worked alone. He had no backup at Patrushev's apartment. His employers wouldn't be anywhere near a target when a contract was being executed. Not to mention, Katkov had incapacitated him, if not killed him. So, no one could have followed Patrushev's car to Alexa's townhouse—which meant they were still tracking his phone. Not using it wouldn't put a stop to it. Nor would shutting it off. He had no choice but to discard it, which, he realized, could work to his advantage—if he *didn't* remove the battery, *didn't* shut it off, and *didn't* remove the SIM card, which not only contained his contacts directory but also the data that identified it as *his* phone.

The Mercedes headed west on Arbatskaya past the Dunkin Donuts and Baskin-Robbins opposite the Dom Knigi bookstore and the Khudozhestvenny Cinema, where the marquee proclaimed *Iron Man 3*, *Fast & Furious 6*, *Man of Steel*, and had just turned onto the Outer Ring when the driver slowed for a traffic signal. The car rolled to a stop next to a tradesman's pickup. Katkov lowered the window and tossed his phone into the open bed that was filled with construction debris. When the light changed and the pickup pulled away, Katkov noticed the region number on its license plate was 76, which meant it was registered in Yaroslaval, an industrial city 160 miles northwest of Moscow. Katkov smiled at the thought of the FSB bloodhounds tracking him to the hinterlands and settled back into the Mercedes' cushy leather upholstery. It wasn't long before his moment of triumph was brought to an abrupt end by a searing pain that shot through his right shoulder.

Chapter Fourteen

Banks of work lights turned night into day along the piers on the Baltimore waterfront, where cargo and container vessels were loaded and unloaded 24/7. Forklifts shuttled back and forth from warehouses transporting pallets of freight to gantries that hovered over the wharves from the decks of freighters. Eighteen-wheelers queued at loading stations, where massive bridge cranes hoisted steel shipping containers, stacking them like building blocks atop those already on deck.

Agent Ruben Diaz, along with two members of the backup team that had worked the busted sting at the train station, had spent the last eight hours inside a battered van on Pier 13 between the Seagirt and Canton marine terminals. They had been staking out the warehouse where the van with the cartons of counterfeit currency had been tracked. Neither it, nor its cargo, nor Bargishev, nor any members of his knuckle-dotted entourage had exited or entered the building. Exhausted by the lack of activity, stagnant air, and general boredom, the three agents had been eagerly awaiting the upcoming shift change.

At midnight, the two backup agents were relieved as planned. When Tom didn't show up, Ruben called his cell phone, desk phone, and home phone, leaving a "Where the hell are you?!" voicemail on each. When neither the JTTF duty officer nor the FBI night supervisor could shed light on Tom's whereabouts, Ruben arranged for another agent to relieve him and headed south on I-95. Instead of returning to headquarters, he detoured to Tom's apartment. It was in one of the new high-rises in Silver Spring, just across the river from McLean. He identified himself to the lobby attendant and asked if he had seen Tom that evening.

"Nope, not since midnight when I came on," the fellow replied with a shrug. "That doesn't mean he didn't come in or go out, because the elevator—"

"Goes down to the underground garage," Ruben interrupted. "I know."

The sleepy-eyed fellow gave Ruben the spare key to Tom's apartment. The plastic tag read 306. "Make a right out of the elevator."

The building was new. The corridors were wide, bright, and quiet. Ruben pressed the buzzer several times, then unlocked the door and opened it slowly. A blue-green glow from the halogen streetlights sent long shadows across the ceiling. He flipped the light switches next to the door and made his way to the living area. Like its occupant, it was neat, clean, and in perfect order, as was the open kitchen. No pile of dirty dishes in the sink, no half-finished cup of coffee on the counter.

"Tom?" Ruben called out, "Hey, amigo, it's Ruben. You here?" He found the bedroom and flipped another wall switch. No soiled clothes tossed about, no kicked-off shoes or dirty socks on the floor. The bed was made, pillows plumped against the headboard. A box of laundered shirts was atop the comforter, along with several suits and sport coats in plastic dry-cleaner bags. The bright-white one on top caught his eye. It was fencing attire. He entered the bathroom and turned on the light. No sign of Tom nor evidence of foul play there, either, nor the pungent scent of death that Ruben had feared. His sense of relief was cut short by a staggering surge of anxiety. It was totally out of character for Tom to just drop off the radar like this, and Ruben's alarm systems were blaring with earsplitting intensity. Before leaving, he checked all the closets, then took the elevator down to the underground garage. Each parking space was identified by an apartment number stenciled on the wall. Space 306 was empty. He walked up the ramp to the street where he had parked his car and had just driven off when his phone rang. His home number was crawling across the screen. "Hi, what's going on?"

"That's what *I'm* wondering," his wife said, sounding miffed. She had fallen asleep with the TV on and an iPad with a spread sheet from the Internet travel agency where she worked in her lap. Several hours later, she stirred and realized Ruben wasn't home. "I thought you were getting off at midnight."

"Me too. I ran into a . . . *un peqeño problema.*"

"The children were upset you didn't call before they went to bed. They miss you." She tossed the covers aside and got to her feet. "Come home, Ruben . . ."

"I can't, babe. It's crunch time. *Muy serio.* I've got to—"

"It's always *muy serio*," she interrupted, pacing about the bedroom. "We need to talk, Ruben. We need to make some decisions. I can't keep doing this."

"I know, babe. I know you're stressed-out, and I know you're homesick. Believe me, I get it. But the numbers have to work before we—*Mierda!*" Ruben hit the brakes and swerved. "*El jodido idiota me cortó! Cambió de carril sin señalización! Tiene que ser un DUI!*"

"Ruben?! Ruben, I have zero interest in the jerk who cut you off, and even less in you wasting your time busting him for driving under the influence! The only thing I care about is that you listen to your wife, hear what she's saying, and get with the program."

"Sorry. Like I said, I get it, but this isn't the time to—"

"It's never the time, Ruben," Julie snapped. "Never. I mean, I can't keep living like this. It's affecting the kids, too, but every time I bring it up, you're either running out the door or brain dead from exhaustion or just unwilling to—"

"Julie? Julie?!" Ruben interrupted. "Lighten up and listen, dammit. Okay?"

"Okay," Julie said with a compliant sigh.

"Tom didn't relieve me. He's MIA."

Julie's eyes widened with alarm. "What? What do you mean?"

"He's missing. Off the grid. That's all I can tell you now. I'm on my way back to HQ. I'll call you soon as I know what's going on."

"Okay. I'm sorry. Really, I-I didn't . . . I . . ."

"It's okay, babe. Forget it."

"I love you. Be careful . . ."

"Yeah. Love you too."

They spoke in English and Spanish as they often did, especially with the children, whom they wanted to be bilingual—which made their lives into episodes of *I Love Lucy* and *Modern Family*. It was the language she and Ruben spoke when they first met. He had just checked into the Sofitel Victoria Regia, an upscale hotel in the Zona Rosa, Bogotá's nightclub district, where Julie worked as a concierge. In addition to the personal services she provided for guests, she also had connections at police headquarters and at a medical clinic with discreet personnel, and, having grown up in the area, she knew who in the teeming local underworld could be trusted and who couldn't. Indeed, as the hotel's "air traffic controller," she knew who was where, who should be where, and who wasn't where they should be at any given moment. "Hi, Julie Moreno, head concierge," she had said, catching up with Ruben as he left the check-in desk. "If there's anything you need . . ."

"*Nada. Estoy bien. Gracias.*"

"Come on, I know why you're here. I can help you."

"Really?" Ruben said, pretending he was baffled. "Help me with what?"

"The two fat cats from Cartagena who are checking in tonight."

Ruben raised a brow and held her look. As an undercover DEA agent stationed in Bogotá, he was casing the hotel in advance of a sting, and though he was an experienced, street-smart cop, Julie had made him in a minute. "*Gatos gordos*, eh? What about them?"

Julie guided him to the concierge's station and removed a tattered paperback from her handbag: *News of a Kidnapping*, Gabriel García Márquez's novel about narco-terrorism and the Medellín Cartel in the 1990s. "Have you read this?"

"I'm *living* it."

"I know." Julie lowered her voice and added, "These bastards are destroying my country. I want to help you nail their asses."

Ruben thought about it for a moment and nodded. "*Bueno.* Make them feel comfortable, secure, special, whatever they want, like they own the place"—he winked—"like they own you."

"Nobody owns me, *Agent* Diaz." Julie fired back. She paused, and with a flirtatious glance, added, "Not yet anyway."

Over the next several days, Julie satiated the drug kingpins with a steady diet of tequila, high-class escorts, and cable porn. They became complacent, cocky, and careless. The sting went like clockwork. Ruben and his team took down a major cartel capo and seized a thousand kilos of pure cocaine.

In the months that followed, Ruben and Julie couldn't get enough of each other. About a year later, when his cover got blown and he was transferring back to HQ, they got married and she went with him. That was ten years ago. And they'd since been living the American dream in suburban Reston with two children, a dog, a mortgage, car payments, and the 24/7 pressure on Ruben to keep America safe.

It was well after three a.m. by the time Ruben reached his workstation at JTTF and checked his inbox. No emails from Tom. None related to his disappearance. After filing an official notice that his partner was missing, he put out an APB for Tom's car and requested his phone be GPS tracked, then headed for the cafeteria in need of coffee.

Several hours later, Ruben awakened on a sofa in the staff lounge. He sat up with a start, then sagged, dispiritedly, when he realized it hadn't been a phone call with news of Tom that had awakened him. A short time later, he was at one of the automated coffee machines in the cafeteria watching his cup fill when Lana approached in her hip-swaying stride. "Hey, Agent Nichols. I was just coming to see you . . ."

"Saved you the trip," Lana said, frowning at his disheveled appearance. "You look like hell, Ruben. What's up?"

"Not here," Ruben muttered, taking the coffee before leading the way to a small conference room. "I gather you and Agent Jones were working together on that Russian railroad thing," he prompted, closing the door.

"Uh-huh. He exchanged emails with that journalist who just got whacked. The one who blew the whistle on the Kremlin investing in our financial markets."

"I know," Ruben said, settling into one of the chairs. "You and Tom been in touch? I mean, yesterday, last night, maybe this morning?"

Lana smiled at the innuendo and leaned her *medaille d'or derrière* against a sideboard. "Yeah, I got back from Vegas yesterday afternoon. Met him at the Grille around seven to catch up. We had a couple of drinks. He said he was going to be relieving you on a stakeout. Why?"

"He never showed up . . ."

"You serious?" Lana gasped.

Ruben nodded grimly. "MIA, AWOL, whatever. Phone dead, apartment empty, he's nowhere to be found. Did he seem distracted, troubled in any way?"

"Well . . . he *was* really bummed out over a busted sting."

"Makes two of us . . ."

"He mentioned guys with knuckle dots. Thought they were Chechens."

"They *were*. Last time I saw Tom . . ." Ruben paused and shifted uneasily at what he was about to say. "He was pulling a roll-aboard with five million in cash."

"The op money?" Lana said, having no idea what had happened to it. "You saying Tom didn't return it?"

Ruben nodded.

Lana's eyes narrowed in confusion. "What about the transponder? I mean, there's got to be one built into the roll-aboard or hidden in the bundles of cash."

Ruben nodded, glumly. "There is. Not a peep. Destroyed, turned off, whatever."

"Then what? You saying you think that Tom—"

"Might be sunning himself on a topless beach in Rio mainlining piña coladas?" Ruben interrupted, his head bobbing with uncertainty.

"Tom?" Lana scoffed. "No way. He's as straight an arrow as they come. Not a mendacious bone in his body. He was probably an Eagle Scout . . ."

Ruben nodded sagely. "He was, but it wouldn't be the first time an Eagle Scout . . . I mean, you never really know about people, do you?"

"Hey, if this business teaches you anything . . ."

"Takes some longer than others." Ruben said, his eyes coming to life. "Couple a years ago I took the wife and kids up to New York at Christmas to see family, heading down to Bogotá this year to see Julie's. Anyway, we did the whole Big Apple cha-cha-cha: Radio City, Rock Center, Macy's, the museums. So, we're in the MoMA. My seven-year-old is staring at this Picasso. The one with the woman in front of the mirror, but she and her reflection don't match, you know?"

Lana nodded and smiled. "One of my favorites . . ."

"I said, 'Amelia, what do you think's going on here?' And she says, 'Well, Papi, sometimes the way a person looks on the outside isn't the way they are on the inside.'"

Lana's brows went up. "Precocious, isn't she?"

Ruben nodded, his eyes aglow with pride. "Smart as a whip." His expression darkened. His eyes found Lana's. "I'm sure hoping she's wrong."

"Yeah, me too. I mean, Tom? I still can't believe he would—"

Ruben's phone rang, interrupting her. The caller ID read: NCTC Security. "Agent Diaz . . . Great. Where? . . . No way. You sure? . . . Okay. Don't mess with it. I'll be right there." He hung up, and said, "They found Tom's car—downstairs."

"Downstairs?" Lana echoed, appearing to be puzzled.

"Yeah, in the staff lot!" Ruben blew out of the conference room and made a beeline for the elevator bank.

Lana was right behind him.

Chapter Fifteen

After tossing his cell phone into the back of the pickup truck, Katkov was too exhausted to worry if the Mercedes was being followed, and he hoped the tactic would keep the FSB ferrets at bay. Traffic on the Outer Ring was crawling, and it took more than a half hour to reach Lyublinskaya, the long southbound boulevard that paralleled the Metro tracks to the Lyublino District, a pre-Soviet enclave of once-grand homes and estates.

Katkov lived in a weathered baroque mansion that the state had taken over between the wars and divided into cramped apartments. After the Soviet Union fell and laws that allowed citizens to own property were passed, Mrs. Parfenov was swindled by a real-estate developer who claimed to have title to the building, but the feisty babushka produced ownership documents that were upheld by the courts. Katkov—who preferred the charm of the early 1900s mansion to mass housing units built by the state—moved back into a larger unit with a separate bedroom. Little in the area had changed, and the industrial stacks across the river in Brateyvo still belched smoke round the clock. The gray haze hung in the stillness, shrouding the power lines that stretched to the horizon.

The driver parked in front of the old mansion and helped Katkov from the car. "Already taken care of," he said, seeing Katkov fumbling with a fistful of rubles. "Can I give you a hand?"

"I've still got *one* that works," Katkov said. "Thanks." He adjusted the position of his sling and climbed the steps to the wrought-iron entrance. His apartment was on the parlor floor, overlooking the grounds. He unlocked the door, used a hip to close it, and dropped his bag on a chair in the darkened foyer. His hand was reaching for the light switch when he noticed an incandescent glow coming from the living room. The air was warm, given the temperature outside. Katkov hadn't been home in days and couldn't imagine that he'd left a light on and the electric heater going all that time. "Vera? You here?" he called out, though there was no scent of perfume in the air.

"Welcome home," Churkin said, startling him. The CI was sitting in the wood-paneled living room, reading the day's edition of *Novaya Gazeta*,

a cigarette pinched between his fingers. An ancient, German-made heater was whirring behind him. "It was a bit chilly when I got here. Hope you don't mind I turned it on."

Katkov sagged with exhaustion. "Those were *your* guys tailing me in the Arbat?"

Churkin shook his head no. "FSB. We routinely monitor their comm traffic; picked up some chatter about tracking your cell phone in the direction of Yuroslaval." He snickered and added, "Nice touch. I couldn't imagine why you'd be going to that grime-encrusted burg, and figured if your phone was heading there, you were heading here. Looks like one of your wings got clipped."

"Your powers of observation are astounding, Chief Investigator," Katkov retorted, glancing around the apartment. As Mrs. Parfenov reported, it had been given a thorough going-over. Every cupboard and closet had been searched. Books had been removed from shelves and tossed aside. The drawers had been rifled. The file cabinets emptied. What are you doing here? Admiring your handiwork?"

"I didn't sanction this," Churkin replied, sounding like he meant it as he helped Katkov out of his parka. "And just to be clear, I didn't sanction *that* either," the CI added, gesturing to Katkov's sling. "I warned you . . . I warned you as a friend."

"This? Dislocated my shoulder," Katkov said with a sly smile. "Light one of those for me, will you?" he asked, prompting Churkin to use the cigarette he was smoking to light another. Katkov took a deep, satisfying drag and dropped onto the sofa. "I'm fading fast. Let's cut to the chase. What do you want?"

"You mean, other than the identity of Ms. Grafinskaya's killer?"

Katkov's eyes rolled behind his wire-framed lenses. "Get real . . ."

"My Lubov story," Churkin snapped, brandishing the newspaper. "Where the fuck is it?"

"Come on, I've been up to my ass," Katkov replied, exhaling a stream of smoke.

"That makes two of us, dammit!" Churkin exclaimed. "That story's really important. Whether you believe it or not, RIC is totally committed to prosecuting corruption in the Kremlin, but we're a new agency—at it less than a year. We need publicity. Notoriety. Headlines that scream we're kicking ass! I figured you're the guy who could make it happen. I gave you an exclusive, and I haven't seen a fucking word!"

"The Grafinskaya story took precedence."

"As it should. But it's *my* ass that's on the line with this Lubov thing!" Churkin erupted. "Zerevski was gun shy," he went on, referring to the head of the RIC. "I used your exposé to convince him that busting someone with Lubov's power and connections was worth the risk, that it would make headlines, that it would prove RIC has clout and should be taken seriously! I need those headlines! And I need them now!"

"You're beating up on a one-handed typist, Sergei."

"Dictate it and have one of your hot little *Novy-Gaz* interns type it up! And make sure it's front page, and above the fold with a seventy-two-point headline!"

"Hey, I hear you, but I'm brain dead. I need to get a night's sleep before I—"

"Make it a nap!" Churkin snapped. "A short one." He slipped into his topcoat, set the Borsalino at a jaunty angle, and slammed the door as he left.

Katkov flinched, then swept his eyes over his trashed apartment. "Bastards," he muttered with a painful grimace. His shoulder was killing him. But none of it mattered. The only thing he really cared about was locked in a secret room behind the walnut bookcases that flanked the fireplace. Each section was framed by molding with a motif of carved rosettes. The one immediately to the right of the fireplace swung inward when unlocked and given a forceful push. The only evidence of its existence was a tarnished brass keyhole centered in one of the rosettes, making it barely visible. An armchair and side table piled with books in front of it further concealed it from view. So, Katkov wasn't surprised that, unlike all the other closet doors in the apartment, this one was closed. He stepped behind the chair and pushed on the section of bookcase. It didn't budge. He sighed with relief and was fishing his keys from a pocket when his desk phone rang. It was a combination telephone and answering machine with a cordless handset. He lived on his cell phone. No one called his landline anymore. He set his cigarette in a butt-filled ashtray and answered it. The numeral 2 was winking dimly in the dusty message window.

"Niko. Thank God," Vera said in a shaky voice. "I've been calling you for hours. I left voicemail on your cell and on your machine too."

"Sorry. I had a little problem to take care of," Katkov said, deciding not to burden her with the details. "What's going on?"

"Did you use my computer when you were here?"

"No, I used my laptop, why?"

"The FSB confiscated it. They pulled me off my shift and interrogated me."

"Agh! They knew I was there, figured I might've used it."

"Come on, they've known for twenty years that we're lovers . . ."

"No, no, they've been tracking my mobile."

Vera groaned. "Get rid of it."

"I did. Go to the table where I was working. Pull out the drawer most of the way and see if you feel something taped to the bottom."

Vera did as instructed. "Yeah, yeah, I feel something."

"Good. Bastards didn't get it."

"Get what?"

"Grusha's flash drive. It's in an envelope. Leave it there."

"For godsakes, Niko! If . . . if they'd found it, I'd be on my way to the Gulag!"

"But they didn't. I'm sorry about your computer. I'll get you another one."

"You can get me another job too! I've been suspended—without pay!"

"Oh . . . well . . . hey, you said, you were thinking about retiring. Maybe you—"

"Retire on what?! They're threatening to take away my pension!"

"Did you say. Take. Away. Your. Pension?" Katkov prompted in a cryptic cadence as an unnerving thought struck him.

"Yes. What's wrong with you, Niko? Aren't you listening to what—"

"Hold on, hold on," Katkov interrupted, his mind racing. He slipped the handset inside his sling, freeing his hand to retrieve his keys, then crossed to the section of bookcase that concealed the secret room.

The awful possibility he was contemplating had first occurred to him when Mrs. Parfenov told him the FSB was searching the apartment, but there wasn't anything he could have done to stop it. Furthermore, he knew from experience that vindictive retaliation wasn't a tactic the FSB employed when the Kremlin felt vulnerable and threatened by instability, when potentially damaging information wasn't under their control. No, they didn't ransack his apartment to teach him a lesson. That would happen after they had regained control and wanted to deter others who might challenge them. This had been a search for names, the names of sources, of disloyal public servants the Kremlin believed had committed treasonous acts. And since the FSB had seized Grafinskaya's computer, Katkov knew, they had them. But now . . . now that Vera had said it, he sensed the awful possibility had become a reality.

He slipped behind the armchair, inserted the key into the lock, turned it, and pushed. The entire bookcase swung inward on forged hinges that creaked with age. His hand found the wall switch. A bare bulb overhead illuminated a small, windowless room that Katkov imagined had once housed valuables, or literature and works of art deemed subversive by the state. Moscow's old mansions were full of these nooks and crannies, and this one, tucked in the space beneath a second-floor stair landing, was why he decided to rent *this* apartment and not return to his old one when he moved back into the building. A small table and chair stood in the middle of the room. The walls were lined floor-to-ceiling with shelves—shelves that were empty! Every last one of the long narrow boxes with alphabetized labels that Katkov kept on them were gone. Not only had the FSB picked the lock and taken the boxes, they had turned off the light and locked the door to the empty room when they finished. It *was* like them, and their sly, self-satisfied cleverness.

Katkov's gut felt hollow as he tugged the handset from inside his sling. "The fucking FSB already took mine."

"Already took your what?" Vera asked, mystified.

"My pension," Katkov replied, scanning the empty shelves forlornly. "My entire comic-book collection is gone."

Chapter Sixteen

An NCTC security vehicle, roof flashers whirling, was parked on the far side of the JTTF staff parking area next to a black BMW. Two uniformed officers in NCTC windbreakers were posted nearby. Ruben and Lana identified themselves, then approached the car and peered into the windows.

"Set of keys and a CAC on the seat," Ruben said, the latter the mag-striped common access card needed to access JTTF parking and the headquarters building. "You guys have gloves?"

One of the security officers retrieved a fistful of blue surgical gloves from his vehicle.

Ruben slipped them on and opened the driver's-side door. It was unlocked. He leaned inside, sniffed the air, and backed out, leaving the items untouched. "Nothing." He lived with it for a moment, then pulled the trunk lever. The lid rose slowly as Ruben and Lana circled to the rear of the car. The sight of a man's naked body in a fetal position stopped them in their tracks. His head was tucked into a corner of the trunk next to a gym bag. His face was concealed by pieces of clothing that had been thrown in after him. Ruben lifted them, then turned to Lana, ashen-faced, and nodded. "It's him."

"Tom? You sure?"

"Be my guest," Ruben said, stepping aside. "See if you spot any birthmarks, tattoos, scars—you know . . . identifying features of which you have intimate knowledge."

Lana glared at him. "What the hell does that mean?"

"It means, I figure, you're the only one here who's had the pleasure of seeing him *desnudo* . . ."

"Very funny . . ."

"We all deal with these things in our own way. Get over it." Ruben leaned back into the trunk. "Looks like . . . like his throat's been cut," he said, his voice breaking. "Box cutter on the carpet there next to him. Dried blood on it."

Lana winced and appeared to be surprised. "My God. That's . . . that's horrible."

Ruben nodded grimly.

"I'm sorry. Give me a minute, will you?" Lana said, emitting a convincing whimper as she turned away and pretended to be composing herself.

One of the security officers approached Ruben. "Better get the locals into this. I'll contact the Fairfax County ME's Office and—"

"*No*, no locals," Ruben interrupted sharply. "I don't need a medical examiner to tell me I'm looking at a homicide. The victim's one of ours—an FBI Special Agent—and FBI will handle it. Cordon off the area. Don't move, touch, or breathe on anything."

"Hey, I know it's a bummer, but we have a protocol we're supposed to—"

"No!" Ruben snapped. "No. He's my partner. My fucking partner! Somebody cut his throat and tossed him in there like a piece of luggage! Now, back off!"

The officer's jaw tightened. A tense moment passed before he nodded.

Ruben peeled off his gloves, then stepped aside with his phone and reported the incident, arranging for FBI forensics and ME teams to be dispatched. His eyes widened at a thought as Lana joined him. "Somebody drove Tom's car here, right?" he prompted, brightening. "Swiped his CAC to get in."

Lana nodded, knowing where he was headed. "Good chance one of our CCTV cameras caught his fifteen minutes of fame. My screening room or yours?"

"Mine. I'll spring for the coffee. You run the search."

A short time later, they were settled in front of the computer in Ruben's workstation. The news crawl on one of the panoramic monitors overhead read CANADIAN PACIFIC RAILWAYS AND CSX RUMORED IN MERGER TALKS. The latter, a major American railroad based in Jacksonville, Florida, serviced the entire eastern half of the country as well as the Canadian provinces of Ontario and Quebec.

Lana clicked on the center's CCTV program and entered Tom's CAC number in the search window. "Last swiped at 3:18 a.m.," she said when the time stamp appeared. She accessed the digital surveillance server, selected the camera that covered the parking security kiosk, and entered 3:15 a.m. An image of the JTTF staff parking area filled the screen. The time counter began advancing. Headlights swept through the tree-lined turns on Tysons McLean Drive. A black BMW approached the kiosk and stopped next to the reader. A hat and dark glasses concealed the driver's identity.

"Stop it . . . *there*," Ruben said as the driver reached out the window and swiped a card. The time stamp read 3:18. "Zoom in." After several mouse clicks, the card reader and driver's hand filled the screen. "See any knuckle dots?"

"No. Gloves. He's wearing gloves."

"*Mierda*. Zoom back out and keep going . . ."

The sequence resumed: The security gate lifted. The BMW crossed the half-empty parking lot to the spot where Tom's car had been located. It was on the periphery of the camera's range. The lighting was poor. The image lacked detail. The driver left the car, closed the door, and, without pausing to get his bearings, walked off in the darkness.

"Gives us nothing," Lana said, running a hand through her hair as if frustrated.

"I don't know," Ruben countered, his head cocked in thought. "The guy didn't hesitate a beat. It's like he had picked his parking spot and worked out his escape route in advance. We're dealing with someone with knowledge of the grounds."

Lana nodded and took a sip of coffee, then shivered as if chilled. Her eyes appeared to be moist with emotion.

"Hey, you okay?"

"Yeah, just thinking about Tom. He . . . he made a joke about Chechens being handy with box cutters," she said, sounding as if she were shaken by the irony.

"Yeah, it's their calling card."

"I know, but what's with the naked thing?" Lana wondered, segueing into a cover story she had concocted with Julian and her mother.

Ruben groaned with frustration. "I'm drawing a blank."

"Some kind of message, maybe?" Lana said as if working it out. "I mean, Tom said he thought his cover was blown. Right?"

Ruben nodded curiously.

"So . . . so, maybe it's kind of like they're saying he's been exposed, revealed. We know he was working undercover . . ."

"Not bad," Ruben said, raising a brow. "Looks like they stripped him before they cut him. I mean, his clothes should be covered with blood, but not a drop on 'em."

"Or on *him,* for that matter."

"So . . ." Ruben went on, thinking it through. "They grab him. Take him somewhere. Pump him for information, whatever. Get him naked. Go to work with the box cutter, and then . . . What? Toss him in the shower? Why?"

"Beats me," Lana replied, and, changing the subject, asked, "You think maybe whoever killed him took the five million?"

"The Chechens . . ."

"Yeah, brazen bastards. It's like they're twisting the knife," Lana said, using the unexpected turn of events to embellish the scenario. "Who else but those chest-thumping primates would have the balls to leave him *here*?"

"Well, whether our favorite Eagle Scout was planning to relieve me or catch a flight to topless heaven, he never made it. Better run his email, cell phone, credit cards before it goes cold. His personal effects too."

"I'll get a geek squad into it," Lana said with feigned nonchalance. From the moment she flicked the blade across Tom's throat, she knew this was coming, knew that *she* was the geek who had to run the data, knew she had to finagle the assignment so she could scrub the emails, files, and electronic records not only from Tom's computer and the JTTF mainframe but also from the systems of personal service providers that could incriminate her. What she had just suggested was dangerous, but it was the JTTF protocol, the expected response. "If anybody can find out where he's been, who he was talking to, what he was up to, it's the comp-tech geeks," she went on, studying Ruben out of the corner of her eye. "I mean, if . . . if you feel comfortable with that . . ."

Ruben leaned back in his chair, studying her. "No. No, I'm not comfortable at all, and you damn well know it, don't you?"

Lana tilted her head and smiled.

"A busted sting is a disappointment," Ruben went on. "*This*—this is a disaster. The kind that begins with finger pointing and ends with a scapegoat being hung out to dry. I'm not looking for a turf war. I'm looking for someone to cover my back." He locked his eyes onto Lana's and said, "And that someone is *you*—you should run them. You're the Amtrak computer geek in chief. It's right in your wheelhouse. Not to mention you're already working the case."

Lana winced as if wrestling with a dilemma. She sensed Ruben felt exposed, and she had taken a calculated risk that paid off. What she wanted—what she desperately needed—was within her grasp, but she didn't want to appear eager. "I don't know, Ruben. I'm running low on bandwidth," she said, then sighed as if reconsidering it. "But, hey, I mean, if it's that important to you . . ."

"Bet your great ass it is," Ruben said with an emphatic nod. "Done deal?"

"Done deal."

"*Bueno*," Ruben mumbled, sounding distracted by a thought.

"What're you thinking?"

"Just a feeling. I mean, Tom's working undercover to sting a Chechen counterfeit ring . . . Contacts Russian journalist investigating corruption in the Kremlin . . . *She* gets whacked . . . *He* gets whacked. I can't help wondering if there might be some connection."

"I don't know . . ." Lana said, drawing it out with uncertainty. "The K in cahoots with the knuckle-dot gang? Sounds like a stretch. I mean, the Kremlin's been at war with Chechnya for decades. They hate each other's guts."

"*Hated*," Ruben corrected. "You're forgetting Kadyrov's been sucking up to Putin big-time, and vice-versa."

"A marriage of convenience headed for an ugly divorce," Lana said, dismissing it. "Besides, counterfeiting's small potatoes compared to putting Russian pensions on the line in some megabillion takeover scam." She locked her eyes onto Ruben's and, with convincing outrage, added, "That said, I'll do anything to catch the bastards who did this to Tom."

Chapter Seventeen

The past seventy-two hours of Nikolai Katkov's life had left him reeling. Though a staggering blow, the loss of his priceless comic-book collection and the prospect of being penniless upon retirement paled in comparison to the wrenching shock of Grafinskaya's assassination and the trauma of being shot by NASCAR Cap. Physically exhausted, his right arm immobilized by the sling, Katkov took another round of antibiotics and painkillers, then shut off the ringer on the desk phone and crawled under the covers. He could've slept for a week, but despite the back-to-back doses of medication that could put a plow horse into a coma, six hours later he was wide-awake.

The fact that Grusha was dead, that his former lover, colleague, and mother of a daughter he never knew he had was gone, *gone forever*, struck with full force. The thought was devastating that he would never hear her voice again, never again be amazed by her incisive intelligence, nor collaborate on exposés of government corruption, suppression of dissent, or disregard for human rights. His battered psyche was gripped by overwhelming sadness. His bullet-torn shoulder was throbbing with pain. He plucked a blister pack from the nightstand, then scowled and tossed it aside. The medication made him drowsy and eroded his mental acuity. He could live with the pain. What he couldn't live with was the feeling of vulnerability that the FSB's search-and-destroy mission had intensified. He picked his way through his trashed apartment, made some coffee, and went to his desk to do what he always did when so besieged. He couldn't type, but he could write, and, as Churkin had demanded, he began outlining the piece on the RIC's bust of Igor Lubov in longhand on a legal pad.

He and Churkin were perfectly matched, Katkov thought. They hated each other's guts and admired each other's courage, each the means to the other's end. Indeed, in exchange for the exclusive Churkin had given him, Katkov would champion his unrelenting pursuit of government corruption. The impact of Lubov's arrest would go well beyond the lurid aspects of the story—which would get people to read it—fueling public outrage at Grafinskaya's fate and that of others who took on the Kremlin. Furthermore, if Katkov had any hope of recovering his pension assets, Churkin was the key to it, but he couldn't raise the subject until the RIC's takedown of Igor Lubov was splashed across the front page of *Novaya Gazeta* complete with tabloid-style photos. And there was no better way to honor Grusha's memory than to continue to expose the oligarchs and former KGB generals who had turned Russia into a kleptocracy. Katkov covered page after page in his left-handed scribble, and by the time the first rays of light were streaming through the windows, he had a draft:

Several nights ago, in the posh Tverskaya District, a crack RIC assault team, under the command of Chief Investigator Sergei Churkin, arrested Igor Lubov, CEO of TeknoKratka, the government technology conglomerate, on charges of corruption, graft, and bribery. On entering the luxurious apartment, Churkin's team sent the naked, cocaine-snorting party-goers scurrying for cover, and, in an ironic twist, it was Lubov's whip-cracking dominatrix who was wearing the handcuffs as officers extricated her client from a leather harness that hung from the ceiling. CI Churkin said that the former KGB general, handpicked by President Putin to run the company, is but one of many corrupt Kremlin cronies he has targeted for prosecution. Churkin also said . . .

Katkov reviewed the hastily written pages, made a few revisions, then took a long, triumphant drag on his cigarette and called Vera. "Hi, it's me. I need your help."

"I know, Niko! I know!" Vera exclaimed. "Alexa just called. She said you'd been shot. Why didn't you say something last night?"

"I didn't want to worry you."

"That's ridiculous. You should've asked me for help."

"I just did. I wrote the Lubov piece—by hand. I need you to type it up."

"I'm sure I can find the time," Vera said with a sarcastic chuckle. "By the way, we're putting together a memorial booklet for Grusha. Mika wants to get your input."

"Sure. Soon as we get this Lubov piece knocked out, I'll—"

"Yeah, well, Alexa said she was heading over to your place to see how you were doing and offered to pick us up. We're on our way now."

"The three of you?"

"Uh-huh. Be about a half hour."

I'm not sure I'm ready for this, Katkov thought as he launched into a one-handed effort to straighten up his trashed apartment. By the time he'd worked his way across the living room to the windows that overlooked the street, the black Mercedes was pulling to the curb. Without waiting for the driver to open the door, the three women piled out and hurried toward the building. Alexa in a classy leather coat, a doctor's bag clutched in her fist. Vera in a down vest and sweater, and Michaela, more subdued than her trademark Pussy Riot chic, right on Alexa's black patent heels. Moments later, Katkov heard Vera's key in the lock, and they were parading through the foyer.

"Nikasha," Michaela said, her eyes glistening as she ran into his arms.

"How're you doing?" Katkov prompted, still unable to believe she was his daughter. Though recent events had intensified the pressure to broach the subject, they also mandated he wait for a more appropriate time. "You hanging in there?"

Michaela nodded sadly. "My father's still a no-show. But Sasha's been great. I'm more worried about you."

"Yes, my God, Niko, look at you," Vera said, touching his cheek with concern.

"He'll be fine," Alexa said with professional authority. "As long as he takes his medication, gets a lot of rest, and eats well. Now, let's have a look at that shoulder."

"I'll be even better after this Lubov piece gets filed," Katkov said, handing Vera the legal pad. "Laptop's in my bag in the foyer."

As Vera went to fetch it, Michaela showed Katkov a paste-up of the memorial booklet. "See? It's going to have Mom's picture on the cover, your obituary, some testimonials, and a packet of soil from her garden."

"It's . . . it's beautiful," Katkov said, the words catching in his throat.

"Slava has one of his designers working on it," Alexa chimed in as she removed Katkov's sling. "And a printer who owes him big-time's covering the production costs."

Michaela forced a smile, then emitted a frustrated sigh. "Now, if I could just get those idiots at RIC to release Mom's . . . Mom's . . ." Her voice broke and she let it trail off.

"Her remains," Katkov prompted gently.

Michaela lowered her eyes and nodded.

"Have you called Churkin?"

"Uh-huh. I keep getting voicemail."

Katkov nodded. "Hand me the phone, will you?" Michaela retrieved it from the desk where Vera was setting up the laptop, and he thumbed out a number.

"Katkov?!" Churkin growled, seeing the name in his caller ID. The chief investigator was in his chauffeured Lada, scanning *Novaya Gazeta*'s morning edition en route to the office. "I was just going to call you. Where the hell's my story?!"

"It's being typed up as we speak. It'll be online today. In print tomorrow."

"About time."

"And it's about time you guys released Grusha's remains," Katkov retorted, his tone softening as he went on. "The family needs closure, Sergei. They need to sit shivah and have a funeral service, but—"

"You know we can't do that," Churkin fired back. "Forensics is still at it, and the ME hasn't finished her work. No way I can release them until we identify her killer."

"Have you been to Number 16 Boyevsk Ulitsa, yet?"

"No. Why? The hit man lives there?" Churkin prompted with a sarcastic chortle.

"No, but I'm hearing rumors he may have—*died*—there."

"What?" Churkin blurted.

"Check out Apartment 4A."

"Katkov, are you saying that—"

"Apartment 4A, Sergei," Katkov repeated. "A as in apparatchik." He hung up and smiled at Michaela. "You should be able to make your arrangements soon . . ."

"What a guy, huh?" Alexa teased, rolling her eyes. "Can we get on with this now?" She loosened Katkov's shirt, exposing his shoulder, and began picking with a manicured nail at the tape that secured the dressing. "How does it feel? You still have pain?"

"It hurts like hell."

Alexa looked puzzled. "Are you taking the medication?"

Katkov waggled a hand. "The painkillers make me brain dead. I had work to do."

"Make damn sure you take the antibiotics, or the rest of you will be dead too." Alexa slipped on a pair of surgical gloves and removed the gauze pads, exposing the wound. "Looks good. Already starting to heal. By the way, how're you fixed for groceries?"

"Are you kidding?" Vera called back over her shoulder. "You can bet the Mercedes his cupboards are bare."

"Well, I'm not due at the clinic till this afternoon," Alexa said, cleansing the wound with disinfectant. "Soon as I'm finished, I'll have my driver run me over to the market and pick up a few staples. Anything else you need?"

Katkov's eyes came to life with a thought. "Yeah, a contact at RZD. I mean, there must be a *siloviki* or two among your *private* clientele who's connected over there."

"At RZD?" Alexa tilted her head, then shrugged. "No, not really. Why?"

"I need to locate someone who worked there," Katkov replied, choosing his words carefully. "Someone who . . . who doesn't want to be found."

"Slava might know someone . . ." Alexa mused, dressing the wound. "His agency did their graphics program a couple of years ago. They're working on a new ad campaign now. He probably has lots of connections there."

"I'll bet he does," Katkov said with a facetious grin.

Alexa forced a smile. "Who are you looking for?"

"One of Grusha's sources. High up in the RZD hierarchy. Very close to Yakunin."

"And . . ." Alexa prompted. "I mean, a name might be helpful."

Katkov winced. "The fewer people who know it, the better."

Alexa frowned. "So what do I tell Slava?"

"Tell him it's a woman," Katkov replied as Alexa buttoned his shirt and went about securing the sling. "There are few at that level. If she hasn't been whacked by the FSB, she's in hiding. Chances are she has more information, but, with Grusha gone, doesn't know what to do with it. I need to get word to her to contact *me.*"

"Not enough. Never happen. Not without a name. Take my word for it."

Katkov nodded in capitulation, leaned close to her, and whispered, "Nadia Nysenko."

"Got it. I'll ask Slava to . . . to look into it."

"*Tell* him to look into it," Katkov retorted, his tone sharpening. "I need this, Alexa. I need you to make it happen. I need everything I can get before I go to Washington. I'm not letting this stop me. I'm going, and I'm going soon."

"You're not going anywhere till after the holidays. Now, if you'll excuse me, *I'm* going marketing."

Several hours later, the apartment was no longer in disarray, the cupboard had been stocked, the funeral arrangements were in the works, and the Lubov story had been typed, proofed, and emailed to Katkov's editor at *Novaya Gazeta*. Vera was about to shut down the laptop when Katkov realized he hadn't checked his emails.

The news crawl at the bottom of the screen read PUTIN TIGHTENS GRIP ON MEDIA: WARNS PROKHOROV, OWNER OF BROOKLYN NETS AND RBC MEDIA EMPIRE TO STOP INVESTIGATING STATE-RUN BUSINESSES.

"Unbelievable . . ." Katkov hissed. He's murdered Grusha, shut down *Lenta* and *TV Rain*, and turned over *RIA-Novosti* to that clown Kiselyov at *Russia Today*! Now he's going after *RBC*?! There'll be no independent media left!"

His Inbox was jammed with run-of-the-mill correspondence. The one titled "Editorial Meeting Agenda" was a business-as-usual communication from Vitaly, who—along with Churkin, the RIC, the militia, the Kremlin, and the rest of Moscow—didn't know what had happened at Patrushev's apartment the previous evening. To Katkov's disappointment, the email he had been waiting for wasn't there. Several days had passed since he forwarded Grafinskaya's sleeper-agent email to Agent Tom Jones, and he still hadn't gotten a reply. He had no way of knowing his fate, and was about to forward it again when he was startled by a pounding on the door. "Moscow Militia! Open up!" a man shouted. "Police! We know you're in there. Open up!"

Apprehensive glances darted between Katkov and the women. He shut down the laptop, then took a deep breath and went to the door. A wall of uniformed officers, brandishing weapons, drove him back into the apartment when he opened it.

"Nikolai Katkov?" the one with the sergeant's stripes on his epaulets asked.

Katkov nodded, his eyes narrowing in recognition. *The stocky build, the massive, snarling St. Bernard head.* "Cujo! The Lubov bust!"

"Ah, yes, the Pussy Riot pimp."

"Very funny."

"Nothing funny about this," Cujo retorted, using a threatening snap of his wrist to present Katkov with a packet of folded pages.

"What the hell is that?"

"A warrant for your arrest."

Katkov look puzzled. His gut tightened. The bravado went out of him. "My arrest?" he asked warily. "On what charge?"

"Accessory to murder." Before Katkov had a chance to protest, Cujo grasped his good arm by the wrist, wrenched it atop the injured one that protruded from the sling, and went about binding them with a zip tie.

"Hey! Hey careful with that arm!" Alexa protested, clearly alarmed. "I'm this man's doctor, and—"

"His doctor?" Cujo echoed with a disdainful snort and a powerful yank on the zip tie. "He'll need his *lawyer* to fix this." He straightened and let his chest fill, then swept his eyes across the three women who had gathered behind Katkov and, with a self-satisfied smirk, said, "Looks like you've got a little *Pussy Riot* of your own going here." He turned to the officers massed behind him, and barked, "Cuff 'em. *All* of 'em."

Chapter Eighteen

Dick Farrell, the JTTF Chief in McLean, worked out of a corner office that overlooked the sprawling counterterrorism complex and the freeways that sliced through the surrounding countryside. A bank of monitors with live feeds from global hot spots and communications apparatus covered one wall. Photos of a smiling president and a stern-faced FBI director hung on another.

Farrell had a trim physique and carried himself with military bearing. His lined face had mournful eyes that left no doubt he had seen it all: as commander of a rifle company in the Gulf War, as an FBI agent who joined the bureau right out of Brooklyn Law School, and as the father of a daughter killed in action in Afghanistan whose memorial flag he kept in a display case on his desk. Still, he needed a moment to come to grips with what he had just heard. "Naked—in the trunk of his car—with his throat cut—in the staff parking lot. Smells like Chechens. We talking Bargishev here?"

"That's how it looks, sir," Ruben replied, hedging it. "We figured the sting went south because Tom's cover was blown. If we're right, Agent Nichols has an interesting angle on the parking-lot scene."

"Agent Nichols," Farrell said, drawing it out. "Got that cybersecurity thing where you want it?"

"Yes, sir. DefCon proved to be a valuable resource."

"Good," Farrell grunted. "Your angle on the scene in the parking lot?"

"I think it's a message, sir," Lana replied, sitting straight-backed on the edge of her chair. "And that message is: We know he was an undercover agent. We exposed him. We blew off your sting and took the ops money to rub salt in the wound."

Farrell's brows rose in tribute, then fell in painful reflection. "Yeah, and it stings like hell. Penetrating insight, Nichols. Good work," he went on, getting past it. "And you're involved because . . . the op was going down at an Amtrak station?"

"The location was tangential, as I understand it, sir," Lana replied evenly. "I'm on board because Agent Jones spotted an article in *Novaya Gazeta* and initiated an email exchange with the journalist who—"

"Grafinskaya," Farrell interrupted with a grimace. "Ugly business. Agent Jones copied us on it. We shared with Langley. The DCI included it in a daily brief."

"Well, in her reply to Agent Jones," Lana resumed, undaunted, "Grafinskaya implied the Kremlin might be conspiring to take over one of our railroads. Agent Jones wanted to run it past someone on our Amtrak team. Ruben suggested me."

"Good. That's how it's supposed to work around here," Farrell enthused with a fist pump. "Well, it sounds like you two have things in hand."

Ruben nodded emphatically. "Forensics'll be moving on to Tom's place soon as they wrap it up here. I'll keep working the stakeout. One way or the other we'll nail the Chechen bastards who did this . . . *assuming* they did this."

"What the hell does that mean?" Farrell asked, jumping on it.

"Just a feeling, sir. I've no evidence to support it, but my gut keeps telling me there might be a connection between agent Jones's murder and Grafinskaya's."

"Christ," Farrell exclaimed, getting to his feet "If you're right, if it's not the local knuckle-dot gang, the scope of this thing becomes global."

Ruben winced. "Yes, sir, it sure as hell does."

"I want a complete media blackout," Farrell declared. "What happened to Agent Jones *hasn't* happened. Not until we know what we're dealing with. He's on special assignment. Whatever. What's your next move?"

"Bargishev," Ruben replied. "Agent Nichols will be running Tom's credit cards, phone records, emails, et cetera to flesh this mess out, and—"

"*No.* No way. Time for a reality check," Farrell snapped, his mind churning. "This goes way beyond Tom's personal and JTTF data into that journalist's notes and records, not to mention her sources. We could end up hacking into the goddamned Kremlin. Give it to one of the geek squads over in comp tech. You know the drill."

Farrell's first three words were still in the air when the surge of adrenaline struck Lana. All the pieces were in place. Now the carefully crafted house of cards was about to collapse and bury her! Having finessed Ruben into giving her the assignment, she had planned to go from Farrell's office to Tom's workstation and scrub the electronic records of incriminating data. This was a lethal threat, an all-or-nothing moment that, despite the risk of making her appear desperate, had to be seized—and seized boldly.

She took a deep breath and exhaled slowly—as her mother had taught her—which suppressed the rising tide of panic and concealed her anxiety. "I know the drill too, sir," she said, locking her eyes onto Farrell's. "Agent Diaz assigned it to me because, as the ranking SAC on Amtrak's comp-tech team, I know it better than most."

Farrell winced and glanced at his watch. "I'm due at Langley. Big ISIS powwow with the NSC gang. You made the call on this, Ruben. Give me the bullet points."

"One: These murders may be linked. Two: Both victims were onto what might be a Kremlin scheme to take over one of our railroads. Three: I agreed with Tom it was a credible threat and suggested he bring in Agent Nichols. Ergo, the geek most qualified to tackle this, is already working the case."

"Net-net Agent Nichols has the best shot at determining if this is all part of the same puzzle or not. Correcto?"

"Correcto," Ruben replied with an emphatic nod.

Farrell's lips tightened into a thin line. "Sure you have room on your plate for this?" he asked, shifting his focus to Lana.

"Yes, sir. I'd *clear* my plate for it."

"Okay, young lady, you got it. For what it's worth, sounds like more than a few pieces to that puzzle are missing."

"I'll find them, sir," Lana said, concealing her relief. "Oh, I'll need Agent Jones's workstation and mainframe user IDs and passwords."

Farrell looked to his assistant, Celia Sexton, a fine-boned, taciturn data sponge whose best friend was her iPad. "Make sure Agent Nichols gets whatever she needs." He slipped some files into his attaché, then headed for the door. Halfway through it, he paused and turned back to Ruben. "Any news on that suitcase full of cash?"

"Nada. Transponder's still dead."

"Chrissakes. Keep me posted."

A short time later, user IDs and passwords in hand, Lana made a beeline for Tom's workstation. Ruben headed back to the staff parking lot.

The area around Tom's BMW had been cordoned off with crime-scene tape and traffic cones. An FBI forensics team was marking bits of debris on the pavement with numbered flags and dusting the car for prints. The medical examiner had approximated time of death, photographed Tom's corpse, and was removing it from the trunk along with his fencing bag and other personal items.

Ruben worked his way through the scene to a folding table on which plastic evidence bags were being aligned in neat rows. Among the bagged items were Tom's wallet, wristwatch, key ring, iPhone, CAC card, JTTF ID badge, and the blood-smeared box cutter found in the trunk.

A forensics technician placed Tom's fencing bag on the table and began removing its contents—shoes, mask, tunic, breeches, and glove among them. Despite having been severely bloodstained, the neatly folded garments were now pristine and blinding white in the daylight. Ruben's eyes narrowed—not from the glare but in recollection of something he had noticed in Tom's apartment. He slipped on a pair of surgical gloves and spent a few moments examining the tunic, then headed into the building.

Lana had spent the time at Tom's computer scrubbing files that might incriminate her. A folder labeled "Novaya Gazeta" contained three emails: Tom's initial query about Grafinskaya's article. Her reply that raised the issue of the Kremlin's railroad takeover scheme. And the email Katkov had forwarded about an FSB sleeper agent embedded in the U.S. national security apparatus.

Lana knew Tom had discussed the first two with Ruben, and that the data had gone up the chain to the president. Deleting them would not only be moot but also raise suspicion. The third email presented a serious threat. Three people knew it existed: Tom and Grafinskaya were dead. Katkov was in Moscow. She forwarded it to an account she used for clandestine work, deleted the original from Tom's inbox, and forwarded a copy from his Sent folder, then did the same in the JTTF mainframe. Before signing out, she wrote a few lines of code diverting any emails sent to Tom's account to her own.

Next, she hacked into the Capitol Grille's CCTV system and deleted the footage of Tom transferring his gym bag from his car to hers and getting in next to her. The footage of her car exiting the parking lot wasn't a problem because the high angle from the rear depicted her behind the wheel but not Tom in the passenger seat. Before disengaging, she revised the time stamp on the footage of his BMW exiting the lot, making it appear that it had departed shortly after hers. The driver Julian had sent to fetch it was of Tom's height and build and wore Tom's clothes, reinforcing the deception.

While in hacking mode, Lana accessed Tom's wireless provider's records. The search for "Lana Nichols nee Nikolshevskaya" that he made from the fencing club in Bethesda was the last one listed. The time and wireless tower accessed would raise questions about what Tom was doing in that area at that hour. She was about to delete it when Ruben returned. To her relief, he entered his own workstation and leaned on the partition separating it from Tom's. "How you making out?"

Lana waggled a hand. "Been running his phone and email records. Nothing out of the ordinary," she replied coolly, deleting the threatening record with a mouse click. "Far as I can tell he was off the grid from the time we left the Grille."

"What time was that?"

"Somewhere between eight thirty and nine. He went to his car, I went to mine, and . . ." Lana let it trail off with a sigh and splayed her hands.

"So he was abducted between then and midnight, when he was supposed to relieve me. "Chances are the Grille's got CCTV . . ."

"Good catch," Lana said, deciding to let him take the credit. "I'm on it."

"Great. By the way, your fencing outfit, when it gets soiled, how do you—"

"It's called a kit," Lana corrected.

Ruben's head bobbed with impatience. "Okay, kit. When your *kit* gets soiled, laundry or dry cleaners?"

"Laundry. I usually do it myself. If I don't have the time, I drop it at the fluff-and-fold down the street. Why?"

"I checked-out Tom's apartment last night. There was some stuff that had come back from the dry cleaners on the bed: box of shirts, couple of suits, and a fencing *kit*—wire hanger, plastic bag, ticket stapled to it . . ."

"Well, you know Tom. Mister knife-edge creases. No fluff-and-fold for him."

"Yeah, but forensics just found another kit in a gym bag in the trunk of his Beemer. Has that fluff-and-fold smell. Like it was laundered."

"Maybe there wasn't time to send it out and he did it himself. Some detergents make your things smell like they spent the night in a bordello. I use an unscented, nonallergic one. My skin's very sensitive, so . . ." She let it trail off with a flip of her hair, suggesting the rest was obvious.

So I've heard, Ruben thought, resisting the temptation to say it. "Come to think of it, the smell was more like . . . like bleach than soap. Clorox. You know?"

Lana nodded. "Uh-huh, I do my kit with my whites . . . toss in a cup of bleach."

"Yeah, but the smell was strong, really strong . . . *muy fuerte.*"

"Where you going with this, Ruben? I mean, you suggesting these Chechen thugs who make a living wallowing in gore brought in a scrubber? Some guy who did the Oxi Clean number on victim, clothing, and location?"

Ruben was entertaining a thought and managed a distracted nod.

"Because, why?" Lana went on, as if she were thinking it through. "Because they . . . they didn't want us to know he was wearing his kit when he was killed?"

Ruben winced. "Chechens, knuckle dots, box cutters—fencing?"

"Doesn't compute, does it?" Lana prompted, trying to reinforce Ruben's uncertainty.

"Sure as hell doesn't . . ." Ruben replied, his expression brightening. "Which is why it intrigues me."

Chapter Nineteen

The militia van taking Katkov and his female entourage to police head-quarters made its way north from Lyublino to the Boulevard Ring, circling the congested streets of Central Moscow. Cujo accompanied them. The van turned into Petrovka beneath the wire grid that powered the electric buses and approached the stolid, ochre-and-beige fortress at Number 38. The block-long complex enclosed a courtyard where the bust of Felix Dzerzhinsky, the notorious founder of the KGB, had been returned to its place of prominence after decades in politically correct storage.

"Volodya strikes again," Katkov said in somber exclamation upon glimpsing it.

Vera nodded in bitter agreement. "They tossed that thing in the basement just after I started working here. Now, *I'm* gone and *he's* back!"

"There's talk of putting him back in Lubyanka too," Michaela chimed in. That statue of Dzerzhinsky had been toppled by protesters outside KGB headquarters after the Soviet Union fell. "How could they even think of—"

"Iron Felix was a great man!" Cujo interrupted, glaring at them.

"He was a monster," Alexa retorted. "A vicious psychopath who—"

"That's enough!"

"Hey, we have every right to voice our opinions!" Katkov countered.

"Not in there, you don't," Cujo said sharply as the van turned into a driveway and went down a ramp into 38 Petrovka's underground garage, where a tunnel led to the CID's windowless In-Processing Center.

The women were booked first. All personal items, including Alexa's spiked heels, which were considered weapons, were confiscated. Two burly female guards with five-o'clock shadows, who Katkov imagined had once been Olympic weightlifters, marched them through a door, where a sign proclaimed: WOMEN'S DETENTION.

After being processed, Katkov was taken to a solitary holding cell that rivaled the KGB's Lubyanka for infamy, including lack of heating, and bunks without mattresses or blankets. The in-processing officers confiscated his wallet, watch, cigarettes, and lighter, but also, as safety protocol mandates, his belt, shoelaces and, in this case, his sling. Katkov sat on the bunk in the fluorescent glare and slipped his wrist inside his half-zipped parka to take the weight off his shoulder.

Hours passed before the clank of a dead bolt startled him. Cujo opened the steel door and marched through it. A patch on his uniform depicted Saint Basil astride a white steed, slaying a cowering dragon. Katkov never thought of journalists as dragons who needed slaying, but after what happened to Grusha, he knew the Kremlin did, and he cowered in agony when Cujo grasped his injured arm and cuffed his wrists behind him once more. He marched Katkov down a corridor into an interrogation room and locked the door after him. The walls were green and bare. One had a mirrored window. A table and two chairs stood in the glare of the light fixture overhead. Warm air came from a floor vent.

Katkov paced the room's perimeter, then paused at the mirror and squinted, as if trying to see what was behind it. He had just settled in the chair nearest the heating vent when Churkin strode through the door, carrying a newspaper, his topcoat billowing about him like a cape. He saw Katkov's wrists were cuffed and glared at Cujo, who accompanied him. "Get those off him and get your ass out of here."

Cujo wasted no time doing as instructed.

"What is going on, Sergei?" Katkov asked as the cell door slammed shut.

"You're a suspect in a murder investigation."

"Bullshit," Katkov said, rubbing his wrists. "The women, too, for chrissakes?"

"Relax," Churkin counseled, smiling at what he was about to say. "All the members of your harem have been questioned and will soon be released."

"Very funny. Since when is the militia doing your dirty work?"

Churkin tossed the newspaper on the table. A photo of a naked Igor Lubov in his bondage harness was splashed across *Novaya Gazeta*'s front page beneath the headline: RIC CHARGES CORRUPT KREMLIN CRONY WITH CORRUPTION! "A story like this powerfully enhances RIC's stature. On the other hand—"

"Not to mention yours," Katkov fired back.

"Yes, I came off quite well. Thank you," Churkin said, allowing himself to preen. "I was about to say, a police blotter story on page ten—'RIC Busts One-Armed Journalist'—diminishes it. Enter the militia." He sat down opposite Katkov, produced a pack of Sobranie Blacks, gave him one and lit it, then lit his own. "Apartment 4A. The tenant is Mikhail Patrushev. Name ring a bell?"

"Sounds familiar," Katkov replied, suppressing a smile.

"It should. He's Bortnikov's right-hand man," Churkin said with a thoughtful exhale. "When I got there, I found some guy in a NASCAR cap hanging out the bedroom window. Looks like the sash fell and crushed his skull."

Katov raised an amused brow. "Sounds like he was unlucky."

"Whatever, he got unlucky with a pistol in his fist. Any idea why?"

"Why are you asking me?"

"A witness saw two men run out of an alley next to the building," Churkin replied, getting to his feet. "One guy's description fits Patrushev to a tee. The other guy had curly hair, wire-frame glasses, and was clutching his bloody shoulder. They got into a Lada and drove off at high speed."

"Guess the other guy was doing the driving," Katkov said with a sarcastic grin.

"Forensics removed several rounds from the window frame and wall," Churkin pressed on. "Any chance they might have bits of your DNA or blood on them?"

"I told you I dislocated my shoulder. It comes out when I put my hands behind my head while I'm thinking. I'm pretty good at putting it back in myself."

"Maybe you should stop thinking," Churkin said with a thin smile. "If you weren't at Patrushev's last night, how did you know about it?"

Katkov exhaled a long stream of smoke. "My sources."

"I thought your little insider—Miss Federenko, isn't it?—was on suspension."

"She is. These things have a way of getting in the wind."

"Did it get in the wind that ballistics tests on the bullets that killed Grafinskaya and the ones recovered from Patrushev's apartment came from the same gun? The one Mr. NASCAR Cap was holding in his cold, dead hand?"

"They did?!" Katkov exclaimed, feigning he was surprised. "Wow! That's great news. I mean, if you've identified Grusha's killer, you can release her remains, right?"

"Done," Churkin grunted, his focus elsewhere. "Patrushev's place looked like he and his wife left in a hurry. Anything *in the wind* as to their whereabouts?"

Katkov flicked his ashes on the floor. "Maybe they took a cruise. Look, it's no secret Patrushev was one of Grusha's sources. *I'd* be on the run. Wouldn't you?"

Churkin nodded. "But there has to be more to it. Bortnikov's frantic. He's got his people turning the city upside down looking for him. Any idea why?"

"Why don't you ask Bortnikov?"

Churkin's lips tightened into a thin line. He slipped the Sobranie's gold-tipped filter between them and took a deep drag.

"He won't tell you, will he?" Katkov taunted.

Churkin exhaled and nodded in frustration. "If I knew what it was, I could position him. Make a deal to keep it under wraps as long as he keeps his nose out of RIC and lets the anti-corruption chips fall where they may."

"Yeah, like all over the Kremlin," Katkov said, relishing the thought. "But I haven't heard anything, and if I did, I couldn't tell you."

"Please, don't give me the old 'If I tell you, I'll have to kill you' routine."

"No, I'm giving you the old 'If you try to blackmail Bortnikov, *he'll* have to kill you' routine. You can thank me now."

"For what?"

"Saving your life," Katkov replied, laughing at his own joke. "By the way, the FSB not only trashed my apartment, they stole my pension."

Churkin was the one laughing now. "Even the old babushkas don't keep their rubles in the mattress anymore."

"It wasn't rubles in the mattress, Sergei. It was a very valuable book collection."

"First editions? Signed by the authors?"

"*Comic* books. Been collecting since I was a kid. I planned to sell them when I retired. Unlike muckraking cops, muckraking journalists don't qualify for pensions."

"Why are you telling this to me?"

"I figure Bortnikov took it to blackmail me. I get it back if I promise to stop beating the anti-Putin drum. *You* get it back for me—no strings attached—and I'll give you what you need to blackmail *him* nine ways to Sunday."

"You just said he'd kill me."

"Welcome to the club. If he knew what Patrushev told me, he wouldn't be wasting time on comic books."

Churkin stared at him, then softened. "You've got a deal."

"Not until I have my walking papers and a guarantee I can leave the country."

Churkin looked puzzled. "Leave the country? What does that have to do with this? I mean Grafinskaya's killer is dead, and—"

"It's *killers*, Sergei. Plural, with a K as in Kremlin," Katkov interjected, getting in the CI's face. "And they're alive and well and living *here with impunity*, but their motive is *there*, in Washington, DC. *That's* why Bortnikov's frantic. Grusha endangered something bigger than 'Russian Pensions to Create American Jobs.' Much bigger. And *that's* why they killed her. *Killed her!*" he repeated, his voice breaking with emotion. "And they're not getting away with it."

"You're just going to walk into that insidious human cesspool called Washington, DC, and figure it all out by yourself?!"

"I have contacts. People I'm working with. Your counterparts, so to speak."

"FBI? You want to get in bed with those snakes?"

"Last time I hooked up with one of their law-enforcement agencies, I came out on top."

"Might be smart to quit while you're ahead."

"Not in my genes."

Churkin's shoulders slumped in surrender. "What do you want me to do?"

"Call Bortnikov and get this thing fixed."

"Which thing? Pension or passport?"

"Passport. You'll have plenty of time to work on the pension while I'm gone."

Churkin rolled his eyes and made a call.

Less than a mile away, Alexie Bortnikov's Mercedes S was crawling in traffic on the Boulevard Ring. Two bodyguards traveled with him at all times. One behind the wheel. The other in the back seat next to him. The FSB chief had his phone pressed to his ear. "Of course. I know how much it means to her," he said, trying not to sound annoyed. "Magda, Magda, I wouldn't miss Arisha's recital if Putin himself . . . Yes, I'm en route, but traffic is—" He flinched at the call-waiting tone and saw Churkin's name on the screen. "I have to take this . . . Yes, yes, I'll be there." He took the incoming call, cutting her off. "What is it? I'm up to my ass in this Patrushev thing. And I'm late for my daughter's violin recital . . . Uh-huh . . . Uh-huh . . . Yeah . . . Yeah . . . Yeah," he grunted, his eyes narrowing in disbelief. "Release him?! Let him leave the country? Why?"

"Because he's a pain in the ass. Better to let the Americans deal with him," said Churkin.

"Point taken," Bortnikov said, starting to waver.

"And if push comes to shove," Churkin pressed on, "if Katkov creates any trouble, I'm sure your assets there can deal with him."

"And blame it on the Americans," Bortnikov added, sparking to the idea.

"On the *FBI*," Churkin corrected. "Who, as you may know, were in contact with Grafinskaya, and are in contact with Katkov now."

"They've always been the perfect scapegoat," Bortnikov said, making his decision. "Okay, I'll get with MVD, make sure Katkov's cleared through aviation security and give our assets in DC a heads-up."

"Good. I'll keep you posted." Churkin pocketed his phone and smiled at Katkov. "Done. You're on your way to Washington, DC."

"After what I just heard, I'm not sure I should thank you."

"I got you what you wanted, but I can't protect you. Not here and certainly not there."

"In other words, you just set me up to get whacked."

"Hey, everything has its price," Churkin said with a sarcastic chuckle. "You might not need that pension after all"—his eyes hardened and locked onto Katkov's—"which is why neither of us are leaving this room until you give me what I need to blackmail Bortnikov."

"The kryptonite . . ." Katkov said with a grin.

Chapter Twenty

From the discovery of Tom's naked body in the trunk of his car to the intense brainstorming sessions with Ruben and the unnerving meeting with Farrell, Lana had spent the day flirting with disaster, and it was her unshakeable equanimity and nimble mind that had averted it. Having parried threats that could have blown her cover and exposed what Bortnikov had shrewdly code named the Adamov Op, she returned to her Foggy Bottom apartment to celebrate with a couple of Ketel Ones, and spent the weekend preparing for her meeting with the Cyber-Borgen tiger team.

Monday morning, Ruben was at his workstation reviewing a surveillance video when she came striding beneath the overhead screens. One of the news crawls read CLINTON NOT PRESSED ON SERVER SCANDAL BY SANDERS AND O'MALLEY IN DEBATE. "What's going on?" he mumbled as she breezed past him.

"Want to make sure I didn't miss anything," Lana replied, slipping into Tom's workstation. The double meaning struck her the instant she said it, and she almost added, *I mean, about what happened to Tom*, but she caught herself. "And you?"

"Had a couple of drive-bys," Ruben replied, indicating the video. It depicted the warehouse on the Baltimore waterfront where the maroon van and cartons of counterfeit currency were concealed. A fast-moving town car came down the access road and slowed as it passed. "My gut tells me I'm close to nailing Bargishev's ass."

"Yeah, looks like he's making sure the coast is clear before making his move."

"And I'm living in a hot, sweaty van until he does." Ruben got to his feet and leaned on the partition. "Want to keep me company?"

"Hey, hot and sweaty can have its moments," Lana replied with a flirtatious smile, "But Cyber-Borgen's in town. Got a meeting over at the Ritz at eleven."

Ruben shrugged. His head tilted in reflection. "You remember that riddle yesterday: Chechens, knuckle dots, box cutters—*fencing*?"

Lana sat at Tom's desk. "Like you said, doesn't compute."

"No. No, I said, that's what intrigues me. Still does. This may sound weird, but what are the chances Tom was killed in some kind of a duel?"

"In a duel?" Lana scoffed, her pulse quickening. "After which he's stripped naked and tossed in the trunk of his car? 'Slim' and 'none' comes immediately to mind. Not to mention modern fencing blades have dull edges and button tips."

"Yeah, well, Tom mentioned something about, you know, real ones. He said—"

"*Vintage* ones," Lana corrected. "The kind gentlemen once used to defend their honor."

"Uh-huh, he said they're still used at exhibitions and charity things sometimes."

"They are, but it's all costuming and showmanship. Nobody's out to draw blood. It's not a duel to the death. Gave up on it being connected to the Grafinskaya hit, huh?" Lana prompted, taking the opportunity to test him.

"No way. Still a big blip on my radar. If you get a minute, check out the ME's wound analysis. Was the blade razor sharp? Serrated? Slash or a stab? Up angle or down? Righty or—"

"Lefty. I got it, but my money's still on a box cutter."

"Humor me," Ruben grunted as he left his workstation and headed for the elevator.

"Good luck!" Lana called out after him. "Go nail those Chechen bastards!" She entered Tom's user ID and password into the computer, spent the next hour verifying she hadn't missed anything incriminating, then headed for the parking lot.

Early that same morning in Bay Ridge, Brooklyn, Pashwan Al-Attas left his apartment opposite the Arab American Association storefront on Fifth Avenue, lugging his laptop case. It had been days since his family's horrific deaths, he had yet to visit the apartment he had rented for them on the floor above, which was filled with cardboard cartons, shipping crates, and recently delivered furniture. Pash's colleagues at Cyber-Borgen had doted on him, encouraging him to come into the office. And Pash did so on occasion, arriving late and leaving early. As was his habit, he got a container of coffee at the Yemeni restaurant en route to the subway on 69th Street. The N train had just pulled into the station, and passengers were pushing their way aboard. Normally, Pash would have taken the steps two at a time and slipped between the doors as they were closing, but, as of late, he'd been content to wait for the next one. Trains came frequently during rush hour, and he was soon crossing the Manhattan Bridge, staring at a dirty window on which someone had scratched *Nuke Mecca*. Instead of changing for the local at Fourteenth Street for his usual trip to the office on Twenty-Third Street, he stayed on the express and continued on to Thirty-Fourth. The unseasonably warm weather extended north into New York City, and he walked the long block to Penn Station in a balmy breeze.

Caitlin Roarke and the members of her Cyber-Borgen team had met in the Main Hall at the escalator that led down to Track 15, where the Acela Express to Washington, DC, was scheduled to depart at 7:00.

"Maybe we should call him?" one of them prompted.

"I did," Caitlin said. "Got voicemail. Must've been in the subway." She shot an anxious glance to the digital clock atop the Arrivals and Departures board, then fished her phone from her handbag. "Might as well try him again. Nothing to lose . . ."

Pash was on a down escalator from the Seventh Avenue entrance. It deposited him in the Main Hall amidst the crush of commuters scurrying to the exits. Several moments passed before he spotted Caitlin and the others on the far side of the hall. He had just begun walking in their direction when his phone rang. Caitlin's caller ID was on the screen. He sighed as if wrestling with a decision, his thumb poised between Accept and Decline.

"Voicemail," Caitlin announced when he didn't answer. "I'll call from the train. See how he's doing."

Pash winced with uncertainty, then began threading his way through the crowd to the escalator. Caitlin and the others were gone by the time he got there.

The Ritz-Carlton Tysons Corner was in the upscale business and shopping district anchored by the Galleria, a short drive from the JTTF headquarters. The hotel featured posh accommodations, state-of-the-art conference facilities, and a fitness center and spa where guests could luxuriate in professional pampering. Christmas was ten days away and the entire complex was festooned with glittering strings of LEDs, Christmas décor, and shop windows extolling holiday sales.

Lana left her car with a parking valet and made her way to the mezzanine level, where the hotel's private meeting rooms were located. Andy Grabowski, Amtrak's chief of computer operations, was waiting for her. "Sorry. Traffic's a mess. We're in here," she said, directing him to one of the conference rooms.

"Hey, Lana, good to see you," Caitlin called out as they came through the door. "And this must be the legendary Mr. Grabowski."

"The legendary Andy, please," Grabowski corrected with a grin. He was a broad-shouldered, powerful-looking man with an easy smile you'd want on your side in a bar fight. "It keeps the *Big Lebowski* wisecracks to a minimum."

"Not to worry, stand-up's not our strong suit," Caitlin joked in her snappy brogue, guiding them to their seats. "We're hoping Pash is up to joining us. In the meantime—"

"Pash? He's here?" Lana interrupted. "I'm sorry, but after what happened, I thought he'd have gone back home."

"No, and it's killing him he couldn't, but he had no guarantee they'd let him out of Yemen, or that the U.S. would let him back in. He wasn't sure if he was up to this. Almost missed the train." Caitlin raised an uncertain brow, causing the safety pin that pierced it to catch the light. "We'll see if he comes down. While we're waiting: Mark Wallace, browser security. Alice Saunders, targeted threats," she went on, introducing her colleagues who peered from behind their laptops. "If Pash doesn't show, I'll pinch hit on anti-malware."

"Looks like you won't have to," Lana said as Pash pushed through the door with his laptop case. "Pash . . ." She sighed, noticing the sparkle was gone from his eyes. "I'm so sorry. I'm . . . I'm still at a loss for words."

"Please, no need to a-a-apologize," Pash stammered in his British-inflected English. "Everyone's been immensely supportive."

"So . . ." Caitlin said, forcing a smile as Pash took a seat. "Since our meeting in Vegas we've analyzed the threat landscape and launched an all-out cyberattack on Amtrak's computer network. The good news is, your security is cutting-edge. All systems—those that monitor rolling stock, those that manage payroll and pension, real estate and infrastructure, and the routing and scheduling of trains from commuter lines to the shipment of hazardous materials—are secure and virus free."

"Ditto for ESR, PTC, and RCRM?" Grabowski prompted, rattling off the acronyms for the programs Lana had highlighted in Vegas and in her mission statement as the key to the safe operation of the nation's railroads.

"Ditto! All three. Burned into our brains!" Caitlin fired back with an impish grin, rolling her Rs. "You'll be sleeping like a baby."

"Way to go," Lana enthused. It was perfect, she thought, admiring the tactical synergy she had devised. Almost poetic how the three programs were also the key to the execution of her mission. "As I said, they're my primary cybersecurity concern."

"And mine . . ." Grabowski said wryly, "as Caitlin so delicately pointed out."

"Before we congratulate ourselves," Caitlin warned, "the *bad* news is that some of the services I just enumerated are provided by outside contractors, which brings us to—"

"Zero-day exploits," Grabowski interjected.

"Zero-day exploits," Caitlin echoed with a snap of her head. "Pash. . . ?"

Pash looked distant. He stared at his laptop without acknowledging her.

"Pash? Pash, I thought you might want to take over from here," Caitlin prompted again. "Zero-day exploits?"

"Ah, yes, yes, zero-day exploits," Pash repeated, his fingers poking at his keyboard. "These flaws that are inadvertently built into operating systems are harmless until discovered by a hacker. At which point, they can be exploited until detected by a software developer or user. I've no doubt Amtrak's operating system could bloody well be ta-ta-taken over by one."

"We talking Shellshock?" Lana prompted. "The Heartbleed bug?"

"Actually, your system proved quite impervious to both, but it *is* vulnerable to back-door access via a self-replicating vi-vi-virus called Plesk th-that . . ." Pash paused and took a deep breath, trying to collect himself.

"I believe it allows hackers to access servers without a username or password," Lana said, coming to his rescue.

Pash forced a smile. "And once a website is penetrated, data can be uploaded to a server con-con-controlled by the hacker, then deleted, revised, and downloaded back into the system, giving the hacker c-control over Amtrak's entire network,"

"Way I see it," Grabowski said crisply, "it comes down to whether or not you guys can write a program to keep Plesk from infecting our system."

"That's a yeah-but," Caitlin cautioned. "*Yeah* we can, *but* there's another way in, and that way in is"—she nodded to a young woman with precise cornrows—"Alice?"

"Via software used by service companies with remote access to your systems," Alice replied. "HVAC maintenance. Billing and human resources management. Office-supply sellers. Even vending-machine operators monitoring which drinks and munchies need restocking. If *their* software's been infected with Plesk, the hacker is in and can control your entire network."

Browser expert Wallace nodded sagely. "Last year, we busted a guy who noticed that workers at a big oil company ordered Chinese takeout online. He hacked the *restaurant's* website, and the next time Big Oil placed an order, he owned their network."

"So, what do we do, Pash?" Lana prompted, trying to get him to reengage.

Pash flinched, then straightened in his chair. "You mean how do we stop this cyber carnage? How do we prevent these monsters from un-un-unleashing wholesale destruction? From indiscriminately destroying communities?" he challenged, becoming more agitated with every word. "Not to mention in-in-in—"

"Maybe this would be a good time to take a break," Caitlin said.

"*Incinerating* innocent women and children," Pash charged on. "Who-who . . ." He groaned, then put his head in his hands and began weeping softly.

"It's okay, Pash," Caitlin said, circling toward him. "But it might be best if we—"

Pash bolted upright from his chair. "What might be best?!" he challenged, his voice taking on an edge. "How can you presume to know? How can any of us? We are so obsessed with ridding the cyber world of ma-ma-malware that we can't see the malware in ourselves, let alone in our corporations, governments, or their heartless leaders."

"Pash . . ." Caitlin pleaded. "Pash, we know you've been through a lot and—"

"*Been* through?" Pash interrupted. "It's not over, Caitlin. It's happening *now*. Every minute of every day and every night! I see the faces of my dear parents, of my relatives and friends, of my sweet wife, who was with ch-ch-child. I see her laughing and then I hear her screams!" He took a moment to marshal his indignation, then locked his eyes onto Lana's and, in precisely articulated phrases, asked, "Do you really think—I give a bloody damn—if Amtrak's operating system gets hacked?" He didn't want an answer, and didn't wait for one. Before anyone could react, he charged across the room and out the door, leaving his laptop behind, and the others in stunned silence.

"I'm sorry," Caitlin finally said. "Poor guy hasn't been himself since it happened. He's so fragile. Loses his concentration. Has this stammer. As I said, he didn't want to be here today. But I pleaded with him to come. Told him I couldn't do this without him. I mean I thought it would be therapeutic. Obviously it was a mistake."

"Don't beat yourself up," Lana said, her mind racing. In her line of work, every event, incident, moment, even word was identified as a threat, asset, or opportunity, and she realized that Pash's state of mind might be useful—if she could convince Caitlin to keep him on the team. "No, I think you were right," Lana said with quiet authority. "Pash should be engaged. Be reminded that he has value and can contribute."

Caitlin emitted a demoralized sigh. "I don't know. He embraced the American dream and it betrayed him. His entire family was murdered by his adopted country for godsakes. He's angry and vengeful. He wants some time off. Maybe he should have it."

"To do what?" Lana challenged rhetorically, realizing she'd have to be more forceful to prevail. "Pace about his apartment? Sit alone in the dark contemplating painful memories? It might only further alienate him. Even . . . even radicalize him."

"Pash? I don't think there's any chance of that. He's so gentle and sweet . . ."

"Well, is he gentle and sweet? Or angry and vengeful? Which is it?"

Caitlin shrugged. Her posture slackened. "I'm not sure . . ."

Lana's eyes softened. "I'm sorry, Caitlin," she said, making a strategic retreat. "I didn't mean to be so strident. My point is that Pash can get over this and put his life back together. It will take time. But the five stages of grief somehow get you there."

"He's already well into stage two, Lana, and I—"

"Thanks to Skype," Lana interjected. "After seeing it happen in real time, he had little choice but to skip denial and go straight to anger."

"I better make sure he's okay," Caitlin said, turning toward the door.

Lana touched her arm, stopping her. "Wait. Wait, an outsider might have a better chance of reaching him. I mean, I've had some . . . some personal experience he might be able to relate to, that, you know, might help him cope."

"But his anger was aimed directly at you, Lana."

"Yes, it was, and it stung," Lana said, her eyes glistening. "But I'm willing to take the chance, and you've got nothing to lose . . ."

Caitlin nodded. "Pash is all I care about right now. If you think you can help him . . ."

Lana was striding across the meeting room before Caitlin finished the sentence. She blew through the door and dashed along the mezzanine in search of Pash. She was about to veer off in the direction of the escalators when she spotted his slight frame through the glass doors that led to the bridge between the hotel and the Galleria. He was standing mid-span at the railing, staring down at the shopping levels far below.

Chapter Twenty-One

Despite Churkin's influence, the 38 Petrovka bureaucracy moved slower than a prisoner being dragged to the gallows. Katkov spent the weekend in a holding cell. It was after midnight when he was released. Unshaven, his clothes soiled, hair unkempt, eyeglasses smudged as if licked by a dog, his right arm in the sling, the other clutching his parka, he pushed through the door from Out-Processing and brightened at the sight of Vera, clutching a sweater in her fist. "What're you doing here?"

"Thought I'd take you home and tuck you in," Vera replied, embracing him.

"What's with that?" Katkov asked, recognizing the sweater.

"The Kremlin cold snap," she replied, joking that the weather, like everything else in Russia, was government controlled. "Last couple of nights have been single digits, *and* I thought you might need some help getting put together tomorrow."

"Tomorrow?" Katkov prompted as she draped the sweater over his shoulders.

"Grusha's funeral. You're giving the eulogy, remember?"

"Oh God," he groaned as they began walking down the corridor toward the exit.

"Yeah, oh God," Vera echoed, sweeping her eyes over him. "You look like . . . like the homeless who panhandle on the Metro. You need a complete makeover."

Katkov rolled his eyes. "Tell me about it. Ever try buttoning a shirt or knotting a tie one-handed? Don't know what I'd do without you. Thanks."

"Hey, *I* should be thanking *you*. I'm on the midnight-to-eight tomorrow."

"You've been reinstated?"

"Yup," Vera replied, clearly delighted. "Getting my computer back too."

"It's Churkin's doing. His head gets screwed on backwards once in a while, but his heart's in the right place."

"Guess that's why he didn't do the cavity searches himself, huh?" Vera retorted.

Katkov stopped walking. He looked stunned. "I'm sorry. Was . . . was that plural?"

Vera nodded. "Alexa and Mika too."

"The butch weight lifters with mustaches . . ."

Vera nodded again.

Katkov winced, then looked off in thought.

Vera sensed what was on his mind. "Yes, the flash drive is still taped to the bottom of the drawer. I checked again when I got home."

Moscow was a festival of light during the holidays. Buildings were outlined with strings of glittering bulbs. The multicolored domes of St. Basil's Cathedral were bathed in brilliant light. Despite the bitter cold, the streets were busy with Muscovites making the weekend last until sunrise when Katkov and Vera emerged from 38 Petrovka. He scanned every face, read every gesture, and kept glancing over his shoulder, quickening his pace as they walked to the Metro. "Come on, step it up. Before the attack dogs are let off their leashes."

"Lighten up, Niko. You're a free man, a citizen of the world. You know?"

"Yeah, but do *they*? Bortnikov may have signed off on it, but did the Rottweilers get the word?! Maybe they're so pissed off over that wild goose chase I sent them on, they *don't* want to get it!" They were approaching the Pushkinskaya Metro stop when Katkov realized he didn't have his shoulder bag, laptop, or phone. He was lost without the latter, but there was nothing he could do about it at that hour. His anxiety level was abating when a face he'd seen before, but couldn't place, sent it soaring. The heavyset thirtysomething with the brush cut was leaning against a parked car in jeans and warmup jacket, smoking a cigarette. He flicked it into the gutter before pushing off and following them. Katkov was hustling Vera into the Metro when he realized he'd last seen Brush Cut with Churkin in the lobby of Grafinskaya's building, straining the seams of his suit. A train was in the station as they came off the escalator and slipped into the last car as the doors were closing.

"Who was that guy?" Vera asked as they stumbled to their seats and the train pulled out, leaving Brush Cut behind.

"Zhukich. Churkin's gofer."

"I thought Churkin was on our side. Why would he be following you?"

"Because they think I'll lead them to Grusha's RZD source. Maybe the kid's trying to score points for the other team because the pay is better, like maybe he'll get recruited. I made him look bad in front of Churkin. Maybe it's just personal."

Lyublino was at the far end of the line, and there were few passengers on the train. A couple at the opposite end of the car caught Katkov's eye. The woman didn't resemble the dog walker who followed him from Gorky Park, and her escort wasn't wearing sunglasses and a NASCAR cap. But his winter warmup suit and their body language made him uneasy, and he was relieved they didn't get off at his stop.

Katkov went straight to his desk when he and Vera entered his apartment, and he was relieved to see his laptop next to it. He was anxious to plan his itinerary to Washington, DC, and email it to Agent Jones. But his local punch list came first: Phone. Funeral. RZD source. Not to mention he was exhausted and his shoulder had stiffened. He headed for the bedroom with Vera in tow, took a double dose of painkillers, and fell onto the covers fully clothed. She removed his shoes and settled next to him.

In the morning, Katkov awakened to the smell of perfume and coffee. Vera handed him a steaming mug and he went about checking his emails. The one he was looking for still wasn't there. His shoulder had regained some mobility, and he was able to set his wrist on the laptop and type with both hands.

> *Dear Agent Jones,*
>
> *I am of the opinion that the email I forwarded you recently, referencing a sleeper agent, provided you with valuable information. Furthermore, I have reason to believe my colleague, Nina Grafinskaya, who wrote, but never sent, that email, may have been terminated to keep that agent's mission from being compromised. I am pursuing this line of inquiry in Moscow, and plan to come to Washington, DC, in several weeks with additional information. I will forward my itinerary as soon as I have it and would very much like to meet with you at your convenience.*
>
> *Yours truly,*
> *Nikolai Katkov*
> Investigative Journalist, Novaya Gazeta

Katkov attached his public key, ensuring the recipient could decrypt it, and sent it, then scrolled past an email from Vitaly, Subject: **Editorial Meeting Agenda** to one from Michaela, Subject: **Grusha's Funeral**.

Hi Nikasha,

Been trying to reach you. Hope you're not still in 38 P. Just a reminder: Mom's service is today, 2:00 p.m. at the Choral Synagogue. You're giving the eulogy, right?

Katkov clicked on Reply, and typed:

Right. Sorry. Released from 38 P last night. Vera's with me. We'll be there.

With Vera's help, Katkov showered, shaved, put on a white shirt, dark suit, a pair of dusty wing tips, and a subdued tie, which she knotted expertly. "Can't tell me and Alexa's driver apart," he joked, posing in front of the mirror.

"*You're* the one with the sling," Vera said with a laugh.

The street was lined with snowed-in cars as they headed for the Metro, but none had men in warmup suits slouching in them, nor was Zhukich lurking in his undercover guise. Vera transferred at Kurskaya to go home and dress for the funeral. Katkov went two stops beyond and walked past the shops on the Inner Ring to Dmitrovka. A bright-red sign over a sleek storefront read MTS. Holiday window displays touted mobile phones, tablets, and other wireless devices as *Ideal'nyy Rozhdestvenskie Podark!*—the perfect Xmas gift. An amalgamation of T-Mobile and Siemens, MTS was the largest telecom company serving Moscow.

After hearing Katkov's tale of woe, the sales tech recommended an iPhone 6. "It's intuitive, has idiot-proof icons, fingerprint ID, no password necessary, 13 LTE bands, a 64-bit A7 chip with Airdrop for multitasking, and M7 coprocessor that knows if you're walking, running, or driving. Last but not least, the iSight camera with continuous-burst mode, not to mention nine hundred thousand mobile apps, email, text, and web browsing."

"Can I use it to make phone calls?" Katkov asked, deadpan.

"Some people do," the tech replied with a grin. "Keeping the same number?"

"Yeah, bad enough I lost my contact list." Katkov didn't explain that, old number or new, the Rottweilers would be tracking his phone the instant it was activated.

"You recall if your phone was on when you lost it?" the tech asked.

Katkov nodded. "Why?"

"If the battery hasn't died . . ." The tech let it trail off, plugged Katkov's new iPhone into a computer, and dialed his number. It rang several times and went to voicemail. After sending a coded signal, he handed the phone to Katkov, who was delighted to see his contacts scrolling down the screen as they were being downloaded.

At about the same time Katkov left MTS, *Novaya Gazeta*'s editor in chief and several members of his staff were in the conference room reviewing the day's breaking stories. The mood was appropriately funereal.

"Okay, what do we have?" Vitaly asked rhetorically. "Putin orders investigation into Grafinskaya assassination. Calls it an outrage. Vows to bring killers to justice."

"Yeah, he's going to arrest himself," one of the editors cracked.

Vitaly pressed on without cracking a smile. "Kremlin pays billions on contracts to companies that exist only on paper. Khodorkovsky claims Putin is leading Russia to stagnation and collapse. Putin pressuring Ukraine to repay a $30 billion loan. And—"

"Yeah, that he stole from our pension funds," a reporter interjected. "A unilateral decision. No committee meetings, no votes taken."

"As somebody famous once said," Katkov piped up, overhearing as he came through the door, "go get the bastards!"

"Looks like the bastards got *you*," Vitaly fired back, eyeing Katkov's sling. "I emailed, texted, left voicemails. Where the hell have you been?" He swept his eyes over Katkov's suit and tie, and added, "At your tailor?"

"Yeah, he works out of a cell in 38 Petrovka," Katkov replied, unable to keep from laughing. "My laptop was at home. My phone was touring Yuroslaval in the back of a pickup. Just got a new one. More bells and whistles than an organ grinder's monkey, but the international app might come in handy soon as I can flap both wings."

"You won't be flapping anything without a visa," Vitaly challenged.

"A visa?"

"Yeah, this isn't the '90s. Journalists are having a tougher time getting them than terrorists." He nodded at Katkov's sling. "How'd you do that, anyway?"

"I tracked down Grusha's FSB source. So did their hit man. Like I said to my-ex, bullets don't bounce off like they used to."

"You get anything before it hit the fan?"

Katkov swept his eyes over the staff. "Nothing I can discuss among friends."

"Give us a few minutes," Vitaly said, prompting the others to depart.

"The sleeper is an American," Katkov said, sotto voce. "Born and raised there."

Vitaly pursed his lips in tribute. "The Kremlin's scored quite a coup. The source didn't happen to mention the nature of the operation?"

"No, just the agent's codename: Pochtalska."

"Pochtalska?" Vitaly repeated with a derisive chuckle. "Whatever the Kremlin's up to, if they run it like they run our postal system the Americans have nothing to fear!"

Katkov forced a smile, then looked over the top of his glasses and locked his eyes onto Yarshevsky's. "That's not for publication, Vitaly. None of it is."

"Yet," Vitaly grunted. "You said Grusha had two sources. FSB and. . . ?"

"RZD."

"You know who he is?"

"*She*," Katkov corrected. "And yeah, I do, but so does Bortnikov. His Rottweilers are in full manhunt mode. She's either on the run or in the Moskva."

"If she *isn't* sleeping with the fishes, you've got to find her first."

"I've got someone working on it. It's dicey, delicate, and—"

"Pressure them, dammit! It's a front-page story, and—" Vitaly groaned in frustration and glanced to his watch. "We're going to be late for the service."

Most of the staff had already left to attend the funeral. They were scurrying through the newsroom toward the elevator when Katkov's phone rang, stopping them. "Hi. We're leaving now . . . What? . . . No way . . . Christ! . . . Yeah, yeah. See you there . . . I hope." He saw Vitaly's look, and said, "Vera. She got a heads-up from a friend on the day shift. Militia's on the way with a warrant for your arrest."

"Told you they'd bring me in to testify."

"To be *interrogated*," Katkov corrected. He went to a window that overlooked the parking lot. Two militia cruisers were pulling in. "They're here," he exclaimed as Cujo lumbered toward the building, his team of uniformed officers hurrying to keep up. "The stairs. We'll never get out of here otherwise."

"Yeah," Vitaly grunted as they changed direction and hustled down the corridor toward the landing. "No way those bastards are making me miss Grusha's funeral."

"It's your own you should be worried about . . ." Katkov let it trail off then, with a sarcastic snort, prompted, "Have you thought about applying for a visa?"

Chapter Twenty-Two

After spotting Pash on the bridge that connected the Ritz-Carlton's mezzanine to the Galleria, Lana took a moment to compose herself, then slipped through the door and approached, slowly, to avoid startling him. "Pash? It's okay, Pash . . ."

He stiffened. His hands tightened on the railing. A tense moment passed before Pash's head turned. His shy eyes were watery. His cheeks streaked with tears.

Lana stepped closer. "I'd like to help you, if you'll let me . . ."

Pash's posture slackened. His face became a remorseful mask. "Lana, I am so sorry. I had no right to speak to you in such a di-di-disrespectful manner."

"So much for the painless dentist," Lana said, getting a weak smile out of him.

"Please, my behavior was shameful. My dear mother would be appalled. I lost my *karama*, my . . ." He paused, searching for the word. "My *dignity*. I am unworthy of help."

"No, no, you're being too hard on yourself, Pash. Your feelings are honest and appropriate. Don't deny them. Express them. Let them play out . . ."

Pash nodded, knowingly. "Ah, you have been sent, as you Americans say, to talk me off the le-le-ledge, but I have lost everything I had to live for. I've nothing left. You are well intended, Lana, but how could you possibly know . . ."

"Because I've been there," Lana replied, letting her voice break. "I went through it as a child with my mother."

The sadness in Pash's eyes deepened. "I'm so sorry to hear that," he said, relaxing his grip on the railing.

Lana made her eyes as sad as his, then touched his hand. "Yes, like you, she lost everything. Her whole life was gone, but unlike you, she had only herself to blame. Why don't we take a walk, and I'll share it with you. I think it might help."

Moments later, they had descended to the promenade between the Galleria and the hotel. "My mother had a good life when she was growing up," Lana began as they walked beneath a canopy of oaks, their bare branches dotted with sparkling LEDs. "Her parents were world-class fencers from well-to-do families in Saint Petersburg, and she followed in their footsteps. Like other Soviet athletes and performers who spent time in the West during the Cold War, she was taken with its many freedoms and sense of hope."

Pash nodded. "As was I, thanks to the Internet and time I spent in London."

"Well, my mother didn't have that kind of reinforcement. But one day in 1976 during the Montreal Olympics, she saw her chance and defected. She wasn't a famous ballerina who could sell out Carnegie Hall, or a UN diplomat with access to top-secret documents. She was an immigrant, left to fend for herself. She used her good looks and athlete's body to do what women have always done to survive, and, well . . ." Lana stopped amid a stand of trees, and let her eyes find Pash's. "She had a child out of wedlock. More than once, she found herself on a ledge, but she persevered and made a wonderful life for herself, and as you can see, for her daughter."

"You are very fortunate, Lana . . ." Pash said with a wistful sigh.

"Yes. I am," Lana said, humbly, looking off in reflection. "We were kind of like Thelma and Louise there for a while."

Pash looked puzzled.

"*Thelma and Louise*? The movie? You've . . . you've never seen it, have you?"

Pash pursed his lips and managed an apologetic shrug.

"It's about two women in bad relationships who kill a rapist and are being chased by the police. Rather than surrender they drive off a cliff. The point is, I've been there. I know what you're feeling, what you're thinking: *I'm a good person. My parents, my siblings, my sweet wife were all good people. If there is a God, how could He possibly let this happen?*"

"Yes, my mother used to say the many gods embraced by mankind have one thing in common—they work in ways we are not able to understand."

"It sounds like she was a very wise woman," Lana said as they resumed walking. "Someone who believed even the most tragic things in life happen for a reason."

Pash nodded sadly. "Yes, yes, indeed she did."

"Then you must believe it, too, and one day your life will have purpose and take on new meaning." Lana let him sit with it a moment, then added, "Perhaps if we continue working together, I can help you find it . . ."

A shy smile brightened Pash's face.

"And from what you've told me, I think your mother might approve."

"Yes, I rather imagine she would. As would I . . ."

"Good, then her wisdom lives on through you," Lana said spiritedly. She had him now, she thought. Had made the emotional connection she needed to manipulate him, and rather than risk overplaying the moment, she decided to disengage. "Speaking of mothers," she went on, brightening, "I'm having lunch with mine today."

"I'm sorry. Please don't let me detain you any longer."

"Oh, I'm always running late. She'll understand. I'd like for you to meet her one day when you're up to it, Pash. I mean, I think you'd really like her."

"Yes, one day, perhaps," Pash said softly. "I'm sure I would."

"In the meantime, Pash," Lana said, allowing her eyes to glisten with emotion, "if you need anything, *anything*, I'm here for you. Okay?"

Pash nodded. He didn't see the sly smile that tugged at the corners of Lana's mouth as she turned and hurried down the leaf-strewn path, and had no idea the entire story was a bald-faced lie that she had been perfecting since childhood.

Indeed, Katia Nikolshevskaya began schooling her daughter early on. She taught her and tested her, and by her teens, Svetlana had become highly skilled in the ways of clandestine tradecraft, in the art of manipulating people, and in the choreography of deception. Pash may not have seen the smile. But Lana's mother had. Many times. She knew what it meant. Knew since the first time she saw it. Since the day Lana outfoxed *her* with what, thereafter, was referred to as the "existence of God" performance—the one by which all others had, since, been measured.

Lana was fourteen at the time. She and her mother—by then known as Kate Nichols—were living in Alban Towers, a prewar complex of textured brick on Massachusetts Avenue in Cathedral Heights. Lana was attending Deal Middle School, where her mother worked as a part-time teacher and fencing instructor. Deal had one of the highest ratings in the DC public school system. Its students came from upper-middle-class families, and the job not only paid the bills but gave Kate Nichols access to their parents, who worked at government agencies, defense contractors, law firms, and lobbying organizations. The contacts were invaluable, the gossip information-rich, and the potential for espionage prized by her Moscow Centre handlers. Several days a week, Kate spent after-school hours coaching the girls' fencing team. One day, Lana missed practice, slipping into the gym as her teammates were heading to the locker room.

"Where were you?" her mother challenged, tossing her a sporting épée.

Lana dropped her backpack and caught the blade by the handle. "Study hall. I told you I was going with Sally to cram for a math test."

Her mother raised a skeptical brow. "You and Sally were *studying* . . ."

"Uh-huh," Lana replied, flipping her flame-red ponytail with an emphatic nod.

"That's not the truth, is it, Lanichka?"

"Yes, it is," Lana replied with a defensive pout. "I'm not lying. I'm not."

"Yes, you are. *I* know you are. And *you* know you are," her mother said calmly.

Lana's posture stiffened with defiance, then slackened. "Okay," she said in an adolescent moan. "We were studying . . . with Sally's boyfriend, Erik. He's in tenth at Wilson, and, like, he's really good in math. Really good, you know? Me and Sally went with him and his friends for pizza after. He's got a really cool car. You saw him pick us up, right? That's how you knew."

"No, I knew you were lying because you blinked and looked away when you answered, then put your hand to your mouth. I've told you many times how important—"

"Mom," Lana whined, making it into two syllables, "I've got loads of homework. Okay? I mean, can we skip the lecture so I can—"

"A *lesson*," her mother corrected. "*Maskirovka* is the key to our work. It's—"

"*Maskirovka*?" Lana interrupted. "It means to lie? Be deceitful?"

"Precisely. And it's very important to our work. You know that. Yes?"

Lana nodded grudgingly, toying with the handle of the épée.

"Good. It's like feigning a *kontrataka* to position your opponent," her mother said taking the sword from Lana and demonstrating. "To be effective, a feint must appear like an attack. And a lie must appear to be the truth. You establish your sincerity with your eyes and speak as if what you're saying is a deeply held belief. Like a . . . a priest extolling the existence of

God." She held her daughter's look and added, "Just remember, it will never work with me."

Lana nodded again. The sly smile turned the corners of her mouth.

"You've got nothing to smile about, young lady. I don't care that you lied. What I care about is that you lied—*and got caught.* As I've often told you, reverse psychology is the *kontrataka* of choice when so positioned: When all else fails, tell the truth."

Lana scoffed. "That's what I did."

"What do you mean by that?"

"Well, I mean, like, I didn't *really* get caught. Okay? The truth is, Sally *doesn't* have a boyfriend named Erik who goes to Wilson. He *didn't* help me with my math, and we *didn't* go for a ride with him and his friends for pizza in his car. I made it all up."

"You made it all up," her mother repeated evenly.

"Uh-huh. I *told* you the truth, but, like, you didn't believe it, so I lied. I mean, I made up something that I thought you *would* believe—and you did." Lana was standing sideways, chin raised slightly, the way teenage girls do when they know they've got the upper hand. She let the smile turn the corners of her mouth again. "Pretty cool, huh?"

Her mother steeled herself, her anger suppressed by an overwhelming sense of pride. A little mentoring goes a long way, she thought. Not to mention the right genes.

Twenty years later, Lana was now waiting for the Ritz-Carlton's parking valet to retrieve her car. She checked her emails and was jolted by one addressed to Tom that had been intercepted by the code she had embedded in the JTTF mainframe and diverted to her clandestine account. The line in her inbox read:

Sender: nkatkov@novayagazeta.ru

*Subject: **Previously Forwarded Email***

Lana had already deleted the email about the sleeper agent to which Katkov referred, and it was no longer a threat, but his intention to travel to Washington to pursue the matter was unsettling. Farrell was right. Some puzzle pieces *were* missing, and one had just turned up. Lana closed the email and called her mother. Not because she was late. No, they *weren't* meeting for lunch. That was a beguiling lie, as was the promise of Pash joining them one day, a graceful way to disengage and set yet another emotional hook in him—the grand finale of an existence-of-God performance second to none. No, she was calling her mother because, thanks to Katkov—and the looming Ruben/Bargishev and Caitlin/Pash scenarios—Lana needed to meet with Kate and Julian immediately.

Chapter Twenty-Three

After clambering down five flights from *Novaya Gazeta*'s offices, Katkov and Vitaly Yarshevsky charged out the service entrance at the rear of the building into the street. Katkov held his right arm against his body in the sling, pumping his left as he ran. They had reached the street when Cujo and several militia officers emerged from the building in pursuit. The fleeing journalists dashed into oncoming traffic and piled into a cab that stopped to avoid hitting them. Ten minutes later, it turned onto Spasoglinishchevskiy, where traffic slowed due to the large turnout for the funeral and made its way to the Choral Synagogue, where a hearse was parked. Built in Central Moscow at the turn of the nineteenth century, the synagogue was a short walk from the Kremlin. Its yellow-and-white neoclassical façade was topped by a silver dome that capped an ornate, Moorish-themed interior decorated with Arabesque moldings and murals.

Mourners bundled against the cold were streaming toward it and climbing the snow-swept steps to the entrance. Cujo and his militia clones hadn't shown up yet. But the Kremlin's Rottweilers had. Katkov sensed them lurking in the latticed alcoves and filigreed lofts that encircled the synagogue's luminous sanctuary. Nameless, cold-eyed men who had traded in their Nike warmups for drab business suits were watching and waiting on the fringes. Fleeting shadows, there and not there, out of sight but never out of mind, they made their presence *felt*.

Indeed, as Katkov expected, they had resumed tracking him the instant his new phone was activated, but his presence at Grusha's funeral was predictable, and thanks to the deal Churkin had made with Bortnikov, he no longer required such high-tech monitoring. So why are they here? Katkov wondered. Is the Kremlin's agenda somehow threatened by an assassinated journalist's funeral? The mere fact of it was proof that Grafinskaya's agenda, as journalists say, had been *spiked*. No, it was because the threat lived on in her sources, in Patrushev and the RZD insider Katkov desperately wanted to contact. Was *she* their target now? Was *that* why the Rottweilers were there?

Grafinskaya's closed casket stood in front of the Holy Ark, where the Torah scrolls were kept. The embroidered parochet had been drawn back and the ark opened as was customary during services. Hanukkah had ended the previous evening, and a menorah with eight burned candle stubs stood nearby. Katkov and Vitaly joined the group of mourners at the simple wooden coffin: Michaela; her fiancé, Sasha; Vera; and members of the *Novaya Gazeta* staff. Colleagues from the international press corps, along with relatives and friends filled the pews behind them to capacity. Churkin was observing from the sidelines. There was no sign of Zhukich straining the seams of his suit. The CI appeared to be working alone.

Michaela appeared distracted, her watery eyes darting about as she accepted condolences from arriving mourners. She saw Alexa striding down the aisle and excused herself. "Where's Slava?" she asked as they hugged.

"Regrets and condolences, I'm afraid. He's into this RZD *thing* for Nikolai. Why, what's wrong?"

"The memorial booklets aren't here yet."

Alexa looked puzzled. She slipped her phone from her purse and made a call. "Hi, it's me . . . Yes. *I* am, but the memorial booklets *aren't,* and Mika's very concerned that—Oh. Oh, okay . . . Uh-huh . . . Uh-huh. Great. I'll tell her." Alexa clicked off and smiled. "They were delivered hours ago. Slava said he and the rabbi worked out a special sequence of events for the service. They'll be in the sanctuary when the time comes."

Michaela was sighing with relief when the rabbi came through an ornate doorway off to one side of the ark and walked to the lectern at a solemn pace. Everyone took their seats, and the service began. The rabbi was all business. He said Kaddish, the traditional prayer for the dead, made a few perfunctory remarks about Nina Grafinskaya's strength of character and journalistic integrity, and introduced Katkov as the eulogist.

"You'll be fine," Vera said, making sure Katkov's yarmulke was in place.

He was approaching the lectern, his sling making a hospital-green slash across his suit coat, when two women came through the doorway next to the ark, pushing a small table on casters. One, bent with age, had her hair tucked under a lace kippah. The other, tiny and precise, wore a plain black dress and low heels. Her only adornment was a silver-and-white silk tallit that covered her head and shoulders, concealing her face. They rolled the table across the sanctuary and parked it off to one side of the casket.

Michaela brightened at the sight of the booklets stacked on it in neat piles. They were the size of a slim paperback and bound in black leather on which *Nina Grafinskaya August 14, 1970–December 8, 2015* was stamped in gold leaf. About a dozen of them had been set aside from the others and were personalized with the name of each recipient, also stamped in gold leaf, in the lower-right corner of the cover: Michaela Grafinskaya, Nikolai Katkov, and Vitaly Yarshevsky among them.

The older woman left the sanctuary immediately.

The one with the prayer shawl took several personalized booklets from the table and presented Michaela with her copy, then walked toward the lectern. Despite the shawl, Katkov got a good look at her face—mid-thirties, tense features, intelligent eyes that belied an anxious wariness—and recognized her at once. As with Patrushev, he had found her name in Grusha's files, downloaded her photo from an online bio, and had no doubt she was Nadia Nysenko, Grusha's RZD source. Katkov's spirits soared as he peered over his glasses and acknowledged Alexa with a nod. Not only had Slava located Nadia and delivered Katkov's message, but he had also arranged for her to be involved in the ceremony, to contact him in a public forum, which minimized her risk of being identified or, like Grafinskaya, assassinated.

On reaching the lectern, Nadia offered Katkov his personalized booklet but held on to it, prolonging the moment, and, in a rapid-fire whisper, said, "Top Secret RZD file. Cybercode: N5Y7T0E5P. Yakunin's eyes only. Need to talk. There's a café that—" Nadia's eyes darted in alarm to an alcove on the other side of the sanctuary. Katkov followed her look to a man who was staring at her from behind the grillework. But it wasn't one of the Kremlin's Rottweilers. It was Zhukich! He looked from Nadia to an image on his phone and back. She pulled the prayer shawl tighter around her face, whirled from the lectern, and scurried back through the doorway next to the ark. Zhukich made a call and spoke two words. It was hard to be certain, but Katkov thought he said, "She's here." He looked across the sanctuary at Churkin. He wasn't on his phone. Zhukich hadn't called *him*!

Katkov was on the verge of panic, torn between his need to honor Grusha's memory, bring her killers to justice, and keep Nadia from becoming their next victim. He wanted to go after Nadia, get her to safety, ask her to repeat the cybercode—it had become a tangle of letters and digits he couldn't recall—and pepper her with questions as he had Patrushev.

But a packed synagogue was waiting for him to deliver Grusha's eulogy. He couldn't just run off without a word. His mind was racing when he looked from his prepared speech atop the lectern to the memorial booklet in his hand and began speaking extemporaneously. "Thank you for being here on this sad day," he said, his eyes glistening with emotion. "There is so much to say about dear Grusha, but it's hard to speak of this *unspeakable* tragedy, because it would force me to accept that she is . . ." His voice broke and he fought to maintain his poise. "Is forever gone, which is beyond comprehension and, indeed, beyond words. So, I will let my obituary, which expresses my sentiments with heartfelt, if not literary, eloquence speak for me. It has been reprinted in these booklets and I hope you will all read it. Thank you." Katkov stepped aside, turning over the lectern to Michaela, but instead of taking a seat, he slipped his booklet into a pocket and went through the doorway next to the ark.

A confused murmur rose from the assembled mourners.

Michaela looked puzzled as she stepped to the lectern, and it took her a moment to come to grips with Katkov's abbreviated eulogy and mysteriously hasty departure. "My . . . my mother was the salt of the earth, of her country, and of the Russian people, whose human rights she fought so fiercely to protect," she finally began, her voice ringing through the domed sanctuary.

The doorway led to the synagogue's administrative area. Katkov found himself in a maze of corridors that were flanked by offices. He peered through glass partitions and doors that were open, and pushed through those that were closed in search of Nadia. One led to a janitor's closet, several to restrooms. He came upon a delivery area, where two women were discarding corrugated cartons labeled "MPC." A line of type below the logo read "The Moscow Printing Company." One of them was the woman with the kiffah who had rolled the table into the sanctuary with Nadia. "Excuse me?" Katkov called out as he approached. "The woman with the prayer shawl. Did you see where she—"

"They would've been there before the service began," the woman interrupted. "But the rabbi told us to wait until after he said Kaddish and the eulogist was at the lectern before we—"

"I'm sorry, but this is an emergency," Katkov interrupted. "Did you see where she went when she returned?"

"Down there," the woman replied, pointing to a corridor. "It goes around to the vestibule. "She seemed upset. I asked her if I could—"

"Any other way out of here?"

"Yes, but they're locked. We all use the main entrance. Even the rabbi. For security." She eyed him from beneath her kiffah. "She deserved better, you know . . ."

"Pardon me?"

"Your eulogy. Terrible. One of the worst I've ever heard."

Katkov forced a smile and hurried down the corridor.

In the sanctuary, Michaela was concluding a moving tribute to her mother: "There's so much more I could say about her exemplary life and about what a loving parent she was—but I want you to have something *more* . . . something that was truly a part of her. I'd like each of you to have one of these." She held up her copy of the memorial booklet, and added, "Along with her picture, Nikasha's obituary, and testimonials from friends and colleagues, these booklets also contain a packet of soil and seeds from my mother's roof garden. As you know, the earth is considered sacred by the Russian people. Many take pots of it with them when leaving the Motherland or journeying to a new home, and my . . . my"—her eyes filled and tears rolled down her cheeks—"and my mother will be taking some on her journey today to the farm where she grew up and where she will be buried next to my grandparents." Michaela removed the packet of soil from a recess inside the front cover, broke the seal, and sprinkled the contents atop her mother's casket.

Katkov had made a one-armed sprint down the corridor that circled to a service door. It opened into the main entrance vestibule that was packed with departing mourners. He spotted Vitaly holding court amidst a group of journalists and pulled him aside. "The booklet lady . . . the small one in the shawl. Have you seen her?"

"Uh-huh. She came running out of there a few minutes ago and got lost in this scrum," Vitaly replied, pointing to the door from which Katkov had just emerged. "What was going on in there? You look frantic. I mean, who was—"

"I *am* frantic. She's Grusha's RZD source," Katkov interrupted as Nadia's voice began echoing in his head: *Need to talk. There's a café that . . .*

What café?! Where?! Across the street? Down the street? On the Arbat—in GUM?!

138

"She's out there somewhere," Katkov continued, silencing his thoughts. "We have to find her before the attack dogs do!" He and Vitaly began pushing their way through the crowd. The sight of militia cruisers parked in front of the synagogue and uniformed officers deploying at the entrance had stopped the exiting mourners in their tracks, creating a backup. Katkov saw Cujo coming up the steps and held Vitaly back. "Wait! There are other ways out of here. They're locked, but maybe we could—"

Vitaly shook his head no. "Time for me to face the music, Nikasha," he said with a rueful smile. "That's why I get the big bucks."

"You sure?" Katkov prompted, his eyes darting about in search of Nadia.

"Positive. At least the bastards didn't stop me from being here for Grusha."

Katkov winced with uncertainty and nodded.

Vitaly bit a lip and surrendered to Cujo.

The brawny sergeant yanked Vitaly's arms behind his back and looped a zip tie around his wrists.

"Come on!" Katkov growled. "No need for that!"

"I'm doing him a favor," Cujo retorted. "He's a journalist. If he can't type, he can't get into trouble." He burst into laughter at his own joke and yanked hard on the zip tie. "I'd do the same for you, but your friends in the Kremlin won't let me."

Katkov glared at him over the tops of his glasses. The members of the *Novaya Gazeta* staff were seething as Cujo perp-walked their editor in chief down the synagogue steps to a police cruiser. They surged after them, voicing angry protests. As did the other members of the press corps.

"No! No, that's what they want!" Katkov cautioned sharply, prompting the angry group to back off as Cujo muscled Vitaly into the cruiser.

The incident unleashed an onslaught of unsettling memories that rocked Katkov to his core: The pounding on doors in the middle of the night. The citizens beaten and taken away by KGB thugs. The ever-present threat of arrest, interrogation, torture, and the Gulag. Twenty-five years had passed since the Soviet Union had fallen. Since the onset of Perestroika and the birth of the fledging Russian Federation and its promise of democracy. Twenty-five years and nothing had changed! Katkov couldn't believe it. Couldn't believe the right to free speech, freedom of the press, and life, liberty, and the pursuit of happiness were being so wantonly violated, if not eliminated. Couldn't believe he had that gnawing ache in his gut again as he fought his way to the congested exit and pushed through the crowd of mourners spilling from the synagogue.

"There you are!" Michaela called out as he hurried down the steps, looking for Nadia. "What happened?" she sobbed as he whirled in response and she lunged forward, embracing him. "Why did you go off like that?"

"I'm . . . I'm . . . I'm sorry," Katkov stammered, his eyes darting about frantically. "I mean, there's something that I—something really important that—"

"It's bad enough my father never showed up," Michaela interrupted, sobbing.

"He's here," Katkov said, aching to tell her the truth. "He's—he's—he's here in spirit," he went on, wanting to get past it and continue his search. "I'm really sorry. Emergency. Got to go. No time to explain." He hurried off, leaving Michaela encircled by a group of mourners offering condolences.

The street was crowded with people going to their vehicles and the Metro station on Kitay-Gorod. A few women wore prayer shawls. Katkov's eyes darted from one to the next to the next. But Nadia Nysenko wasn't one of them. *There's a café that . . .* What café? Dammit, where?! Where the hell had she gone?! Katkov was on the verge of giving up when he glimpsed a wind-blown prayer shawl fluttering in the distance. The woman was nearly a block away, walking quickly down the long street. She was tiny and wore a black winter coat and low heels. He couldn't be sure it was Nadia. But if his comic-book collection hadn't been confiscated, he'd bet Wonder Woman No. 1 it was. Katkov crossed the street, dodging the oncoming vehicles. He was still a half block away, when, in an effort to change her appearance, the woman removed the shawl and tossed it aside, letting her hair fall to her shoulders. The wind caught the square of billowing silk and sent it sailing high overhead as she reached the corner and turned into the side street.

Katkov hurried after her. By the time he reached the corner Nadia was getting into a faded blue Skoda on the opposite side of the street. "Nadia?!" Katkov shouted as she slipped behind the wheel. "Nadia, wait!" But the traffic noise and the whine of the Skoda's engine as she drove off drowned him out. Katkov took a few steps after it, then gave up, his shoulders sagging in defeat. He was standing in the middle of the street when a sedan came screeching around the corner and nearly clipped him from behind.

Two Rottweilers in warmup suits were in the front seat. The one in the passenger seat was gesticulating and yelling at the driver to go faster.

"Hey! Hey!" Katkov called out in futile protest as the sedan fishtailed past him on the slushy pavement and accelerated in pursuit of the Skoda. "Bastards," he muttered to himself, his heart pounding with anger and disbelief. He was close, so close. Just another ten yards and he could have stopped her, could have gotten in the car with her! But Nadia was gone— along with whatever information she would have given him, and the letters and digits of the cybercode he couldn't recall: NT5P7? E7Y5N? 7YN0P? He took a moment to catch his breath and was heading back in the direction of the synagogue when he noticed the wind-blown prayer shawl had become snagged atop a fence. He reached up, stretching to his full height to get hold of it and freed it from the rusting pickets.

Chapter Twenty-Four

Thirty minutes after the valet retrieved her car, Lana was north of the Potomac angling into the Burning Tree off-ramp. The trees that lined the drive to the Bethesda estate were bare, and dried leaves swirled across the grounds as she parked beneath the sign that proclaimed: *Sentiment Du Fer.*

The fencing club was alive with the whispers of steel slicing air, the thumps of thrusting and parrying, and the pings of electronic scoring. Julian and her mother were engaged on the center piste. There was a sense of urgency in Lana's stride as she approached. "There have been some developments. I need to talk."

"As do I," Julian said as he and Kate slipped off their masks. "I haven't had a chance to call because your mother keeps evening the score. She's still very good."

"In more ways than one," Kate said with a seductive smile as she shook out her hair. An attractive woman in her early sixties, she still had a fencer's lithe figure and bristling energy. "Have you time for a bout?"

"No. My meeting ran long. Kind of bizarre. I've got a lot to cover and—"

"*Non, pas ici,*" Julian interrupted with a shake of his head. He and Kate unplugged their body wires and secured their blades, then left the club and crossed the courtyard to the main house with Lana. The interior was decorated with lavish flower arrangements and antique furnishings. Windows of handmade glass in Julian's study overlooked a pond. A high-tech workstation displayed global financial data on Bloomberg terminals that struck a discordant note amid the period décor. The crawl across the bottom of one of the monitors read CANADIAN PACIFIC AND CSX MERGER TALKS PROCEED.

"I'm under siege," Lana said as they settled around an eighteenth-century desk. "I've got multiple opponents on my piste: Caitlin Roarke, cybersecurity. Ruben Diaz, JTTF. Khalid Bargishev, Chechen mafia. And, unexpectedly, a Russian journalist named—"

"Katkov," Julian interjected. "Nikolai Katkov, *Novaya Gazeta.*"

Lana looked surprised and nodded. "He wants to come here."

"*Oui, je sais.* The centre just informed me they approved his travel plans."

142

"Typical," Kate groaned. "They're scraping him off their plate onto ours."

"Because he's toxic like Grafinskaya," Lana said. "They just don't know *how* toxic. He'll never get out of Russia when they see these." She accessed her emails, found the one she wanted, and gave Julian the phone. "Grafinskaya wrote that to Agent Jones but didn't send it. After she was terminated, Katkov found it and forwarded it to him.

Julian's jaw tightened as he scanned the text: *Russian sleeper agents . . . arrested in United States . . . not all captured . . . highly skilled asset . . . embedded in U.S. national security agency . . . don't know name of agency . . . or agent's real or cover names . . . code name: Pochtalska.* He winced and gave the phone to Kate. "Katkov knows what *she* knew, and believes the Kremlin terminated her to protect Pochtalska . . . to protect you."

"And our operation," Lana added.

Kate's eyes widened as she read the email. "This threatens you directly, Lana. *Katkov* threatens you directly."

"Tell me about it. I deleted it from Jones's files and the JTTF mainframe, but when Jones didn't reply, Katkov sent it again. "Thanks to a bit of code I wrote, it was diverted to my account." She took the phone from Kate, scrolled to another email, and handed it back to Julian. "This next one could be really nasty."

"*Oui, très méchant*," Julian said through clenched teeth as his eyes raced across the text: *email I forwarded . . . referencing sleeper agent . . . believe Grafinskaya terminated to keep mission from being compromised . . . pursuing this line of inquiry . . . plan to come to Washington, DC . . . with additional information.* "The salient point is, Katkov doesn't know Jones is dead."

Lana nodded. "Very few people—even at JTTF—do. Farrell ordered a total blackout. Officially, Jones is away on special assignment."

"Then that will be your reply to Katkov's email," Julian said with crisp authority. "Furthermore, you will explain you're his new contact, and will do everything possible to make his time here productive, et cetera, et cetera . . ."

"Why? Why not use these emails to put him on the Kremlin's no-fly list? Or get the State Department to deny him a visa?"

"Because if another toxic journalist must be terminated, the centre wants it to happen *here*, not there. Fortunately, the only other person who has seen these emails will be under your control, but you'll have to gain his trust first."

Lana nodded, her eyes alive with a thought. "I have some people at INS who can help make that happen. Katkov hasn't set an itinerary yet. Gives me plenty of prep time."

"*Très bon*," Julian said with a glance to the Bloomberg monitors. "Remember he's a journalist, not a trained field agent. He'll be out of his element. You'll still have to convince the powers that be to let you take over where Jones left off."

"Already made the sale," Lana said with a smug smile. "Moving right along, Diaz and Bargishev are joined at the hip. The box-cutter ruse made Bargie and his knuckle draggers the FBI's prime for Jones's murder, but Diaz isn't buying it. He's a shrewd, street-smart cop who lives by his gut, and it's telling him it's connected to what happened to Grafinskaya and the Kremlin's plans to take over an American railroad."

Julian grimaced. "*Merde.* You *are* under siege," he said, the bravado gone from his voice. "Any mention of CSX or the proposed merger with CP?"

"No, but Diaz is real close to nailing Bargie's ass."

"Again? Didn't you just alert him to the sting in Baltimore?"

Lana nodded. "Overheard a bit of shop talk at the Russian Desk. It was pure luck. I'd love to have seen the look on Jones's face when Bargie got my text."

Julian's eyes narrowed. "Does Bargishev know you're his guardian angel? Could he betray you to curry favor if Diaz apprehends him?"

Lana shook her head no. "The text was blind. He doesn't know I exist."

"That's a dangerous assumption," Kate protested. "Once the feds have his balls in a vise, they'll squeeze him for Jones. He'll deny it. They'll flutter him, and when the needle doesn't move, Diaz will go with his gut."

"I'm more worried about Farrell," Lana said. "Somebody wasted one of his boys. He'll never quit. Never. He's my boss. He owns me. He could be a big problem."

"Not without interrogating Bargishev," Julian said smartly.

"So, we either save Bargie's ass again or"—Kate paused and smiled—"we cut him a Chechen necktie. I wouldn't mind a little wet work. Keep my hand in."

"The necktie," Lana said without missing a beat.

Julian managed a tight-lipped nod, then stole another glance at the monitors. "Make it appear to be a rival gang. Brighton Beach, North Miami, whatever." He shifted his look to Lana. "That leaves us with Ms. Roarke. Your meeting was bizarre . . ."

"Totally. The good news is: When subjected to a relentless attack, Amtrak tested at a very high level. Their cybersecurity is impenetrable."

Julian looked confused. "But . . . but *ce serait une problème. Non?*

"*Non.* It makes them overconfident. Makes them feel secure, but their operating system has a weakness that can be exploited."

"But this is a time-sensitive op," Kate countered. "Chances are they'll come up with a patch before we can run it."

"I'm counting on it," Lana said with an enigmatic pause. "*I* do the final design review. Embed a little code here, a little there, and I can control the entire system from a park bench with a laptop, but not without the cybercodes for the CSX servers."

"*Ma première priorité,*" Julian said. "Unfortunately, in the M&A chess match that I am playing, information this sensitive is withheld until the parties develop mutual trust. Montreal is doing the due diligence as we speak."

"The *real* good news is this guy Pash, the malware whiz, is from Yemen, and his entire family, pregnant wife included, was just wiped out in a drone strike."

"The one that has been saturating the media as of late?"

Lana nodded. "He's a gentle soul who signed on to the American dream. As you can imagine he's become a little disenchanted, not to mention confused. Emotionally devastated one minute, angry and vengeful the next—and he trusts me. The bad news is, Roarke doesn't think he's up to running the project and wants to do it herself. That's a nonstarter."

"I'm already signed on for Bargie," Kate said matter-of-factly. "Might as well make it a twofer. Where's she staying?"

"The Ritz-Carlton."

"Top of the line. They have a lovely spa and pool there. It's been a while since I treated myself to a day of beauty. Why don't you suggest she do the same?"

"I don't know," Lana said with uncertainty. "She's, like, right out of Stieg Larsson. All edges, spiked hair, piercings, tattoos. Not the type to pamper herself."

"Sure she is," Kate scoffed. "Any woman who pays that much attention to her body is ripe for pampering. She just needs a reason. I'm sure I can help her find her one."

Julian was nodding when his phone rang. "It's Montreal," he said, eyeing the caller ID. "*C'est Julian* . . . *Oui*, I'm in a meeting. *Donnez-moi les détails. Vite. Vite* . . . Uh-huh . . . Uh-huh . . . No. No. *Non, non, j'ai décidé de passer.* The ROI isn't worth the risk. CP/CSX is much more important . . . *Oui, mon objectif premier. Attendez.*" He crossed to the workstation and tapped a fingertip across a color-coded keyboard, highlighting two ticker symbols: CP, the Canadian Pacific Railway, and CSX, the American railroad headquartered in Florida. "Any progress on the CSX cybercodes? . . . *Non, non, ce n'est pas acceptable!*" Julian snapped. "*Mais oui.* I know they're tightly held, but I'm dealing with a time-sensitive op . . . *Oui, oui, ASAP. Comprenez-vous?!* . . . *Bon.* Don't disappoint me." He hung up and reassured Lana with a snap of his head, then shifted his look to Kate. "We were *pampering* the tattooed lady, as I recall. Sounds like a plan as long as—"

A texting ping interrupted him.

Lana grabbed her phone from the desk. "Fuck!" she exclaimed, bolting upright in her chair at the message on the screen."

Julian's eyes widened. "*Quel est le problème?!*"

"Text from Diaz: Bargishev in custody. Three exclamation points."

Chapter Twenty-Five

The funeral service had gone from unexpected triumph to total disaster. Grusha's RZD source, Nadia Nysenko, had gotten close enough to whisper top-secret information in Katkov's ear, but all he could remember was the fear in her eyes as she bolted from the lectern. Not only had he come up empty and made a mess of the eulogy, but Nadia was on the run from the Kremlin's Rottweilers, Vitaly had been arrested and taken to 38 Petrovka to be interrogated, and Zhukich proved to be a snake. He was heading back to the synagogue with Nadia's prayer shawl when Churkin came bounding toward him.

"Katkov? Katkov, what the hell happened in there?"

"Ask your Boy Wonder."

The CI looked puzzled. "Zhukich? It's his day off."

"He was here. I saw him make a call during the service."

"Not to me."

"I know. I think he's freelancing for the Krem."

Churkin flinched. "How do you know that?"

"He fingered the booklet lady," Katkov replied, brandishing the shawl. "She was one of Grusha's sources, had information for me, but Brush Cut sicced the Rottweilers on her when she tried to pass it. Last I saw of her, she was the rabbit in a car chase."

"Christ. The fat little fuck's working both sides of the street."

"Yeah. He followed me home from 38 P the other night. Better watch your back."

Churkin's lips tightened into a thin line. "Thanks. I owe you one."

"*Two*, counting my collection," Katkov fired back.

By the time Katkov reached the synagogue, Vera had left for her shift at 38 Petrovka, Alexa had hurried off to her clinic, and Michaela, grief-stricken at the sight of Grusha's casket being loaded into the hearse, brightened at the sight of him. After explaining his bizarre behavior, Katkov accompanied her and some of the other mourners to the burial service. The funeral cortege took the M7 out of Central Moscow to Nizhny Novgorod, a large city on the Volga River about a hundred miles east of Moscow, where Andrei Sakharov spent his last years in exile. It was called Gorky then, and as the cortege crossed the frozen river, Katkov smiled at the sight of the building on Gagarina Prospekt where the nuclear scientist and human-rights activist was living when an ambitious young journalist knocked on his door and talked him into being interviewed.

The drive to the Grafinsky farm on the banks of the Volga ended beneath a canopy of bare trees and iron-gray skies. A marker next to the freshly dug grave bore the names of Grusha's parents. Bone-chilling winds buffeted the huddled group as the rabbi said the Mourner's Kaddish. It was late evening by the time Katkov got back to his apartment, still wracking his brain for the letters and numbers of the cybercode Nadia had given him. Grusha's memorial booklet and Nadia's prayer shawl were among the items he'd removed from his pockets. Katkov stared at them for a long moment, then flipped through the pages of the booklet, shook it several times, and sagged in disappointment. The slip of paper with the code hastily scrawled on it that he had hoped to find wasn't there. He spread the prayer shawl on his desk, centered the booklet on it, and folded the silken fabric around its length and width until it formed a neat rectangle that he slipped into a compartment in his shoulder bag.

The next morning, the elusive cybercode was still an irretrievable tangle as he trudged to his desk with a mug of coffee to check his emails. His eyes swept down the bold-type addresses in his inbox and locked onto:

Sender: **United States Federal Bureau of Investigation. lnicholsjttf@nctc.gov**

Subject: **Re: Previously Forwarded Email**

He lit a cigarette, took a deep, thoughtful drag, then opened the email, which read:

Dear Mr. Katkov,

I am responding to your email on behalf of Special Agent Tom Jones, who initiated contact with your colleague, Nina Grafinskaya at Novaya Gazeta. Agent Jones is now on special assignment. In my capacity as Amtrak Special Agent in Charge, FBI Joint Terrorism Task Force, the case Agent Jones opened has been assigned to me. Please direct all further communications to this email address: lnicholsfbijttf@nctc.gov

All of us at JTTF extend our condolences for the tragic loss of your courageous colleague, whose work we admired. Needless to say, the information you and Ms. Grafinskaya have provided is invaluable, and I look forward to working with someone of your stature, which I expect will add momentum to our investigation of the highly sensitive matters she raised and to bringing her killers to justice.

Be advised this information has been classified top secret by the United States government. Therefore, despite the use of encrypted connections, it is important you refrain from repeating or refer-ring to it in any correspondence, sharing it with any persons, or publishing it in any newspaper, journal, or magazine until fur-ther notice. Please keep me informed of your travel plans. I will be happy to secure comfortable accommodations for you and do whatever else might be required to make your stay in Washington pleasant and productive.

Best regards,
Lana Nichols, Amtrak Special Agent in Charge
FBI Joint Terrorism Task Force
lnicholsjttf@nctc.gov

It was written in Russian. Katkov contemplated it for a moment, then replied: Thanks. Looking forward to working with you. I'm told it could take me a month to get a visa. Any chance your State Department could expedite the processing of my application?

He packed up his shoulder bag, got into a roomy parka that accom-modated his sling, and headed for the Metro. The winds that swept across the Siberian permafrost into Moscow at this time of year always brought his mother to mind. "But the air is crisp and clean now, Nikasha," she would say when he came home from school with frostbitten cheeks. "It's good for you." Indeed, enduring the face-stinging gusts was the cost of breathing healthy air. There's nothing new, he thought. "No Pain, No Gain" hadn't been coined by some New Age physical fitness guru but by a wizened babushka.

An hour later, he was sitting bare-chested on the table in the examin-ing room in Alexa's townhouse, his burgeoning girth testing his waistband. She removed the dressing from his shoulder and went about cleansing the wound. "It's healing beautifully," she said, clearly pleased. "But you're still grounded through the holidays. Gives you plenty of time to heal and restore your range of motion."

"Gives Slava plenty of time to get back in touch with Grusha's RZD source too."

"Hmm, I don't recall him mentioning that. He's about to leave for the office. Maybe I can catch him." Minutes later, Alexa returned with her husband. He was dressed in black: jeans, turtleneck, sport jacket, boots, cashmere topcoat, leather briefcase.

The Black Knight, Katkov thought. Like he had just stepped out of one of the ads he had created for Dolce & Gabbana Russia.

"I've had no contact with Nadia Nysenko in the last twenty-four hours," Slava said, his demeanor and tone making it clear this was an imposition.

"I'm starting to think no one ever will," Katkov said grimly.

"Well, if something's happened to her, it's on you," Slava said with a sneer of disdain. "You and your pack of muckraking zealots use people like Nadia to get information, and when it goes wrong, *they* pay the price. Not you!"

"She hasn't paid it, yet, but Grusha *has*," Katkov fired back. "Nadia came to *her*. I was hoping you could contact her, and—"

"No way," Slava retorted. "I'm done with it."

"She was committed to making Russia a better place!" Katkov countered, burning him with a look. "Like Grusha and Alexa and Vera, and me, and so many others. For a while there, I thought you were one of us!"

Slava held his look. "It's become too dangerous. When Alexa came to me I—"

"Tell me about it," Katkov interrupted with a glance to his shoulder.

"I rest my case," Slava fired back. "I should've had her tell you to fuck off."

"But you didn't . . ."

"I decided it was Nadia's call, and contacted her. She was terrified. In fear of her life, but said she had something really important for you, and asked me to—"

"She *did*!" Katkov interrupted. "And right in the middle of the service, she gave it to me, gave me a cybercode for a top-secret RZD file. But she rattled it off so fast I can't remember it. If you don't want to contact her, fine. I get it. Just tell me how to reach her."

"Fuck off," Slava said with a sly smile. He glanced at his watch and turned to Alexa. "My morning's jammed. I'll call you. Okay?" He strode past Katkov as if he wasn't there and left the examining room.

There was a glimmer of admiration in Alexa's eyes when she turned to Katkov. "You can still give as good as you get, can't you?"

"So can he."

"You know," Alexa said as she secured a fresh dressing to his shoulder, "I can't help thinking: Why didn't Nadia just email or text you the code? Or even just—"

"Too dangerous," Katkov interrupted. "It's all monitored. I mean, if the Americans are doing half of what Snowden said, you can imagine what's going on *here*."

Alexa nodded grimly. "I was about to say, or even just scribble it on a piece of paper and slip it into the booklet."

Katkov shook his head no. "I already checked. Besides, it's evidence. If you get caught, they use it against you. She wanted to talk, but the Rottweilers spooked her. I went after her, and . . .." He let it trail off with a disgusted groan.

"Ah . . . everyone was wondering what you were up to."

"Well, I didn't trash Grusha's eulogy because of stage fright," Katkov snapped. Alexa was helping him on with his shirt when his phone rang. Vera's caller ID was on the screen. "Hi. Alexa's checking-out my shoulder. What's going on?"

"I'm looking at a report of a body found in a car."

Katkov's eyes widened. "Male or female?" Nadia was his primary concern, but he wouldn't have been surprised if Patrushev had never made it out of Moscow alive.

"I'm waiting on that," Vera replied.

"Skoda or Lada?"

"Waiting on that too."

"Okay, while we're waiting . . . any news on Vitaly?"

"Word is he's in solitary."

"No visitors?"

"Not a chance. You know the routine. Lock him up. Let him think they've thrown away the key. When he gets to the point he'll say anything to get out of there, they'll *take his testimony* as they call it."

"Yeah, let me know if he gets moved to—"

"Hold it, hold it," Vera interrupted. "It's coming in now: Double-tap to back of head—A woman—Found in . . . in a blue Skoda."

Katkov's shoulders sagged. "That's her. Found where?"

"Moskvoretsky Bridge underpass. Militia units, ME, and Churkin en route."

"Didn't get very far, did she?" He hung up, saw the look in Alexa's eyes, and nodded. "Bastards killed her."

The Moskvoretsky Bridge was old Moscow. Built in the 1930s, the concrete monolith sheathed in pink granite had since taken on a grungy patina. Its arched abutments spanning the Moskva just south of Red Square were flanked by massive staircases that descended to the embankment below and the underpass beneath the roadway, where Nadia's car had been abandoned.

Katkov took the Metro from the Arbat to Revolyutsii Station. A biting wind was coming off the river as he trudged past the Kremlin to the bridge. One traffic lane had been closed, exacerbating Moscow's perpetual gridlock. Militia officers in greatcoats were posted in front of the fluttering streamers that cordoned off the north staircase. Katkov's *Novaya Gazeta* press pass drew a stern *"Nyet"* when he flashed it. Moments later, and 600 rubles poorer, he lit a cigarette and began descending the first of three long flights.

Churkin, Zhukich, Cujo, and other militia personnel were gathered around the faded-blue Skoda when Katkov joined them in the darkened underpass. Nadia was slumped sideways across the front seat. Blood had spattered the windshield and roof liner and pooled beneath her head, spilling down onto the floor mat. The medical examiner went about removing her body and personal items from the car, and placed them on a gurney.

"We'll need a few minutes," Churkin said as he and Zhukich pulled on surgical gloves. The CI began searching Nadia's person and pockets. His assistant began going through her handbag and briefcase. Among the items in the latter was an RZD Employee Access Pass with her name, photograph, and title: Senior Assistant to the Director.

Katkov's mind was racing. Was the elusive cybercode in there somewhere? Scribbled on a piece of paper? In a document? In her smartphone? In her laptop? In her briefcase? Her wallet? He'd never get access to any of it! Let alone her apartment or office at RZD, which he had no doubt were being searched by the FSB.

Some business cards spilled from one of the file folders when Zhukich removed them from the briefcase, and they scattered across the pavement. "Shit!" he exclaimed, crouching to pick them up. The wind sent one of the cards skipping past Katkov, who managed to capture it. Elegant typography engraved on white cardstock proclaimed: *Julian Levenger, International Business Consultant*. His eyes widened on seeing the list of offices: Paris, Montreal, Moscow, and Bethesda, Maryland.

"Hey, that's evidence," Zhukich said, snatching it from Katkov's hand.

"They all look the same to me," Katkov said, eyeing the cards Zhukich had retrieved. "Sure you can't spare one?"

Zhukich scowled. "They're part of the investigation."

"So am I," Katkov replied. "He's CI Churkin. You're DI Zhukich, she's ME Vasilova, and I'm IR Katkov—that's *investigative reporter,* in case you're wondering."

Churkin grinned, plucked the cards from Zhukich's fist, and fanned them like playing cards. "Yes, they *are* all the same. And there are one, two, three, four, five, *six* of them. One for me, one for RIC files, one for militia files, one for Forensics, one for *Novaya Gazeta*"—he paused and gave one to Katkov—"and one for . . ." He let it hang there as he glared at Zhukich, then slapped the card in his hand. "The Kremlin."

Zhukich reddened, swallowed hard, and crushed the card in his fist.

Katkov suppressed a smile, ground out his cigarette with a heel, then stepped aside and googled Julian Levenger on his iPhone. The banner read: About 50,600 results (0.39 seconds). One result, dated September 2012, revealed that Levenger had represented RZD, the Russian National Railway, and its CEO, Vladimir Yakunin, in the billion-dollar takeover of GEFCO, the French Overland Freight Company. Katkov had thought its connection to the Kremlin's interest in acquiring an American railroad too tenuous and had advised Grusha not to include it in her story. But now, on scrolling down the column of Google results, he found one—titled "CP/CSX in Talks"—that linked Levenger's name to the proposed merger, and though neither RZD, Yakunin, nor the Kremlin were mentioned, Katkov knew in his gut that Julian Levenger—whoever he was—was working for his Russian clients again.

Chapter Twenty-Six

Bargishev in custody!!!

Lana stared at Ruben's text, trying not to look shaken. She leaned across the desk and handed the phone to Julian, who winced at the message, then showed it to Kate. "I imagine he's expecting you will be ecstatic," he said in facetious understatement.

Lana bit a lip and nodded.

Julian returned the phone. "Don't disappoint him."

Thirty-five miles north, Ruben was riding shotgun in an FBI van barreling along the Baltimore waterfront in the direction of the interstate. A chain-link screen separated him and the driver from the zip-tied prisoners shackled in the cargo hold. After taking down Bargishev and his crew, Ruben had conducted a search of the warehouse where the maroon van and its counterfeit contraband had been concealed, then released the crime scene to Forensics. He was in his personal fast lane, savoring the triumph, when his phone rang. "Hey, Amtrak!" he said, seeing Lana's caller ID. "Got my text, huh?!"

"Yeah, that's great news!" Lana exclaimed with a glance to Julian. "Congrats!"

"Thanks. Nailed Bargie and his entire crew. The two hundred mil in funny money too."

"And the not so funny money?"

"Nada. No sign of the roll-aboard. We're heading back with Bargie-Boy now. We'll grill him until he gives it up, or burns to a crisp."

"Well, don't turn him into Joan of Arc until he cops to murdering Tom."

"Top of my punch list. How'd it go at the Ritz?"

"Better than expected. Turns out Amtrak's cybersecurity's damn near impenetrable. Couple of issues I'll be working on with Cyber-Borgen," Lana replied, seizing the opportunity to establish it. "So when are we dropping Bargie on the barbie?"

"Probably take the rest of the day to book and bed these lugs. Let's ice him for the night, and turn up the heat first thing."

"Great. I assembled some data we should review first: The Forensics report, the ME's wound analysis, and a couple of other interesting bits and pieces."

"Way to go. Plan on some face time bright and early," said Ruben.

"Bright and early," Lana echoed, ending the call. "We've got work to do," she said to Kate and Julian. Of the threats she had identified, Caitlin/Pash was the only one they had a plan to defuse. The other two—Bargishev/Ruben, and Katkov/Grafinskaya—were still unresolved, loose cannons capable of blowing Lana's cover and her mission, and she felt more under siege as she left than when she had arrived. It was late afternoon by the time she returned to headquarters and found Katkov's email. She clicked on Reply and wrote in Russian:

> *Dear Mr. Katkov,*
>
> *I'm afraid the current level of tension and distrust between our governments makes it all but impossible to expedite the visa process as you requested. Please excuse my brevity, which is due to an overwhelming workload.*

She was about to send it when it struck her that she had come within a mouse click of wasting a valuable opportunity—a chance to ingratiate herself to Katkov, to begin building the trust that would allow her to manipulate him, to make him feel he was in her debt. Lana deleted the last sentence and added:

> *That said, please know that, despite the adversarial climate which prevails, I will contact the State Department and our embassy in Moscow and will do everything in my power—as FBI Special Special Agent in Charge JTTF—to see that your visa application is processed as swiftly as possible. Please let me know if I can be of any further assistance, and keep me posted as your travel plans develop.*

The next morning, Ruben was in his workstation catching up on paperwork and emails when Lana slithered between the partitions and tossed a flash drive on his desk.

"What's that?" he asked.

"A porno flick," Lana replied with a laugh. She plugged the flash drive into his computer. A small window appeared on the screen. Three folders were listed beneath the case number: Forensics Report, Medical Examiner's Report, Capitol Grille CCTV. "You can spend the morning with a copy of Gray's Anatomy, or"—she flipped open a spiral-bound pad—"you can let me bring you up to speed."

"Go for it."

"For openers, Forensics found nothing useful in Tom's apartment. Clean as a whistle, like the guy who lived there. And the chemical on the fencing kit in the trunk of his Beemer was—"

"Household bleach," Ruben interjected.

Lana nodded emphatically. "Kudos . . ."

"It was a no-brainer."

"That's what the ME said," Lana said with a little smile.

"That horny old necro," Ruben cackled.

"Moving right along," Lana resumed, turning the pages of the pad, "no blood residue, DNA, or other evidentiary matter detected on the fabric. No defensive wounds on Tom's hands or arms. The blood on the box cutter was his—which confirms the horny old necro's findings that the wound was caused by a sharply honed blade, most likely a straight razor or box cutter."

"She left out vintage dueling sword?" Ruben said, needling her.

"Well, we all know better, don't we?" Lana chirped, not taking the bait. "Furthermore, the angle, depth, and direction of the slash indicates the killer was right-handed. Last but not least, the Capitol Grille CCTV shows Tom driving out of the parking lot in his BMW shortly after I did."

Ruben cocked his head. "Time to ask Bargishev what happened next."

The interrogation rooms at JTTF were in the subbasement where the holding cells were located. Each room contained a CCTV camera, voice recorder, one-way mirror, and several chairs on opposite sides of a table that was fixed to the floor. Bargishev sat facing the door. His left hand was cuffed to a steel ring bolted to the tabletop. A strategically placed spotlight illuminated his face, emphasizing his prominent brow and cheekbones. Its narrow beam kept the interrogator and perimeter of the room in shadow. When the door opened, Bargishev raised his chin in cocky defiance, then brightened at the sight of Lana. Without breaking stride, she dropped a pad and ballpoint pen on the table and circled to a corner behind him, purposely cutting off visual contact. "You're allowed to take notes."

"I take your number," Bargishev cracked in Russian-inflected English, eyeing her as she passed. He rattled his cuffed hand and added, "But this makes hard to write."

"The only number *you're* getting is going to be on an orange jumpsuit," Ruben retorted, following after Lana. "We ask the questions. You spill your guts. That's how it works." He sat opposite Bargishev and glared at him. "We got you, your crew and the counterfeit twenty-five million. You're still five mil light. Where is it?"

Bargishev looked confused and shrugged.

"The suitcase with five million in cash?" Ruben prompted. "*FBI cash . . .*"

"Have no idea of it."

"Sure you don't."

"Look, I take case from trunk. Throw to ground. Last I see it. *Last.* Ask FBI guy with blown cover what happen to it."

"We would if we could," Lana said sharply. "But somebody cut his throat with a box cutter."

Bargishev's eyes flared. "No! No fucking way!" He yanked at his manacled wrist that prevented him from physically confronting her. "No fucking way you hang on me!"

"Box cutter's a Chechen calling card, isn't it?" Lana taunted coolly.

"Like those knuckle dots he's wearing," Ruben chimed in. "Unbutton your shirt."

"For why I do that?"

"To show off your VVZ merit badges."

"Not your fucking business, asshole," Bargishev retorted with a defiant scowl.

All in one motion, Ruben lunged across the table, grabbed Bargishev's shirt with both hands, tore it open, and pulled it down off his shoulders. The Russian's torso was covered with tattoos: a spider web on one shoulder, a galaxy of stars on the other, a turreted castle centered on his chest, a pirate with an eye patch, and a small dagger on his neck. "High rank, mafia captain, done time, made his bones as a thief and hit man," Ruben said, ticking off their significance. "Done it all, haven't you, Bargie?

Well, almost. I mean, where's your tiger tat?" he taunted, referring to the tattoo awarded for killing a law-enforcement officer. "Haven't had time to get it, huh?"

"Fuck you," Bargishev grunted.

"No problemo," Ruben countered. "I hear they do some fine needle work at ADX. It's the mother of all federal prisons, in case you're wondering—desolate, middle of nowhere, a lot like Siberia; you'll feel right at home."

"I don't earn tiger tat—" Bargishev sneered with a threatening glare. "Yet."

"Come on," Lana scoffed, emerging from the shadows to confront him. "You butchered an FBI agent. Left him naked in the trunk of his car. In our parking lot!"

Bargishev looked startled. The sudden onslaught caught him off guard. "No! Idiot! Fucking idiot! Person who kill federal agent is fucking idiot!" he sputtered. "FBI guy set me up. Sting got blown. I go *my* way. He go *his*. I don't kill him. And I don't have fucking five million."

"You're looking at a death sentence, Bargie-Boy," Lana said, getting in his face. "Be better if you cooperated and copped to the hit."

"Lady's got a point there, Bargie," Ruben said. "Maybe you can plea-bargain it down to getting butt-fucked for life. You have anything to trade, now's the time."

What the hell?! Lana thought, staggered. Plea bargain?! Anything to trade?! She couldn't believe it. Bargie's on the barbie! Getting his ass fried! He takes the fall or it's crispy-critter time! Suddenly, he's looking at copping a plea?!

Bargishev worked his shirt back up onto his shoulders. "Depends on deal."

"Depends on what you're selling," Ruben countered. "Comprende?"

Bargishev leaned back with a cocky tilt of his head, mulling it over. His eyes drifted to Lana's, made contact, then darted back to Ruben's.

Lana's pulse rate soared. Was it intentional? *Did* Bargishev know the blind text had come from her? Was it a warning? *Get this fixed or I give you up?* Or was it just a stare-off in his mano-a-mano with Ruben? She was the tech geek. She knew the odds against it were astronomical. But there was no way she could chance it that Bargishev knew she was a sleeper and, squeezed hard by Ruben, would blow her cover to cut a deal. She had framed him for Tom's murder, and was hell bent on making it stick. Now, in a bizarre turn of events, she had to get him off the hook. She caught Ruben's eye and inclined her head toward the door. "I need a minute."

"Now?" Ruben challenged in disbelief.

"*Right* now." Lana got up and headed for the door.

Ruben wrestled with it for a moment, then followed her into an anteroom, joining Farrell, who was observing the interrogation through the one-way mirror.

The boss looked confused. "What's going on?"

"Ask her," Ruben snapped.

"Agent Nichols?" Farrell prompted, trying to sound impartial.

"He's way over the top, sir," Lana replied evenly. "Turning this guy into a punching bag makes no sense. Agent Diaz needs to lighten up, and—"

"Lighten up?!" Ruben erupted. "He's squirming. He's guilty. He's looking to cut a fucking deal!"

Lana rolled her eyes. "Guilty or not, chances are he's got nothing to trade and is just going to blow smoke up your ass."

"Chances are he was involved in Tom's murder," Farrell retorted in an angry growl. "Chances are we should squeeze his balls until they pop. Chances are he starts screaming: '*Yeah, yeah, I did it! I did it. I killed him!*'"

"Chances *are*" Lana echoed, boldly, knowing the slightest hint of uncertainty would be fatal, "Bargishev would give us his mother if he thought it would save his ass. Besides, Tom's blood may be on the box cutter, but Bargie's prints *aren't*; we have no evidence, forensic or otherwise, that tie him to Tom's murder; and, in case you haven't noticed, Bargie-Boy's left-handed. The ME says the killer's a righty."

Farrell's posture slackened. "So we don't have him for Tom."

"No, sir, we don't," Lana replied. "I'd be looking at his crew. Squeeze *their* balls. Not his. Maybe we get lucky and they give us something."

"Maybe," Ruben grunted, matching Farrell's tone. "Whatever. We can still squeeze him on the counterfeiting charge."

Lana's eyes rolled with mock disdain. "Come on, Ruben. It's a time-waster. Let go of it," she said, keeping the pressure on. "Either way, if he has nothing to trade, he'll just spin you—and, from where I'm sitting, he's got nothing to trade."

"She's right, Ruben," Farrell said, sounding dispirited. "Looking at a murder rap, the incentive to cut a deal is overwhelming. The funny-money thing . . ." He let it trail off and waggled a hand. "It's done. You nailed his ass. He's going down for a long time. Good work. Mission accomplished. The only thing I care about, now, is nailing the bastard who killed Tom. Everything else is a distraction. Focus on Tom."

Lana had prevailed, but her victory was Pyrrhic at best: She got Bargishev off the hook but kept the search for Tom's killer—the search for *her*—alive. "Dotting *i*'s and crossing *t*'s, sir," she said, changing the subject. "Where's the roll-aboard in all this?"

Farrell mused for a moment, then questioned Ruben with a look. "Rube?"

"As I said, last I saw it was when I dropped Tom at HQ after the sting went bust."

"Well, Bargie-Boy or not, the son of a bitch who killed Tom has it now!" Farrell concluded, seething with frustration. "While we're at it, anything new on your hunch that his murder might be connected to Grafinskaya's?"

"No, sir. We're still working it."

"Agent Nichols?"

"Well, I'm not sure it connects," Lana replied, seizing the opportunity to deal with it. "But yesterday, I learned one of her colleagues at *Novaya Gazeta* is planning to come to Washington. His name's Katkov. Nikolai Katkov."

"Yeah, Langley says he's been a thorn in Putin's paw for decades."

Lana nodded. "Sorry, so much going on I haven't had a chance to mention it."

"Doesn't sound like he's coming here to cover the State of the Union, does it?"

"I doubt it, sir. I gather he and Grafinskaya were close. Very close."

"It's personal. Case-related," Farrell concluded.

Lana nodded. "Stands to reason that Katkov knows she was in contact with Tom and is picking up where she left off."

Farrell looked puzzled. "How do you know all this?"

"Well, with the media blackout, Katkov has no way of knowing Tom is dead, and sent him an email. I'm covering Tom's cases, so it came to me."

Farrell forced a smile. "You haven't replied yet, have you?"

Lana almost winced. She knew she should have run it past Farrell first, but when Julian told her that Moscow Centre had signed off on Katkov's travel plans, she felt pressured to get with the program. It was a mistake. There was no finessing this one. She had little choice but to hold Farrell's eyes with all the sincerity she could muster and lie. "No, sir, I haven't. I wanted to be sure we're on the same page first."

"And the page you're on says that we should . . . what?" Farrell prompted.

Lana's mind raced. If the *timing* of her reply to Katkov's email was the problem, its *content* was the solution. She raised her chin slightly and replied, "Sir, the page I'm on says I should tell Katkov Tom is away on special assignment. The case has been reassigned to me. His help will be invaluable. And I'll do everything I can to make his time here comfortable and productive."

"No. Not going to fly," Farrell said decisively. "Katkov's driven by his colleague's murder. We're driven by Tom's, and it's looking more and more like they're connected. He's coming here because he's got something, and I want to know what. Keeping the lid on what happened to Tom isn't going to help. We give him something, he'll give us something. Tell him the truth and swear him to secrecy under penalty of immediate deportation. No. Make that arrest and prosecution—and work him. Agreed?"

Lana suppressed a sigh of relief and managed a smile. "Yes, sir."

"Ruben?" Farrell prompted.

"No problemo."

Farrell shifted his look back to Lana and added, "From the minute he lands, you're joined at the hip. Where he goes, you go. Got it?"

"Way to go, Amtrak," Ruben said with a sarcastic chortle. "Looks like you're going to be this Russkie's personal shopper."

Farrell glared at him. "And *you're* going to be the personal pit bull for the Russkie who killed Tom! I want him. I want his head on a pike. Got it?!" Farrell burned him with a look and headed for the door.

Lana knew Ruben would unload on her the moment they were alone and was right on the boss's heels.

"Hey?! Hey, this isn't over!" Ruben called out after her as the door closed. He groaned in frustration, then glanced through the one-way mirror into the interrogation room where Bargishev was sitting at the table in a cocky slouch.

Chapter Twenty-Seven

The fact that Levenger represented RZD in the GEFCO takeover, and that he was now connected to merger talks between CP and CSX—two North American railroads—convinced Katkov he was working for the Kremlin again. That, and the fact that he'd been spending most of his time at his office in Bethesda, a DC suburb, intensified Katkov's itch to get there. But as Alexa had predicted, he spent the holidays in Moscow recuperating, commiserating with Vera and Mika, and applying for a visa, which meant collecting "The Required Documents": A passport valid six months beyond period of stay. The online Nonimmigrant Visa Application, Form DS-160. The Application Fee Receipt. The Photo. And the Verification of Employment. All in preparation for "The Interview": At the U.S. embassy—a massive edifice that Katkov thought resembled a pile of terracotta and glass LEGOs topped by an American flag. "Did my damnedest to get you expedited," the interviewing officer said. "An Agent Nichols at JTTF really went to bat for you, but these days, this is about as about good as it gets."

During this time Katkov also: Rehabilitated his shoulder. Reunited with Vitaly, who had convinced his interrogators he couldn't identify Grusha's sources and was released from 38 Petrovka. Emailed Lana regarding the details of his itinerary and hotel preferences: *a smoking room, hot shower, and Wi-Fi.* And made an impromptu visit to Levenger's Moscow office in one of the ultramodern towers in Moscow City, the new financial district where, due to the depressed economy, entire floors could be rented for a fraction of their worth.

A plaque proclaimed: *Julian Levenger, International Business Consultant.* The reception area had contemporary furnishings and a panoramic view of the city. The attractive young woman behind the desk explained that Levenger had been working out of his Bethesda and Montreal offices. She had no idea when he would return to Moscow.

As Katkov left the office, a man with faded military bearing emerged from the elevator. Katkov recognized him from photos in the Google hits that connected Levenger to the RZD/GEFCO deal, and identified him as an ex-KGB general—one of Putin's werewolves in epaulets who provided liaison between the Kremlin and RZD during the takeover of the French freight company. The man strode past Levenger's office and entered an unmarked door at the end of the corridor. It's an FSB front! Katkov thought. Not only does Levenger have powerful connections in global financial circles but also in the Kremlin's foreign and domestic in-telligence agencies who, like the CIA and FBI, use legitimate businesses and their facilities as a cover.

Also during that time, Katkov pressed his search for the elusive cy-bercode. Having no access to Nadia's office, apartment, or computer, he hired some geeks at an Internet café in Menezh Mall to hack into Yakunin and Levenger's files, but state-of-the-art firewalls made them impenetrable. Undaunted, he met with individuals he trusted in govern-ment, the media, and the political opposition who might have worked with Nadia and had access to the code. He was still at it when his visa was issued, confronting him with a decision: Depart immediately? Or continue his search for the code? If his theory was right, if Grusha and Nadia were killed because they threatened a sleeper running an opera-tion in the United States, the fact that the Kremlin had acted so swiftly meant the op was imminent, and he decided to act with equal swiftness. Furthermore, Levenger—the link between Grusha, Nadia, RZD, and the Kremlin—was in Maryland, not Moscow.

Terminal D, Sheremetyevo Airport's newest facility, resembled a bird in flight with soaring walls of glass tucked beneath its gracefully outstretched wings. Aeroflot SU-104 was scheduled to depart at 9:20 a.m. The Aviation Security page on the airport's website stated, *Passengers are required to check in for international flights two hours prior to departure, except for U.S.-bound flights, which require three hours.*

It was 6:15 when Katkov exited the elevator in his parka with suitcase and shoulder bag, which contained his economy e-ticket and his passport with a U.S. visa sticker firmly affixed by an officer at the U.S. embassy.

A row of self-check-in kiosks ringed the Level 3 entry zone. Katkov inserted his ticket into one of the readers and was relieved to be issued a boarding pass, but he still had to get out of Russia, and, despite Churkin's assurance that Bortnikov had signed off on his travel plans, Katkov was aware that the Aviation Security website also stated: *Each passenger's luggage and hand baggage are subject to pre-flight inspection. Outer garments, shoes, and items with metal components will be scanned with X-ray endoscopes and metal detectors. The procedure may involve examination by hand to detect any dangerous or prohibited items on a passenger's body.*

All passengers will be interviewed in rooms with video surveillance to identify potentially dangerous individuals and substances. When questioned, passengers should refrain from making jokes. False or threatening statements are subject to prosecution under Article 207 of the Criminal Code of the Russian Federation.

Interviews are conducted by the Airport Paramilitary Security Service (APSS).

Public order is enforced by officers of the Line Internal Affairs Department (LIAD).

Passport control is carried out by officers of the Federal Security Services (FSB)

FSB! That's Bortnikov and his Rottweilers! Katkov thought when he first read it online. After being x-rayed, metal-detected, and interviewed without setting off any alarms, he proceeded to Passport Control. The arc of booths, manned by the dreaded Rottweilers, was the last hurdle in the security gauntlet. Had Bortnikov and Churkin been toying with him? Playing a cruel game of gotcha that they'd spring at the last minute?

Katkov slipped his passport through the slot beneath the bulletproof glass. A young woman in an FSB uniform—with ice-blue eyes that reinforced her intimidating demeanor—studied his face, challenging it to match the photograph. A tense moment passed before she indicated the sticker affixed to it and said, "A United States visa . . ."

Katkov forced a smile and nodded.

"You have plenty of time," the officer said slyly. "Months, as a matter of fact."

Indeed, as Katkov discovered on his last visit, a visa didn't guarantee entry, and its expiration date didn't represent *length of stay* but rather the last day he could present himself to a U.S. immigration officer and request entry. Should it be granted, length of stay would be based on his visa category, proof of employment, and nature of his work.

"Yes, but I need to be there now," Katkov replied, fighting to conceal his anxiety. "It's a media visa, and I—"

"I can see that. What kind of media?"

"I'm a journalist."

"Employed by?"

"*Novaya Gazeta.*"

The officer scowled, flattened the passport, and swept it through a scanner.

Katkov's anxiety soared. Was she checking the no-fly list? The apprehend-and-detain list? The journalists-to-be-terminated list?! Would he end up in the international transit zone like Snowden? In the bowels of Lubyanka?

The officer's brows arched in anticipation, then fell in disappointment. She stamped the passport, and said, "It would be wise to refrain from writing anything about the Motherland that could be considered disrespectful or unpatriotic."

"Oh, I'm just covering the State of the Union Address."

"If the Americans let you in," the officer retorted with a smirk. A flick of her wrist propelled the passport back through the slot.

Katkov palmed it and hurried from the booth. He had run the security gauntlet and survived. A sign, above an intersecting corridor proclaimed Gates 30-31-32. An Airbus A330-200 with the white, red, and blue Aeroflot logo streaming across the fuselage was visible beyond the gate's soaring sheets of glass. The jetliner's upswept wingtips gave it a sense of flight even when on the ground, and its racy look raised Katkov's spirits.

International departures were always delayed, and SU-104 departed two hours behind schedule. As it accelerated down the runway and rose into the heavy overcast, Katkov settled in his seat exhausted by the security check and the lingering shock, anger, and sadness of Grusha and Nadia's executions. He was out of Russia, but, as the icy-eyed Rottweiler had taunted, there was that one last entry hurdle to be vaulted.

Chapter Twenty-Eight

Lana spent the Christmas holidays with Kate and Julian skiing at Mont-Tremblant in the Laurentians, and working from home in marathon email blasts with Caitlin and the Cyber-Borgen team on Amtrak's new cybersecurity program. The chaotic pace enabled her to conceal a gateway through which she could implant the rootkit webcrawler in the final version and take control of the operating system. Pash was a low-key presence at first, but writing code with Lana was a powerful stimulant that raised his morale and nurtured the rapport they'd established on the bridge in the Ritz-Carlton Galleria.

On Monday, Lana went into headquarters. Caitlin and the team were already online when she logged in, and, after another day of nonstop brainstorming Lana was in serious need of a double-vodka decompressor at Le Diplomate, a trendy brasserie in the District. She secured her workstation and headed for the elevator. The news crawl on one of the overhead monitors read CRUZ LEADS TRUMP IN IOWA POLLS.

"Hey, Amtrak?" Ruben called out, intercepting her in the parking lot as she was about to get into her car. "You've been off the grid for weeks."

"I could say the same about you."

"Bargie-Boy," Ruben groaned. "Spent a week in the box, grilling his crew, and got nada. The thrill of busting their asses, the agony of making it stick. I did manage to get the family down to Bogotá for a week."

"Great. Thought maybe you were still chewing on that Bargishev thing."

"Who said I'm not? You were supposed to be covering my back. Instead you—"

"Look, I'm in serious need of a drink. You want to talk about this, get in."

"The Grille?"

Lana shook her head no. "I can't. Not since Tom. You know Le Diplomate?"

Ruben winced. "Yeah. In the District. It's a haul. I've got to pick up the dog from the kennel on the way home. Julie'll kill me if I don't."

Lana slipped behind the wheel and started the engine. "Your call."

Ruben groaned, then hurried to his Jeep and followed as she drove off.

Traffic was moving, and a half hour later, they were settled in one of Le Diplomate's upholstered window banquettes waiting on a couple of double-vodkas. True to form, the place was buzzing with hook-up hopefuls and information-rich chatter.

Ruben took a long swallow the instant the waiter set his drink on the table. "I'm on the clock, so let's just cut to the chase. Instead of covering my back, you sandbagged me with the boss—" He paused and pinned Lana with a look. "I'm listening."

Lana rolled her eyes. "Your heart was ruling your head in there. I want the bastard who killed Tom, too, but you have no evidence—zero, nada—that it was Bargishev."

"Tell me about it. But if not Bargie, who? And more important, why?"

Lana shrugged. "Maybe Farrell's right."

"About what? I mean, he's on the ceiling over this."

"About the roll-aboard with the five million. Stands to reason, whoever killed Tom has it, right? Now, if it turned out it's Bargie-Boy—lefty, righty, ambidextrous, straight, gay, bi, whatever—nailing his ass for Tom would be a slam-dunk."

Ruben nodded, then winced. "How the hell could *Bargie* get his hands on it?"

"Well . . ." Lana mewed, as if envisioning a scenario. "Like you said, Tom had it when you dropped him at HQ, and he was really pissed about the busted sting. Right?"

"You kidding? He was punching walls."

"So, maybe . . . just maybe . . . he heads into HQ to make his report. He sits there, staring at the blank screen. The cursor's flashing like a neon sign: *You blew it! You blew it! You blew it!* And Tom decides, *This isn't over!* He calls Bargie and convinces him—or thinks he does—that he had it all wrong about him being undercover and sets up another meet. Couple of hours later, Tom shows up with the roll-aboard, Bargie does the box-cutter balestra, and . . ."

Ruben looked puzzled. "The box-cutter what?"

"*Balestra.* It's a lethal fencing move."

"I got it. Bargie cuts Tom's throat and keeps the cash," Ruben said, sounding exasperated. "Stay on the grid, dammit. And if you get any more bright ideas . . ."

"I get them all the time," Lana said, sending a seductive glance across the room. "See that dangerous-looking guy at the end of the bar? He could keep me off the grid for a week. So—" A texting ping interrupted her. The message read: *Bad news. Family crisis. Forced to withdraw from project. Back to Ireland tonight. Caitlin.* Lana winced. Her eyes narrowed. "Sorry, I've got to deal with this," she said, the dangerous-looking guy at the bar no longer a priority. "Keep me posted, okay?" She slipped out of the booth and hurried off.

Ruben took a moment to collect himself, then tossed some cash on the table and headed for his Jeep. With the stop at the kennel, it took more than an hour to get home. He pulled into the garage, closed the door, and let the dog out of the car, then went to a wall of shelves that were stuffed with sporting equipment, sleeping bags, camping gear, boxes of toys, Christmas decorations, backpacks, and pieces of luggage. He pulled a black roll-aboard from beneath some suitcases, set it on the workbench, and opened it. His eyes were sweeping across the neatly packed bundles of U.S. currency when the squeak of a hinge got his attention. Julie was standing in the doorway that led into the house. Her hands circled her hips. Her eyes held his like lasers. "I was wondering when you were going to get around to mentioning that."

Ruben stared at her dumbstruck. "How . . . how long have you . . ."

"Since the kids found it."

"*Dios mío,*" Ruben gasped. "The kids?!"

"Yeah. The sleepover at the Penzers? They were out here getting their backpacks. Amelia comes running in: 'Mommy, Mommy! Come see what we found!'"

"*Maldición! Cómo lo manejaste?!*" Ruben exclaimed, clearly unsettled. "*Qué les has dicho? Quiero decir . . . Mierda!*"

"Lighten up, lighten up, it's okay," Julie pleaded. "I told them it has to do with a case you're working and swore them to secrecy. That was the end of it."

"It *does* have to do with a case," Ruben said, still unsettled. "There's a chance it's evidence that'll nail the bastards who killed Tom."

Julie looked puzzled. "That's great, but . . . but you haven't booked it in?"

"Well, it was damn near midnight, and with you and the kids, you know, upset at the hours I've been pulling I . . . I dropped Tom off and came straight here. Left it in the car, and then, well . . ."

"I'm still listening . . ."

"Well, the next morning you were taking the Jeep for the book drive, and I didn't want you driving around with five million of Uncle Sam's bucks. Figured this'd be as good a place as any to park it."

"Just another rolling suitcase . . ."

"Yeah, in plain sight. You know. And then when this thing happened to Tom, I . . . I just left it there. And . . . well . . . I was going to talk to you about it, but . . ."

Julie looked incredulous. "What are you telling me? That . . . that you're tempted?"

"Hey, it comes with the territory, babe, and you know it, but I—"

Julie stopped him with a look. "My mother used to say being tempted means thinking about doing something you know you shouldn't be doing."

"She was right, but *thinking* about doing something isn't a crime."

"And just what are you thinking about?"

"I'm thinking about you. I mean, I know Reston isn't the Zona Rosa, and well . . . it sure as hell would make that move back home happen sooner than later, wouldn't it?"

Julie sighed. She looked deeply touched. "You'd . . . you'd do that for me?"

"I'd take a bullet for you, babe," Ruben replied, his eyes leaving no doubt he meant it. "I'd do anything for you. I mean, I know my being on the job's been tough: The hours, the uncertainty, the anxiety every time the phone rings. Wondering if you and the kids are going to have to go it alone . . ."

"I love you with all my heart, Ruben," Julie said, her eyes glistening. "And I love you all the more for wanting to do this, but there's no way I'd ever let you. You've been on the job for twenty years, and you've played by the rules every damn one of them. No. No way, Jose." She held his eyes and added, "No—fucking—way."

Ruben's posture softened. He sighed with relief and smiled. "I was hoping you were going to say that. I was counting on it. You always keep me centered. Yeah. Yeah, I *have* played by the rules, and no fucking way I'm going to start breaking them now."

"Then get that thing the hell out of here."

Ruben bit a lip. "I can't, not yet," he replied with a troubled sigh. "There's a lot going on with what happened to Tom, and I can't get past this feeling in my gut that it might not be what it seems. It's been bugging me for weeks. I know it sounds kind of off the wall, but that *thing* might come in handy, depending on which way it breaks."

"And you've been hanging on to it until you know one way or the other?"

Ruben nodded apprehensively. "Yeah, it's dicey, I know."

"You going to be okay? I mean, you sure you can pull it off?"

"No, babe, I'm not. I'm terrified," Ruben replied with a self-deprecating laugh. "Hey, it's the story of my life. In the meantime, why don't we take it upstairs, dump the cash on the bed, get naked, and roll around in it for a while?!"

After getting Caitlin's text, Lana drove to her apartment in Foggy Bottom, changed into running clothes, and texted Kate: *Need to go for a run. It'll be good for our health.* The sun was dipping below the Potomac as she made the downhill jog past the Watergate complex and across Rock Creek to the path along the Georgetown Canal. Kate Nichols was sitting on one of the stone walls that contained its waters, smoking a cigarette. "What's up?" she asked as Lana settled next to her.

"Looks like you're off the hook." Lana slipped her phone from a pocket and scrolled to Caitlin's text. "See? My personnel problem at Cyber-Borgen's been solved."

"Yes, I know . . ."

Lana's brows went up. "This was you?"

Kate broke into a satisfied smile. "In a manner of speaking . . ."

"Back to Ireland? Family crisis? Told you she wasn't the spa type."

"*Au contraire,* as Julian would say. The girl with the dragon tattoo had already accepted a complimentary hour of beauty at the Ritz: 'Where the Martini and Manicure Set Go to Have World Cares Melt Away.' Had all my ducks in order, but Julian nixed it."

"Why? The Full-Body Wrap with Death Mask works every time."

"I know," Kate said almost wistfully. "By the time they realize the attendant hasn't poked holes in the Saran and slipped straws up their nostrils, they're barely conscious. But the Ritz isn't some strip-mall massage parlor, and Julian figured the tabloids'd be all over it: 'Kinky Cyber Geek Meets with Federal Agent at Ritz-Carlton Day Spa. Turns Up Dead!' Not to mention the feds."

"So you contracted it out."

Kate nodded. "One of our people in the UK. Likes to play with fire. Set one in the pump house on the Rourke family farm during a thunderstorm. Local officials chalked it up to a lightning strike. No water pressure. Gale-force winds. Intense heat. Propane tanks popping off. Turned 'Mrs. O'Leary' into Dresden. Your cybergirl's daddy had a heart attack fighting it. Not part of the plan, but . . ."

"A convincer, if she needed one," Lana said finishing the thought. "She has an offer from Google Dublin but isn't keen on moving back. This could change that."

In New York City, Axel Carlsen was meeting with his staff in Cyber-Borgen's eighteenth-floor conference room. Weary staffers, working late in the wake of Caitlin's abrupt departure, circled the table covered with laptops, fast food containers, and piles of LEGOs. Carlsen was on the phone when it chirped. "Hold on a sec—Sorry. I need to take this," he said, seeing the caller ID. "Lana? . . . Hi, I was about to call you."

"No need to apologize. It's just that I got this text from Caitlin. Said she was going home because of a family crisis?"

"Yeah, we're all devastated," Carlsen said, shaking his head in dismay. "First Pash. Now Caitlin. This place must be cursed or something," he went on, telling her about the fire. "Her family's okay, but her father had a massive coronary. It's touch and go."

"My God," Lana exclaimed, feigning surprise. "How awful. I had no idea."

"Yeah, Cait's on indefinite leave. Let's put tomorrow's meeting on hold, take a couple of days to regroup, and talk again on Thursday."

"Face-to-face. No phones, texts, telecons, email blasts," Lana said, her voice ringing with authority. "I'll come to you. Be there first thing. Deal?"

"Deal. I'll put you on the guest list with security."

Lana spent the next couple of days fine-tuning the rootkit webcrawler that would allow her to take control of Amtrak's computer network, then headed off to Le Diplomate. Should the stars align, the dangerous-looking guy at the bar might be there. If not, Le Dip was always flush with hook-up hopefuls looking for a nightcap.

The dangerous end of the bar was empty when Lana slid onto a stool and ordered a double-vodka rocks. The bartender was filling a tumbler with ice cubes when a rangy man with chiseled features and tousled hair, wearing a leather rancher's jacket, leaned in next to her. "That's on my tab, Julio," he said in a resonant voice. "Same for me."

Lana shot him a sideways glance and smiled. "So much for opposites attract."

"First they attract and then they attack, or so I've heard."

"Thanks for the warning," Lana said with a saucy hair flip. "But I like a dangerous vibe."

He broke into the predatory grin that had stirred her when she first saw him. "Makes two of us."

"Well, if it turns out you're into sex trafficking, gun running, or computer hacking, I won't disappoint you."

"All of the above," he countered with a jaunty cackle. "Why?"

"I'm an FBI agent," Lana replied with a raised brow and a seductive gotcha grin. "Don't knock it till you've tried it." She raised her glass, ran her tongue across her lips, and whispered, "Cheers."

Chapter Twenty-Nine

Aeroflot SU-104 arced across Western Europe and the Arctic Circle, skirting the coastlines of Newfoundland, Nova Scotia, and the northeastern United States. It landed at Dulles International in the Virginia countryside thirty miles west of Washington, DC, at 2:37 p.m. and taxied to a holding area, where a mobile lounge awaited. These windowed vehicles that transported passengers to and from jetliners had been replaced, recently, by an underground Aero Train system but were still being used for international flights.

Katkov stared, impassively, at the airport landscape as the driver navigated the maze of taxiways to the International Arrivals Building. The cabin rose from its undercarriage and docked with one of the entry portals, allowing passengers to deplane directly into the terminal. Not much has changed, he thought, but there were a few new additions: the massive United States Department of Immigration & Naturalization sign, the ubiquitous No Smoking symbols, and the uniformed INS officers with badges and name tags pinned to their blouses and insignia of rank perched on their epaulets—like the Rottweilers at Sheremetyevo. He was approaching passport control when the PA crackled to life. "Will arriving passenger Katkov proceed to Station Number 6?" a soothing female voice prompted. "Arriving passenger Nikolai Katkov to Station 6, please." Long queues were forming at 1 through 5, and he had every reason to expect FBI Special Agent in Charge Lana Nichols would be waiting at Station 6 to expedite the arrivals procedure, but it had been cordoned off and was manned by an INS officer. Sergeant's stripes slashed his uniform sleeves. His name tag read Garrett.

"Mr. Katkov? Welcome to the United States," Garrett said in fractured Russian. "I'll need to see your passport."

"I'd much prefer we massacre your language than mine," Katkov replied in British-inflected English.

"Spent some time in the UK, huh?"

"Never been there, I'm afraid," Katkov replied, slipping the red-and-gold passport from his bag. A double-headed imperial eagle was imprinted

Greg Dinallo

on the cover, as was RUSSIAN FEDERATION in Cyrillic and English. "My
nanny was from Dover. She spoke Russian to my parents and English to
me," he went on as Garrett matched face to photo. "Worked for our family
for years—until my father decided he loved his country more than his
government and was declared an enemy of the state." Katkov left it there,
deciding not to mention that this pang of conscience had cost his father his
professorship at Moscow State University and their apartment in the House
on the Embankment, an elite pre-WWII complex on the Moskva where he
lived until his mid-teens.

Garrett slipped the passport into a scanner, then turned his attention
to data on a computer screen. "According to our records, you were here
twenty years ago. Correct?"

"Quite correct. I was working on a story, but I was freelance at the
time. As I'm sure you know, I'm *employed* by *Novaya Gazeta* now."

"Yes, we know," Garrett said condescendingly. "According to our Entry
Review Protocol, your approved itinerary was Moscow–DC–Moscow, but
you departed the United States from Miami and traveled by freighter to
Havana."

"Correct again."

Garrett pursed his lips. "The former was a violation of your travel restrictions, the latter of your visa-mandated exit procedure. Kind of stuff'll
get you flagged every time."

"Well, it was unintentional, I assure you, not to mention unavoidable.
I was working with a federal law enforcement agent who—"

"Gabriella Scotto, United States Customs, on loan to FinCEN."

Katkov responded with a cautious nod. "I'm working with another
agent this time. Special Agent in Charge Lana Nichols on loan to the Joint
Terrorism Task Force from Amtrak. She was supposed to meet me here."

"Nichols . . . Amtrak . . . JTTF," Garrett repeated, typing the data into
a search window. "Nope," he finally said. "No hits in my ERP search."

Katkov looked puzzled. "Well, I imagine she'll be able to clear it
up when she gets here. I have copies of our email correspondence that
might—"

"We'll get there," Garrett said, punching a button on his phone.
"Cap . . . Yeah, that journalist from Moscow . . . Uh-huh, Katkov. He says
a JTTF SAC, name of Nichols, was supposed to meet him . . . Yeah, copies

of emails, but nothing in the ERP on it, so . . . What I figured." He hung up, looked at Katkov, and said, "Follow me."

Garrett directed Katkov down a corridor to an interview room, where another officer waited. Her eyes were narrow and quick. Polished captain's bars rode her epaulets. Her name tag read Dixon.

Double déjà vu, Katkov thought. Windowless room. Institutional furniture. One-way mirror. Video surveillance. Police-state personnel—just like Sheremetyevo.

"I'm Captain Dixon," the female officer said. "You mentioned some email exchanges with an Agent Nichols at JTTF to Sergeant Garrett. Have I got that right?"

Katkov nodded. "I'm working on a story, and she—"

"Okay, here's what's going to happen," Dixon interrupted with crisp authority. "I'll review the emails. If they support granting you entry, I'll contact Agent Nichols. If she signs on, we can discuss expunging your previous violations. In the meantime, Sergeant Garrett will conduct a routine search of your luggage."

Katkov nodded again, slipped a folder from his bag, and handed it to her.

Dixon forced a smile and headed for the door.

Garrett unzipped the suitcase and pawed through the contents. "No problems there," he announced, going on to remove the items from the shoulder bag: laptop, phone, notebook, voice recorder, comic-book price guide, and Nadia's prayer shawl. He fingered the silk curiously and unfolded it, revealing the memorial booklet within, which he proceeded to open. His eyes narrowed in suspicion at the clear plastic packet set into the recess inside the cover.

"What's in that?"

"Soil. Rich black Russian soil, along with a few seeds that—"

"Soil?" Garrett interrupted, his brow furrowing. "Soil's a prohibited substance. I'm going to have to confiscate this," he went on, closing the booklet.

"Might we discuss that for a moment?" Katkov asked calmly. "You see, it's a tribute to a colleague who passed away recently. I'm here to complete a project she was working on when she died. The booklet is all I have of her, and I—"

"Sorry," Garrett interrupted. "I don't make the rules. I just enforce 'em."

"Would it be correct to assume that if I removed the packet of soil and gave it to you, I could retain the booklet?"

"Don't see why not," Garrett replied, handing Katkov the booklet. "Go for it."

"You see, she was quite an avid gardener," Katkov explained as he gently removed the packet. "The soil and seeds are meant to be planted, and then the flowers bloom, keeping her memory alive."

Garrett nodded with polite disinterest, put the packet of soil in a plastic bag that he took from a drawer, and went about labeling it.

Katkov was closing the booklet when his eyes darted to something written on the inside cover that had been concealed by the soil-filled packet. Printed in a tiny hand, it read: Топ секретных файлов РЖД. Якунина в глаза только. Кибер код Ы5Н7Т0Е5П. His heart pounded at the message. He suppressed his elation, closed the booklet, and wasted no time returning it and the prayer shawl to his shoulder bag.

"Okaaayyy," Garrett said with a spirited clap of his hands. "Let's see if Captain Dixon had any luck working out that little problem."

"And if she hasn't?"

"I'm not going to sugarcoat it," Garrett replied, sounding ominous. "Best case scenario: you'll be bunking in the International Transit Zone. Worst case: you'll be on the next flight back to Moscow." He opened the door, then paused and added, "Nine times out of ten it's the latter." The door closed, locking Katkov in the interview room. He stood there in stunned silence, his jet-lagged brain staggered by the wrenching irony. Nadia's neat, Cyrillic printing read: *Top-secret RZD file. Yakunin's eyes only. Cybercode N5Y7T0E5P.* Katkov finally had the elusive, if enigmatic, code. Had the Levenger connection. Had a contact at JTTF—and now, because of a twenty-year-old technicality, he was on the verge of being sent back to Moscow without ever getting out of the airport!

Chapter Thirty

The five-a.m. Acela Express from Washington, DC, arrived at Penn Station at 7:45 on Thursday as scheduled. Lana took a cab to Twenty-Third Street, where Broadway slices across Fifth Avenue forming the Flatiron triangle. She hurried into the lobby, checked in at the security desk, was photographed for a visitor badge, and got into one of the notoriously slow elevators. Though the Flatiron's exterior epitomized early twentieth-century grandeur, Cyber-Borgen's headquarters were cutting-edge twenty-first: glass-walled offices, leather-and-chrome furniture, contemporary artwork, and ubiquitous flat-screen monitors without a cable in sight. Most of the staff had yet to arrive, and she continued through the reception area into what they called "the maze" in search of Carlsen. After several wrong turns she spotted him in one of the coveted "point" offices in the building's prow. Arched windows framed Madison Square Park, the Empire State Building, and Midtown's glass-and-steel canyons. He was unaware of Lana's presence. She knocked lightly on the glass door, which was open. "Axel?"

"Lana!" he exclaimed. "First thing! You weren't kidding, were you?"

"Hey, when the going gets tough—the tough get up with the birds," Lana said with a laugh as he helped her off with her coat. "Got it figured out yet?"

Carlsen shrugged. "Not really. Caitlin's the catalyst that makes things happen around here. Without her, the team dynamic fizzles."

"I know, but I'm under enormous pressure to certify that Amtrak's network is secure. I know Pash hasn't been himself, and he doesn't have Caitlin's infectious vitality, but he *is* your anti-malware expert, and familiar with the project. So . . ."

"Best in the business. But I think he needs Caitlin now more than ever."

"Or someone like her. I'd be more than happy to pinch-hit. I've had some personal experiences that helped me relate to what Pash has been going through, and we've developed a bit of a rapport. I think he'd be open to the idea."

"Well, he seems more stable, and I've noticed his stammer's gone. Frankly, he made a similar suggestion the other day. I wasn't sure what to make of it but . . ."

"Great. JTTF's got a deal with Ritz-Carlton. I thought I'd spend the next couple of days working with Pash and the team, and, well . . ." She did a hair flip and let her eyes soften. "We never did get to have that sushi and bottle of bubbly, did we?"

"*Vintage* bubbly," Carlsen corrected, letting his eyes find hers. "I'm sure I've got a few magnums lying around somewhere."

"You're on," Lana chirped. "But first things first. Where does Pash hang out?"

"Other end of the maze. Yemeni flag on the door. I don't think he's in yet."

"Good. I'll surprise him."

Pash's office was a bright, white, meticulously ordered cyber space. A landscape of keyboards, mouse pads, and monitors marched across a work-station opposite a standing desk. Lana spent some time scanning the lines of code scribbled on the wall of whiteboards. It was the only personal touch other than the flag, and a framed snapshot of Pash's family on the desk. Lana was admiring the latter when he arrived. "Lana?" he exclaimed in a mixture of disbelief and delight. "Axel didn't tell me you were coming."

"We thought a surprise might brighten your day after Caitlin's news."

Pash's eyes saddened. "Indeed, we're all quite upset," he said in his British accent. "But yes, you have indeed brightened my day."

"Well, it's about to get brighter!" Lana exclaimed. "Axel really liked your idea of us working together. I know there's no way I could replace Caitlin, but I'll do my best to live up to her standards." She sighed, vulnerably, and added, "There's a lot of pressure on me, Pash, and, well, I guess, what I'm trying to say is, I really need you now."

"That's a lovely compliment, Lana, but I'm afraid it's rather the other way round." Pash tilted his head, entertaining a thought. A smile spread across his face.

"What?"

"I have a surprise for *you*."

"Oh, I love surprises."

"Well, there are times now when I feel terribly saddened, and when the darkness falls, I . . . I seek solace in my work. So, last night as it began closing in, I ran a scan of the program we've been writing, and it really raised my spirits."

"That's wonderful, Pash, but not that surprising."

"Oh, I haven't gotten to the surprise, yet. You see, I—" He paused, letting his chest fill with pride, and proclaimed "I found you out, Lana. I caught you."

Lana was staggered. "Caught me?" she prompted, forcing a smile to cover her rising sense of panic. "I'm not sure I know what you mean."

"Oh yes you do," Pash said, sounding parental. "You tested me. I'm quite certain of it. You wrote a bit of malware into the program to see if I could detect it, didn't you?"

Lana nodded, taking a moment to regroup. "Yup. Guilty as charged. You got me. Hey, I'm a cop, Pash—a cybercop. It's what I do." She let her eyes come alive with a mischievous twinkle. "You have to admit it was a pretty cool bit of code, wasn't it?"

Pash nodded emphatically. "A *brilliantly concealed* pretty cool bit of code—a malware gateway, to be precise—that a hacker could use to access the program."

Lana looked baffled. She couldn't imagine what had given it away. "And just how did you manage to detect such a *brilliantly concealed* gateway?"

"It was quite simple, actually." Pash turned to the workstation and tapped at a keyboard. Lines of code began tracing across the monitor. "You see, each of our primary code writers has a unique identifier, and, when more than one person is working on the same software, an anti-malware filter we've developed intercepts all lines of code not entered by the prima-ry, isolates them in what we call a virtual petri dish, and flags any it deems suspicious. It's somewhat like the Track Changes option in Microsoft Word. Others can make additions and deletions, but they are highlighted in colored text, alerting the original author, who then decides whether or not to incorporate them."

Lana didn't know whether to feel lucky or threatened. "I'm impressed, Pash. Very, very impressed. You passed the test with flying colors."

"The *filter* did," Pash corrected. "As you can see, it isolated all the original code you wrote and revisions you made to mine, but only flagged *that* one"—he pointed to a block of code highlighted in red—"the mal-ware gateway."

"Well, something tells me I just had one of your famous root canals, didn't I? What was it you called it? *Nush det*-something-or-other?"

"*Nushprafh detrush*," Pash replied gently. "That's me, the painless dentist."

"I'll be the judge of that," Lana said with a laugh. "Shall we get to work?"

They spent that entire day into the evening and the next morning with browser specialist Wallace and targeted threats expert Saunders fine-tuning the architecture of Amtrak's new cybersecurity program. Lana searched for a flaw that would allow her to reinstate the malware gateway Pash had deleted, but came up empty. Determined to find it, she headed for Carlsen's office to touch base before leaving. By the time she emerged from the maze, a plan had begun to develop. "Looks like you're going to have to keep that bottle of bubbly on ice," she said, trying to sound chipper.

"Oh?" Carlsen said with a frown. "Thought you were staying the weekend . . ."

"Me too, but the Russians are coming—today! I've got to get back."

"The ones suspected of scheming to take over one of our railroads?"

"That's classified. I can't talk about it."

"Hey, I get it. By the way, rumor has it you and Pash had a very productive time."

"You betcha," Lana said with all the brio she could muster. "Grabowski and the gang at Amtrak are going to be stoked when I tell them about the anti-malware filter that flagged my gateway," she went on, setting her plan in motion. "But I don't want to misrepresent the level of security Cyber-Borgen's providing. So, just to be clear: the unique identifier and your anti-malware filter make the program impenetrable, right? There's no way a hacker could infect it with a webcrawler or rootkit virus and use it to control Amtrak's operating system?"

"No. No way. Any code written without Pash's UI would be isolated and flagged as malware before it could breach a gateway and infect the program."

"And there's no way anyone, not even you—king of the Cyber-Borgen castle—could get their hands on his UI . . ." Lana paused and held Carlsen's eyes. "Because, Axel, if there *is*—if there's even an infinitesimal chance that someone could take control of the ESR, PTC, and RCRM programs, I'm not leaving this room until you tell me how."

"Well, Lana, as much as I'd like you stay . . ." Carlsen said with a sly grin. "No. Not a chance. There's no way anyone could get it."

"Are you saying it's committed to memory, and that's it?"

"Some of it," Carlsen replied, enigmatically. "The joke around here is: it dies with them. But it's not a joke. Believe me Pash's UI is secure." He paused, then smiled at what he was about to say. "The details are classified. I can't talk about it."

"Exactly what I was hoping to hear," Lana exclaimed, lying through her teeth.

Carlsen produced a flash drive and gave it to her. "It's all on there. Do your final design review, get your butt back here on . . . when? What works best for you?"

"Sunday? Gives me a day or two . . ."

"Perfect. Soon as you and Pash encode the revisions, we can test the program against various threat landscapes and work out the bugs. So, hop to it."

"Oh, I'm hopping," Lana replied, knowing the post-installation shake-down was her last chance to hack into Amtrak's operating system and take control of the three programs she would need to execute the Adamov Op, and despite Carlsen's certainty that it was impossible, she was still hell-bent on finding a way to do it—but she had to deal with Katkov first.

Chapter Thirty-One

After locking Katkov in the interview room, Sergeant Garrett entered a control room that was alive with the blinking LEDs of digital surveillance equipment. Two women, seated at a workstation, were observing Katkov on monitors and through the one-way mirror beyond. The one in the uniform was Captain Dixon. The one in the pantsuit with her hair in an all-business bun was Lana Nichols. That morning, after leaving Cyber-Borgen's offices, she caught United 4047 out of La Guardia, arriving at Dulles in time to connect with Dixon and Garrett before Katkov's flight landed.

"That working for you?" Garrett prompted as he came through the door.

"Perfect. I love the bit about the next flight back to Moscow," Lana replied, her eyes alive with mischief. "He'll give me the keys to the Kremlin after this."

Dixon laughed. "Ready to ride to the rescue?"

"A few more turns of the screw first, okay?" Lana slipped two envelopes from her laptop bag. "Belated Christmas cheer!" Dixon and Garrett pocketed them and left. Lana remained behind to time her appearance.

Katkov had spent the time trying to collect himself and was lighting a cigarette when the two INS officers returned. He exhaled and looked up expectantly.

Dixon dropped Katkov's folder of emails on the table and, in a no-nonsense tone, said, "You'll have to put that out. There's an ashtray in the drawer." Katkov took one last deep drag and did as instructed. "It seems Agent Nichols is OTG," the captain went on. "That's agency-speak for off the grid, which means: she's not at her desk, her phone went straight to voicemail, and she didn't respond to my texts."

Katkov groaned in frustration. "But . . . but, we exchanged correspondence," he said, indicating the file folder. "She had my flight data. What's going on here?"

"Stuff happens," Dixon replied with a shrug. "If we haven't reached Agent Nichols before the next flight to Moscow departs—you're going to be on it."

"What about the International Transit Zone? Couldn't I stay there until she . . ."

"That option's off the table," Dixon interrupted. "These decisions are made by people way above my pay grade. They don't tell me why."

Katkov's posture slackened. He stared at the floor, dazed by brain-numbing jet lag.

Several sharp knocks snapped him out of it.

Lana strode through the door, suitcase in one hand, ID in the other. "Lana Nichols, JTTF," she said as if she'd never seen Dixon or Garrett before. "Sorry, hoped to be here in time to escort Mr. Katkov through the process, but my flight got delayed."

"They all do," Dixon cracked, extending a hand. "I'm Captain Dixon, this is Sergeant Garrett. And Mr. Katkov, who I understand will be in your charge—assuming he's granted entry."

"Assuming? Hey, I ran this by your people weeks ago," Lana protested. "I'm really sorry about this, Mr. Katkov. I'm sure we'll find a way to get this little kerfuffle cleared up. Won't we, Captain?"

"Well," Dixon mused. "According to our ERP, Mr. Katkov violated the terms of his previous visa several times. One could argue they're technicalities, but—"

"Twenty-year-old technicalities," Lana fired back sharply. "Citing them to deny Mr. Katkov entry now is pointless. Or has the INS taken to punishing Russian journalists for the Kremlin's current Cold War mentality?"

"Point taken. I seem to recall, there *were* some extenuating circumstances that might justify granting it," she said, pretending to be wrestling with the decision. "Well, I'll probably end up pulling graveyards for this, but—" She pursed her lips, then nodded to Garrett, who stamped Katkov's passport. "Welcome to the United States, Mr. Katkov."

"Thank you," Katkov said with a relieved sigh, getting to his feet. "I was afraid Agent Nichols's efforts to expedite my visa were for naught."

"We're not leaving just yet Mr. Katkov," Lana said gently. "I need to bring you up to speed on a few matters first—classified matters. Captain, is there a—?"

"Room's yours," Dixon interrupted, making the assumption.

Lana raised a skeptical brow. "Thanks, but CCTV central isn't exactly agency protocol. Any chance there's a private office or secure conference room we could use?"

"In this place? Even the broom closets have CCTV."

"Then, it'll have to wait till we get to the hotel." Lana led Katkov from the interview room into the Arrivals Terminal and down a ramp to the lower level. The taxi queue stretched beneath the building's slanted window walls. "Ritz-Carlton, Tysons Corner," she said to the driver as Katkov dropped his suitcase in the trunk. Katkov's watch read 1:25 a.m.—Moscow time. The taxi was on the sweeping approach to the Dulles access road when he nodded off.

A half hour later, he was standing bleary-eyed next to Lana at the check-in desk in the Ritz-Carlton's wood-paneled lobby. It was still decked out with sprays of holly and twinkling LEDs, as were the grounds and adjacent Galleria.

"Reservation for Katkov," Lana said. "It's a JTTF account."

"Katkov . . . JTTF . . ." the clerk echoed, turning to his computer. "You're in 402, Mr. Katkov." He slipped a card key onto the counter. "Smoking room, as requested."

"I also requested a high floor," Lana said with crisp authority.

The clerk frowned. "Doesn't seem to be noted here, but I might be able to—"

"This one's fine," Katkov interrupted, wearily, palming the card key.

"No, it isn't," Lana hissed, taking him aside. "Any room *but* this one is fine. The travel office made the booking weeks ago. It's a given 402's been bugged: By *my* side? *Your* side? *Both* sides? Hey, they can make porno flicks of you in the shower for all I care, but the conversation we're about to have is for our ears only. Got it?"

Katkov nodded, wearily. "As long as it's a smoking room."

Room 1206 was a smoking room. It had all the amenities: king-size bed, marble bath, flat-screen TV, Wi-Fi, gift basket, and ash trays with the Ritz-Carlton logo.

"Not exactly the Paris Hilton," Lana joked as they entered. "But it'll do."

The reference went right over Katkov's head. He lit a Marlboro.

Lana slipped a bottle of wine from the basket. "Join me?"

184

Katkov shook his head no and dragged on his cigarette. "My only vice," he said with an impish grin and a resurgence of energy from his catnap in the taxi.

Lana raised her glass. "One of my many," she said as they settled in a windowed seating area. "Before we get to the nitty gritty, I have a personal question I'd like to ask."

"British nanny," Katkov said without missing a beat.

Lana looked baffled. "Pardon me?"

"I have this accent because I had a British nanny. That *was* your question, wasn't it? Everyone eventually gets around to asking."

"Well, being predictable isn't exactly an asset in my business," Lana said with a self-deprecating laugh. "But actually, Mr. Katkov, I was about to ask why you're here."

"Oh? Sorry. Well, quite simply, I'm a journalist, working on a story. And if I may, my friends and my enemies call me Nikolai . . . among other things."

"Okay, Nikolai. But there's more to your visit than *getting the story*. I mean, it's personal. Your colleague, Nina Grafinskaya, was murdered."

"*Assassinated*," Katkov corrected. "By direct order of Vladimir Putin."

"That's one hell of a headline. Can you substantiate it?"

"Absolutely," Katkov replied with an emphatic exhale. "Grusha, that was her nickname, had a source in Putin's inner circle. He was there when the order was given. I interviewed him just before he fled the country in fear of his life."

"So," Lana said, recapping, "Putin is in Moscow. Grusha was killed in Moscow. The investigator is in Moscow . . . Makes my question all the more pertinent: What are you doing *here*?"

"Yes, yes, it's all in Moscow!" Katkov exclaimed, gesticulating as he broke into Russian: "*Ublyudok, otdavshiy prikaz, killer, sledovatel—vse zdes. No motiv, chto by ni ugrozhalo Kremlyu, zdes!*"

Lana understood every word but had no trouble pretending to be baffled. "I'm not sure I caught that last part there," she said with an engaging smile. "Hey, hey, it's okay. I mean, since my emails were in Russian, you naturally assumed . . ."

"Naturally. And as we all know, assumption is, indeed, the mother of all . . ."

"Kerfuffles?" Lana suggested with a grin. "By the way, Agent Jones spoke Russian. He was quite fluent. I use the translation program. Would you mind?"

"Of course not: I said, 'The bastard who gave the order, the hit man, the investigator, are all there. But the motive, whatever is threatening the Kremlin, is *here*.'" He paused, and with boyish charm added, "I killed the hit man, actually."

Lana's eyes widened. Her brows arched.

"He shot me. It was a matter of self-defense." Katkov's head tilted in reflection. "By the way, I believe you just said Agent Jones *was* fluent, *spoke* Russian. Past tense?"

"Yeah, I was getting to that. The case was reassigned to me, not because Agent Jones is on special assignment but because he was killed in the line of duty."

Katkov look stunned. "I'm . . . I'm quite sorry to hear that . . ."

Lana nodded sadly. "It has us tied in knots. The boss put a lid on it, but he values your initiative and asked me to brief you," she explained, aware that Farrell's decision to share this information could help her gain Katkov's trust. "He and I, and my colleague Agent Diaz, who was agent Jones's partner—and now *you*—are the only ones who know, and it must stay that way until we know what we're up against. *Must*. You understand?"

Katkov nodded. His eyes brightened with intrigue. "In other words, I've stumbled upon the killing of an FBI agent that might be related to my story."

"*Might*," Lana warned. "He'd also been working undercover to sting the Chechen mob. We can't prove they did it, but he was killed with a box cutter, which just—"

"Happens to be their calling card," Katkov interjected with a confused wince. "You're *adding* pieces to the puzzle instead of helping me assemble the ones I have."

"And those pieces are?" Lana prompted, probing the depth of his knowledge.

"One: Agent Jones saw Grusha's story about the Kremlin investing in U.S. financial markets and contacted her. Two: The Kremlin had her terminated because what she wrote threatened them. Three: Whatever they're up to involves a scheme to take over a U.S. railroad, and/or an email she wrote to Agent Jones about a sleeper agent."

"Stop right there," Lana commanded. "It's important you understand that you and I are the only people who know about the sleeper. Not even the boss knows."

Katkov's lips tightened into a thin line. "Another secret that must be kept."

"Yes, *must*," Lana fired back. "The point is, Tom never had a chance to disclose it, and when I got the case and saw the email, I decided to keep it to myself because the sleeper could be someone at NCTC, JTTF, the FBI, or any other USG national security agency. It's possible Tom didn't disclose it because—*he* was the sleeper."

Katkov's eyes widened. "Needless to say, I find that quite astonishing."

"In my business, Nikolai, nothing is astonishing, and no one is above suspicion. As I said, Agent Jones was a Russian-speaker—on the Russian desk—and, per *your* email, the sleeper, like Agent Jones, is a native-born American, not a Russian. Right?"

Katkov nodded and stubbed out the cigarette. "Code name Pochtalska."

"Yes, I saw that," Lana said, matter-of-factly. "Furthermore, the sting Agent Jones was working got blown at the last minute. On purpose? By him? It's more than possible if *he* was the sleeper. It's also possible, that's what got him killed. Further complicating the puzzle, Agent Diaz has a theory that the two killings might be connected."

"Indeed . . . but . . . but if Agent Jones was the sleeper . . ." Katkov let it trail off, confused as Lana intended. "Why would he contact Grusha? What was his angle? To find out if she knew why the Kremlin was scheming to take over an American railroad?"

"Makes sense. I mean, if *I* was the sleeper, I'd want to gain her trust and pick her brain." Lana paused, and, with a casual air, asked, "Did Grusha mention anything else?"

"Yes, that a Canadian billionaire, who brokered the RZD/GEFCO deal for the Kremlin, is working for them again. It's rumored he's using a shell corporation to conceal their involvement. The name Julian Levenger mean anything to you?"

Lana's heart rate quickened at the mention of a Canadian billionaire, and it was racing by the time Katkov named him. She drained her glass, buying a few seconds to settle. "Levenger? Julian Levenger? Doesn't seem to ring a bell."

"He's a formidable player with global presence. It's important I speak with him."

No way! Lana thought. "Hey, easier said than done," she said, forcing a smile. "You have to find him first. He's probably got offices all over the world."

Katkov took Julian's business card from his shoulder bag. "He *does*."

"Then he could be anywhere like . . . like Moscow," she teased with a chuckle.

"But he isn't. As a matter of fact, his receptionist in Moscow said he's spending most of his time at that one." Katkov pointed to an address on the card. "So, the answer to your question is: I'm here to have a chat with Julian Levenger of Bethesda, Maryland."

"Makes two of us," Lana said. She got to her feet and collected her things. "I was hoping we could have dinner, but I got texted in the taxi while you were napping. I'm already running late. My standard operating procedure these days. We hit the ground running tomorrow. The boss is expecting us at eight. I know it's Saturday, but this is a 24/7 business."

"So is mine."

"I'll pick you up at seven thirty. Get some rest."

Katkov double locked the door after her, then took Grusha's memorial booklet from his bag and did what he'd been itching to do ever since he removed the packet of soil and gave it to Sergeant Garrett. His eyes saddened in reflection as he opened it, then brightened at the sight of the cybercode that Nadia had written inside the front cover, at the combination of letters and numbers that had so maddeningly eluded him—N5Y7T0E5P. They were all there in proper sequence now, but the code was still as enigmatic as it was when Nadia recited it, rapid-fire, during the funeral service, and Katkov still had no idea what it meant or how to go about deciphering it.

Chapter Thirty-Two

Lana blew out of the Ritz-Carlton and got into a taxi. "Bethesda. Burning Tree," she said to the driver as she tapped Julian's icon on her phone. "It's me. We need to talk . . . No. No phone, no texts, no emails—On my way. Twenty minutes."

Shafts of light from the windows of the main house and fencing club streamed through the darkness as the cab pulled into the courtyard. The *Sentiment du Fer* banner rippled in a light breeze. Julian and Kate were comfortably ensconced in the eighteenth-century ambiance of his office with snifters of vintage port and the flickering warmth of a fireplace when Lana joined them. The financial markets were closed, and the workstation with its array of Bloomberg terminals was strangely dormant. One of the news crawls read: FORMER KREMLIN INSIDER ESTIMATES PUTIN'S NET WORTH AT 40 BILLION. "When was the last time this place was swept?" Lana asked as Julian handed her a snifter.

"This morning. A daily ritual," Julian raised his glass. *"À votre santé."*

"Santé . . ." Lana echoed, softly, savoring the liquor's lingering warmth. "It's been a long day. Can we get on with this?"

"Avec quoi?" Julian asked.

"Katkov. I just parked him at the Ritz."

Kate rolled her eyes. "Well, we didn't want him but we got him."

"Thanks to Bortnikov," Lana chirped. "Even jet lagged, the guy's a lot of work. Not only does he know about the sleeper—I swore him to silence, by the way—but he also got his hands on one of your business cards, and he knows—"

"Oui, oui, j'ai déjà été informé," Julian interrupted with a wave of his hand.

Lana's eyes narrowed, then brightened with insight. "Moscow Centre."

Julian nodded. "FSB terminated Grafinskaya's RZD source. Several of my business cards were found at the crime scene. Katkov somehow acquired one."

"Christ. I better pick his brain. Find out if she gave him any intel. He already knows you're connected to the K and the CP/CSX merger. You're in his cross hairs."

"Should he be in mine?" Julian fired back.

"That's my question. He's determined to interview you, and I—"

"*Très bien*," Julian said decisively. "*I'll* pick his brain and keep you out of it."

Lana winced. "Where he goes, I go. It could be awkward."

"*Non, au contraire*, it's a perfect opportunity for you to establish your professional savoir faire and act as Katkov's loyal advocate. And for me to *cooperate fully with law enforcement*," Julian added with haughty sarcasm. "Keep your friends close but your enemies closer. Falsely attributed to Niccolò Machiavelli."

Kate nodded emphatically. "'Better they're inside the tent pissing out than outside pissing in.' Lyndon Johnson."

"An extraordinarily gifted wordsmith, wasn't he?" Julian said with a laugh.

"Hey, there's nothing funny about this," Lana protested. "Katkov makes a living connecting dots, and connecting you to the CP/CSX deal endangers the op, dammit!" She sighed and shrugged, apologetically. "Sorry, long day, like I said. I'm just . . ."

"Then take a breath, Lana," Julian counseled calmly, sipping from his snifter. "The CP/CSX merger can't endanger the op, because the merger is dead . . . *un fait accompli*. It was obvious going in neither company would get what it wanted. It was *posé-décollé* there for a while, but while they were blowing their deal"—he placed a flash drive on the desk in front of Lana—"I was closing ours."

Lana's eyes brightened. "The CSX cybercodes."

"The CSX cybercodes," Julian echoed in smug triumph.

"Great. I'll access their op system to verify," Lana said, segueing into a rueful sigh. "I'm afraid penetrating Amtrak's new cybersecurity program hasn't gone as well."

"I was under the impression you had already installed a gateway?"

"I did, but I got caught by Cyber-Borgen's anti-malware whiz. Actually by a filter that detects code not written under his unique identifier."

"Which means what?" Kate asked rhetorically. "You got burned?"

"No, it means I got lucky. He thought I was testing him."

Kate's jaw tightened. "Can you execute the op with just the CSX codes?"

"No. They're the key to the endgame, but, I have to gain control of three Amtrak anti-malware programs first, and that's not going to happen without a gateway."

Julian raised a concerned brow. "You must find a way to get that identifier."

"Tell me about it. Trouble is the code writers keep them in their heads, so—"

"Seduce him. Turn him," Julian snapped. "Do whatever it takes."

"It's not like we can threaten his family," Kate said with a macabre chuckle.

"We're barely a month from launch," Julian warned. He leaned back and steepled his fingers in thought. "Now, this Katkov business. The sooner we assess the threat level the better. Can you arrange the interview for tomorrow?"

Lana nodded. "We're meeting with Farrell and Diaz first thing, but after lunch should work. Speaking of Diaz, I don't know if I can keep him from horning in, so—"

"I should have my nails done," Kate interjected, knowing where Lana was going.

"Precisely. As I've said, he's very sharp, very incisive. He might pick up on something: our speech patterns, gestures, not to mention resemblance."

"*Très bien*," Julian said. "Once we deal with Katkov, you will transport your *medaille d'or derrière* back to New York and deal with that anti-malware expert."

"His name's Pash," Lana said, entertaining an idea as she crossed the room to the fireplace. A painting of a young woman sitting in a chair with her hands in her lap and her head tilted to one side as if she had fallen asleep in the midst of a reverie, hung above the mantel. Lana tilted her head as if mirroring the serene work. "I've always liked this."

"It's a Picasso . . ."

"I know," Lana said, sweeping her eyes across the lushly painted canvas.

"Been in the family for decades," Julian went on. "I've always wondered what was going through her mind as she was dozing off: An *affaire de coeur*? Had she just spent the afternoon with a lover? Un *souvenir d'enfance*? Or—" He paused suddenly, straightened in his chair, and, his tone sharpening, said, "You have no idea how to convince this fellow, Pash, to reveal his identifier, have you?"

"*Au contraire*," Lana said with that little smile. "I'm looking at it."

Chapter Thirty-Three

The next morning, snow flurries were dusting the Virginia countryside when Lana pulled up to the Ritz-Carlton. Katkov was waiting at the curb dressed in a tweed sport coat with threadbare cuffs, and rumpled corduroys. A cold front had pushed south, ending the unseasonably warm weather, and his breath was visible in the January chill.

"What are you, some kind of a polar bear?" Lana asked incredulously as Katkov settled next to her. The collar of her coat was turned up, and her flame-red curls tumbled from beneath a knitted cloche. "You should've brought a warmer coat."

"I did," Katov replied matter-of-factly. "But this is rather balmy compared to a Moscow winter: Twenty-below for weeks on end. The entire city sheathed in glistening ice. The profound silence of heavy snow. Almost something magical about it . . ."

"Yeah, well, it's the *almost* that worries me," Lana said.

The drive to JTTF headquarters at Liberty Crossing took less than ten minutes. Lana led the way across the massive jigsaw puzzle that encircled the flagpole outside the main entrance. "That's what we do here," she said, indicating the interlocking pieces of pavement that were dotted with snowflakes. "Personnel from national security and law enforcement agencies—investigators, analysts, computer nerds, spies—with IQs that are off the scale, racking their brains 24/7 to figure out which of the trillions of bits of intel collected by all the agencies are part of the same puzzle."

Katkov nodded. "I imagine you've read *The Puzzle Palace*."

"*Heard* of it. I mean, I must've been in pre-K when it was published," Lana said with a laugh. "An exposé of the NSA as I recall. Rattled a lot of cages."

"Indeed. Written by an investigative reporter, by the way. I was at Moscow State when one of my professors slipped me a tattered paperback with the covers torn off. It was eye-opening, inspiring, and quite prescient. It was also samizdat—underground literature. I'd have been sent to the Gulag had I been caught reading it."

"Well, it's a different world, Nikolai," Lana said, quickening her step. "For better *and* worse." They picked up his security pass at the visitors' desk in the lobby, and headed for the elevators.

Ruben was pacing in the reception area outside Farrell's office when they arrived. "You must be Katkov," he said, extending a hand. "Ruben Diaz, JTTF . . ."

"And all-around pain in the ass," Lana added with a sarcastic laugh.

"*Nikolai* Katkov," Katkov said, shaking Ruben's hand. "Investigative reporter . . . and all-around pain in the ass."

"Good, I need all the help I can get. The boss is on a call. Shouldn't be long." Moments later, the door behind Ruben opened and Farrell's assistant, Celia, waved them in.

"Okay, let's get right to it," Farrell said with a clap of his hands after the introductions had been made. "Unlike in your country, Mr. Katkov, we practice freedom of the press in ours, and to make certain Mr. Putin and his Kremlin propaganda machine can't accuse us of doing otherwise, I'll neither curtail your movements nor vet the people you intend to contact. But there *are* some rules: One: You don't go anywhere on your own. Two: You don't go anywhere on your own. Three: You don't go anywhere on your own. You and Agent Nichols are joined at the hip. Have I made myself clear?"

Katkov nodded. "Yes, sir. I fully expected she would be my minder."

Lana smiled and crossed her legs, exposing an expanse of thigh.

Katkov's eyes widened in appreciation.

"Keep it zipped," Ruben warned sotto voce. "She's a honey trap waiting to happen."

Katkov raised an amused brow. "The KGB coined that term. As I recall they entrapped more married Western diplomats than divorced anti-Kremlin journalists."

"Hey, there are worse ways to die," Ruben joked.

"And you're real close to being exhibit A," Lana said, burning him with a look.

"At ease. The sand box is closed," Farrell growled, his eyes shifting to reengage Katkov's. "Remember: You don't meet with anyone by yourself. If you talk to other JTTF investigators, NCTC people, government employees, law-enforcement personnel, media reps, railroad execs, the homeless guy who camps out in front of the White House—Agent Nichols will be with you. Don't waste your time trying to lose her, because we'll know where you are at all times."

"Any chance you worked for the KGB in a former life?" Katkov asked wryly.

"In *this* life. And they never knew it," Farrell replied, leaving no doubt he meant it. He gave a curt nod, then glanced at Ruben. "Any news on Tom?"

"Uh-huh. Final Forensics report just came in. Agent Nichols was right the first time: It wasn't Bargie-Boy."

Farrell scowled. "Damn. Why? The left-handed thing?"

"That and whoever cut Tom's throat nicked his jawbone. The lab found shards of metal embedded in it. Furthermore, microscopic—"

"No shit, Sherlock," Lana interrupted with a hearty guffaw. "Obviously from the box cutter we found in the trunk with his blood on it."

"I was about to say, microscopic examination showed the box-cutter blade to be intact," Ruben said with a wily smirk. "And metallurgy analysis determined the shards were hand-forged, eighteenth-century steel."

"Well, I suspect we can all agree that the box cutter was invented sometime *after* the French Revolution," Katkov said.

Ruben nodded. "Yeah, the guys in the silk knickers and powdered wigs were into dueling swords—like the ones you use in charity bouts—right, Amtrak?"

"They were also into thumb screws, torture racks, guillotines, and the ax," Lana replied with a laugh. She knew from the moment Ruben mentioned the scent of bleach on Tom's fencing tunic he suspected the evidence had been manipulated. She also knew just how she would manipulate him, but this wasn't the time, and she lightheartedly added, "The French aristocracy was very creative when it came to instruments of execution."

"So . . ." Farrell said with an exasperated sigh, "the five mil in the roll-aboard isn't the key to nailing *Bargishev* for Tom's execution, creative or otherwise."

"That's how it looks, sir," Ruben conceded glumly.

"Well, find out *who's* got it, and nail *their* ass!" Farrell snapped, shifting his look to Lana and Katkov. "What's your first order of business?"

"A Canadian billionaire," Lana replied. "He brokered the takeover of a French freight company for the Russian Railway Corporation, aka the Kremlin. His name is . . ." She paused, pretending she couldn't remember it.

"Julian Levenger," Katkov said, producing Julian's business card. "I've reason to believe he's representing the Kremlin again through a shell corporation. An *American* railroad is the target this time. He's been linked to the CP/CSX merger talks."

Farrell's brow furrowed. "You've come a long way Mr. Katkov. It's got to be more than the stench of financial chicanery to make this guy a person of interest."

"Indeed. He also links the Kremlin to the assassination of Nina Grafinskaya, my colleague at *Novaya Gazeta* who was killed because she threatened it, or . . . or . . ." Katkov paused as Lana, concerned he might mention the sleeper, caught his eye. "Or something related to it."

"That was a tragedy. Putin's crackdown on dissent is reeking of Soviet-era purges." Farrell shook his head in disgust, then his eyes narrowed in puzzlement. "Why in hell is the Kremlin interested in one of our railroads anyway? Shell corp or not, the regulators and the NSA legal gang'd be all over it in a minute."

Lana nodded sagely. "Railroads connect city centers. Fiber-optic companies pay top dollar for access to the land adjacent to the right of way. It's possible the Kremlin's after the real estate, not the railroad. Just a theory, sir. Agent Jones was working on it when he was killed. Mr. Katkov and I are working on it now."

"As you know, Agent Jones initiated contact with my colleague," Katkov chimed in. "Which is why I suspect the two killings are connected."

Ruben nodded. "That makes two of us. Starting to look like a no-brainer to me."

"So, net-net, Mr. Katkov, you're betting that"—Farrell glanced at the business card—"this guy, Levenger, knows who was behind the killings and why."

Katkov nodded.

"Bethesda. Spitting distance. Good." Farrell handed Levenger's card to Celia. "Run this guy. I want his life story."

Celia allowed herself a wry smile. "It might take a few moments, sir,"

Farrell's eyes locked onto Katkov's. "A word of advice, Mr. K. We never reveal information to suspects or persons of interest. We make them give it to us. You probe, you seduce, you provoke. You make this guy feel threatened, you befriend him, you back him into a corner until he's begging you to let him out and spill his guts. Got it?"

Katkov nodded and forced a smile.

"As I believe you mentioned, sir," Lana said gently. "Mr. Katkov is a journalist. An *investigative* journalist. I'm sure he's more than familiar with the technique."

Farrell responded with a preoccupied nod. "Anything else on your plate?"

"Yes, sir. I have to go to New York again to finalize Amtrak's cybersecurity program. We're installing next week."

"I hear good things about Carlsen and the people at Cyber-Borgen."

"Yeah, Grabowski's very high on them too. He's letting me run with it."

"Smart guy. When do you go?"

"Tomorrow."

"Okay. Ruben's your backup. He'll keep tabs on Mr. K while you're gone."

Katkov smiled at a thought. "So much for the honey trap."

Farrell ignored it and turned to Ruben. "Work for you?"

"No problemo. Other than the missing five mil, my plate's empty."

"Sounds like a plan. You're out of here. Keep me in the loop."

The trio nodded and headed for the door. Farrell intercepted Ruben and, in a tense whisper said, "The backup clock starts ticking now. Keep your distance. Low profile. Real low. Nichols has a lot of balls in the air. Don't undermine her confidence and make her drop one."

Chapter Thirty-Four

"Looks like my ass is on the line for five million bucks," Ruben said as he caught up with Lana and Katkov outside Farrell's office.

"Break a leg," Lana chirped as he hurried off, glad to be rid of him. "Okay, Nikolai, what say we go give Mr. Levenger a poke?"

Katkov looked surprised. "Just like that? Without an appointment?"

"The FBI doesn't make appointments."

"Neither did the KGB."

"Yeah, well, in this game, a little tactical advantage goes a long way. Quantico 101: Surprise 'em. Badge 'em. Grill 'em. Most cooperate. A few slam the door in your face. I doubt Mr. Levenger will do the latter."

"He would if he feared being sent to the Gulag, but you don't have one."

"We sure as hell do. It's called ADX Supermax."

"Sounds like a computer game."

"It's the *endgame*," Lana said with an icy stare. "You go in and never come out."

They were crossing the parking lot when Lana reflected on Julian's strategy. It was vital she appear as unfamiliar with the estate, its main house, outbuildings, interior layouts, and location as Katkov, or anyone who had never been there before, and in Julian's presence, vital that Katkov not sense any connection between them and, therefore, vital that she give Julian no quarter. "You have that business card handy?" Lana asked as they got into her car. "I know Bethesda a bit, but . . ."

Katkov nodded and recited the address on Julian's business card as Lana entered it into her dashboard GPS. A half hour later, when they arrived at the Bethesda estate, a black Bentley Mulsanne was parked in the courtyard between the main house and fencing club. The rippling *Sentiment du Fer* banner caught Katkov's eye as they walked across the snow-dusted pavers. Lana ignored the A/V security panel and knocked on the door, then knocked again more sharply. Moments later, Julian appeared. Tall and aquiline, he looked every bit the master of the universe in a bespoke suit. The knot of a boldly striped tie preened between starched collar points as if challenging anyone who dared question his authority.

"Julian Levenger?" Lana asked, as if she'd never seen him before.

"Sorry," Julian said, closing the door. "Whoever you are, I'm not—"

"FBI," Lana interrupted, badging him. "Lana Nichols. Special Agent in Charge. Joint Terrorism Task Force. This is Mr. Katkov. He's an investigative reporter with a Moscow newspaper. Do you have a few moments to speak with us?"

"No. I don't. As you can see, I'm about to leave," Julian replied with a nod to the Bentley and driver standing next to it. "You show up unannounced, accompanied by a journalist, and expect to be invited into my home?" he went on in an imperious tone. "I can't imagine what could have brought you to my door."

"The cold-blooded murder of an FBI agent," Lana fired back.

"*Mon Dieu*," Julian said, appearing taken aback. "Well . . . that's . . . that's very . . ."

"Unsettling, is the word I believe you're looking for, Mr. Levenger," Lana said. "I'd prefer we talk about this inside. Wouldn't you?"

"*Oui, bien sûr.* I can't imagine how I can help you, but please . . ."

Lana glanced about, appearing to be taken with the luxurious surroundings as they entered, and Julian closed the door after them. "*This* way, Agent Nichols," he said with a thin smile as he led the way to his office and settled behind the antique desk. His enameled cufflinks were emblazoned with the Sentiment du Fer crest.

"I'll be brief," Lana said as they settled admist the eighteenth-century ambience and the Bloomberg terminals. "The bureau has reason to believe the agent's death might be connected to the assassination of a Russian journalist Mr. Katkov is investigating."

"I'm not aware of the former, but the latter was covered by the media as I recall."

"The *latter* was my colleague and friend," Katkov said pointedly. "She was terminated for exposing political corruption in the Kremlin. Putin claims Russia is a developing democracy, but in his misguided zeal to recapture the glory of the Soviet Union, he has turned to violence to crush its newly won civil liberties and anyone who opposes him!" Katkov went on, his voice ringing with indignation. "Vlad the Impaler—a tribute to his ruthlessness, not to mention sexual exploits—has a dacha on a lake near Saint Petersburg, where he and an inner circle of former KGB officers plan their schemes. I rather suspect you've spent time there yourself, Mr. Levenger, in your capacity as—"

"Mr. Katkov?" Lana interrupted. "Mr. Katkov, I'm sure Mr. Levenger appreciates your passion, but we're not here to lecture him on political corruption in Russia."

Katkov tightened his lips, then nodded, taking his comeuppance in stride.

Julian forced a smile. "Merci, Agent Nichols. I am sorry about the death of your colleague, Mr. Katkov, but to be honest, I have no interest in politics, Russian or otherwise. Of the many things that capture my interest, I am most passionate about matters of finance and *l'art de la vinification*. Both are rich in opportunities to be cultivated. Whether the seeds are planted in Russian, French, British, or American soil is immaterial. One produces grapes with the perfect balance of sugar and acidity essential to making *les premier grands crus*, the other, dynamic corporate synergies essential to making windfall profits. Politics doesn't enter into it." He glanced at his watch and winced. "My time is short, and you still haven't explained what this has to do with me."

"The *murdered* journalist," Lana replied, her voice taking on a prosecutorial edge. "learned that the Kremlin, having taken over GEFCO, a French freight company, was now scheming to take over a U.S. railroad. After she was killed, Mr. Katkov began his investigation, and guess whose name turned up?"

"*Oui*, I brokered the RZD/GEFCO deal," Julian said, his voice ringing with pride. "For RZD, not the Kremlin. As you say, a win-win for all parties involved."

"You included," Lana fired back, making it sound like an indictment.

"I said *all* parties made money. That's what I do. And I do it very well."

"Your name also came up in regard to the CP/CSX merger," Katkov taunted.

"*Mais oui.* I've been conducting due diligence on behalf of a client for months."

"RZD, not the Kremlin," Katkov countered with stinging sarcasm.

"I'm not at liberty to disclose that information."

"Of course," Katkov scoffed. "Shell corporations provide anonymity, thereby shielding the parties from regulatory oversight and legal culpability."

"And from members of the media," Julian added with a sarcastic sneer. "It's all perfectly legal, Mr. Katkov . . . though your impertinence suggests otherwise."

"There's nothing legal about a foreign entity acquiring a controlling interest in an American railroad, sir," Katkov retorted, pinning him with a look. "Not to mention assassinating the journalist who threatened to expose it."

"Agent Nichols mentioned that, as I recall," Julian said with haughty disdain.

"She didn't mention that one of my colleague's sources who worked at RZD was also killed," Katkov fired back. "Nor did she mention that *your* business cards were found in the victim's briefcase at the murder scene."

"*C'est assez!*" Julian snapped, his eyes narrowing to angry slits. "You have made one implication too many, Mr. Katkov, and I categorically deny each and every one of them. I have no knowledge of the events you just referenced."

Katkov's eyes flared behind his wire-framed glasses. "I'm quite certain you do! I'm quite certain you know exactly why all three of them were killed, and I'm going to keep the pressure on until I find out."

"What grounds have you for making such an accusation?"

"I'm not at liberty to disclose that information," Katkov retorted with a smug smile. "I *can* disclose that, having visited your Moscow office, I'm quite certain it's an FSB front."

"Really? And what caused you to come to that conclusion?"

"An ex-KGB general who bypassed the main entrance in favor of an unmarked one at the end of the corridor."

"*L'entrée des employés*," Julian corrected brusquely.

Lana's eyes widened. "Mr. Levenger, for the record, are you saying you have an ex-KGB general in your employ?" she challenged, sending a veiled signal he should deny it.

"No, Agent Nichols, I don't. Not to my knowledge."

"His name is Ulov," Katkov replied. "Yuri Ulov. Head of the KGB station in Dresden in the late '80s. Putin was one of his subordinates." He scrolled through the photo library and handed the phone to Julian. "That *is* you and your mate, Yuri, there, celebrating the closing of the RZD/ GEFCO deal, isn't it?"

"He is of no consequence," Julian scoffed on seeing the snapshot of him and Ulov clinking Champagne glasses. "An errand boy at best."

"He looks more like the *poster* boy for Putin's *werewolves in epaulets* to me," Katkov countered. "Is he running errands for the CP/CSX deal too?"

"There is no CP/CSX deal, Mr. Katkov. I determined the ROI wasn't worth the risk, and advised my client to pass."

Katkov looked confused. He ran a hand through his graying curls. "The ROI?"

"Return on investment. As you say, the numbers didn't work. *S'il vous plaît*, Mr. Katkov, I'm a key player in a highly regulated business. The constraints are daunting, and infuriatingly complex. The winners use them to advantage. The losers are, well, losers."

"Once again, Mr. Levenger," Lana chimed in. "Are you saying that playing by the rules is the secret to your success? Is that your statement?"

"My statement? I didn't know I was making one," Julian intoned, as if offended, then, seizing the opening, he pinned Lana with a look and added, "For the record: Yes. I do play by the rules. My business dealings are fully transparent and vetted by the SEC, FINRA, the ERC—whichever regulatory agency has standing. I don't know anything about corruption in the Kremlin, assassinated journalists, FBI agents, or RZD employees." He stood and buttoned his jacket with a flip of his thumb and forefinger. "I am out of time, as are you." He plucked an attaché case from a sideboard, directed them outside into the courtyard, and got into the waiting Bentley.

"What's your take?" Lana asked as the Mulsanne drove off in luxurious silence, leaving dual vapor trails rising in its wake.

"You're the FBI Special Agent in Charge, Amtrak, JTTF," Katkov replied wryly.

"Okay," Lana said with a thoughtful nod. "He's good. Really good. Smooth as silk. Hard as nails. And very smart," she went on, ticking his qualities off like bullet points. "He meant what he said about being apolitical. He's all about money."

"*Kremlin* money," Katkov countered. "He knows everything."

"How can you say that?" Lana challenged. "I mean, how can you be so certain?"

Katkov shrugged. "I can't explain it. It's a feeling. I just . . . *know*. If you'd spent your entire life in Russia, so would you."

"Perhaps. But feelings don't alter facts," Lana countered, attempting to shift his focus. "The CP/CSX deal *didn't* close. Levenger *hasn't* set up a shell corporation. The Kremlin *isn't* trying to take over an American railroad. Whatever the reason, it's moot."

He *does* know everything, Katkov thought, *absolutely* everything. If there is a Russian sleeper in a USG national security agency, there's a better-than-even chance Julian Levenger is running that cell. "The *deal* may be moot, Agent Nichols," Katkov retorted, "but Mr. Levenger *isn't*—and neither is the sleeper."

"Point taken," Lana conceded. "But without evidence that proves otherwise, Mr. Levenger is an accomplished international financial consultant who counts corporations and governments among his clients, and nothing more."

"If *you* can't get the evidence, who can?" Katkov taunted.

Lana recoiled as if she'd been stung. "I don't think I deserved that," she said softly, playing him.

"Sorry, I'm afraid the frustration gets the better of me sometimes."

"Me too," Lana said, sounding as if she meant it. "Drop you at your hotel?"

"Lovely. That would be fine," Katkov said as they got into her car.

They were driving down the long access road from the estate when Katkov's phone pinged. The text from Vera read: *Venice? Paris? Ibiza? All of the above! Puzzled? Churkin just called. A quote: Collection returned end next week. Merry Xmas, Nikasha!* He stared at it for a moment, then brightened. "On second thought, I'd like to go to . . ." He exited the text and brought up his contacts list. "Do you know DuPont Circle?"

"Of course. It's in the heart of the District. What's there?"

"This may sound rather strange, but I'm going to a comic-book store."

"Big Planet?"

Katkov looked surprised. "You've heard of it?"

"Who hasn't? It's famous. Not far from where I live."

"I've been dealing with them for years."

"You're a collector."

"Guilty as charged. A childhood hobby that became an adult obsession."

"Hey, they're the best kind," Lana said. "By the way, you said something back there . . ." she went on, offhandedly, pretending Julian hadn't briefed her. "I mean, unless I got it wrong, you said that *three* people related to your story have been killed. Not two, right? Agent Jones, Grusha, *and* her source at RZD?"

Katkov nodded. "Yes. Her name was Nadia Nysenko. She worked at a very high level. I was convinced she had more information and made contact with her."

"And? Did she? I mean, have more info?"

Katkov shrugged, deciding to keep the enigmatic cybercode to himself until he had a chance to decipher it. "If she did, they killed her before she could pass it."

"Unfortunate," Lana said as the Prius reached the end of the estate's long driveway. She had just made the turn onto the access road when a black SUV pulled out from behind a stand of trees and followed them.

Chapter Thirty-Five

Massachusetts Avenue runs arrow-straight from Bethesda through North-west Washington into the heart of the District. Traffic was always congested on Saturdays, and darkness had fallen by the time Lana and Katkov reached Dupont Circle, where New Hampshire angles off to U Street. It was lined with parked cars and nineteenth-century row houses with stoops rising to parlor-floor entrances. Many were now occupied by an eclectic mix of boutiques, restaurants, nail salons, art galleries, and bookstores. Lana double-parked in front of the one that had startling computer graphics painted on its royal-blue façade. They were the size of trash-can covers and swarmed about its barred windows like a horde of alien invaders. A sign proclaimed BIG PLANET COMICS.

"I'll find a spot somewhere. Call when you're done. I'll come get you."

"I've no problem taking the Metro," Katkov offered. "I purchased one of your smart cards and some cigarettes at the hotel—both much more expensive than Moscow."

"No Metro for you, comrade. Door-to-door service. Those are my orders."

"*Da tovarishch*," Katkov said with mock subservience. "I'll be quick about it."

"No pressure. My inbox is busting. I'll play catch-up on emails." Lana tapped the map on her GPS screen where a location marker was flashing. "That's us, and *that's* the signal from your phone. As the boss said, we'll know where you are at all times."

"Good, then I've no worries about getting lost," Katkov said with a grin. He got out and was approaching Big Planet Comics when a black SUV with a shadowed figure behind the wheel came down the street, slowed as it passed, and continued on.

Lana drove off and called Julian. "Hi, it's me. How'd I do?"

"You were . . . unsettling."

"Yeah, I know," Lana said in a cocky tone. "What's your take on this guy?"

"Unpredictable. A loose cannon. Driven by his heart, not his head," Julian replied. "*Il sera un problème.*"

"He's a journalist. They're always a problem."

"The Centre left it to our discretion to terminate—*si c'est nécessaire.*"

Lana winced. "I don't think we're there yet, Julian."

"Nor do I."

"Good. Because Agent Diaz is going to be Katkov's minder while I'm in New York. If something happened on *his* watch, *he'd* be running the investigation instead of me, which could endanger the op. I'll deal with Mr. K when I get back—if necessary."

The interior of Big Planet Comics was a collector's heaven. Vintage issues of every comic since Superman first outran a speeding bullet and Archie first flirted with Veronica were displayed on the walls and in glass cases. Katkov spent a few moments taking it all in before approaching the counter, where a slight fellow stood in a T-shirt advertising Ben's Chili Bowl.

"Might you be Nick?" Katkov wondered.

"I've been called worse," Nick replied with an easy smile.

"As have I," Katkov said, extending a hand. "Nikolai. Nikolai Katkov. You probably don't remember, but we've done business on the Internet over the years."

"Nikolai," Nick scolded, as if Katkov should know better. "How many collectors you think we have in Moscow, hmm? Quality—you've always been into quality. Into picking up something special, right?"

"Right. But I'm into *selling* something special today." Katkov replied, placing a flash drive on the counter. "Something *very* special."

Nick stared at it, uncertain of Katkov's implication, then went with his gut. "You're . . . you're into selling your entire collection."

Katkov nodded. "If the price is right."

Nick plugged the flash drive into his computer and clicked on the window that appeared. Pages of titles from Action and Avengers to Wonder Woman and X-Men began scrolling up the screen. "Wow. Pricing a collection like this . . . I'd . . . I'd have to get with the owner. Hey, it could take us weeks."

"I rather expected as much. I'm at the Ritz-Carlton Tysons Corner. That's my cell," Katkov added, jotting the number on a slip of paper."

"The Ritz," Nick echoed, raising a brow. "Hey, with a little luck, your collection just might be worth enough to cover your bar tab."

"Might?" Katkov prompted with a laugh.

"Well, and a bowl of chili or two," Nick added, gesturing to his T-shirt. "Ben's. Just down the street. Best in DC. I'll return that soon as I can."

Katkov winced. "I'd much prefer you download the files," he said pointedly.

"No problem." A couple of mouse clicks later, Nick unplugged the flash drive and returned it to Katkov. "I'll be in touch. Feel free to browse."

Katkov could have spent hours at Big Planet but left immediately, calling Lana as he came down the stoop. "It's Nikolai. I hope I wasn't too long."

"No problem. I'm nearby. I'll—"

"Hold on—hold on," Katkov interrupted. The tip of a cigarette glowing in the darkness had caught his eye, drawing his attention to a figure standing beneath the stoop of an adjacent building.

"What? What is it?" Lana prompted. "Something wrong?"

"I'm afraid I'm being tailed," Katkov replied, continuing past the building.

"You sure?"

Katkov glanced over his shoulder. A man in a down vest and watch cap came from beneath the stoop into the glow of a streetlight. He dragged on his cigarette and began walking in the same direction as Katkov. No jogging suit. No NASCAR cap—but Katkov had been through this too many times to dismiss it. "Yes. Positive."

"Go to the corner," Lana commanded. "I'm close."

Katkov turned up his collar and quickened his pace. He was a half block from the corner when the black SUV that had driven past earlier drove past again and double-parked up ahead. Before the driver got out, Katkov crossed the street and began walking faster in the opposite direction. The man in the watch cap did the same. The black SUV made a broken U-turn and pursued.

Damn! Katkov thought, breaking into a jog. I'm not being tailed. I'm being hunted—abducted! His eyes darted to a Metro sign up ahead. He had eluded more KGB agents than he could count in the Moscow Metro, but the entrance was beyond an intersection and the traffic signal was against him. The lights of the cross-traffic were streaking the darkness as he glanced back in search of his pursuers: The SUV was among the vehicles stopped at the traffic signal, but the man in the watch cap was still coming, puffs of breath visible in the wintry air. Katkov darted into the street, clutching his shoulder bag, and zigzagged between the oncoming vehicles, setting off a cacophony of honking horns and screeching brakes. He made it across and sprinted toward the Metro station. The man in the watch cap didn't stop either, he was artfully dodging traffic when the side mirror of a van clipped his shoulder, knocking him off stride. He did a military tuck and roll, and came up running. When the traffic signal changed, the SUV accelerated and reached the Metro station just as Katkov dashed into the entrance pursued by the man in the watch cap. The driver got out sprinted after them.

The station was bustling with passengers streaming through the gates. Katkov merged into the flow with his smart card and got on the escalator. It descended beneath a coffered ceiling that arched above the murals—honoring African Americans who served in the Civil War—that ran the station's length. Katkov was making his way down the crowded platform toward an exit sign at the far end of the station when the sound of a train rose behind him. He looked back into its blinding headlights as it emerged from the tunnel, saw the black watch cap surging toward him, and began walking faster. Watch Cap plunged deeper into the crowd, shoving the passengers aside, and lunged at Katkov, intending to push him in front of the onrushing train, but at the last instant, another man knifed between them, driving Katkov away from the edge of the platform and his assailant toward it. The motorman slammed on the brakes. Katkov's assailant ricocheted off the side of the train as it streaked past back into the crush of horrified passengers waiting to board it. He regained his balance and ran toward the far end of the station. Katkov and his savior had gone sprawling across the platform as the train came to a stop. The latter got to his feet, spotted the fleeing assailant, and went after him.

It had happened so fast that Katkov never got a clear look at either of them. Several bystanders helped him to his feet. Another handed him his glasses and a few items that had spilled from his bag. Despite the pain in his shoulder that had broken his fall, he assured the Good Samaritans he was uninjured and was taking a moment to gather his wits when he was struck by a chilling thought: Someone will call the police. Most likely already had. He knew the routine all too well: Interviews. Reports. Official statements. Media coverage—a time-consuming, intrusive, unpredictable process. Indeed, any connection to a public altercation that involved local law enforcement, not to mention one that threatened to reveal the nature of his mission, could have him on the next plane back to Moscow. He declined further assistance and hurried toward the escalator, trying to call Lana, but couldn't get a signal in the underground station.

Chapter Thirty-Six

Lana was angered and shaken by the news Katkov was being tailed. Hadn't she and Julian just agreed hands off for now?! And her anxiety level soared when he didn't show up as instructed, not to mention that his phone went straight to voicemail, and that its marker had vanished from her GPS screen. She was driving east on U toward Big Planet Comics in search of him when the marker reappeared, placing Katkov—if he was still in possession of his phone—at the Cardozo Metro Station.

The flashers of approaching police cruisers were strobing in the darkness as Lana arrived and spotted Katkov among the passengers emerging from the station's vaulted canopy with his phone to his ear. Hers began ringing as she hurried toward him. "Katkov?!" she called out with a mixture of parental relief and frustration. "What the hell were you doing in the fucking Metro?!"

"Running for my fucking life!" Katkov fired back. "*Ublyudki popytalsya ottolknut' menya pered chertov poyezd!*" he went on, breaking into Russian. "*Izvinite, no ya nemnogo vstryakhivayut, Lanichka, yesli vy ne vozrazhayete!*"

"Chrissakes!" Lana exclaimed. "*Ya skazal vam gde vstreitit'sya so mnoy! Ya—*" She bit it off, realizing what she'd done, that Katkov's tone, reversion to Russian, and use of *Lanichka*—a term of endearment still used by her mother—had triggered her gaffe.

Katkov looked puzzled and splayed his hands.

"What? Tom. Agent Jones. I picked it up from Agent Jones. I told you he was fluent. He spoke Russian all the time. Now, what the hell is going on?!" Lana challenged, attempting to change the subject. "I told you where to meet me!"

"I know . . . I know," Katov replied. "But a vehicle joined the pursuit, forcing me to reverse direction. I tried to evade them in the Metro, but the one tailing me caught up and shoved me in front of a train. A bystander took action that saved my life."

"For the love of Christ," Lana said, clearly shaken. "This is unbelievable. I mean—" She cut herself off, surprised to see Ruben coming from the Metro station. He began walking swiftly in their direction, ignoring several police cruisers that had just arrived. "We're not doing this here," Lana said sharply. She spun on a heel and led the way into an alley next to the Lincoln Theater across the street. A bare bulb at the top of a fire escape sent shafts of light across the pavement and adjacent buildings. "Your turn," Lana said, locking her eyes onto Ruben's. "What the hell were *you* doing in the Metro?"

"Saving his ass and yours," Ruben replied, matching her fervor.

"What?" Katkov blurted. "That was you? You're the one who . . ."

Ruben nodded matter-of-factly. "I was driving west on U when—"

"In a black SUV," Katkov interjected.

"Yeah. Jeep Wrangler."

Lana was seething. Her breaths coming in angry puffs. "I'm listening, Ruben."

"Long story short, I saw this guy tailing Katkov and pursued. He chased Katkov into the Metro. He made his move. I made mine. All hell broke loose. He took off. I went after him. But I lost him."

Katkov's eyes were wide with astonishment.

So were Lana's. She took a moment to collect herself, then burned Ruben with a look. "And what? You just happened to be passing by?"

Ruben winced, wrestling with it. "The boss thought you should have some . . . some . . . backup just in case. Looks like he was right."

Lana's eyes flared. She was on the verge of launching into a tirade about Farrell's insulting lack of confidence and Ruben's unforgivable disloyalty when she was struck by a sobering thought: It was Farrell, not Ruben, who was really backing her up. Who, by assigning Ruben to support her, was enabling her to focus on Amtrak's new cybersecurity system—to develop it and install it—not to mention take control of it and execute the op! "Yeah, sorry," she conceded with a sigh. "The boss *is* right. I've got a lot on my plate. I need all the help I can get. Thanks."

"*De nada,*" Ruben muttered.

"So, now what? I mean, forget the hotel. No way Katkov can stay there now."

Ruben nodded grimly. "Looks like we're talking a safe house."

"A safe house?" Katkov echoed. "The last one I spent time in was called Lubyanka. It was so safe most citizens who went in never came out. If I can't come and go as I please, I'll never accomplish what I came here to do."

"Yeah, but the bed'll be a lot comfier than a slab in the morgue," Ruben said with a sarcastic smirk. He shifted his look to Lana and added, "It'll take some time to set it up. I'll collect his things from the hotel and work it out with the boss."

"Thanks. I'm nearby. He can crash on my sofa tonight, but I'm off to the Big Apple in the morning. He's all yours after that."

"Might I have a word?" Katkov asked.

"No," Lana replied brusquely. "We're out of here."

Katkov was still unsettled when he and Lana reached her apartment. He swept his eyes across its eclectic furnishings with anxious curiosity as she double locked the door and closed the blinds. "You okay?" she asked, sensing his uneasiness.

Katov nodded. "I'm fine. I've been living on edge my entire life, but it does become more unnerving as one gets older, I'm afraid."

"I'm sorry to hear that," Lana said with a laugh. "Something to warm your innards? Port, cognac, Armagnac? I got 'em all. Pick your poison. I'll join you."

"As poisons go, alcohol tends to totally incapacitate me," Katkov said, lighting a cigarette. "*These* will merely kill me—eventually."

"If a hit man doesn't get you first," Lana said, nodding toward the sofa. "Get comfy. It's not a king-size playpen at the Ritz but first night's free, breakfast included." She poured some cognac into a snifter, kicked off her shoes, and settled into one of the club chairs. "So . . . who do you think is trying to kill you?"

"The same psycho who sanctioned Grusha's murder," Katkov replied, massaging his shoulder. "Fortunately, when it came to me, the Kremlin's hit man was a poor shot."

"You're serious, aren't you?"

"Quite serious," Katkov replied with a lengthy exhale. "Grusha threatened them. You saw her email about the sleeper."

Lana nodded. Her brow furrowed. "But if I have the sequence of events right," she said, as if thinking it through, "they killed her before they ever saw it, didn't they?"

"Precisely. They didn't have to see it because they knew—"

"That what she was onto could blow the sleeper's cover," Lana interjected, pretending it had just occurred to her.

"No," Katkov said sharply. "I'm quite certain it's bigger than that. More like it threatened to expose an operation the sleeper's running. And having spent years chasing clandestine shadows . . ." Katkov paused and locked his eyes onto Lana's. "Chances are *Monsieur* Levenger is running the cell."

"Really?" Lana said, savoring the cognac's heady warmth to cover her reaction. "What makes you think that? You have any proof?"

"No, but I'm working on it. At the moment it's just gut instinct."

"And your gut's usually right."

"Unfortunately. That's what makes the Kremlin assassinate journalists."

"And since you've inherited Grusha's story, you're their next target."

"I'd bet my life on it," Katkov said with a wry smile.

"Thank you, Nikolai. Now, not only do I know *why* you're here—I'm *glad* you're here." She set the snifter aside and got to her feet. "If you'll excuse me, I need to pop into the girls' room." She scooped up her bag, then whirled back to Katkov and commanded, "Be here when I get back." She headed into the bathroom, closed the door, and leaned her back against it, then took her phone from her bag. "What the hell's going on!" she demanded in an angry whisper when Julian answered. "Didn't we just decide not to terminate our erstwhile journalist?"

"*Absolument.* What are you trying to tell me?"

"Somebody tried to push him in front a Metro train."

"*Merde,*" Julian grunted, sounding uncharacteristically troubled. "It wasn't one of our people, Lana. Not by my order. *Je le jure.*"

"Well, it wasn't one of mine," Lana fired back. "Bortnikov?"

"Who else? Probably one of his wet-work specialists from the *rezidentura*, which suggests Mr. Adamov is demanding he take neither chances nor prisoners. Considering this is a priority-one op, one might argue he made the right call."

"Especially since Katkov suspects *you're* running it, but I'm his—"

"*Mon Dieu.* He's a clever one, isn't he? Shame they *didn't* terminate him."

Lana's eyes flared. "I'm his minder, dammit! Killing him now would put the spotlight on *me.* Or have you forgotten why you decided not to terminate Caitlin Roarke?"

"*Touché.* I'll contact Moscow Centre and remind them."

"Do it now, Julian. Right now," Lana commanded. She flushed the toilet, rinsed her hands, and ran her wet fingers through her hair before leaving.

Katkov was at the fireplace admiring the vintage dueling sabers on the mantel when Lana returned. He hadn't removed one from the cradle and examined it and hadn't seen the name of its eighteenth-century maker or the personalized engravings in Russian.

"Beautiful aren't they," Lana said, joining him.

"Indeed. I thought Ruben was teasing you about these, so to speak."

"He was. It's agency gamesmanship. The entire staff plays it. We use it to kind of keep each other sharp. On our toes. Match-tough . . . so to speak."

"Ah, well, investigative reporter that I am . . ." Katkov said with self-deprecating charm "they lead me to suspect, quite strongly, that you're a fencer."

"I *was* . . . in college. National champion. No time for it now. Just the occasional charity bout. Did you know Agent Jones was a fencer?"

Katkov shook his head no.

"Uh-huh. A very good one. Thanks to the Russian coach he had as a kid," Lana prompted, taking advantage of the moment to finesse it. "So . . ."

"Ah, yes, the source of his fluency . . ." Katkov let it hang there for a moment, then added, "And yours."

"Far from it, but that's quite a compliment, coming from you. Thanks."

"Pozhaluysta," Katkov said with a magnanimous gesture. *"Eto legko skazat' pravdu. Vy govorili dovol'no khorosho."*

Lana's brow furrowed as if she were working out the translation. "I'm not sure I got all that: You're welcome? And something about telling the truth and speaking well?"

"That's rather good. I said, 'It's easy to tell the truth,'" Katov explained. "By the way, I noticed a banner hanging from a building on Levenger's estate. It had a crest with some words in French above crossed swords."

"Yes, I saw it too. Probably a private club. Way out of my league."

"Did you notice he was wearing cuff links with the same crest?"

Lana nodded. "Which, I imagine, leads you to suspect, quite strongly, that *he's* into fencing too," Lana said sarcastically. "What about you?"

"I've done a little in my day," Katkov replied with an oblique smile.

"Épée, foil, saber?"

"The pen," Katkov replied, deadpan.

Lana rolled her eyes.

Katkov raised an amused brow and nodded. "My legendary *rapier* wit."

Not only had Katkov alluded to her language gaffe, Lana thought, but also to Ruben's needling her about her vintage sabers. She was searching for a way to deflect his threatening curiosity when she recalled his keen observation of details at Julian's estate. "You know . . . considering Levenger's wealth and many passionate interests, one of which appears to be fencing, it wouldn't surprise me if he had a world-class collection of vintage dueling weapons. And if he *is* running the sleeper . . ." She let it trail off, suggesting the conclusion was obvious.

"Ruben's gamesmanship might, actually, be a penetrating insight into Agent Jones's murder."

Lana's eyes brightened. "Exactly. Tom knew about the sleeper. Right? Maybe he got into it. Maybe he got too close, and the microscopic specks of three-hundred-year-old steel found in Tom's wound came from one of the sabers in *Levenger*'s collection."

"Well," Katkov said, mulling it over. "Your theory is teetering on a wobbly foundation of ifs, buts, and maybes, but there's something about it that feels right."

Lana suppressed a relieved smile and nodded. It was a no-brainer, she thought. Katkov's fix on Julian was right on target, and it made perfect sense to reinforce it. Having acquired the CSX cybercodes, Julian had served his purpose. Indeed, Moscow Centre's priority-one op could proceed without him, but not without her. Besides, she knew Julian would relish "fencing" with Katkov, using the disinformation to keep him occupied while she executed the mission.

Chapter Thirty-Seven

The next morning, the temperature had dropped, and a biting wind was coming off the Potomac fulfilling forecasts of more wintry weather. Katkov was standing in front of Lana's townhouse hunkered down into his turtleneck and sport jacket. Lana stood next to him, hands stuffed into the pockets of her stadium coat. A sedan with an Uber logo in the window was parked nearby, motor running. "It's about time," Lana muttered when Ruben's Jeep turned the corner and pulled in behind it. He got out and tossed Katkov his parka. "Thought this might come in handy," he said and, with an amused grin, taunted, "Looks like you two made it through the night unscathed."

"I'm more interested in making my train," Lana fired back with an anxious glance at her watch. "God help you if I miss it."

"Lighten up, Amtrak. I skipped breakfast to beat the traffic, but—"

"Whatever," Lana interrupted. "I've got to dash. Make sure you keep our boy out of trouble." She tossed an overnight bag into the back seat of the Uber and got in after it. The driver closed the door, slipped behind the wheel, and drove off.

"Rest of your stuff's in the back," Ruben said as he and Katkov got into the Jeep.

"Thank you for collecting it. Might I ask where we're going?"

"The Skillet. It's a bacon-and-egg joint over by GWU. Work for you?"

"Can I smoke?"

"Not legally, but the short-order cook has a two-pack-a-day habit."

"Actually, when I asked where we were going, I was referring to the safe house. As I said, I can't be locked up 24/7 and do my job."

Ruben nodded. "Yeah, well, I went to bat for you with the boss on that. Got me promoted from backup minder to backup minder/driver/bodyguard: Where you go, I go, and where I go, you go . . . which means I get to take you home when I clock out."

Katkov looked incredulous. "Pardon me?"

"Ditto. We'll take it a day at a time. If the wife and kids can't handle it, it's hasta la vista baby for you."

All the parking spots outside the Skillet were taken. Ruben angled into a bus stop and tossed a card with the agency's seal onto the dash. The diner's windows were wet with condensation. A smoky haze and the acrid smell of grilled onions hung in the air. A few patrons, on fixed stools with duct-taped cushions, hunched over the worn counter. Katkov and Ruben had just settled into a booth when the waitress arrived with her Silex pot and filled their cups. Ruben greeted her by name and grunted, "The usual." Katkov ordered, "Sausages and home fries."

"So how'd it go yesterday?" Ruben prompted as the waitress hurried off. "You and Amtrak rattle that Canadian billionaire's cage pretty good?"

"Indeed," Katkov replied, following it with a swallow of coffee. "Though I'm afraid mine got rattled too. He's a slippery fellow, dripping with European swagger and smug entitlement. I went after him with everything I had and came rather close to losing it. Agent Nichols, as you might imagine, was quite the professional: cool, incisive, and politely unrelenting. Nothing got past her."

"Good cop/bad cop, way to go . . ."

Katkov's brow furrowed. "Come to think of it, I don't recall mentioning we were going to see Levenger."

"You didn't. I was backing up Nichols, remember? I followed you to Bethesda, to the comic-book store, and down into the Metro."

"Needless to say, I'm quite appreciative of your heroic effort, but be advised that my aversion to be being terminated is matched only by my aversion to being put on the next flight back to Moscow—which could very well happen should local authorities or the media learn of my involvement in that incident."

"Not gonna hear it from me. They're both on the agency's no-leak/no-speak list." Ruben raised a brow and broke into a salacious grin. "So, did our girl spring the honey trap last night? I mean, was it *Sex and the City* or Snooze on the Sofa?"

"I can assure you the queen bee had no intention of sharing any of her honey with me. I have a feeling she sees me more like a father figure than a one-night shag. Though I imagine it might be worth risking her sting."

"Hey, it's not *her* sting that'd worry me, it'd be my wife's."

Katkov grinned sagely. "By the way, there *are* a couple of vintage dueling swords prominently displayed in her hive. Quite beautiful, actually."

Ruben nodded matter-of-factly. "I know. Agent Jones told me about them."

Katkov's eyes narrowed. "So you weren't just needling her. I mean about the bits of three-hundred-year-old steel the medical examiner found in his wound."

"I wish. It's keeping me awake nights."

Katkov looked troubled. "Are you saying that you think Agent Nichols could be complicit in his death?"

Ruben winced. "I know it sounds bizarre. I mean, she's sharp as they come, the best cybercop in the business, but there's something about her and Tom's murder that keeps bugging me. I just got this . . ." He paused as the waitress slipped their plates in front of them and, without breaking stride, moved on to another table. "I don't know . . . I've just got this thing in my gut that keeps telling me the pieces don't fit."

"Well, as someone who lives on gut instinct, I suspect it's possible they don't fit because they might not all belong to the same puzzle. A fresh eye often helps. Why don't you run them past me?"

"Nothing to lose," Ruben replied, launching into it: "According to the medical examiner, Agent Jones's throat was slashed with a razor-sharp blade. A box cutter with his blood on it was found next to his body. But those pesky bits of vintage steel were found in the wound—and our girl owns those sabers. The killer was right-handed—so is she. And Tom had his fencing outfits dry cleaned; the one found with his body smelled of bleach."

"Suggesting it was laundered to clean up the bloodstains and cover up the fact that he was wearing it when he was killed."

Ruben nodded emphatically. "Furthermore, Agent Nichols was the last person to see him alive, she made sure she took over the case, and zeroed-in on a Chechen gang leader as the killer. Pushed him real hard as a prime, then torpedoed it—not to mention *me*—in front of the boss. Now she's pushing the Chechen on me again. It all just feels weird."

Katkov winced. "Well, it's all quite intriguing, but, I'm afraid I was wrong. Whether or not the pieces belong to the same puzzle is of no consequence because they seem to be circumstantial. You have no hard evidence of Agent Nichols's complicity."

"Come on, Katkov. She's got means, method, opportunity . . ."

"Indeed, everything to make *her* a prime—except a motive."

Ruben nodded grudgingly. "One minute I feel like we're clicking. The next like she's playing me. Christ, I'm really starting to hate this job."

"Well, for what it's worth—" Katkov cut himself off, wishing he hadn't said it.

"What?" Ruben asked, jumping on it. "Come on, come on, *venga*. Spit it out."

Katkov used a swallow of coffee to buy some time, then put down the cup and centered it in its saucer. "Sorry, I'm trying to decide whether or not I should trust you."

"At this point I don't think you have a choice. What's the hang-up?"

"Agent Nichols swore me to secrecy."

"Christ. What about?"

"That the Kremlin has a sleeper in a U.S national security agency, and based on everything I know, *my* gut's telling me it's yours."

Ruben's eyes widened. "How the hell did Little Miss Amtrak get onto that?"

"Grafinskaya put it in an email to Agent Jones, but she never got the chance to send it. So *I* did, and after *he* was killed, Agent Nichols—"

"Took over the case, and the emails came with it," Ruben interjected. "You're positive you and Nichols are the only ones who know about it?"

Katkov broke into a Cheshire smile. "Not any longer, I'm afraid."

"Christ. Why would she do that? I mean, be secretive."

"Because if the sleeper *is* embedded in this agency, she didn't want to tip them off it might be someone close, like Farrell, or Agent Jones, maybe even you—"

"Maybe even *her*!" Ruben erupted. "Nichols fences, right? And has those vintage sabers. Maybe she's the sleeper!"

"Well, that *would* explain a few things, wouldn't it?" Katkov's eyes widened at what he was about to say. "Are you aware she speaks Russian?"

Ruben looked stunned. "What?"

"Yeah, she claims she picked it up from Agent Jones."

"Well, he *was* fluent," Ruben said, equivocating between sips of coffee. "They hadn't been working together very long, but they did have a fling. Guess she could have picked up a few phrases between the sheets."

"I wouldn't attribute her proficiency to an exchange of bodily fluids," Katkov said with a mischievous laugh. "Even if they'd been shagging for twenty years, she couldn't have learned her Russian from Agent Jones."

"What makes you so sure of that?"

"Her accent. It's aristocratic. Not what one would pick up from an American Russian-speaker. I'm quite certain she learned hers from whoever raised her."

"And who raised you? The Archbishop of Canterbury?"

"No. An expatriate British nanny."

"You know, I'm not rooting for my gut on this. What you're telling me about her is breaking my heart."

"Well, Agent Nichols did concoct a rather plausible theory about vintage dueling swords and microscopic bits of three-hundred-year-old steel that might just mend it."

"I'll bet she did," Ruben said sarcastically.

"Which brings us back to *my* gut and *my* prime."

"Levenger."

Katkov nodded. "We both noticed he's a passionate collector—not only of companies that strike his fancy, but of antiques, works of art, fine wines, and has a private fencing club on his estate—which caused Agent Nichols to hypothesize . . ."

"That Levenger just might also collect vintage dueling swords."

"Precisely."

"What's *his* motive for killing Tom?"

"The *Kremlin's* motive," Katkov corrected. "Not only for killing him but also my colleague. You made it quite clear yesterday, you're convinced they're connected."

Ruben nodded emphatically. "Been my gut instinct from the get-go."

"It's been mine too. And when I found Levenger's business cards with the body of a third, Grusha's source at RZD, I became convinced he's the key."

"Why?"

"Because I think he's running the sleeper."

"For chrissakes, as guts go, yours is sure full of surprises, isn't it?"

"Not really. It stands to reason that if Agent Jones *wasn't* the sleeper, he could have come to the same conclusion I did and pursued it, and it cost him his life."

Ruben's eyes narrowed. "But we were both on the Russian desk, working these Chechen *cabrons*. If Tom knew about a sleeper, no way he would've kept it to himself."

"Either way, the first order of business is to find out whether or not Levenger has a collection of vintage swords. The background check should cover that, right?"

"It should . . ." Ruben replied, with a pregnant pause. "When we get it. Rumor has it Levenger jet-sets about on a Gulfstream that he parks at Dulles. I'd better get in his face again before he jet-sets out of town."

"No way, Jose," Katkov retorted with a mischievous grin. "You're the backup minder/bodyguard/driver in chief. Where I go, you go, and where you go, I go. *Da?*"

"Yeah, *da*," Ruben said, forcing a scowl. "Thanks for reminding me."

"Don't mention it. You know, between your gut and mine, who knows what might turn up in Levenger's cage if we rattle it hard enough."

Ruben brightened and nodded emphatically.

Katkov lit a cigarette and emitted a satisfying exhale, adding to the smoky haze overhead that came from the grill. "Now, finish your breakfast so we can get on with it."

Chapter Thirty-Eight

Lana dashed aboard the Acela express minutes before it departed from Union Station. She'd had little time to review the final version of Amtrak's new cybersecurity program on the flash drive Carlsen had given her, and had just begun scrutinizing it on her laptop when a stunning thought struck her: Pash entered his UI from memory via keyboard each time he accessed the program. Could it be embedded somewhere in the lines of code?! An hour later, all the searches she ran had come up empty, but she still had every reason to believe that the idea inspired by the Picasso in Julian's office would convince Pash to reveal it, and she turned her attention to another flash drive—the one with the CSX cybercodes—and accessed the railroad's operating system. She opened the RCRM—Rail Corridor Risk Management—file that determines the safest routing for cargo with high levels of risk, zeroed-in on those scheduled on eastern seaboard routes, and reviewed their dates of departure and arrival, and destinations. None met her criteria precisely, but she identified several that she could redirect to the target from her laptop.

She arrived at Cyber-Borgen's headquarters just after noon. Pash was all business when she joined him, and they spent the afternoon double-checking every line of code that made up the security system's key programs and tuning up those sections that Lana had flagged during her review. "Don't know about you, but I'm burned out," she said after they had locked the program and certified it for installation. "I need some cultural refreshment. You ever go to MoMA?"

"Where?"

"The Museum of Modern Art?"

"Oh, yes, of course. Not as often as I'd like, I'm afraid."

"Makes two of us. It's been ages. I was a member when I was on the job in New York. Went every chance I got. My treat!"

They were emerging from the Flatiron's entrance when a taxi pulled to the curb and dropped off a passenger. A short time later, they were whirling through a revolving door into the museum's lobby. Lana purchased the tickets and led the way to a coat-check line. Pash folded his arms and studied her for a moment. "You have a special reason for wanting us to come here," he finally said. "Don't you?"

"Yes, I do," Lana replied, palming the coat-check tag. "Come on, I'll show you."

They took the elevator to the fifth floor, where many of the world's most acclaimed works of modern art were on display. Lana led the way past Cézanne's *Bather* and Van Gogh's *Starry Night* to an adjacent gallery, where Picasso's *Girl Before a Mirror*—the boldly painted abstraction in which the reflection in the mirror bears little resemblance to the figure standing in front of it—hung in solitary grandeur.

"One of my all-time favorites," Lana gushed. "You know, I have a colleague whose young daughter was quite taken with it, and when he asked her what she thought it was about, she said: '*Sometimes people are different on the outside than they are on the inside.*'"

"Indeed, your colleague is blessed with a precocious child. We have a saying in Arabic—*La tsta an tqwl ktaba mn ghlafh*—much akin to your 'You can't tell a book by its cover.'"

"Yes, much akin," Lana echoed, mimicking his accent with an infectious giggle that made him laugh.

They drifted from the provocative Picasso past an equally powerful de Kooning and a spirited Pollock into a gallery filled with the more soothing canvases of Matisse. "So, which one are you, Pash?" Lana asked as they settled on one of the benches in a corner of the gallery. "The person in front of the mirror or the reflection that doesn't match? Are you the gentle soul who seems to have accepted the horrible tragedy that befell his family? Or the wounded hero who, swept up in the churning narrative of dramatic events, comes upon his destiny and seizes it?"

"Well, I'm afraid I'm not quite up to seizing anything as of late, Lana," Pash replied with a weary sigh. "I'm just taking it one day at a time."

"Of course you are," Lana said, her tone dripping with empathy. "But you and your family bought into the *American* dream, and an *American* drone destroyed it. You know, after you ran out of the meeting that morning, Caitlin told me you'd been very angry, even vengeful, but I haven't seen it."

"Yes, that is true," Pash said somberly. "My emotions were quite raw and my anger extreme, but, fortunately, short lived."

"Well, I want you to know that if you've been keeping it to yourself because you thought I'd disapprove, you're wrong. I won't judge you, Pash. Nor would Caitlin. There must be a part of you that's crying out for justice . . . that wants to even the score."

Pash nodded, digesting it. "I don't believe I'm crying out for anything, Lana, but I do cry quite often," he replied, his eyes brimming with sadness. "Picasso used his extraordinary talent to express a penetrating insight. Mine, though perhaps not as profound, reflects my belief that vengeance should be left to God and justice to man and his institutions, and—since neither can give me back what I've lost—if I am ever to be at peace, I would be wise to accept what happened and move on."

Well, *that* went well! Lana thought sarcastically, her mind racing in search of a face-saving reply. If Picasso couldn't get Pash to take the bait, what could?! "Yes, Pash," she said, making her eyes glisten. "You are being very wise, and you do seem to be more at peace, and I apologize if anything I said upset you. I guess I just got caught up in the empathy I feel for what you've been going through. For what you . . . you . . ." She let it trail off as if she couldn't find the words and wiped a tear from her cheek.

"Please, Lana, I'm sure you were well intended," Pash said, his eyes coming alive with an idea. "If you really want to know who I am, you should go to Yemen, to the neighborhood in Sana'a where I grew up. Unfortunately, I can't take you there, but I *can* take you to Brooklyn! It has the largest Yemeni population in the United States!"

"Oh, Pash! What a great idea!" Lana said with feigned enthusiasm. *Whatever it takes!* she thought. *I'll go to Yemen and ride a camel down the main street of Sana'a stark naked if it'll get you to tell me your goddamn UI!*

Chapter Thirty-Nine

After leaving the Skillet, Katkov and Ruben piled into the Jeep and headed for Bethesda. Thirty minutes later they were south of Burning Tree at the turnoff that led to Levenger's estate.

"By the way," Katkov said offhandedly, "Agent Nichols told me the FBI never makes appointments. Assuming Levenger *does* have a collection of vintage dueling swords, sabers, whatever they're called, dare I ask about an *order na obysk?*"

"A who?"

"A search warrant. Even the FSB pretends to respect a citizen's right to privacy."

"So does the FBI," Ruben said with a snort. "But we have no evidence linking him to Tom's murder. So, no judge worth his wing tips would sign off on it."

"So, we need the evidence we're looking for before we can look for it?"

"Yeah, it's called a catch-22. Sometimes just asking for cooperation does the trick."

"Levenger's not the cooperative type, I'm afraid."

"We'll, there's the easy way and the hard way," Ruben said, guiding the Jeep into the courtyard between Julian's mansion and the fencing club. "It's his call."

Katkov stepped to the A/V security panel, thumbed the button, and identified himself when challenged. A moment later one of Julian's assistants came to the door and led the way to his office. The Asian markets were open and several traders sat staring at the rapidly changing data on Bloomberg terminals.

Tall, trim, and precise, his hair flowing back over his ears in perfect waves, Julian eyed them with undisguised displeasure. "You've come in the heat of the trading day this time, Mr. Katkov. Every minute I spend with you will cost me money—a lot of money—*beaucoup d'argent!*"

"We'll endeavor to keep your losses to a minimum, sir. We just have a—"

"Who are *you*?" Julian asked, cutting Katkov off as he shifted his steely gaze to Ruben in his leather bomber jacket and jeans. "And why are you here?"

"Special Agent Ruben Diaz, FBI, JTTF," Ruben replied, badging him. "The FBI agent who was killed was my partner. I'm looking for the bastards who murdered him."

"Well, you won't find them here," Julian snapped.

"We just have a few questions," Katkov said, stepping between them.

"*Très bien*, because I just have a few *minutes*," Julian fired back with a snarl.

"We understand you're into fencing, sir," Katkov prompted gently. It was obvious Ruben was on the verge of losing it, and Katkov realized he'd be wise to play good cop this time. "Is that correct?"

"That's one way of putting it. *Oui*."

"And that you're also a collector," Katkov said, raising a brow. "*Oui?*"

Julian nodded curiously. "Of many things."

"Might vintage dueling swords—épées, foils, sabers—be among them?"

Julian nodded again. "*Oui*, but what does that—"

"My partner's throat was slashed!" Ruben interrupted, his voice quavering with anger. "He was stuffed, naked, into the trunk of his car! And—"

"What does that have to do with me?!" Julian interrupted, matching his tone.

"He was investigating the illegal acquisition of an American railroad being brokered by you for the Kremlin!" Ruben fired back. "And he was a fencer. Microscopic bits of three-hundred-year-old steel were found embedded in his jawbone."

"Ah, *bien sûr*, therefore you wish to examine my collection. Correct?"

"Correct. And confiscate suspect weapons for DNA testing."

"I doubt that will be necessary," Julian countered with a smug smile, leading the way from the office. "But since examining my collection will disprove your scurrilous allegations, I've every reason to cooperate."

They were crossing the courtyard to the fencing club when Ruben leaned over to Katkov and whispered, "Told you."

The ping of electronic scoring machines and the metallic scraping of blades came from a few matches that were in progress. Julian led them down a circular staircase into an underground armorer's lair equipped with precision metalworking tools. Several vintage dueling weapons were spread across a worktable, where a fine-boned man in a suede apron was honing the elegantly engraved blade of a vintage saber.

"We have some visitors, Gilles," Julian said as they entered. Then, noticing the saber, he added, "That one seems to have come up even better than I expected."

Gilles nodded, gripped the saber in one hand, picked up a sheet of paper in the other, and sliced it into thin ribbons with a few flicks of his wrist.

"Excellent, Gilles. Now, we'll need you to open the vault, if you will."

Gilles stepped to a steel door and entered a numerical code on a security pad. It opened with a pneumatic hiss, revealing a long, narrow, climate-controlled room. Racks of vintage dueling foils, épées, and sabers, along with military long swords and a variety of medieval weapons that dated to the Crusades ran the length of the walls.

As Julian anticipated, Katkov and Ruben appeared staggered by the enormity of the task. "All yours, gentlemen," he said with feigned magnanimity. "If you'll show your search warrant to Gilles, he'll be happy to fetch the 'suspect weapons.'"

"We don't have a warrant," Ruben conceded grudgingly. "We were hoping to do this the easy way. There's always the hard way, the litigious way. It's your call."

"*Mais oui*. And I've already made it: *Facile* for me. *Difficile* for you," Julian said. Then, as if dealing with incompetent underlings, he added, "Leave the premises, obtain a search warrant, and make an appointment—with my attorney."

Ruben looked chagrined as Julian led them upstairs and outside to the courtyard. "Don't say it, Katkov," he warned as the door closed behind them. "*Silencio*."

Katkov suppressed a smile. "Rather shrewd son of a bitch," he said as they drove off. "Warrant or not, he knows we haven't a chance of examining all of them."

"Yeah, well, I can think of two other vintage sabers I wouldn't mind examining."

"And they're not in Levenger's vault, are they?" Katkov added.

"No. But I'm getting you checked in to the Diaz Hilton first."

Casa Diaz was on South Shore Drive in Reston on Lake Anne. "It's the fancy hacienda on the corner there with the Olympic-size pool, tennis courts, and putting green," Ruben said facetiously as the Jeep came through a turn and approached a mid-'60s split-level ranch situated in a grove of bare trees.

Katkov was laughing when something up ahead caught his eye. "Keep going!" he said, slouching down in his seat, "Keep going. Don't stop!"

"What? What the hell're you talking about?!"

"Green Mercedes in the trees beyond the turn. Keep going."

Ruben took the road that ran along the lakefront and pulled into a parking area that overlooked the choppy water. "Way to go, Katkov. You did good. *Muy bueno.*"

"When I was growing up, learning to spot the KGB was a rite of passage. Nothing's changed except the acronym."

Ruben nodded and called Julie. "Everything okay?"

"I'm fine. In case you're wondering the green sedan's been there for three hours."

"*Mierda.* Cancel our guest's reservation . . . Yeah, yeah I'll keep you posted." He hung up and turned to Katkov. "The boss is really going to be pissed. I don't have a clue where the hell I'm going to park you now."

Katkov's head tilted in thought. Actually, he had five women in his life, not four. He hadn't seen the one that had just come to mind in twenty years, but he knew he could trust her. "*I* have one . . . assuming she'll have me."

"An old flame, huh?"

"Rather more like an old fantasy. We worked on a case together."

Ruben looked incredulous. "She's on the job?"

Katkov nodded. "Deputy director of FinCEN. Couldn't tolerate being chained to a desk. I was her excuse to get back into the field. That was twenty years ago."

A knowing smile broke across Ruben's face. "You know the Bensonhurst Bombshell? I can't believe you worked a case with Gabby Scotto! Real piece of work."

Katkov nodded and grinned. "Sounds like you worked with her too."

"Drug-cartel thing. I was undercover. Gabby was following the money."

"I'm quite certain she was. We followed a half a billion in cash in a shipping container from Baltimore to Moscow via Havana."

"The lady can take care of herself. Any idea where she's at?"

Katkov shrugged. "I seem to recall a Christmas card. Ten years ago? She and her husband were building a house somewhere in Virginia. Near a river. Started with an A?"

"Arlington? Alexandria? Annandale?"

"Alexandria. I'm quite certain that was it."

"Maybe HR has something on her," Ruben said, tapping an icon on his phone. "Hey, hon, Ruben Diaz. How're you doing? . . . Tell me about it. Quick question: Gabriella Scotto. FinCEN. Ring a bell? . . . Yeah, yeah, hard to forget. Any contact info on file? . . . Great. I owe you one." He hung up and said, "She's been on indefinite leave for the last—" A texting chime interrupted him. Scotto's phone number and address in Alexandria were on the screen. He showed it to Katkov, who went about entering the data into his phone. "Take us about forty-five minutes. Better call and give her a heads-up."

"Not a terribly good idea, I'm afraid. I learned a long time ago that unpredictability is the key to longevity. I'll take a cab."

"No way. Where you go, I go, where I go, you go. Comprende?"

"*Da*, but that's why the *rezidentura*'s hit men are counting on you to lead them to me. I've been doing this a long time. Every once in a while I intercept a bullet or walk into a fist, but I always land on my feet. That said, should what you're planning go awry, I'd be on the next flight to Moscow. Ergo, I'd be wise not to participate."

"Bet your Russian ass," Ruben fired back. "Covert ops are best left to covert operatives."

Chapter Forty

The days were shortest now, and Midtown's canyons were awash in a harsh LED glare when Lana and Pash left the museum, catching the R train at Fifty-Seventh Street. It angled southeast beneath the city to Bay Ridge Avenue in Brooklyn. Winter had finally arrived, and a cold wind buffeted them as they walked the few blocks to Fifth Avenue, Little Yemen's Main Street, which was lined with two- and three-story prewar buildings. Most of the signs on storefronts and in shop windows were in Arabic. Residents were going about their daily routines. Some wore down-filled parkas or woolen coats over traditional Middle Eastern attire, others over clothing right out of the L.L.Bean catalogue. Many women wore headscarves, a few peered from behind veils.

"Something smells really good," Lana said, inhaling the heady aroma that came from a nearby restaurant. Its blue awning proclaimed YEMEN CAFÉ in English and Arabic. A card in the window boasted an "A" rating from the city's health department.

"It's hawaji. A traditional Yemeni spice," Pash said with a hint of pride. "That used to be a Scandinavian diner. I get coffee there every morning. The food is wonderful."

The café's interior was plain and familial. A row of sturdy tables ran along the side walls. A few customers sat chatting in Arabic over the hiss of cast-iron radiators. Photographs of Sana'a's Old City were hung on the yellowing walls, but the aroma coming from the kitchen more than compensated for the lack of ambiance.

Lana and Pash had just settled at a table when a middle-aged waiter in a stained apron approached. He greeted Pash by name, but his demeanor and harsh, disapproving tone during the exchange in Arabic that followed made Lana uncomfortable. Pash seemed to be holding his own and managed to have the last word, which softened the waiter's expression. He nodded to Lana, then gave them menus, took a deferential step back with a slight bow, and hurried off.

"What was that about?" Lana asked in a concerned whisper.

"He's my dear wife's uncle," Pash replied with a sad smile. "And though Islam obliges women to mourn their husbands but puts no such burden on men, he thought I was being disrespectful to her memory. I explained that you're a business associate, that I have no interest in having another wife in this life, and will be happily reunited with Safia in the next."

"So, I shouldn't worry your uncle will poison my food?" Lana joked in an awkward attempt at levity.

"I'll be your taster, if you wish," Pash replied, seeming distracted.

Lana spent a few moments scanning the menu. "It's all Arabic to me. Why don't you order for us. Pash?" she prompted when he didn't respond.

"Oh, forgive me, Lana. I'm afraid our discussion at the museum about seeking vengeance has suddenly taken hold of me. I keep getting this strange feeling that you had something specific in mind."

"No, no, not at all," Lana replied, pleased that he seemed to be circling the bait. "You remember me saying one day your life will have purpose and take on new meaning?"

"Of course I do," Pash replied curiously.

"Well, I just thought, perhaps, doing something to ensure your family won't be forgotten might be a good start. They gave their lives for their adopted country—indeed, were sacrificed by its government before they ever got here. No one knows. No one cares. It seems unfair, doesn't it?"

Pash emitted an ambivalent sigh. "Yes, I imagine it does, but there are no guarantees that life will be fair." He paused and tilted his head in reflection. "You know, there's an old Arabic saying: When you want everything, you lose everything. And I'm afraid I sowed the former and have reaped the latter."

"True, but you still have a right to even the score."

"Yes, but some rights are best left unclaimed. Vengeance is not mine, Lana. I've come to know myself and to accept it."

Lana was beside herself. What was the *kontrataka* of choice? she mused, hearing her mother's voice. *The truth! When all else fails, tell the truth!* "No, Pash, you're right, Vengeance isn't yours," she replied, letting her countenance soften. "That's exactly what I was hoping you'd say," she went on enigmatically, setting the hook. "I couldn't be happier."

Pash winced and looked baffled.

"I know that's confusing. Give me a chance to explain, okay?"

Pash's eyes widened with cautious insight. "You tested me again, didn't you?"

Lana lowered her eyes and nodded. "I'm sorry, I had no choice. A few days ago, one of our assets picked up intelligence that a terrorist organization is planning to strike the American homeland. It's raw data that has yet to be vetted, but if accurate, it represents a cyber threat with potentially catastrophic consequences."

Pash looked stunned. "My God, how awful."

Lana nodded grimly. "Didn't make my day either."

"Catastrophic is a frightening modifier. I can't imagine what the threat could be."

"And *I* can't tell you. It's been classified top secret. But I *can* tell you that I've been assigned to counter it, that it involves *our* work, and that, if and when the intel is verified and determined to be active, I'll be fighting a real-time move/countermove cyber war, and there's no way I can do it without your help." She gave him a moment to process it, then added, "As you can see, there was no way I could've shared this with you if you were blaming your misfortune on the United States and wanted to even the score." She found his eyes and held them as if pleading for confirmation. "I had to know, Pash. I hope you understand."

A tense moment passed before Pash blinked several times and nodded. "Yes, of course I do," he replied, his eyes brightening at a thought. "I guess I was right, wasn't I?"

"About what, Pash?"

"That you had something specific in mind I could do to memorialize my family."

Lana nodded. Her smile was beneficent. "Just remember, this is top secret, Pash. Tell no one. Not Carlsen or any other member of the Cyber-Borgen team. Not even Caitlin, if you happen to have contact with her. No one."

Chapter Forty-One

Katkov caught a cab at the stand in Reston City Center. Forty minutes later and seventy-five bucks poorer he was in Alexandria, a city of narrow streets lined with a charming mixture of period houses. Some were still decorated with Christmas lights and had evergreen wreaths on their doors. Scotto's Craftsman, with its peaked roof and brick pillars, was within sight of the Potomac on South Lee Street opposite Jones Point Park. Katkov had the driver drop him off next to its heavily wooded grounds. He flipped up the hood of his borrowed parka and made his way through the trees to a vantage point directly across the road from Scotto's house. The casement windows gave him a view of the main room, where she snuggled under a blanket in a lounge chair reading a book. A steaming mug sat on a side table. Katkov watched for a few moments, then called her.

"Ready to hop another freight?"

"What? Who is this?" Scotto asked, sounding annoyed by the intrusion.

"How many Russian men with British accents do you know who have grabbed you by the seat of your britches and hauled you up into a moving boxcar?"

Scotto rolled her eyes and scowled. "Katkov? Nikolai Katkov? No fucking way."

"Guilty as charged, I'm afraid."

"I don't know what you're after, but this isn't a good time for me."

"Nor for me. If you put that book down and come to the door, I'll explain."

Scotto's eyes arched in disbelief. "You fucking serious?"

"Yes, and if that's a mug of hot coffee, I'd love one. It's freezing out here."

Scotto pulled herself out of the chair and went to the door. Katkov was coming down the walkway with his suitcase and shoulder bag. The hollows beneath her eyes were gray. Her complexion was pale. And her hair unkempt. "Not a good time, indeed. I'm sorry to say, you appear rather . . . rumpled."

"You haven't exactly found the fountain of youth yourself," Scotto cracked, leading the way inside.

Katkov swept his eyes over the Stickley and Frank Lloyd Wright–style furnishings that had been carefully arranged beneath the cathedral ceiling. "And you aren't exactly living out of the trunk of your car any longer, are you?"

"No. And you're the last person I expected to find knocking on my door."

"That's what I said to the hit man who's trying to kill me."

"You shouldn't have opened the door," Scotto snapped snidely.

Katkov looked puzzled. He ran his fingers through his graying curls and followed her into the kitchen. "Am I detecting a certain lack of marital bliss in the air?" he wondered in an amused tone. "Dare I speculate your husband is pissed because you're still trashing vacations in the Caribbean to chase miscreants?"

"None of your fucking business," Scotto snapped, pouring coffee into a mug.

"In case you're wondering, I much prefer it black."

"Good because that's how you're getting it. I mean, what the hell gives you the right to come barging in here after twenty years and ask questions about my personal life? Drink your coffee, warm your bones, and get the hell out before I lose my . . . my . . ." She faltered, and her eyes welled. "I'm . . . I'm sorry, Katkov. Like I said, it's not a good time."

"Care to elaborate? Or am I really being thrown back out into the cold?"

Scotto ran a sleeve over her eyes. "Sit down and behave yourself." She took a moment to regroup, then lit a cigarette and inhaled deeply as if in search of sustenance. "Okay. Make it fast. What do you need?"

"One of *those,* for starters."

"Still hooked, huh?" Scotto said, tossing him the pack.

"And still sober." He lit a cigarette, adding to the smoky haze that hovered between them. "You're quite clearly not yourself, Gabby. We'll discuss my needs, but only after you tell me what's going on with yours."

Scotto sighed in concession. "You were right. It's Marty." She took another deep drag of her cigarette and exhaled slowly. "Son of a bitch went and died on me."

"Oh, oh my God, Gabby," Katkov said, the words running together into a long sigh. "I've quite obviously put my foot in it, haven't I? I'm sorry . . . I'm . . . I'm so sorry."

"Me too. Life was good. Really good. Marty's career took off. We bought this property. And he built his dream house. Every architect has one burning inside him. Then one day, something else started burning inside him." She dragged on her cigarette and sighed despondently. "He lasted about a year. I'll spare you the ugly details."

"The wound seems quite fresh . . ."

Scotto nodded solemnly. "Couple of weeks before Thanksgiving."

"I'm sorry. I'd no idea. I didn't mean to be so flippant."

"No way you could've known. It's been tough. Old habits are hard to break. I mean, I roll over in bed at night to snuggle with him. I make comments about the news to an empty chair. The other morning I took the newspaper back to bed with *two* mugs of coffee. I'm living with a ghost. Life's a bitch. I've been trying to pick up the pieces and get on with it. And look who the cat dragged in."

"Well, for better or worse, Gabby, history has a way of repeating itself. I just might be the answer to your prayers."

"Get over it, Katkov. I'm an atheist. So, who's trying to kill you this time?"

"Same bastards who assassinated my colleague at *Novaya Gazeta,* along with one of her Moscow sources and an FBI agent who had been in contact with her."

Scotto's eyes flared. "Jesus H. fucking Christ."

"No, actually it's Vladimir H. fucking Putin."

"Yeah, the little turd's been strutting his stuff lately, hasn't he?"

"Not to mention trying to buy an American railroad."

"Oh no," Scotto groaned. "No way. Not trains. Not again."

"Not to worry, we won't be riding the rails. It's a cybersecurity thing. I'm up to my knickers in it with some people at JTTF. One of them, an Agent Diaz, says he's worked with you."

"Ruben?" Scotto echoed, her expression brightening. "The bureau's answer to Don Quixote?"

"That's him. The murdered FBI agent was his partner. They were working to sting a Chechen counterfeiting operation, but—"

"The box-cutter gang," Scotto interjected. "Nasty bunch."

"That's what Agent Diaz thought at first, but we're both quite certain, now, it's connected to the other two Kremlin-sanctioned hits."

"I'll bet," Scotto said, chuckling at a thought. "And relentless investigative reporter that you are, you've worked your way to the top of the Kremlin's hit list."

"I'm afraid so. The JTTF team thinks I should be in a safe house."

"Good idea," Scotto said with a grin. "Wish I'd thought of it back when."

"Seriously, they decided to park me at Ruben's place—with his family—but the hit team was parked down the street when we got there. So . . ."

Scotto's eyes widened in disbelief. "You came here?!"

Katkov nodded sheepishly. "I'm not sure who I can trust, I'm afraid."

"Christ, you're a pain in the ass," Scotto said, becoming uneasy. "Ruben was as solid and smart as they come, but that was a lot of years ago, and the job has a way of changing people. I'd factor that in." She went to a window and studied the wooded landscape across the road. "All of a sudden I'm feeling a little exposed." She took her pack of cigarettes and directed Katkov into a den with shuttered windows. It was equipped with a multiscreen computer workstation, shelves stuffed with briefing binders, and tack boards covered with photographs, printouts, and notes from cases she had worked. Firearms, body armor, and night-vision goggles were neatly arranged behind the glass doors of a cabinet. Scotto opened it and removed a 9mm Glock .42. The double-action pistol was less than six inches long and weighed less than a pound. She ejected the magazine, checked the chamber, then slapped it back into the handgrip and set the weapon on a desk. "If you don't mind me asking," Scotto said, settling behind it. "These agents you're working with are putting it on the line 24/7 for their country—not to mention yours. What made you distrust them?"

"Information," Katkov replied, eyeing the pistol, "that's made me quite certain one of them is a Russian sleeper."

"Jeez, Katkov!" Scotto exclaimed, caught off guard. "You've always had a way of getting my attention. I'm listening."

By the time Katkov ran it all past her, Scotto felt as if she had just run a 10K. "Whew . . . can't imagine what you'd have shared if you trusted them."

"I had little choice at the time, I'm afraid. How's your Russian these days?"

"Rusty. Why?"

"I haven't shared *this* yet." Katkov slipped Grusha's memorial booklet from his shoulder bag, opened the cover, and handed it to Scotto. Her eyes narrowed at the sight of Nadia's handwritten note and cybercode:

Топ секретных файлов РЖД.

Якунина в глаза только.
Кибер код Н5Ы7Т0Е5П.

"What do you make of that?" Katkov prompted.

Scotto studied it for a moment, then, working it out as she went, said, "Top-secret RZD file—Yakunin's eyes only—Cybercode: N, Five, Y, Seven, T, Zero, E, Five, P."

"Not bad. I'm quite certain the op is imminent, and that code's the key to it."

Scotto nodded. Her eyes narrowed with concern. "Guess we'll just have to find a way to break it. Won't we?"

Chapter Forty-Two

The green Mercedes that had been parked opposite Casa Diaz was gone when Ruben returned from dropping Katkov at the taxi stand. "I'm back!" he called out as he came through the door. "Julie?" he prompted when there was no response. The dog glanced up from a bowl of kibble as Ruben circled through the kitchen and bounded up the stairs. He heard the shower and leaned into the bathroom. "I'm back," he called out again to avoid startling her. "Running late, aren't you?"

"Not really," she replied over the rush of running water. "Didn't want to be in here with that car out there."

"It won't be back."

"Why not?"

"Their target's gone," Ruben replied, eyeing her lithe figure through the steamy glass enclosure. "Need a hand in there?"

"Among other body parts," Julie replied with a seductive giggle, pressing her body against the wet glass.

They spent the afternoon making love, moving from the shower to the bed, and were cuddling beneath the comforter in the afterglow when Julie raised a brow. "You're working tonight," she said with a knowing smile.

Ruben nodded. "One-man op. Shouldn't take long."

"It better not," Julie countered, then, with a rueful sigh, she traced a fingertip across his cheek, and said, "Sorry, Rube. I take that back. Just be safe for me, and savor every minute of it, okay?" She knew her husband chafed at the time he spent at his workstation, at the brain-numbing analysis of Russian crime organizations, and at the endless strategy sessions and filing of reports. Fieldwork was in his genes, and tolerance for twelve-hour stakeouts in claustrophobic surveillance vans wasn't a dominant chromosome. He sorely missed the intrigue, the sense of danger of undercover work and clandestine operations, and, lying next to him, she realized the mere thought of the upcoming op had reinforced his sense of worth, not to mention his sex drive. "Those guys who were out there . . ." she said, her voice rising the way it always did when she wanted to get his attention.

"*Si?* What about them?"

237

"Well, I was just thinking, maybe . . . maybe, they were waiting for me to leave."

"*Por qué?*"

"So they could check out the garage," she replied, letting it hang there for a moment before pointedly adding, "You know, the place where we keep our luggage?"

"Oh," Ruben muttered, having missed the inference. "No, no, way they could know it's out there."

"I was hoping you'd say it wasn't."

"I know. Trust me. I'm working on it. One way or the other it's getting booked into the evidence vault."

"*Bueno.* The sooner the better."

"Yeah, well," Ruben said with a lascivious grin as he slipped a hand between her thighs. "My mind's on other things at the moment."

After dinner he drove to Foggy Bottom, parked in an underground garage in the GWU complex, and took a black plastic attaché from the Jeep. A baseball cap concealed his face from the District's CCTV cameras as he walked the few blocks to Queen Anne's Lane, where Lana's apartment was located. It took less than twenty seconds to pick the entry lock and slip into the lobby. A carpeted staircase led to Lana's apartment on the second floor. He slipped on surgical gloves and swept the door frame with a device that would have detected alarm sensors had any been present, then picked the lock and entered the apartment, taking a moment to let his eyes to adjust to the darkness. Lana's desk was piled with documents, communications gear, a laser-jet printer, keyboard, and twenty-inch monitor. Its webcam light, which would have been a compelling beacon in the darkness, was off. Ruben placed the attaché on the coffee table and opened it. Among the items in its well-organized interior were two evidence-collection kits—one for latent fingerprints and the other for DNA samples—an array of precision hand tools, and an LED headlamp.

The latter projected an intense beam on the vintage sabers as Ruben approached the fireplace. He removed one from the cradle on the mantel and brushed black magnetic powder on the grip and upper part of the scabbard, but it raised no prints. He removed all traces of the powder with a magnetized wand, then slipped the saber from the scabbard. Its razor-sharp blade appeared pristine. Not the slightest trace of dried blood was visible, nor was the scent of a bleaching agent present. He dipped a DNA swab into a vial of sterile water and ran it the length of the blade's honed edge. Though no traces of blood appeared, he slipped the swab into a collection vial and set it aside.

He was about to return the saber to its scabbard when he was struck by an intriguing thought: Had the bloody saber been slipped back into its scabbard immediately after use and scrubbed at a later time? Improvising, he taped the stem of a fresh swab to the edge of the blade, letting it extend past its tip, then moistened it with sterile water and slowly slipped the blade into the scabbard almost to the hilt, then moved it, gently, this way and that as he withdrew it. His eyes widened at the sight of a pale, rusty-colored smear on the swab. He removed it from the blade and sealed it in a sterile tube, then slipped the saber into its scabbard and returned it to the cradle atop the fireplace. He repeated the procedures on the second saber, with similar results, and was returning it to its scabbard when his phone began vibrating against his chest. He set the saber aside, took the phone from a pocket in his field vest, and winced at the sight of Lana's caller ID. Was she back in the District?! On the street approaching her apartment?! "Hey, what's going on, Amtrak?" he asked, trying to sound nonchalant. "Where the hell are you?"

"Heading back on the train."

"I thought you were going to be up there for a couple of days?"

"Went faster than I thought," Lana chirped, settled comfortably in one of the Acela's first-class loungers. "Turned out great. So, how'd it go with our boy?"

"You mean *before* we spotted the hit team parked near my house, or *after*?"

"Chrissakes!" Lana exclaimed. "These Russian bastards mean business."

"Bet your ass they do."

"Forget *my* ass, dammit, and tell me about Katkov's!"

"It's in protective custody, so to speak."

"What the hell does that mean?"

"He parked himself in Alexandria with a federal agent who lives down there."

"Scotto. FinCEN. Right?" Lana fired back.

"How do you know that?"

"Their little adventure turned up in his entry-review protocol. Damn near twenty years ago. She worked a Russian money-laundering scam he was covering."

"Worked one with me too."

"Well, at least he's in her hair and out of ours. See you at the shop first thing."

"Yeah, give us a chance to catch up," Ruben said, pocketing the phone. He returned the second saber to the cradle above the fireplace, packed up both test kits, and made certain every item on the table and mantel were exactly as they were when he arrived. Katkov had all but convinced him Lana was a Russian sleeper embedded in JTTF, turning the vague feeling in his gut that she had killed Tom into one of absolute certainty. He hurried from Lana's apartment, anxious to get the evidence that could prove it to the lab.

Chapter Forty-Three

"What say we try the easy, obvious way first?" Scotto suggested. She typed the cybercode—N5Y7T0E5P—into a Google search window and hit Enter, which produced: *Your search did not match any documents. Suggestions: Make sure all words are spelled correctly. Try different keywords. Try more general keywords.*

Entering just the letters *NYTEP* produced: *about 12,800 results (0.54 seconds) Did you mean NYATEP?* Among them were websites for "New York's Next Top Event Planner" and the "New York Tar Emulsion Project" in the 1920s.

Entering just the numerals "5705" produced: *15,500,000 results (.41 seconds).* Among them were contact information for several physicians, a website for the Powers of Arbitrator New York Consolidated Laws, and one for OSHA accident investigations.

"Maybe it's a date," Scotto said. Entering May 7, 2005, produced: *53,700,000 results (0.47 seconds).* Among them were birthday facts, horoscope projections, and famous people born on that date. No notable events were listed.

"Well, that went well," Katkov said with a laugh. "You know, it rather reminds me of strategic game moves. Chess, for example. N7 to Y5. T0 to E5, et cetera."

"Yeah, yeah, et cetera. That's it," Scotto joked. "Chances are the Kremlin's geek squad invented an encryption key for whatever game they're playing."

"If I'm right about Agent Nichols being a sleeper, they're not playing a game."

Scotto bit a lip and nodded. "Speaking of sleepers, I don't know about you, but I'm beat. Time to go hug my pillow. In the meantime, I've got a—"

"Come on, Gabby," Katkov snapped. "You know how the Krem operates. They've already liquidated three people. They're protecting an endangered op. I mean—"

"Hey, hey, lighten up," Scotto interrupted. "While we're sleeping on it, I've got a couple of code-breaking programs that'll be *working* on it. Okay?"

"Whatever you say," Katkov replied with a shrug.

Scotto entered the cybercode into each program's search window, narrowed the parameters to railroad-related concepts: words, phrases, terminology, and events, took the 9mm Glock from the desk, and strode off. "Bathroom's through that door. Sleep tight."

Katkov spent a restless night on the foldout sofa, one eye on the monitors where the decrypting programs were running endless permutations. Early the next morning, he was dragging on a Marlboro and staring at the data-filled monitors when Scotto entered the den, carrying two mugs of coffee. She was dressed for action: jeans, boots, turtleneck, and the Glock, riding on her hip. Her eyes were brighter. A bit of color had returned to her cheeks, and her hair was damp from the shower. "Morning . . ."

"Morning," Katkov echoed, eyeing the two mugs. "One of those for me?"

Scotto broke into a wistful smile. "Yeah, guess it makes a little more sense than when I'm alone."

"*Are* you alone? I mean, no family, no . . . no . . ." Katkov winced, letting it trail off.

"Children?" Scotto prompted with a shake of her head. "Never part of the game plan. Hard to be chasing after toddlers and miscreants at the same time. You?"

Katkov sipped his coffee, then responded with a hesitant nod. "A daughter . . . with Grusha. Michaela. She's twenty-one. Getting married in the spring."

"So, you and Grusha were. . . ?" Scotto prompted, splaying her hands.

"Young lovers," Katkov replied. "She told me the same day those bastards killed her. Mika doesn't know. I'm Dyadya Nikasha to her."

"Uncle Nikolai."

Katkov nodded. "I'm giving her away at the wedding—assuming I live long enough."

"Oh dear." Scotto sighed as she settled at the keyboard and began scrolling through the results. Secret Code Breaker had produced ten decryptions of N5Y7T0E5P that were rated from -1.122 through -2.567 in descending degrees of certainty. Among the results were N5A7D0 T5H, F7 T5H0E5 O and I7C5K0 T5R.

Katkov and Scotto stared at the data, shaking their heads. "Moving right along," she said, scrolling through a glossary of railroad terms. None contained any of the code's numerals—7505. Each started with one of its letters—NYTED.

E: Ejector, Electric Multiple Unit (EMU). Electro-Motive Diesel (EMD).

N: Narrow gauge. Northern type. Notch 8 or Run 8.

P: Permissive signal. Piston. Positive Train Control (PTC). Prairie type 2-6-2.

T: Tank car. Texas type 2-10-4. Through routing, Track circuit. Transition motor.

Y: Yard. Yardmaster. Yellow thing.

A list of the ten largest railroad companies in North America followed: Union Pacific. BNSF. CSX. Norfolk Southern. Canadian National. Canadian Pacific. Kansas City Southern.

"Last but not least," Scotto announced, "The Vigenère Cipher Codebreaker. It's an algorithm that decrypts codes written in the Roman alphabet and the numbers one to twenty-six."

"That's more like it," Katkov enthused. "What is an algorithm, anyway?"

"A set of problem solving instructions that tells the computer what to do and how to do it," Scotto replied, squinting at the deciphering key—N=5 Y=13 7=U T=1 0=O E=18 7=U P=6—that had transposed the cybercode N5Y7T0E5P to an equally puzzling 5N13U11O1846. "I take the problem-solving part back. You know," Scotto said, taking a deep breath and tilting her head in thought, "I'm thinking, maybe it's time we got JTTF into this. Anyone come to mind?"

"Yes. A brilliant Amtrak cybercop who just happens to be a code-writing whiz."

"Wait, don't tell me: Agent Nichols—who you and Ruben suspect is the sleeper."

Katkov nodded and ran a hand through his graying curls in frustration. "Anyone over there you *trust*?"

"Agent Diaz," Katkov replied without missing a beat. "I'm aware of what you said, but we've a rather good chemistry."

"And the boss? I mean, Dick Farrell's got more smarts and more integrity than just about anybody I've run across in this game. Not to mention the agency's decrypting programs can do in a day what takes mine a week."

"Really?" Katkov exclaimed, suddenly energized. "Best take yes for an answer."

"Best give Ruben a heads-up," Scotto said, mimicking him. "He'll be—"

The ring of Katkov's phone interrupted her. "Guess who?" he said, glancing at the screen. "Thought you'd forgotten about me. I'm quite crushed."

"Mission accomplished," Ruben reported. "That ought to brighten your day."

"The warrant for Levenger's collection?" Katkov prompted.

"No," Ruben groaned. "The forensics sweep on Nichols's sabers. Figured it'd be smart to put the warrant on hold till we get the results from the lab. So, how goes it down there? You two getting along? Another snooze on the sofa?"

"What do *you* think?" Katkov replied with a laugh. "I was about to call you. I'm in possession of some rather significant information. Scotto suggested we get together with you and Farrell. Hold on." He raised a brow and gave the phone to Scotto.

"Agent Diaz . . ." Scotto enthused, drawing it out. "Been a while . . ."

"Yeah, not much has changed. Up to my ass. How about you?"

"Well, it isn't every day a Russian journalist knocks on my door with a Kremlin cybercode that needs to be cracked. Looks like a real game-changer. We're thinking it's the key to a major code-red covert op."

Ruben's eyes widened with alarm. "To a *what*?!"

"You heard me," Scotto fired back, "We have no fucking clue as to vector or target and, therefore, no fucking choice but to assume launch is imminent. So give Farrell a fucking heads-up. We'll be there in less than an hour." She gave the phone to Katkov, crossed to the shuttered windows that overlooked the street, and peered through the slats. "What was the color of that sedan staking out Ruben's place?"

"Green," Katkov replied. "Green Mercedes."

"Second time it's driven by. I spotted it from the kitchen before. Couple of guys with thick necks and shaved heads."

"Not quite how I like to start my day."

"I figure they're trying to figure out how to come at us. So before they do—pack up. We're outta here."

Katkov gathered his gear. Scotto tugged a barn jacket from a hook in the mud room en route to the garage, and they piled into her Land Rover. Moments later, she was accelerating down South Lee. "So much for plan A," she said with a glance to the mirror. "They're right on our tail," she went on, making a beeline for Memorial Parkway that ran north toward the District. "It's your phone. They're GPS-tracking it."

"Bastards," Katkov growled. "So much for your Constitution's precious right to privacy."

"The guys who wrote it couldn't spell 'Geographical Positioning System,' let alone imagine it," Scotto cracked. "Shut it down and remove the SIM card." She pointed to the dash panel in front of him, and added, "And open that when you're finished."

"The glove box?"

"It's not a glove box," Scotto replied as Katkov went about disabling his phone. "It's the field agent's emergency catch-all. The only gloves in there are made of latex. There's a phone in there somewhere. Don't use it unless ten guys with guns are chasing you. Number 1 auto-dials me. Number 2 auto-dials 911."

"What's 3, the coroner?" Katkov said, slipping the phone into his bag.

"There's a black metal cylinder in there too. Find it."

Katkov rummaged in the glove box and came out with a silencer.

Scotto pulled the Glock from its holster and handed it to him. "Screw it on that."

"You're going to challenge these thugs?"

Scotto nodded. "At the next stoplight."

Traffic was moderate as the Rover approached the Madison Street intersection, joining a line of vehicles waiting for the light to change. The Green Mercedes was several vehicles behind it. Scotto took the Glock from Katkov, got out, and walked swiftly past them, holding the pistol behind her thigh until she reached the Mercedes, then opened fire. In the time it would take to say *pffft, pffft, pffft, pffft, pffft* she fired five shots: one into the right front tire, two through the distinctive grille into the engine block, and one into the left front tire, one through the center of the windshield that crackled like a network of spider webs—and hurried back to the Rover.

"You actually terminated them?" Katkov asked in astonishment as the light changed and they drove off.

"Crossed my mind," Scotto replied, matter-of-factly as the sound of blaring horns rose behind them and smoke seeped from beneath hood of the crippled Mercedes that was blocking the road. "But whacking them isn't as much fun as frustrating them."

Chapter Forty-Four

The return trip on the Acela always seemed to take twice as long as the trip to New York, and it was nearly midnight when Lana got back to her apartment. The tense day had ended well, and she was confident that, when faced with the need to prevent a catastrophic cyberattack, Pash would reveal his unique identifier.

Five hours had long been her default sleep pattern, and she made a beeline for her lifesaving espresso machine as she did every morning upon awakening. Double-shot in one hand, cell phone in the other, she left the kitchen and was crossing the living room when something caught her eye. She paused, then stepped to the fireplace. One of vintage sabers in the cradle atop the mantel wasn't tight into its scabbard. Lana was certain that after Levenger's armorer cleansed the murder weapon—wiping down its blade with bleach, scrubbing it with detergent, and washing it with steaming water to remove the scent of chlorine—she had slipped it and its mate fully into their scabbards, the underside of each guard tight to its mouth. A hollowness began growing in her stomach. She moved swiftly to her desk, settled in front of the computer, and clicked on Security Program, selecting Video Surveillance from a dropdown menu.

Unlike those who stick a Post-it or piece of tape over the lens on their computers to prevent hackers from observing them, Lana had state-of-the-art systems in place to ward off such threats, and having programmed the webcam to serve as the all-seeing eye of a motion-sensitive surveillance system, she had placed a black adhesive-backed dot over its pilot light to prevent it from alerting an intruder that the camera was activated.

Lana bit a lip as the video began to play out on the screen: A man in a baseball cap, carrying a black attaché, crossed the darkened living room, which, bore no signs of being burgled. Indeed, it appeared untouched, as did the rest of the apartment, and though her initial discovery had caused her to suspect that the sabers might, somehow, have been tampered with, she was shaken to her core when the intruder—who donned a headlamp before making his way to the fireplace and engaging in his evidence-gathering activity—turned out to be Ruben.

Lana knew that he had been nursing a gut feeling about what had happened to Tom and had teased her, mercilessly, about her vintage sabers, but having planted the box cutter with Tom's blood on it in the trunk of his car, she had underestimated the depth of Ruben's suspicion, and never imagined that he would take such drastic action.

Had he shared his suspicions with Farrell? Lana wondered, her eyes riveted to the screen where Ruben was, busily, dusting for prints and swabbing for DNA. Had the boss approved his clandestine evidence-gathering expedition? Had Ruben mentioned it to Katkov? Her level of anxiety had risen, steadily, as the video progressed, but the sight of Ruben taping a DNA swab to one of the blades and slipping it deep into its scabbard sent it off the charts. *No! No! Oh my God, no!* she thought, struck by a terrifying thought. Had she, in the adrenaline-charged moments of the aftermath, slipped the bloody saber into its scabbard?! Prior to removing all traces of Tom's blood and DNA from the blade?! Had she just watched Ruben obtain a sample of blood that the lab would certify contained Tom's DNA?! Her neatly crafted plan was coming apart at the seams, threatening to blow her cover and, ultimately, her ability to execute the op. She was pushing back in the chair, expecting her time-proven equanimity to kick in and counter the unnerving surge of adrenaline when her phone rang. Lana stared at the caller ID for a tense moment before picking it up. "Axel?" she said in a fragile voice.

"Yeah, hi, it's me. Sorry if I woke you, but I wanted to catch you first thing."

"No, no I had a mouthful of coffee. Is there a problem or something?"

"On the contrary. Caitlin called last night. Turns out her father's coronary wasn't as serious as they thought. He's going to be okay."

"Wow, that's . . . that's fantastic," Lana said, sounding like she meant it. "You can wake me anytime for news like that."

"The best part is Cait gets in this afternoon. She'll need a little time to get up to speed, but she's a quick study. I've no doubt she'll be match-tough for installation and shakedown."

Lana stifled a gasp, glad Carlsen couldn't see her reaction. "That's . . . that's great, but after all she's been through . . . I mean, the program's changed dramatically. She'll have lot of catching up to do. Rest assured Pash and I have it in hand if she can't."

"Hey, I don't mean to take anything away from you guys, but Amtrak was Cait's baby from the get-go. I think it'll do her good to see it through."

"I'm sure you're right," Lana said with an apprehensive roll of her eyes. "We're good to go at this end."

"Great. See you tomorrow."

Lana hung up and stared at the surveillance video on the computer screen, where Ruben was packing up his equipment. "Fuck, fuck, fuuuuck!" she exclaimed in an exasperated shriek.

The video ended. The computer screen went black. Lana stared at it, taking a moment to regain her composure, then, took several deep breaths and texted her mother: *911! Must meet at J's ASAP!*

Kate replied, *J hosting tournament in Montreal. 10:30 departure. Meet at Signature instead.*

Lana knew exactly what that meant, and wasted no time heading for the shower.

Chapter Forty-Five

Dick Farrell kicked back in his desk chair in astonishment at what he had just heard. "Are you kidding me? The Kremlin has a sleeper in JTTF? In *my* shop?!"

Ruben nodded solemnly. "That's how it looks, sir."

"How the hell do you know that?"

"Katkov," Ruben replied. "Grafinskaya put it in an email to Tom but didn't send it. Katkov found and forwarded it to him. When *he* was killed, Nichols—"

"Took over the case," Farrell interrupted. "Why didn't she put it on my radar?"

"Whoever it is, I figure, she didn't want to alert them. I'd've done the same."

"Makes three of us. You think Nichols knows who it is?"

Ruben shook his head no. "I'm looking at a suspect, but I'm waiting on a forensics report that will prove whether or not I have it right."

"Forensics on what?"

"A possible murder weapon. I dusted it for prints, came up empty, took some DNA swabs too. A couple had visible stains that could be human blood."

Farrell looked puzzled and countered, "The *box cutter* had Tom's blood on it."

Ruben waggled a hand. "My gut's telling me it was planted."

"And this *possible* just fell into your lap? What is it? Where'd it come from?"

"I can't tell you that, sir."

Farrell's eyes burned like angry lasers. "Don't play games with me, Ruben."

"I'm not, sir. I don't want to reveal the suspect's identity until I'm certain."

Farrell's eyes brightened with insight. "Because the suspect's in-house . . ."

Ruben nodded. "The tar goes on a lot easier than it comes off."

"Okay, I get it. But I want that lab report today."

"It's priority one, sir. I'll keep on it."

"Keep on Katkov too till Nichols gets back, and then—"

"She's back. Wrapped up the cybersecurity thing faster than she thought."

"Good. Speaking of Katkov, where the hell is he?"

"A safe house," Ruben replied apprehensively, "in Alexandria."

"I thought I told you to park him at your place."

"You *did*, sir. But a wet team was waiting to welcome him to the neighborhood. He and his minder are on their way in now."

"His minder?"

Ruben nodded. "Gabby Scotto. Remember her?"

"Yeah, a lot of steel in her, but a real pain in the ass. How'd she get into this?"

"She and Katkov stung the Russian mob for half a billion . . . before your time. They've been trying to crack a cybercode he came up with. I'm thinking it's connected to the sleeper."

Farrell's brows went up, "Christ. Soon as they get here, we pick Katkov's brain, and—" A texting ping interrupted him. He glanced to his phone. "We won't have to wait long. They're on their way up."

Moments later, Celia knocked and showed Katkov and Scotto into the office.

"Old home week, hey?" Farrell said with a chortle. "Looking good, Gabby."

"You too, sir. Not to mention Don Quixote, here."

"My wife thinks *I'm* more insane than *he* was."

Scotto laughed. "Smart lady . . ."

Farrell rolled his eyes, then locked them onto Katkov's. "Talk to me about this sleeper. Why do you think he/she, whoever the hell it is, is in my shop?"

"As you know, Agent Jones contacted my colleague about a story she wrote. Shortly thereafter, they were *both* terminated."

"Because they threatened to expose the sleeper," Farrell prompted.

Ruben winced. "Looks like it's more than that, sir. Katkov's thinking they threatened a code-red, priority-one, Kremlin op that the sleeper's running."

Farrell looked stunned. "A code-red . . . priority-one . . . Kremlin op?" he repeated, his volume rising with each phrase. "And everybody knows about it but the boss?!"

"That's on me," Katkov said. "Agent Diaz and I have developed a rapport, which led me to confide in him even though Agent Nichols said doing so might—"

"Tip off the sleeper. I know," Farrell interjected. "Now, assuming it's *not* me, what's the target? Do we know?"

"Nothing, sir. Not a clue," Ruben replied.

Farrell groaned and shifted his look to Katkov. "You said this guy Levenger is brokering an illegal takeover of one of our railroads for the K, and that he's a party to the CP/CSX merger talks. Anything in that?"

"I was quite certain there was, until the merger fell through." Katkov took a sheet of paper from his bag. The single typewritten line read TOP SECRET RZD FILE—YAKUNIN'S EYES ONLY—CYBERCODE: N5Y7TOE5P. I'm convinced cracking that code will provide the answer."

"Because?" Farrell challenged.

"Because the Kremlin terminated my colleague's source for passing that to me."

Scotto nodded emphatically. "That code's the key. We need to break it."

Farrell's brows arched. "You knew about it too. Why didn't I?"

"Look," Scotto said, trying not to sound impertinent. "It's no secret Katkov's at the top of the Kremlin's hit list. So he—"

"Gabby, Gabby," Katkov interrupted, shifting his look to Farrell. "I doubt I'm at the *top* of their list. But Agent *Diaz* did engage one of their hit men in the Metro, and Agent *Scotto* was forced to engage several more this morning. In addition, you have a sleeper in your shop. So, as you might imagine, I felt the need to confide in people I've come to trust."

"Make sure I'm one of 'em, dammit!" Farrell snapped. "If you have a problem with that, I'll take your security pass right now and book you on the next flight to Moscow. So . . . are we good to go?"

Katkov looked over the top of his glasses and nodded emphatically.

"Moving right along," Scotto said. "We ran that through a couple of code-breaking programs." She indicated the page with the typewritten code. "Came up empty. I figured one of your geek squads would have a better shot at it."

Farrell nodded. "We already have a geek on this. It's right in Nichols's wheelhouse. Get on the horn. And tell her to get her ass in here."

Ruben was trapped: He didn't want to reveal Lana was his suspect, but if he was right, she was the last person he'd entrust with the cybercode. He almost blurted: *Not until I get that lab report!* But he bit a lip and made the call.

Farrell glanced at his monitor and checked his inbox. The news crawl below read: TRUMP DOUBLES-DOWN ON MUSLIM BAN. TAKES LEAD IN GOP PRIMARY FIELD.

Lana's Prius was moving fast on the Dulles access road when her mobile rang. She saw Ruben's caller ID, ignored the call, and took the Windsock Drive off-ramp to the Signature Flight Support complex where private and corporate aircraft were housed and serviced. Lana badged the security personnel at the Departures Desk and was cleared to board Julian's Gulfstream. She dashed across the tarmac and up the airstair built into the jetliner's door, joining him and Kate in its posh lounge. "Brought a little entertainment," she said, plugging a flash drive into her laptop.

"Sneaky bastard, isn't he?" Kate prompted as the video of Ruben doing his forensics sweep of Lana's vintage sabers played out.

Julian looked more puzzled than concerned. "As I recall, Gilles thoroughly scrubbed your blade. It would be impossible for Agent Jones's DNA to be detected. I fail to see the problem."

"The scabbard," Lana fired back tersely. "I can't remember if I sheathed the saber before Gilles scrubbed it. Do either of you?"

Kate shook her head no. "It was all a blur then, and still is, now. I've no idea."

"Nor I," Julian replied, visibly concerned. "If you *did* sheathe, if they *did* get a sample of his DNA from the scabbard—" He gave an ominous sigh.

"I'm burned."

Julian scowled, his mind racing for a few moments before his eyes brightened. "You can execute the op from anywhere with a laptop. *Oui?*"

"*Mais oui. Anywhere.* Long as I can get a Wi-Fi or cellular connection."

"We should pull her out now," Kate declared. "Take her with us. We have more safe houses in Montreal than tacky French bistros. No way they could track her there."

"Not going to work," Lana said decisively. "I'm still missing a key piece of data, and there's no way I can pull this off without it."

"You mean the unique identifier, don't you?" Kate prompted.

"Yeah, and I'll never get it if I vanish before the new security system's installed."

Julian looked puzzled. "I was under the impression the Picasso in my office made something click? That it, somehow, held the key to manipulating him."

"Makes two of us, but it didn't. So . . ." Lana paused and smiled at Kate. "I told the truth, told Pash that a massive terrorist cyberattack is in the works, and that I can't counter it without him. He sees it as a way to honor his family and is eager to help."

Julian's brows arched. "We're thirty-six hours from launch. That's a very fine line. Is Agent Diaz aware of this video? Or that you know he suspects you?"

Lana shook her head. "He doesn't have a clue."

"Excellent," Julian concluded. "That's your advantage. Make use of it. Return to headquarters and take care of business—our business."

"How long will you be gone?"

Julian waggled a hand. "It's a two-day tournament, and the reception is tonight, but it's possible the flight crew has timed out."

Lana packed up her laptop and left the aircraft, returning Ruben's call en route to her car. "It's me," she said when he answered. "Sorry, late night. I was in the shower. What's going on?"

"I'm with the boss," Ruben replied. "Katkov and Scotto are here. We're having a group grope on a cybercode. He wants your input."

"Great. On my way."

"She's coming in," Ruben reported. He was pocketing his phone when Celia entered with a sense of urgency and handed him a file folder.

"The lab said you're waiting on this."

Ruben scanned the data. His eyes fell. His posture slackened. "My suspect's been cleared. A couple of the DNA samples were clean. The others were too degraded to produce any meaningful—"

"Degraded?" Farrell interrupted. "You said the stains looked like human blood."

"*Sí*. They *were* human blood," Ruben replied, disappointed his hunch hadn't paid off, but strangely relieved that the evidence didn't implicate Lana as Tom's killer. "Three hundred-year-old human blood."

"What the hell kind of weapon was it? A medieval disemboweling claw?" Farrell cracked, hurrying to add, "Don't answer that. You made the right call."

"Looks like it's back to square one," Scotto said, sounding frustrated.

"Not exactly," Katkov said, his expression brightening. "We still have the cybercode."

"Yeah," Farrell said with a clap of his hands. "And I'm counting on Nichols to crack it."

Chapter Forty-Six

Katkov, Ruben and Scotto were in a conference room pondering the cybercode—*N5Y7T0E5P*—along with other phrases they had written on a white board when Lana arrived. "Sorry, got here as fast as I could," she said with a glance at the data: *Top Secret. Yakunin's eyes only. RZD cybercode. RZD = Russian Railroad Corp. Levenger. Plot to take over an American railroad. CSX. Amtrak. Code red, priority one, Kremlin op.*

"You must be Agent Nichols," Scotto said, extending a hand. "Gabby Scotto, deputy director FinCEN. I've heard a lot about you."

"Uh-oh," Lana said with a laugh. "That can be a disadvantage in our business."

"Not when it comes to cracking that," Ruben said, stabbing a finger at N5Y7T0E5P on the whiteboard. "Boss said it's right in your wheelhouse."

"A real brain teaser, huh?" Lana said with a laugh. "I love puzzles. Looks like fun."

Katkov burned her with a look. "I'm sure the young woman the Kremlin terminated for passing that to me would find it hard to agree."

"Sorry, just a figure of speech," Lana said, managing to sound remorseful.

Katkov absolved her with a nod. "Keep in mind, it wasn't because she threatened to expose the sleeper, but for—"

Lana looked surprised. "The sleeper?" she interrupted, scolding Katkov with a look. "Sounds like you let the cat out of the bag."

"With good reason. As I was saying, she wasn't terminated to protect the sleeper, but to protect a code-red, priority-one op that the sleeper is about to launch."

"What?" Lana exclaimed, having no trouble appearing to be shocked. "Sorry, that's really scary. I'd no idea. Do we know what we're up against?"

"We will when you crack that cybercode," Katkov replied.

"Oh boy," Lana sighed, sounding overwhelmed. "I'm installing Amtrak's new security system with Cyber-Borgen tomorrow, and I'm running the preinstallation punch list this afternoon, but I'll give it a shot in my spare time."

Katkov offered her the typed copy of the code. "This might come in handy."

"N5Y7T0E5P," Lana recited as if memorizing it. "Burned onto my hard drive. Guess I better get cracking, huh?" She gathered her things and headed for the door. "Pun intended!" she called back as it closed after her.

"Any thoughts?" Katkov prompted.

"Her usual perky self," Ruben replied with an ambivalent shrug.

Katkov nodded. "She didn't seem at all threatened. Quite oblivious, actually."

"Too oblivious," Scotto retorted. "Both of you suspect she's the sleeper and killed Agent Jones, right? But the lab report just cleared her. Why am I picking up signals neither of you believe it?"

"For the same reason you don't," Katkov said. "Because my gut instinct is telling me otherwise."

"And because I'm pretty damn sure I can prove it," Ruben snapped.

Katkov shot him an incredulous look. "Prove it? How might you do that?"

"Don't ask," Ruben replied, annoyed with himself. "I shouldn't've said it. Both of you, just forget that I ever—" His phone rang interrupting him.

"Nichols with you?" Farrell asked in an urgent tone when Ruben answered.

"No, she just left with the cybercode. Why?"

"Got something hot. Stay put. I'm on my way."

Lana felt more anxious than threatened when she left the conference room. The launch date was close, but the target and the forces she would be unleashing to destroy it were converging at a point in time that was inexorably fixed. She went into one of the supply rooms, locked the door, and called Pash. "Can you talk?"

"I'm briefing Caitlin with Axel, but I can step aside . . ."

"I've got bad news," Lana said in a trembling voice. "The intel has been vetted and verified. We could be under a devastating cyberattack at any time."

"Oh dear," Pash whispered. "I'll do whatever I can to help."

"I know you will, Pash. I need you here with me."

"I'll be there. The entire team's coming this evening. Caitlin too, of course."

"I know, but we have a lot of work to do that can't wait until then. There's an Acela at noon. Gets in about three. Can you make it?"

"I . . . I guess," Pash replied, caught a little off-guard. "Yes, yes, I'll be on it."

"Good. I'll meet you at Union Station. Tell Carlsen I need help running the preinstallation punch list." She ended the call and made another.

Levenger's Gulfstream was in the air when Kate's phone rang.

"Julian was right," Lana said when she answered. "I just met with Katkov, Diaz, and a new player, an Agent Scotto. There was talk of a sleeper and a Kremlin op, but no mention of DNA swabs. They actually gave me the cybercode to crack."

"Sounds like you've got it under control."

"Seems so. But I need a little field support. The *rezidentura* owes us one for going rogue on Katkov in the Metro. Julian can arrange it with a phone call. Put him on."

Katkov, Ruben, and Scotto hadn't a clue as to what was coming when Farrell blew into the conference room, brandishing a folder. "The background report on our favorite international deal broker," he announced, having little trouble getting their attention. "Julian Levenger. Born 1949, Montreal, Canada. Mother Russian. Father French Canadian. He's fluent in French, Russian, and English. Finance major McGill University. MBA Harvard University. Began his career at the Bank of Montreal in Mergers and Acquisitions. Raised money for the 1976 Summer Olympics. Sponsored Katya Nikolshevskaya, who was a member of the USSR's Olympic Women's fencing team when she defected to the West."

"Nikolshevskaya?!" Katkov blurted, breaking the stunned silence. "She Americanized it."

Farrell winced. "Not the first time the K used a defector to plant an agent."

"Yeah, and her fucking daughter followed in her footsteps," Ruben cracked.

"Their fucking daughter," Farrell corrected. "Svetlana. Born Boston Mass, 1981. Mother: Katya Nikolshevskaya. Father: Julian Levenger. He was running the bank's M&A operations in Bean Town at the time, went on his own in the late '80s."

"So Nichols is a genuine born-in-the-USA American," Scotto said with a smirk.

Farrell nodded dispiritedly. "Their documents had to be flawless."

"KGB forgers were writing the book on it back then," Katkov said with crisp authority. "But this information was there for anyone to find. Why didn't it turn up before now?"

"No way it didn't," Scotto replied. "But it would've been meaningless back then."

Ruben looked baffled. "But rising through the ranks . . . Amtrak to the bureau to JTTF, Nichols would've been fluttered more times than Aldrich fucking Ames."

"And lied through her teeth each time," Scotto chimed in. "Obviously she's real good at keeping that little stylus on the straight and narrow."

"I put Tom onto her," Ruben said, sounding crushed. "He'd be alive if I hadn't. Time we busted her ass!"

"Busted for what?" Farrell challenged. "Maybe we're getting ahead of ourselves here. Let me play devil's advocate for a minute: We have no evidence Nichols killed Tom, no evidence she's a sleeper. She's an American. A brilliant cybersecurity expert and accomplished law-enforcement officer with a mother who happens to be of Russian descent and a father who happens to be an international financial consultant and numbers the Kremlin among his clients. So does Goldman Sachs. It's all circumstantial. Where does that leave us?"

"Well," Scotto said, thoughtfully, "we could confront Nichols head-on. If Katkov's right, and an op is imminent, it might muck it up a bit, but there's no guarantee it'd stop it. Maybe we should just play her for a while, keep her under surveillance. And if she is the sleeper, we slam the door on the op and roll up the entire cell."

"That wouldn't give us Svet-lana for Tom," Ruben said, emphasizing it as if spitting out an expletive. "We won't get her for him, or for Katkov's people either. As long as I'm working this case, there's no way I'll ever—"

"Ruben?! Ruben, take a breath," Katkov interrupted sharply. "Despite the lack of evidence that one of her vintage sabers was the murder weapon, might Tom have been killed in a duel?"

"I ran that theory past her once," Ruben scoffed. "She laughed and said vintage dueling swords are only used in exhibitions and charity events."

"But yesterday, I believe you mentioned Tom's tunic smelled of bleach, suggesting it had been laundered after he was killed."

"Yeah, so?" Ruben retorted. "Where the hell you going with this?"

"To Levenger's fencing club. I mean, if he was killed in a duel, might it have laundry facilities?"

"Yessss!" Farrell exclaimed, firing a look at Ruben. "Get a warrant. The slightest trace of Tom's DNA in a washer, drain hose, plumbing line, and we've got them."

"Now that that's all done and dusted," Katkov said, brightening at what he was about to say. "If I was breaking this story with my editor, he would ask me three questions: What do we know? What don't we know? And what do we do to find out?"

"Smart guy. Must've taken my class at Quantico," Farrell said with a sly grin. "Okay, we all know what we know. Time to cut to the chase and tackle what don't."

"Like damn near everything," Ruben replied. "We don't have a clue about the target or the nature of the threat, and if Katkov's right, if it's imminent . . ."

Farrell rolled his eyes. "I can no longer allow sentences that begin with 'If Katkov's right' to go unchallenged. What makes you so damned sure it's imminent?"

"Experience," Katkov fired back. "The K wouldn't have gone to such lengths to protect a sleeper. They'd bring her in from the cold, get her out of country, but they'd move heaven and earth to protect a code-red, priority-one op."

"Yeah, but we don't know what's going to happen. Where it's going to happen. When it's going to happen," Scotto countered. "And if it is Nichols, we don't know if she's a lone wolf or running a pack she's trained to carry out the op."

"Moving right along," Farrell charged on, taking over. "What do we do? We get the com-tech geeks to monitor her texts, emails, and phone, and like Gabby said, we make her feel secure, part of the family. I don't want anybody spooking her, because, if she is the leader of the pack, we need her to nail them."

Katkov nodded. "As somebody famous once said: Keep your enemies close . . ."

Ruben emitted a sarcastic snort. "Nichols just walked out of here with the cybercode, Katkov. That close enough for you?"

Scotto groaned. "Yeah, and in a couple of days, she'll claim she cracked it and give us some decrypted junk to throw us off the track."

"Good catch," Farrell said. "And here's what else we're going to do: We are going to put our best geek squad on it to keep her honest. We going to put all rail carriers, train yards, and terminals on alert. Last but not least, Cyber-Borgen's in town tomorrow installing the new security system. Their input could be invaluable. We're going to bring them up to speed on everything except our suspicions about Nichols. Got it?"

"If I may . . ." Katkov said deferentially. "Since she is your Amtrak point person, wouldn't it serve our purposes to allow her to conduct that briefing?"

Farrell scowled, then his eyes crinkled with delight. "Yeah, see how she handles it. Good." He shifted his look to Celia and said, "Let Carlsen know I want him and his team in here at eight o'clock sharp tomorrow for a briefing. And let Nichols know she's running it. Questions?"

"Just one," Ruben replied. What are we doing in the meantime?"

"You're getting that search warrant for the fencing club. We're all going to focus on: "What, Where, and When. And Scotto will be Katkov's permanent minder."

"Not that I don't appreciate Gabby's willingness to risk breaking one of her nails," Katkov said, "but might that not make Agent Nichols suspicious? Why not maintain the status quo? If she and I remain 'joined at the hip,' as you initially decreed, I'd be your sleeper, your spy. Why change horses now?"

Farrell locked his eyes on to Katkov's and replied, "Because she'll kill you."

Chapter Forty-Seven

"Guess we've got our marching orders," Scotto said after Farrell left.

"Sure as hell do," Ruben said, heading for the door like a man on a mission.

Katkov swung Scotto a puzzled look. "Okay, where does that leave us?"

"Well, the boss made me your permanent minder, and he wants Nichols kept under surveillance . . . Looks like we're working together again."

"Joined at the hip," Katkov said with an impish grin, then his eyes hardened and locked onto Scotto's. "Be advised, Gabby, I didn't come here to get a story, I came to get justice for Grusha and others the Kremlin cold-bloodedly murdered." He paused and, measuring each word, added, "This one is personal."

Scotto's lips tightened with determination. "We'll get them. I promise."

"I know. That's why I came to you. What's our next move?"

"Acquire the target."

"I can identify her car. I know where she lives. And I know the location of Levenger's estate," Katkov said, ticking them off. "You're the professional. Pick it."

"The parking lot," Scotto replied without missing a beat.

Katkov had no trouble locating Lana's Prius. Scotto's Land Rover had a sightline from visitor parking, and they had just settled in with the engine running and heater blasting when Lana spun through a revolving door, strode swiftly to her car, and drove off. Scotto waited until it had cleared the security kiosk before following. A half hour later, they had crossed the river into the District and were approaching Union Station.

"Hope you brought your toothbrush," Katkov said with a laugh. "Looks like we're riding the rails again."

Scotto rolled her eyes. "She's traveling light. With luck, she's just meeting someone. Yesss!" she hissed with a relieved sigh as Lana pulled into a street-level parking area. A sign proclaimed AMTRAK CORPORATE HEADQUARTERS, AUTHORIZED PERSONNEL ONLY. "There is a God." Scotto parked in a loading zone and tossed a FinCEN placard onto the dash. She and Katkov hurried into the terminal, tailing Lana through the streaming crowd of travelers. Instead of queuing for the airport-like security check, Lana went straight to Gate G adjacent to the Acela Club Lounge—the gate from which arriving passengers would emerge. A uniformed guard with an anxious German shepherd at his side was posted in front of the glass doors. He forced a smile and tugged the canine aside as Lana badged him and, without breaking stride, pushed through the doors and strode down the platform in search of Pash.

Katkov and Scotto remained in the terminal and blended into the crowd. As passengers began coming through the doors, they saw a slight a young man neither could identify standing on the platform with an overnight bag, waving at Lana.

"Hi, right on time! That's a first!" Lana exclaimed as she joined Pash and hugged him. "Come on, I'm parked just outside." She led the way into the terminal, passing the information kiosk and concession stands that flanked it. "We've got a lot to—" She stopped short, her eyes darting to two men who were coming up behind them at a determined pace. "Don't look back. I think we're being followed."

Pash's eyes widened with concern. "Followed? Are you certain?"

"Trust me. Two men: Black leather jacket/shaved head; Down vest/ watch cap," Lana replied with a glance over her shoulder. "And one of them's got a gun!" She and Pash took off through the crowded terminal. The two men quickened their pace. Black Leather thrust his pistol between some travelers blocking his way and fired two shots. Both missed his fleeing targets. Passengers began screaming and running from the area.

Katkov and Scotto were in the midst of the pandemonium when they spotted Lana and Pash dashing between the Shake Shack and the Mexican Grill a short distance ahead of the hit men, who were knifing between frightened passengers in pursuit. Scotto lunged at a cart piled with luggage, sending it rolling at high speed into the path of the onrushing assailants. The collision knocked both of them off their feet and sent the shooter's pistol skittering across the ground. He grabbed it as they ran off in opposite directions.

Dusk was falling as Lana led Pash to the Amtrak parking area. "Who are those men?" he asked, looking back anxiously. "Why do they want to kill you?"

"To kill *us!*" Lana corrected sharply. "My boss gave me a Russian cybercode to crack. It's the key to countering the cyber war we'll be fighting. Somebody sent them to stop us," she went on as they dashed to her car.

"Where are we going?" Pash asked, clearly shaken, as he dropped his luggage in the hatchback.

"Someplace safe where we can talk," Lana replied, suppressing that little smile.

They were long gone by the time Katkov and Scotto reached the Amtrak parking area. "That went well," he muttered, hunkering down into his parka as they walked to where Scotto had parked the Land Rover. "So much for keeping her under surveillance."

"That's on me," Scotto said as a light snow started to fall. "Those were the guys in the Mercedes this morning. I should've taken *them* out instead of their car."

"Forget it," Katkov growled with a dismissive wave. "The Kremlin has an endless supply of psychopaths. I'm quite certain the fellow in the watch cap tried to kill me in the Metro, but why would they target Nichols? They're on the same side."

"Sure as hell are," Scotto fired back, her eyes alive with insight. "They could have whacked her *and* her buddy—if they wanted to. I'm thinking it's a setup, a charade to manipulate him. Make him think they're in danger. Like they're in this together."

"They *are* in it together. His laptop case had a Cyber-Borgen logo."

"Good catch," Scotto said with a fist pump. "Then, chances are, whatever scheme the Kremlin's cooked up, Nichols needs *him* to pull it off."

They got into the Rover and slipped into the traffic lane, the wipers sweeping across the snow-dotted windshield. "Where do you think they're going?" Katkov wondered. "Her apartment? Levenger's estate? Headquarters?"

Scotto shrugged. "Six of one, half a dozen of the—" Her eyes darted to the dash. "Boss didn't waste a minute, did he?"

"That *does* seem to be his nature, but I'm not sure I follow."

"Follow *that*," Scotto said, pointing to a marker flashing on the GPS screen. "That's our girl's cell phone. She's heading North on Massachusetts."

After leaving Katkov and Scotto in the conference room, Ruben went to the fourth floor, where the offices of the federal prosecutors were located.

He briefed one of the staff attorneys on his investigation into the homicide of FBI Agent Tom Jones, provided her with copies of relevant forensics tests, and requested she prepare and file an affidavit with a federal judge for a search warrant of Levenger's estate, then headed home.

Julie was at her computer booking reservations for a client when Ruben leaned into the den. "Clocked out early, again, huh?" she said. "I'll never get this lobbyist and his twinkie on a flight to Rio if you're thinking what I think you're thinking."

"Well . . . I'm thinking"—Ruben sat on the corner of her desk—"that we're going to have to put that move back home on hold."

Julie nodded. "You got it figured out? That thing in the garage . . . you're taking care of it?"

Ruben nodded, looking into her eyes.

"Nice to know you still listen to your wife!"

"Well, that and . . ." Ruben paused, setting up the qualifier. "The fact that Nichols convinced the boss whoever has the roll-aboard with the five mil killed Tom."

Julie looked incredulous. "Are you serious?"

"Yeah, but I know who killed him," Ruben said with a laugh, savoring the irony. "And I've got the evidence to prove it."

Chapter Forty-Eight

The signal from Lana's cell phone was moving swiftly up Massachusetts on the Rover's GPS screen, leading Katkov and Scotto into the heart of the District. Lana took Fourteenth to Le Diplomate and left the car with a parking valet. Scotto drove past and parked around the corner. Katkov left her in the Rover and trudged off in the swirling snow.

Lana and Pash were greeted by a cacophony of voices and raucous laughter when they entered the brasserie. Waiters were snaking between tables with trays of sparkling cocktails, foaming beers, and platters of hors d'oeuvres chaud. Her favorite Le Dip stud—whom Lana had nicknamed Danger Man—was at the bar, and he caught Lana's eye as they followed the maître d' to a booth.

Katkov pulled the hood of his parka over his head and went to a window that gave him a clear view of the bistro's bustling interior. He watched as Lana and Pash settled in, then stepped away from the window and called Scotto. "Looks like cocktails for two. I must say, the food appears rather appetizing."

"Thanks a lot. I'm starving. Get a menu; we'll call for takeout."

Katkov laughed and returned to the window.

A waitress was taking their order. Pash squirmed with impatience and swung Lana a puzzled look as soon as she departed. "Perhaps I misunderstood, Lana, but didn't you say someplace safe where we can talk?"

"It's Thursday. TGIF rush night. No one's paying attention to us. They're all looking for a weekend hook-up and think we're doing the same."

"We called it a Saturday-night shag when I was in college in London."

"I'm sure it was, but as far as we're concerned, it's called hiding in plain sight."

"But those men knew you were meeting me at Union Station," Pash protested. "Whoever is behind the cyber strike must be surveilling us, monitoring our phones."

"I know," Lana said, studying him as if making a decision. "Okay, you'll hear it at tomorrow's briefing anyway: There's a sleeper embedded in JTTF."

Pash looked uncertain. "A sleeper? What do you mean? What is a sleeper?"

"A spy—a *Russian* spy. Probably living in the United States for decades. Maybe even born here. Highly intelligent. Well educated. Worked in law enforcement, excelled at every level, and was assigned to JTTF. We've no idea who it is."

"But you're quite certain that's who sent those gunmen to kill us?"

Lana nodded. "A journalist from Moscow named Katkov alerted us to the situation. But I suspect he came here to collaborate with the sleeper, not catch him."

"My God. It sounds as if this catastrophic cyber strike is . . . is *beyond* catastrophic."

"Way beyond. As I said, the boss gave me a Russian cybercode to decrypt. It's—"

"The key to countering it," Pash interjected feverishly. "Yes, yes you told me. Do we know its nature? Its target. Its timing?"

"No. Leave that to me and focus on the punch list. We're going to be fighting a move/countermove cyber war, but our hands are tied until the new system is installed. My biggest concern is—" Lana stopped short and forced a smile as the waitress arrived with their drinks.

Katkov turned from the window and headed back to the Rover, bent into a stinging wind. "Make that *serious* cocktails for two," he said as he joined Scotto. "*Very* serious . . . and intense. She's got him positioned and is closing the deal. You were right." He lit two cigarettes and gave one to her. "I find it's becoming more and more difficult to satisfy one's vices," he said, inhaling deeply. "I suspect I could grow rather fond of stakeouts."

"Tell me about it. I can smoke at home and behind the wheel. That's it."

"Indeed. Since I've been on the proverbial wagon, my addiction to nicotine is the only vice I have left . . . along with women and my comic-book collection."

Scotto shot him a strange look, then exhaled through her nose and mouth, and cracked open a window.

When the waitress left, Lana took a long swallow of her drink and locked her eyes onto Pash's. "As I was saying, my biggest concern is that if something happens to me, you'll be fighting that cyber war by yourself."

Pash nodded and toyed with his iced tea. "Perhaps, but you said they intended to kill *both* of us. What . . . what if something happens to *me*?"

"I was getting to that," Lana said, relieved he had taken the bait. "I have every confidence our people will make sure it doesn't, but we can't take any chances. I know it will be difficult, but . . ." She paused and, with an apologetic sigh, said, "The time has come for you to share your most sensitive professional secret with me."

"I expected as much, Lana, but one *can't* share what one doesn't know."

"Oh?" Lana blurted, her heart rate surging. "I'm sorry. I'm not sure I understand. I thought your UI was committed to memory."

"No, I'm afraid not. Each one is a prime number that is generated by our mainframe. They're quite lengthy and impossible to memorize, therefore . . ." Pash produced a flash drive from his laptop case and held it up in mock triumph.

"Perfect. I'll need a copy."

"I'm afraid it's locked and can't be opened, read, or copied, but—"

"What if it got corrupted?" Lana challenged. "Or the drive got lost or misplaced?"

"I was about to say, Axel can generate one from the mainframe. So . . ."

"Good. Tell him it got corrupted. Make sure he does it today and brings it with him."

"Of course, but there is one more precaution: To guard against the flash drive being lost or stolen, the file can't be downloaded or run by the program until I enter my personal activation code, which *is* committed to memory." Pash palmed his phone and quickly typed: 1662014. "I just emailed it to you."

Now Lana knew what Carlsen meant by "Some of it" when she asked if Pash's UI was committed to memory. "Thank you. I trust I'll never need to use it."

"And, should Allah be so inclined, *I* trust you will open it only should He decide to grant my most fervent wish. You see I—" He paused, his lips trembling with emotion. "You see, I . . . I chose . . . I chose the day my dear Safia and I were married as my PAC, and my longing to be reunited with her is such that I often pray to Him for deliverance."

"Well, I hope Allah doesn't take action anytime soon," Lana said with a laugh, trying to lighten the mood. "I mean—" Her cell phone pinged. The text read: *Can you come by later?* She flicked a sideways glance to the bar, where Danger Man was perched in a predatory slouch, then replied: *Can't. Working a source. Will call.*

"What is it, Lana?" Pash asked anxiously. "Is there a problem?"

"No, just one of my people checking in," Lana replied, draining her glass. "Time we got over to Amtrak HQ and ran that punch list. Drink up."

A short time later, a parking valet brought Lana's car to the curb. "Better call Carlsen about the flash drive now," she said to Pash as they drove off. "Don't mention what happened at the station. I haven't had a chance to run it past my boss yet."

Katkov and Scotto tailed them back to where they had started—the Amtrak headquarters parking area at Union Station. Scotto pulled into a no-parking zone with an unobstructed view of the main entrance.

"Perhaps it's time to give Farrell a heads-up," Katkov prompted.

"About what?"

"The shooting incident in the train station."

"Bad idea. It could change the dynamic," Scotto said decisively. "If Devil's Advocate Dick was right and Nichols is clean, *she'll* report it at the meeting. Better to say nothing and see where she takes us tomorrow."

Katkov nodded. "Actually, I'm curious to see where she takes us *next*."

"Whatever, wherever, my gut's telling me it's going to be a long night. All kinds of fast-food joints in the terminal. Call me if they're on the move."

"Might there be a Ben's Borscht Bowl?" Katkov asked as she popped the door. "I believe there was one across from the Metro Station on U Street."

"That's Ben's *Chili* Bowl," Scotto corrected with a hearty laugh. "Shake Shack or Mexican Grill? Forget it. I'll surprise you."

In the Amtrak HQ lobby, the guard at the security desk swiped Lana and Pash's IDs through a reader, then directed them to a restricted-access elevator that descended to Central Computer Control beneath the massive train station. Andy Grabowski was waiting for them. The vast space, big enough to accommodate a jetliner, was permeated by the pungent scent of ozone and the hum of electronics from the rows of servers that filled nearly half of it. A maze of high-tech workstations, manned by technicians monitoring and controlling the movement of rolling stock, filled the other half. High above, on a panoramic tracking board, a zigzagging tangle of multicolored graphics charted the progress of passenger and freight trains on rail lines that traversed the United States and parts of Canada. Lana and Pash spent the next several hours with Grabowski and a team of Amtrak technicians running the preinstallation punch list.

It was close to nine thirty p.m. when the express from New York arrived at Gate G several levels above. Carlsen, Caitlin, and the other members of the Cyber-Borgen team went directly to Amtrak HQ in the southeast corner of the station. After being cleared by security, they took the elevator down to Computer Control, pulling suitcases and hefting overnight bags.

"Caitlin!" Lana exclaimed the moment she spotted her. "I'm so glad your dad's going to be okay," she went on, running into a mutual hug-fest.

Caitlin was beaming. "Yeah, it was touch and go. Never thought I'd make it."

"So are we good to go?" Carlsen prompted as Pash and the others encircled them.

"As good as it gets," Lana replied with unbridled enthusiasm. "Right, Pash?"

"Right. Good to go!" Pash echoed.

"Sure as hell are," Grabowski chimed in.

"Great!" Carlsen exclaimed with a clap of his hands. "We've got an early start at JTTF tomorrow. Then it's back here to download, install, and shake down." He high-fived those around him, then took Pash aside and gave him the duplicate flash drive that contained his UI. "Lose this one and you'll be working customer support at Microsoft."

"You know very well I didn't lose it, Axel. The file got corrupted."

"Yes, Pash, I know," Carlsen said with a gentle smile. "Just yanking your chain."

A short time later, the group took the elevator to the lobby. Lana and Pash hung back as the others headed outside.

"Guard this with your life," Pash whispered, slipping Lana the flash drive.

"With all nine of 'em!" Lana said, palming it. "Drop you at the hotel?" she asked as they joined the others outside.

"Thanks. I'll tag along with the team."

Lana nodded, then called out, "Bright and early, everyone!" She went to her car and drove off, buoyed by the fact that she had everything she needed to control the three programs in Amtrak's operating system. The ESR, PTC, and RCRM programs that, in conjunction with the CSX cybercodes, would enable her to execute the Kremlin's code-red, priority-one op.

Chapter Forty-Nine

Katkov and Scotto were trying to stay warm and awake in the Land Rover when Lana pulled out of the parking area. "Gabby? Gabby!" he said, poking an elbow into her ribs. "It seems we have some action here."

"What? Oh, oh yeah, great, she's on the move," Scotto said, shaking out the cobwebs. She swept some fast-food containers from the console, slammed the Land Rover into gear, and pulled into traffic a distance behind the Prius.

Lana took Constitution on the north side of the Mall. Twenty minutes later, she was on Twenty-Sixth, approaching Queen Anne's Lane, when her eyes widened with alarm at the sight of multicolored flashers tracing through the treetops and across the façades of the brick townhouses. A convoy of black sedans, SUVs, and vans with light bars ablaze and FBI logos on their doors were in front of her building. Bold typography on one of the latter proclaimed: EVIDENCE RESPONSE TEAM. Instead of making the turn, Lana slowed and rolled through the intersection. Agents with luminescent logos on the backs of their field jackets were removing file boxes, computer equipment, and other items from her apartment. One cradled her vintage sabers, which had been wrapped in plastic evidence bags. Another hefted a black rolling suitcase she recognized as the type used in sting operations and placed it in the ERT van. Other agents gathered round as he opened it, revealing the bricks of hundreds within. Lana's heart sank. She felt like she was trapped in a falling elevator as she accelerated in the direction of Rock Creek Park.

"This looks rather familiar," Katkov said as the Land Rover approached the intersection. "I believe her apartment is just down the next street."

"What the hell's *that* all about?" Scotto exclaimed on seeing the FBI circus.

"*Onya bula razoren,*" Katkov replied wryly. "Which means—"

"Her cover's blown. I know," Scotto interjected as Lana accelerated and beat the K Street traffic light. By the time the Rover got there, a tractor-trailer was blocking the box. "Fuck!" Scotto exclaimed, hitting the brakes. She bounced a fist off the steering wheel, then glanced to the locator from Lana's phone on the GPS screen and settled.

At JTTF headquarters, Dick Farrell was getting off the phone when Ruben blew into his office. "Bad news on the warrant. No probable cause. Nothing ties Tom to the club. CCTV from the Grille shows him driving off by himself. If forensics matches those specks of steel to one of her sabres, we might get her for Tom, but—"

"We just did," Farrell fired back. "That was com-tech on the horn. They picked up the transponder signal from the roll-aboard with the five mil—it was in Nichols's apartment under the bed."

"No way," Ruben exclaimed, pretending to be surprised. "Then the bitch really did kill Tom, didn't she?"

Farrell nodded grimly. "Yeah . . . and she did that one-eighty on Bargishev because *she's* the sleeper. You called it. IA's running with it."

"Have they picked her up?

"Not yet." Farrell's phone rang. "Scotto," he said eyeing the caller ID. "Gabby?" he growled. "What's going on?"

"The FBI's all over Nichols's apartment.

"I know."

"She's rabbiting. We're tailing her."

"Way to go. What's your location?"

"Pennsylvania and Rock Creek Parkway. Heading north."

"You have eyes?"

"No. Truck cut us off. We have her on GPS."

Farrell tapped an icon on his keyboard. "So do we," he said, as the GPS map with a flashing locator filled his computer screen. "Stay on her."

In Julian's art-filled penthouse atop the sleek YUL Towers in heart of downtown Montreal, he and Kate were hosting the reception for the Sentiment du Fer Annual Charity Tournament. Fencers and financiers from around the world were chatting in clusters with Champagne flutes and hors d'oeuvres plucked from passing trays.

Kate, a stunning presence in an elegant sheath, was holding court amongst a group of young acolytes when her cell phone vibrated. She saw Lana's caller ID and excused herself.

"Hi, got it where you want it?" she asked cheerily as she moved aside.

"Net grebany put'! No English! *Govorit' po-russki!"* Lana said, commanding her to speak Russian. "My cover's blown. The FBI's all over my apartment."

"Why? Lanishka?!" Kate exclaimed sotto voce, in Russian. "What happened?"

"Somebody planted evidence to prove I murdered that FBI agent."

"What . . . what about your webcam?" Kate sputtered. "Wouldn't it show that—"

"Nyet!" Lana interrupted. "It doesn't cover the foyer or bedroom. It was a rolling suitcase. Probably under my bed. That's where I'd put it if *I* was planting it. I've got everything I need to launch, but if you don't pull me out now, it'll never happen!"

"Christ. Hold on, we're in the middle of the reception." Kate slithered between the partygoers, slipped up behind Julian, and whispered, "Lana, 911. Her cover's blown. We have to pull her out, now." She led the way to an alcove behind the bar.

Julian winced and took the phone. *"Non, c'est impossible!"* he said with harsh finality, going on to add in Russian, "The flight crew timed out as I thought. Best case ETA seven/eight o'clock tomorrow night. You'll have to go to ground until then."

"Where?!" Lana challenged, beside herself. "FBI'll be all over your place and Kate's, too, and one swipe of my credit card at a hotel and—"

"The embassy," Julian interrupted sharply. "Go to the embassy."

"And risk spending the rest of my life in there like Assange in London?!"

"Lanishka, this is no time to—"

"Wait, Dzhulian, wait, slow down," Lana interrupted, her eyes brightening at a thought. "I just need to vanish for a while. And I know just how." She hung up and made another call. "Hey there," she said in a breathy voice. "That source I was working was a waste. Your place, half hour?"

"On my way," Danger Man replied. "I'm still at Le Dip. If you get there first, fine bottle . . . Pomerol . . . in the—" The call started breaking up and went dead.

"Hey? Hey, you there?" Lana prompted. "I'm in the car. Must've hit a dead zone. I'll call you back." A few moments later she tried him again. Nothing. Neither voice nor text responded. She tapped the email icon. The message on the screen read: *This email account is no longer active.* She knew what that meant, knew that the agency had shut it down, knew that she'd been cut off from all communication, that she couldn't access Pash's Personal Activation Code, that the flash drive that contained his UI would be useless without it. She steeled herself against the rising feeling of panic, suddenly aware that her phone, though useless to *her,* was just what the com-techs tracking it, needed to locate her. She took the Massachusetts off-ramp, pulled into the parking lot behind St. Sophia Greek Orthodox Church, and popped the back off the phone.

Several miles south on Rock Creek Parkway, the GPS tracking flasher vanished from the screen in Scotto's Rover.

"Damn!" Scotto exclaimed. "We lost her."

Katkov scowled. "That's odd. I recall even a deactivated phone can be tracked."

"Long as it has a SIM card and a battery," Scotto fired back.

Katkov scoffed and splayed his hands. "Then we would be wise to conclude that Agent Nichols's phone no longer has either."

Lana had been traveling north when she pulled into the church parking lot. It was on a corner where Massachusetts and Wisconsin avenues intersect at an acute angle. Lana abandoned her car and hailed a cab that was heading south on Wisconsin. She was still under siege, but she had a plan of attack now. Indeed, she knew exactly where she was going, and also knew where they would *think* she had gone—and stop looking for her! She had executed a perfect *kontrataka-zahavat*: a counterattack with an engagement of the blades that forces an opponent's weapon into a new line. "Georgetown. Waterfront Park," she said to the driver.

Scotto made the transition from the parkway onto Massachusetts and handed her phone to Katkov. "Your turn to give the boss the bad news."

"It appears Agent Nichols has disabled her phone," Katkov said when Farrell answered. "The locator just vanished from our screen. I'm afraid we lost her."

"I'm afraid I already know that," Farrell said, mimicking him, his eyes riveted to the GPS map on his monitor. "Last known location a Greek Orthodox church on Massachusetts and Garfield."

"Maybe she sought refuge there . . ." Katkov said, letting it trail off with a sarcastic chuckle. "Maybe she is confessing her sins."

"To the Russian ambassador!" Farrell fired back. "That church is around the corner from their embassy. *Your* embassy! Get your asses back here, we've got work to do." Farrell slammed the handset back into the charger.

"If she's in the embassy, no way we can touch her," Ruben said.

Farrell's lips tightened into an angry line. "No way that briefing can wait till tomorrow," he said decisively. "Scotto and Katkov are coming in. Get hold of the geek squad, the GPS and CCTV gangs, the Cyber-Borgen crew, and the head of Amtrak computer ops. Andy Grabowski. I want 'em all in here now. ASAP!"

Chapter Fifty

Danger Man lived in a brick-and-stone manse a short walk from the river in Georgetown. A row of dormers at the roofline bathed the artist's studio below with northern light. A high brick wall enclosed a parking area and an adjacent yard at the rear of the property, where the bare branches of several gnarled oaks clawed at the darkness.

Lana usually parked between his F-150 pickup and vintage Porsche whenever she had some time to come by. Tonight she got out of the cab a few blocks away near the Francis Scott Key Bridge. A cold wind was coming off the river, sending litter spinning across the pavement and snow-dusted grass. Clusters of students, fists stuffed in the pockets of parkas and ski jackets, were shuffling in and out of Gypsy Sally's, a popular hangout opposite the park. Lana pulled her hood up and walked down the alleys behind the buildings, avoiding any CCTV cameras in the area. Both of Danger Man's vehicles were parked in the yard when she slipped through the side gate and entered the house via the kitchen door as she always did.

"Honey, I'm home," Lana called out, forcing a laugh as she joined him in the great room. Powerful abstract paintings covered the walls. A grand piano presided over one corner where photos spanning several generations were displayed: some in black and white, others in vintage sepia, a few in living color, suggesting decades of family service to government and the arts. Floor-to-ceiling bookcases spanned the shuttered windows and flanked a massive stone hearth where Danger Man was tending to a picturesque fire. "Sorry, I tried calling you back, but my phone crashed," she went on with a pout, kicking off her Uggs. "Totally useless."

"It might just need to be reset. Want me to give it a shot?"

"I'm a tech geek, remember? I do this stuff for a living."

"How could I forget? You're welcome to use mine if you need to make calls."

"See? I knew you'd come to my rescue."

Danger Man's eyes narrowed. "Well, you know, you do seem . . . I don't know . . . a little skittish. Not your cocky FBI-agent self. Something going on?"

"Case I'm working." Lana dropped onto the shabby-chic sofa, and shook out her hair. "Nothing a little TLC wouldn't cure," she said with a come-hither smile.

"Ah, *that's* why you come here," Danger Man said, feigning a moment of insight. "The code's 1973," he went on, offering her his phone. "Year I was born."

"Thanks," Lana said, declining. "I need to be off the grid for a while."

"Well, *this* was born in '89," Danger Man said, picking up the bottle of Pomerol he had opened earlier, allowing the dense, ruby-purple Château L'Évangile to breathe. "Great now. Fantastic thirty years from now," he went on, pouring two glasses. "Guaranteed to take you to a better place."

"Lucky for me you live for the moment."

"That's *two* things we have in common," he said with a lascivious grin, handing her a glass. "Cheers!"

"Cheers!" Lana echoed as they both sipped the smooth, bracing Bordeaux.

He put his glass on the table and settled next to her, momentarily captured by the alluring emerald sparkle of her eyes, then kissed her forehead and wrapped an arm around her shoulders, embracing her protectively.

Lana burrowed in next to him and emitted a weary sigh.

"Tough day, huh?"

"Very. I can't think of any other place I'd rather be, or of anyone else I'd rather be with right now . . ."

"Well, as you know the Danger Man TLC Center offers two restorative programs: the casual great-room starter, and the more intense bedroom advanced."

"I vaguely recall signing up for both," Lana replied, slowly unzipping her sweater as she sat up and turned to face him, revealing a bare breast that swayed across the V-shaped opening beckoningly.

Danger Man raised an appreciative brow, then caressed her breasts, and began kissing his way across their peaches-and-cream whiteness until his lips found their target, encircling it as he began, gently, coaxing it to life with the tip of his tongue.

Chapter Fifty-One

It was after midnight by the time Katkov and Scotto, along with Carlsen, the Cyber-Borgen team, and Grabowski gathered in the windowless situation room opposite Farrell's office. A grid of flat-screen monitors alive with cable news stories and satellite images of the world's hot spots covered one wall. One of the banners read: IRAN NUCLEAR DEAL TO BE IMPLEMENTED THIS WEEKEND. On an adjacent wall, a similar grid displayed data from a line of computer stations where JTTF tech teams were at work: The GPS geeks were retracing the movements of Lana's phone to determine if she had gone to the Russian embassy. The CCTV geeks were searching for footage of her and/or her Prius. And the code-writing geeks, who were trying to crack the cybercode, had covered the wall of white boards with indecipherable scribbles.

"Okay, people," Farrell said, getting down to business. "We have a full-priority situation. It's a major personnel security breach that must be dealt with now. Right now, and it's a tough one: Agent Lana Nichols has been exposed as a Russian sleeper agent. She's on the run and may have taken refuge in the Russian embassy. Wherever she is, she is intent on launching a catastrophic cyberattack—target, modus operandi, and precise timing unknown."

The stunned silence that followed was broken by a collective gasp when Ruben added, "And she murdered one of our agents in cold blood."

"That's . . . that's hard to believe," Carlsen finally said. "I'm at a loss for words."

"As am I," Caitlin said, equally shaken. "My God, are you sure?"

Farrell nodded grimly. "We don't make these accusations lightly. She was one of our own. A member of the family. A highly trusted agent who has done exemplary work. Unfortunately, she was doing it on behalf of the Kremlin."

"Russian hackers . . . they're good," Carlsen said grudgingly. "They've infiltrated our banks, financial markets, power grids, and interfered with elections in Ukraine and other Eastern European countries. I can't believe Agent Nichols would be capable of such duplicity."

"She's an American," Farrell fired back, unable to contain his anger.

"I'm afraid, I'm . . . I'm having trouble processing this too," Pash said, his voice breaking. "We were attacked by two gunmen at Union Station this afternoon. Thanks to Agent Nichols's quick thinking, we escaped unharmed. I just can't—"

"Yeah, we heard about that," Farrell interrupted. He shot a look at Katkov and Scotto and pointedly added, "Though not from any of our people on the scene."

"Guilty as charged, sir," Scotto said, getting the message.

"We thought it prudent to give Agent Nichols a chance to brief you," Katkov chimed in. "That it might serve as a—"

"A test?" Farrell challenged.

Katkov and Scotto nodded apprehensively.

"Well, she failed it big-time didn't she?!" Farrell snapped, shifting his look to Pash. "So did you!"

"No. No, she instructed me to keep it to myself until . . . until, as Mr. Katkov just said, she could brief you," Pash stammered defensively. "She also confided to me that there was a sleeper in JTTF who sent those gunmen to Union Station."

"Well, she oughtta know," Farrell scoffed.

"But we worked together, closely," Pash protested, wracked with ambivalence. "She supported me at a time when I had no reason to live. She *literally* saved my life. I trust her totally. I still can't believe what you're saying . . . that . . . that she would do such things."

"Welcome to the club," Farrell said, gesturing broadly.

"But she warned me of the cyberattack you just referenced. And . . . and said she needed my help to prevent it. Why would she do that if she was the perpetrator?"

"Because she's a covert operative committed to undermining our democracy. They're masters of deception and beguilement. They befriend you, share confidential information to gain your trust, then swear you to secrecy so they can manipulate you."

"But why? Why would she do that? I'm afraid I still don't—"

"Because she can't execute the cyberattack without your help. Now, why the hell not?!"

"I'll field that one," Carlsen said before Pash could reply. "Because no one can hack into a Cyber-Borgen security program or the operating system it protects without the original code writer's unique identifier and personal access code."

"No way Nichols can pull it off without them," Grabowski added. "Correct?

"Correct," Carlsen replied, struck by a thought that made him wince. "Pash? Pash, I need you to tell me your UI flash drive was really corrupted."

Pash bowed his head in shame. "I'm sorry, Axel. I'm afraid I can't. I gave the duplicate to Agent Nichols."

"You idiot!" Carlsen erupted, beside himself.

"I am not an idiot," Pash protested, unable to contain his frustration. "She infected the program with malware, and I caught her. It was flagged by my UI. But I—"

"Christ!" Carlsen interrupted. "That was a bright-red fucking flag! Wasn't it?!"

"No, it wasn't," Pash replied evenly. "I thought she was testing me, testing us, testing the new program. I would have done the same. I had no reason to think otherwise. Nor would you."

"Damn," Farrell grunted. "We're in deep shit, aren't we?"

"Maybe, maybe not," Carlsen replied, waggling a hand. "The flash drive is useless without the code writer's PAC. Did you give that to her too?"

Pash nodded again. "I emailed it."

"When?!" Farrell interrupted, jumping on it.

"Earlier this evening. We were at a restaurant. She said she—"

"Did she open it?"

"No. She said she hoped she wouldn't have to use it, and would delete it if—"

"Time frame?!"

"Six thirty, seven o'clock . . ."

Farrell sighed with relief. "Her email account had already been deactivated."

"Thank God," Grabowski said, equally relieved. "I think it's time to get back to where, when, and how. What's the threat matrix? What has this got to do with Amtrak?"

"And CSX," Katkov added. "Nichols's handler was involved in the CSX/CP merger talks. Are you familiar with the name Levenger? Julian Levenger?"

Grabowski shrugged. "Doesn't ring a bell. Besides, that deal went bust."

"Yes, but the due diligence required of such mergers gave Levenger access to information he couldn't otherwise obtain," Katkov replied. "*That's* what he was really after. The merger was merely a smokescreen."

Grabowski's brows rose with intrigue. "What information?"

"I've no idea, but I *can* tell you the answer to that question and many others is in this cybercode"—Katkov stabbed a finger at N5Y7T0E5P written on the whiteboard and added—"and we have to find a way to crack it."

"It's in the works," Farrell replied. "We're running a full-court press . . ." He burned the geek squad with a look. "Right?"

The geek in chief swallowed hard. "Yes, sir. No three-pointers yet."

"Ditto," Scotto said. "Katkov and I took several shots at it. Ran a number of—"

"Wait, wait, don't tell me," Caitlin interrupted, her brogue thickening. "Googling it produced company names and titles of legislation. Running it through a glossary of railroad terminology proved equally useless. Code-breaking programs produced deciphering keys that were a total waste. Last but not least, the Vigenère algorithm transposed it into codes even more baffling than the one we need to break."

"Sounds like you've done this before," Scotto said, clearly impressed.

Caitlin nodded humbly. "A childhood hobby. On a farm, one can only clean out so many barns and bale so much hay without totally losing one's mind."

"We ran 'em all," the geek in chief said defensively. "No hits on Amtrak, CSX, Julian Levenger, RZD, the Kremlin, nothing—no relevant results."

Caitlin's eyes brightened at a thought. "What if it isn't a code? What if it's just a sort of shorthand someone made up? I mean, maybe we're overthinking this."

"Of course we are!" Katkov exclaimed. "And I'm the prime offender. If I remove myself from the enigmatic world of spies and clandestine operations and put my well-worn journalist's cap back on, it becomes embarrassingly clear that if we set aside the numerals"—he stepped to the whiteboard and wrote *NYTEP*—"we are left with that!" He paused then, erasing the last two letters, concluded: "And I promise you, for more than a hundred fifty years, there hasn't been a newspaperman on this planet, who, upon seeing these three letters, doesn't automatically think: *New York Times.*"

"Okay, smarty-pants . . ." Ruben said, locking his eyes onto Katkov's. "What's EP? Extreme politics? Endless pontification? Excruciating pain? Easy pickings?"

"I suspect the phrase you're so desperately after, Ruben, is 'editorial page.'"

"Yeah! And the numbers are the date: May 7, 2005," Scotto exclaimed as fingers started dancing across keyboards. "But why the hell did they wait so long?"

"Because she was probably in grad school, and it took a decade of patience and planning and career development to plant her *here*," Farrell replied as the *New York Times* editorials for that date appeared on the monitors: Building on Ground Zero, Tony Blair's Third Term, The Jobs Report from 30,000 Feet.

Puzzled expressions, furrowed brows, and a chorus of groans followed.

"Way to go, Katkov," Ruben chided.

"Please, don't spare the accolades, but I'm afraid you've the wrong date. You see, you Americans write: Month/Day/Year. In my country, as in many others, we write Day/Month/Year. I suggest you try July 5, 2005."

The image on the monitors changed. In 24-point Cheltenham the title of the 7/5/05 lead editorial proclaimed: WASHINGTON'S DEADLY BRIDGE. The first paragraph read: *The weakest point in America's defense against terrorism may be an inconspicuous little bridge a few blocks from the Capitol. Rail tanker cars filled with deadly chemicals pass over the bridge at Second Street SW on their journey up and down the East Coast. The bridge is highly vulnerable to an explosion below, and if deadly chemicals were released on it, they would endanger every member of Congress and as many as 250,000 other federal employees and local residents.*

Farrell scanned the following sentences, reading them aloud in bursts. "'A single chlorine-filled tanker could kill or seriously harm 100,000 people.'"

"And that's just *one* tank car!" Katkov exclaimed.

"'Terrorists could wait for a shipment to reach the bridge and then explode a truck bomb from below,'" Farrell charged on. "'Causing them to derail and crack open releasing their deadly contents.'" He paused, scanning the text, then with a sigh of relief, added, "The city council in Washington passed a law prohibiting the transport of ultra-hazardous material within 2.2 miles of the Capitol. But CSX, the railroad that operates the two main lines through the District has gone to court to challenge the law."

"Great. That bridge is within spitting distance of Capitol Hill!" Ruben exclaimed. "These shipments have dozens of tanker cars! If even half of them ruptured . . ."

"Yeah, and SOTUS is tonight," Farrell concluded glumly.

"SOTUS?" Katkov echoed. "Sorry, I'm afraid I'm somewhat in the dark here."

"It's government-speak for the State of the Union speech," Farrell replied. "The president, vice president, the entire cabinet except for the designated survivor, every member of both houses of Congress, the Supreme Court, Joint Chiefs—the entire USG would be wiped out."

"Well, in light of its current level of vitriol and dysfunction," Katkov said with a mischievous twinkle, "there are those who might argue they'd be doing you a favor."

"I doubt the other 250,000 victims would agree," Farrell fired back. "We're already on high alert with SOTUS, and as I recall, I believe that editorial led to a deal between the USG and CSX. Help me out here, Andy. You're the expert on this."

"Right," Grabowski, echoed. "The railroad agreed not to ship any hazardous materials over the E Street Bridge, or through the DC area, during the State of the Union, presidential inaugurations, and events that attract large groups of people."

"See that, Katkov?" Farrell taunted with evident glee. "Our dysfunctional government in action." He turned to Celia and added, "Now that we know where, when, and how, protocol mandates we notify the White House, Secret Service, FBI, NSC, Joint Chiefs, et cetera, et cetera . . . You know the drill."

Celia's slim fingers were tap-dancing across her iPad as Farrell spoke. She nodded and said, "Done, sir."

"Before we deploy the Third Army," Ruben said with a sarcastic laugh, "maybe we should try blocking access to that underpass."

Farrell nodded and glanced at Celia.

"Done," she said, tapping away on her iPad.

"Great idea," Scotto said facetiously. "But a *truck* bomb wouldn't be Nichols's IED of choice. Would it? It'd be some kind of a . . . a *cyber*-bomb. No?"

"A cyber-*knife*," Pash corrected. "She would hack into the operating systems that are used to schedule hazmat shipments and control the trains transporting them and . . . and . . ." He paused, struggling to maintain his composure, then added, "And if . . . if you're right about Agent Nichols, that's why she needs me to 'pull it off,' as you put it. Isn't it?"

Farrell nodded emphatically. "And you can bet your ass we're right about her."

"Right down to her being a cold-blooded killer," Ruben added.

Pash shivered as if chilled and drifted aside, trying to come to grips with the unimaginable magnitude of Lana's deception, and his own naïveté.

"Whatever she is," Grabowski said evenly, "I just checked this week's hazmat shipments. CSX and CLX have several scheduled on eastern seaboard routes, but none moving through the DC area, let alone across the E Street Bridge within a six-hour window that brackets the president's speech."

"Did I hear C-L-X in there somewhere?" Farrell prompted.

Grabowski nodded. "It's the stock ticker symbol for the Clorox Corporation."

"Christ, we're talking liquid chlorine, per the editorial, aren't we?!"

Grabowski nodded again. "We'll get the new program installed ASAP and monitor the hell out of that rolling stock all day tomorrow."

"It *is* tomorrow!" Farrell snapped in a voice hoarse from the hours of nonstop conversation "Get your asses over there now!" He shifted his look to the three tech teams and grunted, "Full-court press. Full fucking court!"

It was three in the morning when Carlsen and his entourage left the situation room. Farrell trudged into his office with Katkov, Scotto, Ruben, and Celia in tow, fell into his desk chair, and stared at his daughter's memorial flag, his weary eyes glistening.

"What is it, boss?" Ruben prompted. "You always do that when you're looking for answers: What happened? If it happened? Why it happened?"

"Time of year," Celia said, softly with a knowing glance at Farrell.

"Yeah, something about cold weather," Farrell said, getting past it. "Nichols is cunning beyond cunning. I got an ugly feeling this embassy thing might be a ploy."

"But the CCTV geeks haven't had any hits over there."

"I don't think she went to the front door and rang the bell, Rube," Farrell cracked. "But if she manages to pull this off, everyone within a three-mile radius of ground zero could be killed, and, if she's in the embassy, chances are she'll be one of 'em." Farrell's lips tightened. "I rest my case. It doesn't compute."

"I agree," Katkov said, pushing his glasses up into his hair and rubbing his eyes. "Russian spies tend to be Patton-esque. You know, make the other poor bastard die for his country. The idea of dying for their own isn't in their DNA."

Ruben nodded emphatically. "Sure as hell isn't in hers. If Nichols *is* in there, she's lining up tactical support, transportation, and field operatives to smuggle her the hell out of there . . ."

"I want eyes on every way in and out of that place. I want her, Ruben, I want her alive, and I want her prosecuted."

"Yeah, and no death penalty cop-out. After what she did to Tom, Miss Nikolshevskaya's going to be spending the next fifty years at ADX in extreme solitary."

"Let's catch her first," Farrell warned. "Better give Centerville a heads-up—if she hasn't been smuggled in there already." Centerville was a Georgian-style mansion on the Corsica River in Maryland about an hour's drive from the District that the Russian government had owned since the Cold War. Ambassadors and high-ranking officials and their families spent weekends and vacations there, but American intelligence agencies—aware that the sprawling compound was used to conduct electronic surveillance and launch clandestine operations—kept close tabs on it. "And, crazy as it sounds," Farrell concluded, "in case Nichols somehow manages to get her ass out of the country, better issue a Red Alert."

"Not so crazy," Ruben said, agreeing an Interpol international arrest warrant was in order. "Better keep tabs on Levenger's Gulfstream too."

"Good catch. Where is it now? Parked at Dulles? En route to Montreal? Paris? Moscow? Any flight plans filed? Whatever, I want it grounded."

Ruben hissed with uncertainty. "That'd take a court order, boss. I mean, we got Nichols for Tom, but it's *Levenger's* plane, and, like you were saying, we've got nothing on him or Kate Nichols. Besides, even if we did, we'd never get the CO in time."

"Nothing's easy, dammit!" Farrell growled, popping a fist off his desktop. "Check it out anyway. I want to know where it is now and where it's going next."

Chapter Fifty-Two

The next morning, Lana awakened, alone, in Danger Man's antique brass bed. He was always up before dawn, and she always took advantage of the rare chance to sleep in. She slipped into a silk robe she'd left behind on a previous visit, then climbed the staircase to the top floor, where the heady scent of linseed oil and turpentine greeted her. The studio was awash with morning light that came from the dormers and spilled through the open door as Lana approached. Canvases in various stages of completion leaned against the walls. Finished ones were signed *Whitlock* in the lower-right corner.

Danger Man stood at an easel encircled by worktables that held a collection of paint cans and spattered buckets. Some were stuffed with brushes of all sizes and textures, others with a collection of palette knives, drawing instruments, pens, pencils, and markers. Paint-filled bucket in one hand, a wide brush in the other, he was sizing up a large, powerfully structured abstraction that evoked a violent, storm-tossed seascape.

Lana stopped outside the door, taken with his posture and sharply angled profile. Like a fencer about to engage an opponent, she thought. "Hey there . . ."

"Hey," Danger Man echoed, his attention remaining on his work.

"Who's winning?"

"I'm not sure yet," he replied before attacking the canvas with several bold strokes. He stepped back, assessing their impact, then nodded toward the windows that overlooked the yard. "Your car's not down there. Where'd you park?"

"In a bad neighborhood," Lana replied. "Gone in sixty seconds."

"You serious?"

Lana nodded glumly.

Danger Man looked puzzled. "But you called from the car. Didn't you? I mean . . ."

"Yeah, I did. But I made a stop on the way over."

"That source you were working . . ."

Lana nodded. "Bastard's info was bogus. Car was gone when I came out."

"Any chance it was towed?"

Lana shrugged. "Yeah, I guess . . ."

"Why didn't you say something?"

"I don't know. I just . . ."

"Did you report it?"

"My phone crashed, remember?"

"I offered you mine. They'd be able to tell you if it was towed or not. I mean . . ."

"Hey, hey, lighten up. Okay? Like I said, I need to be off the grid for a while."

"Sorry. Didn't mean to be pushy. You came in the back way, so I just assumed . . ."

"Force of habit," Lana explained as she pirouetted toward him, the robe billowing about her lithe figure, her long, flame-red hair whirling through the air. "Time for your morning break, isn't it?" she prompted with a grin. She tapped the tip of his nose and pressed her naked body against him.

"Well, I've got a meeting with my gallery rep . . . but . . ." He tapped the tip of *her* nose and smiled. "It's time I hit the shower. Give me a couple of minutes."

"Conserve water . . ." Lana said with a seductive giggle, pulling free and beckoning him to follow. She pranced toward the door, passing a workbench next to it. Her eyes drifted across the carpentry and paper-cutting tools scattered across the bench's scarred surface. Several matte knife blades that had spilled from a box glimmered amid the clutter. She did a little turn, confirming Danger Man was preoccupied, and palmed one as she left the studio.

A short time later, Lana was shampooing her hair when Danger Man slipped into the glass enclosure. The bubbling foam was slithering down across her shoulders and glistening torso as she whirled into his arms and kissed him, then locked her legs around his waist as he lifted her off her feet—her gold-medal buns cupped in his hands, her back arched, exposing her breasts to the powerful spray that made her nipples tingle. Now, as she eagerly anticipated, he was, patiently, bringing her closer and closer with his slow, rhythmic thrusts. She shuddered as an intense rush radiated from deep inside her, infusing her flesh with an electrifying sizzle that attended to every pore. Lana waited until Danger Man quickened his pace and threw his head back with a cry of ecstasy as she knew he would, then, all in one motion, she slipped the matte knife blade from beneath the soap dish in the shower caddy and drew its finely honed edge across the side of his neck, severing the carotid artery that was throbbing with unbridled passion. He felt no pain, just a linear, burning sensation that made him shudder as his eyes widened in confusion and the life began draining out of him. Within seconds, his strength had ebbed and his grip had weakened, allowing Lana to disengage and guide him to the floor, where a crimson whirlpool was swirling down the drain.

"I'm sorry," Lana whispered as his eyes glazed in a puzzled stare and his lips pursed in silent supplication. "You were special, but I can't take any chances." She stepped over him and stood beneath the shower, rinsing off his blood, then slipped from the enclosure, wrapping a bath towel around her torso as she returned to the bedroom to dry her hair and get dressed.

Lana's feelings of helplessness had been replaced by a growing sense of empowerment. She knew what she needed to survive, and she had it: a phone that wouldn't be tracked, an anonymous vehicle that wouldn't be targeted by an APB, and a lovely antique and art-filled townhouse in Georgetown where she could spend the day without fear of being discovered. Indeed, having left her car in the church parking lot, she had no doubt that Farrell, Ruben, and other federal agents who were hunting her had concluded she had sought asylum in the nearby Russian embassy and was, therefore, literally and legally beyond their reach. Last but not least, she had everything she needed to launch the code-red, priority-one, Kremlin op—almost.

Lana went into the great room, poured the remainder of the Pomerol into a fresh glass, and settled on the sofa deep in thought: For a few hours she *did* have everything she needed to carry out the op, had it until her email account was shut down, denying her access to Pash's Personal Activation Code. There was nothing she could do about it now, but the shooting incident at the train station had convinced Pash to share his UI with her, and she knew just how she could convince him to do so again.

Lana was back in control of the bout now—*Gotov atakovat!* Ready to attack! She plugged the flash drive with the CSX cybercodes into her laptop, accessed the railroad's operating system, and opened the RCRM program. She was reviewing the shipments she had flagged earlier—the ones that required rerouting to the target—when her eyes darted to a newly scheduled one that *didn't*. Like the others, train CSXT 5415 was prominently flagged as Hazmat but was routed directly over the E Street Bridge during the president's speech! But Lana knew that CSX had agreed not to schedule hazmat shipments during such events, and, as she feared, a safety plan had been enacted. Train CSXT 5415 was the perfect weapon of choice one minute and useless the next. *Gotov atakovat!* Or not?! she thought, pumping herself up. Yes! Yes, ready to attack! It was too good to give up without a fight, and upon scrutinizing the details of 5415's routing, Lana realized that the logistics of the delay, the very linchpin of the safety plan, was its flaw—a flaw that, in a move/countermove cyber war, could be turned to advantage. It was the perfect *kontrazaschita*!

Lana was savoring the moment when the crunch of gravel and the slam of a car door, followed by footsteps on the back porch, got her attention. Whoever the visitor was knocked on the kitchen door. "Dan? Dan it's me," a woman's voice called out. "Dan?" The clack of the latch was followed by the squeak of hinges. "Dan? It's me," she went on as she came through the door and closed it. "It's Fiona."

Lana was crossing the great room when a woman in her early thirties with a pixie haircut and an excess of nervous energy came from the kitchen, lugging a backpack. "Oh, sorry. I . . . I didn't know Dan had company," she said, surprised to see Lana. "I'm Fiona. Fiona Highsmith. His gallery rep."

"Lana, Lana Nichols. His on-again/off-again/on-again . . ." Lana said with self-deprecating charm.

"Sounds like Dan the Man to me," Fiona said with a haughty laugh. "He asked me to come by to review some new work. Spring show I'm putting together."

"Oh, right, he did sort of mention he had something, but . . ." Lana let it trail off with a shrug, and added, "No details. Sorry, I had no idea you were coming by."

"No problem. Need to make a quick pit stop before I get started." Fiona smiled, turned on a heel, and headed in the direction of the master bedroom.

Lana's heart pounded. Her mind raced. "Fiona? Fiona, he's in the shower," she called out, unable to believe what she had just said. "You can use the one upstairs."

"Sure, I'm heading up there anyway."

"Great. I'll tell him you're here."

Fiona picked up her backpack and crossed to the staircase in the foyer.

Lana took a moment to regroup and went about gathering her things, giving Fiona time to use the toilet, get settled in the studio, and concentrate on the job at hand. Then she headed for the stairs in a determined stride.

Fiona was studying one of the finished paintings that leaned against the walls and jotting notes on a pad when Lana joined her.

"He's getting dressed," Lana reported cheerily. "Said he'd be right up."

"Great," Fiona chirped, turning back to the painting with her notepad.

Lana forced a smile, slipped another matte knife blade from those spilled on the workbench, and took two quick steps toward her.

Chapter Fifty-Three

The meeting in Farrell's office broke up just after two a.m. Katkov didn't dare return to the Ritz-Carlton. Scotto wasn't up to the drive to Alexandria, and they bunked in the All-Nighter Marriot, which was how JTTF personnel referred to the staff lounge. Katkov spent a few hours making notes on his laptop, then reinserted the SIM card and battery in his cell phone and called Vera.

"Nikasha!" she exclaimed, relieved and delighted. "I've been calling and calling. There must be something wrong with your phone."

"Sorry, the KGB was using it to track me. I had to disable it."

"KGB? I think you meant FSB or SVA . . ."

"No, I meant KGB," Katkov fired back. "They are still KGB here—only worse."

"Well, for what it's worth, I'm at your apartment with Churkin. He has an inventory of everything FSB confiscated and is returning your entire collection."

"He'd better be. From the minute I got here, the bastards have been trying to kill me. He sold them on letting me leave the country because it would be smarter to terminate me here than there. I was in no position to argue."

"Maybe he feels guilty . . ."

"No fucking way! We made a deal. I get the collection back and he gets what he needs to nail the Kremlin's ass. I knew the story was here, Vera—and it was. I found the bastards responsible for killing Grusha, and the FBI agent who contacted her, and I found out why too."

"That's wonderful. I'm so happy for you, Nikasha. When are you coming home?"

"Soon. If I can stay alive long enough. Things are moving quickly. With luck it will be over tonight. Watch the president's speech. If there's news about this . . . well, then you'll know."

"I will," Vera said with an anxious sigh. "I miss you, Nikasha. I can't wait till you get back. I've been on all the travel websites. Paris is wonderful, but Venice . . . Oh, Niko, Venice is just amazing! We could rent a little *appartamento* on a canal. Take the vaparetto to the Lido. Go to the opera at La Fenice, Vivaldi concerts in the churches, and—"

"Vera? Vera, I can't do this now," Katkov snapped, wishing he hadn't. "I'm . . . I'm sorry, but the pressure's been nonstop. I've barely slept in days. And I've been worried sick about Mika. How is she? Is she managing to cope?"

"As well as can be expected. She's been going through Grusha's things. Closets, drawers, boxes and more boxes. I'm helping her. We laugh. We cry. It's very hard for her. Knowing her mother's killers will be brought to justice should bolster her spirits."

"Let's hope so," Katkov said with a weary sigh. "I'm sorry. I have to go. I'll be a basket case if I don't get some sleep."

"Take care, Nikasha. Be careful, please."

"I promise. I'll call soon as I can."

In the morning, Ruben slept late, had breakfast with Julie, and made the mistake of suggesting that her dream to return to Bogotá might be unrealistic. Shortly thereafter, he found himself on the GW Parkway heading into the District.

Farrell was on the GW doing the same but had to make a stop first. He'd lost his marriage to his career, and his only child to the war in Iraq, and each year, on the anniversary of her death, he joined his ex-wife, Carol, at their daughter's gravesite in Arlington National Cemetery. The uniformed officer at the gate noted the Permanent Vehicle Pass on the windshield and waved him through. Section 60, where those who were killed in Iraq and Afghanistan are interred, was just off Eisenhower Drive a short distance from the gate. A slight woman huddled in a winter coat was standing along the roadside next to a car, clutching a bouquet of flowers. Farrell parked and joined her. Without a word, she took his arm, and they walked between the headstones that marched in perfect alignment across the snow-covered landscape to one that read: Maryanne Farrell— Sgt.—U.S. Army—July 14, 1976–January 12, 2004. Heads bowed, eyes glistening, they had been standing in silent prayer for several moments when Farrell noticed a tear rolling down Carol's cheek. He was brushing it with a fingertip when his phone rang, piercing the solemn silence. Carol flinched at the sound. Farrell glanced at the caller ID. "Not a good time, Ruben. What? . . . Uh-huh . . . Uh-huh . . . Won't be long."

Carol eyed him knowingly, the lesson of her experience leaving little doubt she was about to be disappointed. "We have to reschedule," she said, referring to their annual ritual of catching up over lunch.

"I should've called you," Farrell said with a heartfelt sigh. "I'm sorry."

"Priority-one situation."

Farrell nodded grimly. "Stay out of the District tonight. That's all I can tell you."

Carol nodded, glanced up at him with a wistful smile, and kissed his cheek.

"I'll be in touch," Farrell said in a raspy whisper. He gave her arm a little squeeze and hurried toward his car.

Carol stared at her daughter's grave, her eyes glistening, then bent forward and placed the flowers on the pristine whiteness at the base of the headstone.

Carlsen, Caitlin, Pash, and the tiger team had spent the night deep beneath Union Station in Amtrak Computer Control, installing and shaking down the new cybersecurity program with Grabowski and the Amtrak computer techs. The lack of sleep, unnerving pressure, and heady scent of ozone along with the constant hum from the rows of servers and computer workstations had taken their toll. It was late morning when Katkov and Scotto joined them, and well past noon by the time Farrell and Ruben arrived.

"So, we up and running?" Farrell asked, his voice reduced to a craggy rasp.

Carlsen nodded crisply. "All cybersecurity programs up and running. All Amtrak operating programs monitored and protected."

"We've also given CSX and CLX a heads-up," Grabowski chimed in. "They're keeping an eye on things from their end."

"That heads-up includes the CSX antiterrorist and rapid-response teams?"

"Sure does," Grabowski replied. "They're coordinating with Amtrak police and local law enforcement." He pointed to the panoramic tracking screen and added, "We're keeping an eye on all hazmat shipments that Nichols could reroute to the District, those in Pennsylvania and Maryland, for example, but we're keeping real close watch on CSXT 5415—the bright-red one there. It's a sixty-five-tanker shipment, heading north from the Clorox plant in Georgia through the Carolinas and Virginia to the Seagirt terminal in Baltimore. Many shipments have a—"

"Baltimore?!" Farrell echoed, visibly alarmed. "Only way to get there is through the District on that damned bridge."

"Right, after which it uses the Virginia Avenue Tunnel to bypass Union Station," Grabowski said, matter-of-factly. "As I was about to explain, many shipments have fixed delivery dates and times in their contracts. So, instead of being held in the Atlanta Yards, CSXT 5415 departed on schedule, but an hour before the president's speech, the train will be shunted onto a siding in Virginia twenty miles from the Capitol and held there until he finishes. By the time 5415 starts rolling again, the Capitol Building and surrounding areas will be vacated."

Farrell looked unmoved. "That's getting a little too close for comfort, Andy."

Grabowski sighed and splayed his hands. "Look, if it'll make you feel better, every locomotive has an electronics package that communicates with the signals network and this control room. A program that contains 5415's data—the number of tankers, gallons of chlorine, weight and length of the train, along with speed restrictions, grade, curves, signals, and switches, including the hold on the siding—has been downloaded into the computer. If the train deviates from those parameters, the engineer gets a warning on a screen above the engine's dash. For example, if it's exceeding the speed limit and he doesn't respond, the alerter starts screaming at him; if he still doesn't respond, Positive Train Control kicks in, automatically slows the train, or applies the emergency air brakes and shuts it down."

"As long as our girl can't hack into that computer and take control of the train," Farrell retorted. "Right?"

Grabowski nodded grudgingly. "Right."

"But remember," Carlsen chimed in. "She'd have to hack into the new cybersecurity program first, and she can't do that without Pash's personal access code. And we know she doesn't have it. Right, Pash?"

Pash nodded. "And she never will."

"I'll try to keep that in mind," Farrell said. He motioned Katkov, Scotto, and Ruben aside, and in his raspy voice confided, "I can't get past this thing in my gut that Nichols checking into the Russian embassy is a head-fake."

"Yeah, but we've got eyes on it now," Ruben protested.

Farrell emitted a frustrated groan. "The point is, if she's gone to ground somewhere else, we could bust her ass and put an end to all this . . . this craziness."

"I'm with *you*, boss," Scotto said. "I mean, she must have a life. I'd be cooping with a girlfriend, or some guy I'm hooking up with, maybe even a coworker . . . somebody we wouldn't have under surveillance."

Katkov nodded in agreement. "Indeed, perhaps she has a favorite pub, a place where she prefers to wind down."

"There is this joint in the District," Ruben said, reflecting. "Nichols dragged me there once. Got the feeling it was her default watering hole. Le Diplomate. You know it?"

"Heard of it," Farrell grunted. "Not exactly my scene."

"Gabby, isn't that where Nichols took *him* yesterday?" Katkov prompted, gesturing to Pash in the maze of computer workstations.

"Yeah, yeah we followed them there from Amtrak HQ and back."

Ruben's head cocked in thought. "Come to think of it, she had the hots for this guy at the bar, was about to make a move, but she got texted and buzzed on out of there."

"You know who he is?" Katkov asked.

Ruben shook his head no.

"Then maybe you ought to buzz on *over* there and find out," Farrell fired back. "Chat up the bartender. See if she's a regular, who she hangs with, whatever . . ."

Ruben had just turned to go when his cell phone pinged, stopping him. "Okay, listen up," he said, scrolling through the text. "Levenger's Gulfstream is parked at Montreal International. Cockpit crew's timed out till five. No flight plan filed as of yet."

"Great. Keep on it," Farrell said as Ruben hurried off.

"Dick? Somebody you should meet," Grabowski called out as he approached with a colleague in tow. "Mark Ingles, Amtrak hazmat specialist—Dick Farrell, Chief, JTTF. Mark can bring you up to speed on the cargo we're dealing with here."

"I'm not sure I want to hear this," Farrell said glumly.

"I'm not sure you do either," Ingles said, leaving no doubt he meant it. "We're talking ultra-hazardous cargo. Each tanker carries thirty thousand gallons of highly concentrated liquid chlorine, which, when exposed to air, quickly boils into a highly toxic gas. Think: First World War. It's heavier than air, stays close to the ground, and flows into every nook, cranny, crevice, and orifice. Eyes, nasal passages, tracheas, and lungs can be severely damaged or destroyed. Imagine sixty-five chlorine-filled tankers rupturing in a derailment or crash. That's sixty-five times thirty thousand. We're talking damn near two million gallons of the nasty stuff. Bottom line, there's enough CL in that rail shipment to turn DC into a ghost town."

Farrell took a deep breath. "Thanks. Now give me the bad news," he cracked, glancing at a TV monitor tuned to one of the cable news stations. The countdown clock read: 02:45:36 to SOTUS when his phone rang. The caller ID belonged to the White House chief of staff. "Got your wake-up call yesterday," McDonough said when Farrell answered. "More lead time would've been nice."

"Sorry, sir, per protocol we alerted all relevant agencies soon as the intel was confirmed and the target identified. We didn't want to cry wolf or create a panic."

"Makes two of us," McDonough said sharply. "But this is the president's final SOTUS. His best chance to remind the nation and the world that he rescued the economy, passed healthcare reform, blocked a nuclear Iran, reformed Wall Street, brokered a climate-change agreement, and eliminated Osama bin Laden. When you tack on Putin's moves in Syria, Ukraine, and Crimea; the threat from ISIS; and the hot-button issues of the primaries, it's crucial he command center stage. Canceling and retreating into the nuclear bunker would fuel claims that his cautious leadership has caused us to lose respect around the world and endanger his legacy. I need to know now, right now, that the chance of a hazmat catastrophe in the District tonight is zero. Yes or no?"

Farrell winced. "That's a tough call, sir. The vector has been identified and compromised, but not terminated, and I'd be—"

"Yes or no?" McDonough interrupted. "I need the answer now."

"The *right* answer," Farrell retorted. "I've got cybersecurity, computer, rail shipment, and hazmat experts here. Let me run it past them and get back to you."

"Not on your life," McDonough fired back. "I'll hold. Make it fast."

Farrell gathered the group and held up his phone. "President's chief of staff. He needs an immediate, go/no-go on tonight's speech. Can we guarantee that the commander in chief, the members of our three branches of government, and the hundreds of thousands of people within the kill zone won't be annihilated by a toxic cloud of chlorine gas? Yes or no?"

A half dozen pair of weary eyes darted about anxiously. No one spoke.

"Axel?" Farrell prompted. "You're on point here. Talk to me."

Carlsen's lips tightened. "As I've said, as long as Nichols doesn't have Pash's PAC, the system is secure. Yes, we could guarantee that."

"And as *I've* said, she doesn't have it, and never will," Pash added sharply.

"You sure? Positive? A thousand percent?" Farrell challenged.

"Ten thousand," Pash replied.

"Andy?" Farrell prompted.

"Definitely . . . Long as that train's parked on a siding twenty miles away."

"Everybody else on board?" Farrell prompted.

Another tense silence followed as Pash, Caitlin, and the other techs wrestled with it, then nodded one by one.

Farrell put the phone to his ear. "I'd still prefer to err on the side of caution, but the consensus is unanimous. We can guarantee it."

"Excellent," McDonough chirped smartly. "The president will be pleased."

Farrell pocketed his phone and glanced at the panoramic tracking screen. CSXT 5415 had left North Carolina far behind and was well into Virginia. He swept his eyes across the team gathered round him, and said, "God help us if we missed something." He sat with it a moment, then cocked his head and called Celia. "Don't you ever go home?"

"JTTF is my home away from home, sir."

"Mine too," Farrell said wearily. "Not to mention Nichols has us thinking the Russian embassy is *hers*. Put out a fugitive alert. Airports, train stations, you know the drill—and then go home. That's an order."

Chapter Fifty-Four

Traffic on Massachusetts was at a crawl, and it took Ruben forty minutes to get to Le Diplomate. The bistro was buzzing when he badged the maître d', who stepped aside with a condescending nod. Ruben made his way through the crowd to the far corner of the bar where Julio was running the show and waved him over with his ID case.

"Agente Diaz," Julio intoned eyeing it. *"Elige tu veneno."*

"Pick my poison?" Ruben retorted, placing his phone on the bar. A photo of Lana he downloaded from her HR file filled the screen. "How about *her*? Been around lately?"

Julio's eyes narrowed, then widened. "Yeah, oh yeah, Red's a regular. Not easy to forget. Lot of guys looking to poke *her* in the panties."

"I'm interested in the guy who did."

"Well, there was this one she hooked up with sometimes . . ."

"He have a name?"

Julio cocked his head, then nodded. "Dan, yeah, yeah, it's Dan."

"Dan who?"

"This is a first-name business, you know?" Julio replied with a shrug. "But"—he pointed to a painting on the wall adjacent to the bar—"that's one of his masterpieces over there. Pretty sure it's signed."

The signature at the bottom of the energetic abstraction was written with a crisp flourish. Ruben gave Julio a thumbs-up, then typed Daniel Whitlock into the DMV search window on his phone, got the Georgetown address, and hurried outside to his Jeep.

The cable news countdown clock on the TV above bar read: 01:51:16 to SOTUS.

It was 7:15 when Lana hurried down the back stairs of Danger Man's townhouse, clutching a fistful of keys. One of them had a worn Ford logo. Fiona Highsmith's car was parked between the Speedster and Ford pickup. Lana tossed her laptop case into the latter and drove off. Minutes later, she had crossed the Francis Scott Key Bridge and was heading west toward Dulles. In less than a half hour she was on the ramp that led to the

Signature Flight Support complex. She left the pickup in the parking lot, hurried beneath the gray canopy that welcomed Signature's well-heeled clients to the sleek terminal, and badged the security officer at the Departures Desk. "Hey, how're you doing," Lana said cheerily. "Weren't you on the last time I was here?"

"I'm always on," the agent replied with a laugh. "Doing a double today."

"Makes two of us."

The agent checked the arrivals log on her monitor, informed Lana the Gulfstream had arrived, and cleared her to board. She left the terminal in a jaunty stride, then dashed across the tarmac and up the airstair, joining Julian and Kate in the jetliner's lounge. After setting up her laptop, she reinserted the battery and SIM card into her cell phone and got to work. The crew wasted no time queuing for takeoff, and the Gulfstream was in the air by the time the Fugitive Alert with Lana's photo popped onto the monitor at the Departures Desk and on monitors in terminals throughout the airport.

In northern Virginia, the sixty-five chlorine-filled tankers of CSXT 5415 were slithering through the darkness like a mile-long yellow-and-blue snake. The steel rails glistened in the beam of the locomotive's headlight as the train navigated a series of switches that directed it onto a siding just south of Alexandria twenty miles from the capital. From the moment the train departed the Clorox plant in Georgia, the electronics package in the locomotive's cab had been constantly reporting its precise location and status to Amtrak Computer Control beneath Union Station.

Katkov, Scotto, and Farrell were monitoring the train's progress on the tracking screen with Grabowski. The alphanumeric indicators above the screen read: CSXT 5415. SPEED: 005—004—003. In the maze of computer workstations nearby, Carlsen, Pash, and Caitlin were monitoring the cybersecurity program for alerts. When the indicator read 000, Grabowski glanced to the TV monitor, where members of Congress, the Supreme Court, the Cabinet, and their guests were assembling in the House Chamber in the Capitol Building. The cable news countdown clock read: 01:03:12 to SOTUS. "Right on schedule," Grabowski said with a clap of his hands. "So far so good."

Katkov winced and pushed his glasses up into his hair. "Perhaps rather too good. As my mother was fond of saying, be careful what you wish for . . ."

"Yeah," Scotto chimed in. "Mine used to say, don't put the *malocchio* on it."

Katkov looked baffled. "The what?"

"The evil eye, the horns," Scotto explained, waggling a hand with index finger and pinkie extended.

"Well, mine preached the power of positive thinking," Grabowski countered with a wry smile. "Of course, growing up in Poland during the '60s, she had little choice."

"Yeah, well, as mine would say . . . you're all full of shit," Farrell cracked, eliciting laughter from the others. They were all starting to relax when his cell phone rang.

"Bad news, boss," Ruben said when Farrell answered. "I tracked down that guy Nichols was hot on. But she found him first. Throat slashed, naked, in the shower."

"Chrissakes," Farrell hissed. "Sounds familiar, doesn't it?"

"Yeah, his name's Whitlock. There's more. Second victim. Female. Mid-thirties. Throat slashed in upstairs studio. I got a CSI team coming in."

Farrell winced and bit a lip. "She's on the loose, dammit."

"I ran Whitlock's DMV. He's got a Porsche, and a Ford pickup that's gone."

"And she's driving it. Good work. We'll put out an APB, and—"

"Hold on, boss, hold on," Ruben interrupted. "FAA text coming in. Gulfstream did a touch and go at Dulles twenty minutes ago."

"Dammit. Didn't they file a flight plan?"

"Yeah, in Canada with the TCCA. I'm looking at it now."

"FAA was supposed to notify us!"

"They just did. But there's always lag time between agencies, boss. Montreal/Dulles is just an hour and a half. So—"

"Fucking bureaucracy," Farrell growled. "Nichols isn't on the loose. She's on that plane."

Chapter Fifty-Five

On the overhead TV monitor in Amtrak Computer Control, the First Family had just arrived in the House Chamber balcony and were greeting friends and honored guests. CNN's Wolf Blitzer appeared in split screen and reported, "We just received word that the president is en route to the Capitol and will be arriving momentarily."

In the maze of workstations, Pash was hunched over his computer, monitoring the cybersecurity program for alerts when his phone rang. His eyes widened at the sight of Lana's caller ID.

"It's me," Lana said when he answered. "Can you talk?"

"Give me a moment," Pash replied, moving out of earshot of the others. "Where are you?"

"In hiding. The hit team from the train station came at me when I went home last night. The sleeper is trying to stop me from countering the cyberattack."

"I . . . I don't know how to say this, Lana," Pash said, his voice quavering. "But . . . but Farrell and the others are telling me it's you. They're saying you're . . . you're the sleeper."

"Of course," Lana scoffed. "They've all been taken in. That's what sleepers do. They control, manipulate, and frame others for their misdeeds, not to mention getting them to shut down my email account."

"In other words, you haven't been able to gain access to my PAC."

"Exactly. That's why I'm calling. You have to share it with me right now."

"Why is it so important? I'm in Computer Control monitoring the security program with Carlsen and the team. All is well. It's running perfectly."

"Not for long. They're good, but, together, you and I are better, much better. The cyber war is about to start, and we both need control of the ESR and PTC programs if we're to fight it. You have to share it with me, Pash. You have to. Hundreds of thousands of people are going die if you don't!"

"They're telling me hundreds of thousands will die if I do!"

"They're lying. They're using you," Lana said, tapping FaceTime on her phone. "I need to see your face, Pash, and I need you to see mine. Look at me, Pash. Look at me. Look into my eyes and you'll know I'm telling you the truth."

Pash lowered the phone and stared in troubled silence at Lana's image.

"Pash? Pash are you there," she prompted, trying not to sound desperate.

"Yes, Lana, I am."

"Good. Look into my eyes, Pash. This cyber catastrophe is going to happen. There's a train with sixty-five tankers of lethal chlorine out there headed for the District. We have to stop it. I can't do it without your help."

"We have stopped it, Lana," Pash said evenly. "The train is parked on a siding twenty miles from the Capitol and will remain there until it's safe to proceed."

"Look at me Pash. Look at my face. If you don't share your PAC with me now, right now, a lot of people are going to die. You have to believe me. You understand?"

"I'm sorry Lana," Pash replied with a pained wince. "I *am* looking at you. I see mendacity in your eyes, and hear desperation and deception in your voice. I'm . . . I'm afraid you're not the person I thought you were."

"Of course I am," Lana said softly. "Please, I'm trying to prevent a disaster. As I've been saying all along, I can't fight this cyber war without your help."

"That's right, Lana, you can't, and, yes, as you've been saying, we will be fighting a move/countermove cyber war, but we will be adversaries not allies."

"That's ridiculous," Lana snapped. "How many times do I have to say it? I can't do this without you."

"Precisely. Which is why I am unwilling to—"

"You all right?" Katkov interrupted. He'd been observing Pash's animated conversation with growing concern, and he made his way through the maze of workstations.

"Hold on," Pash said, covering the phone as he turned to Katkov. "A cousin in Yemen. Things have been going quite badly there as of late," he explained, having little trouble sounding unsettled.

Katkov was nodding with empathy when Pash returned the phone to his ear, inadvertently giving him a fleeting glimpse of Lana's image. "I'll take that!" Katkov exclaimed, snatching the phone from Pash's hand. "It's Katkov!" he barked into it.

"I can see that," Lana said smugly. "You look angry."

"Try outraged. How could you do this? How?! How could you?!"

"Because I love my country!" Lana replied, glancing across the Gulfstream's lounge to Julian and Kate. "I've got Russian DNA in my genes and Russian blood in my veins!"

"So do I!" Katkov retorted. "It's *my* country too! You're just helping Putin and his henchmen to destroy it!"

"Traitors like you, who conspire with the Americans and Europeans, already have! Volodya is a great man. A true patriot who wants to reclaim the Motherland's rightful place in the world order, to reclaim the dignity and respect she deserves, and has too long been denied!"

"Spare me the Kremlin propaganda. Your Volodya is a murderous thug. If you really cared about Mother Russia, you would be supporting those who want it to become a true democracy, not assassinating them!"

"Sorry about your colleague, Nikolai," Lana said over the steady hum of the Gulfstream's engines. "But she knew the risks, and took them."

"While you spent your life in the world's most developed democracy!"

"Guilty as charged," Lana fired back snidely. "What does that tell you?"

"It tells me you've been brainwashed, and that you're not the person I thought you were."

"Thanks for the compliment. That's twice today. I rest my case."

"You *have* no case. You'd know that if you'd been living in Russia all your life, but you've never even been there, have you?"

"Sorry, I don't have time for this . . . this propaganda!" Lana retorted, spitting it back at him. She hung up with an exasperated groan and looked off deep in thought, the sound of air rushing past the cabin filling the silence.

"Well, that went well," Kate finally said with a sarcastic grimace.

"*Merde*," Julian grunted. "You still don't have everything you need, do you?

"No. No, I don't, but I'm not beaten yet!" Lana replied, her expression brightening as she went to work on her laptop.

In Computer Control, Katkov handed the phone to Pash and burned him with a look. "She was trying to convince you to reveal your PAC, wasn't she?"

Pash lowered his eyes and nodded solemnly.

"And you gave it to her . . ."

"Of course not."

Katkov looked incredulous. "Why should I believe you? You just lied to me."

"Yes, and I'm quite sorry. I lied because I feared you would think *I* had called *her.* I promise you, I didn't."

"And why should I believe *that?*"

"Because you and the others opened my eyes to the truth. Agent Nichols said we would be fighting a move/countermove cyber war together. I just told her that she was quite correct—but it will be against each other." He sighed and glanced to his workstation. "Believe what you like. I'm sorry, but I should be monitoring the security program for alerts," he said as he turned and hurried off.

At the far end of the vast space, Ruben popped out of an elevator and came running over to Farrell. "The CSI team's working the scene. What's going on?"

"Nichols just tried to convince her favorite mark to cough up his PAC."

"And?"

"Looks like the kid hung tough," Farrell replied, his head cocked at a thought. "Confiscate his phone. Find out where that call came from."

On the TV monitor overhead, the sergeant-at-arms took his position in the center aisle that led down to the floor of the House Chamber. "Ladies and gentlemen, the president of the United States!" he announced with great fanfare as the president appeared to rousing applause. He made his way through the crowd that surged from both sides of the aisle and engaged in the time-honored ritual of handshakes, hugs, backslaps, finger points, and shoutouts en route to the podium, then he waved, acknowledging the applause, and raised his hands several times to dampen it.

"Mr. Speaker, Mr. Vice President, members of Congress, my fellow Americans," he began as the applause faded. "Tonight marks the eighth year I've come here to report on the State of the Union. And for this final one I'm going to try to make it shorter. I know some of you are antsy to get back to Iowa."

Chapter Fifty-Six

In Amtrak Computer Control, Katkov, Scotto, Farrell, Ruben, and Grabowski, along with Carlsen and the Cyber-Borgen team, had all gathered in the workstation maze below the tracking screen and were starting to believe they had the situation under control. The red line extended from Georgia through the Carolinas and into northern Virginia, where CSXT 5415 had been parked on the siding twenty miles from the Capitol since eight p.m. It had been there for more than an hour and twenty minutes when Katkov craned his neck and stole a glance at the screen, then did a double-take, squinting at it from behind his wire frame glasses. *Was the red line creeping forward?* The alphanumeric indicators read: 5415—SPEED 000—002—003. "Am I daft?" he said to Grabowski. "Or is that train moving?!"

Grabowski looked up at the screen and winced. "Sure as hell is!"

Katkov whirled to the workstation where Pash was hunched over his keyboard monitoring the cybersecurity program. "Nichols played you, didn't she? She convinced you to give her your PAC."

"No. On my dear mother's soul, she didn't," Pash replied. "Why?"

"Because that train's moving!" Katkov pointed to the screen and pinned him with a look. "Then, what?! She accessed your email account? Hacked your Sent file?"

"Impossible," Pash replied. "It has impenetrable protection. I do recall mentioning my PAC was the date of my wedding. I suspect it was the New York City Records Bureau that she—"

"Who cares how she got it?!" Grabowski interrupted. "That train's moving! It's picking up speed!" He slipped on a wireless headset with pipe-stem mic and said, "Amtrak Control to CSXT 5415. Control to 5415. What's going on, Al? Come on, talk to me! What's the hell's going on?"

"Beats the hell out of me," the engineer in the lead locomotive replied, sounding frantic. "These locos, they just . . . just came to life and started rolling," he went on, shouting over an earsplitting screech. "The alerter is screaming like crazy. I've got no control. I can't shut her down! It's like someone's controlling it remotely."

"Someone *is*!" Grabowski exclaimed, the red line snaking slowly through a series of switches onto the main spur, where it began picking up speed. "They're controlling the signals and switching systems too!"

The alphanumeric indicator now read: CSXT 5415. SPEED: 005-006-007 MPH.

"Twenty-two miles to the E Street Bridge," Grabowski calculated. "It'll take fifteen of 'em to get up to notch eight."

Farrell looked baffled. "Notch eight?"

"Wide-open throttle. With the load that train's pulling, speed'll max out somewhere between ninety to a hundred miles per hour. At which point it'll be five minutes from the E Street Bridge."

The indicator now read: CSXT 5415. SPEED: 16 MPH

"We're twenty minutes from ground zero and counting?!" Farrell said, visibly alarmed. He pulled his phone and stared at his contacts list. "Damn!" he said, throwing up his hands. "The NSA and everybody else are at that damned speech."

"Better alert somebody!" Grabowski fired back. "Must be a couple thousand people in that building! There's got to be some kind of an evac plan."

"Evac?! To where? The street? Into a cloud of lethal gas?! No way they'd clear the three-mile zone in time."

"Boss?" Ruben called out. "Nichols's call was relayed from a com-sat that covers aircraft in the East Coast corridor—got to be the Gulfstream."

"What I figured," Farrell said decisively. "Wanted to be sure she's on board before I made the call. Only way to stop her now is to take out that plane."

"I want her alive, boss," Ruben protested.

"Me too. But I want the government and 250,000 people alive more!" Farrell countered. "It got screwed up on 9/11, but it's not going to get screwed up this time!" he went on, convinced of the fact that the air-defense procedures that failed during 9/11 had been rectified. He called the National Military Command Center, identified himself to the duty officer, and said, "We have a priority-one national security emergency. Target is a Gulfstream in the East Coast corridor. It needs to be taken out immediately."

"The SOD would have to sign off on that, sir," the duty officer explained, referring to the secretary of defense. "It's—"

"There's no time for that, dammit!" Farrell interrupted. "He, and anybody else that matters, is at the State of the Union."

"I'm sure you're aware of the designated survivor, sir, Perhaps—"

"No way am I letting the *secretary of education* make this call. If we don't take that aircraft out in the next fifteen minutes, the president and the entire USG, along with anyone within a three-mile radius of the E Street Bridge is going to be dead!"

"I understand, sir. Do you have coordinates or tail number?"

"Hold on." Farrell turned to Ruben and barked, "The tail number. Get the tail number off that flight plan."

Ruben found the text and gave Farrell the phone. The screen read NJL1KS.

"Got it," Farrell rasped into his phone. "November, Juliet, Lima, the numeral one, Kilo, Sierra.

"Copy that," the duty officer said, and repeated it.

"Take out that aircraft now, son," Farrell growled, buttoning it. "I mean now! And get me patched in to fire control at Joint Andrews."

Since the air-defense miscues of 9/11, rotating two-pilot teams of the 121st Fighter Squadron at Joint Andrews Base in Camp Springs, Maryland, as well as other air force bases across the country, had been on 24/7 alert. Tests were run regularly, but this was *real world*, as military air-traffic-control personnel referred to it. In minutes, two pilots had scrambled, donned flight gear, and slipped into the cockpits of their F-16C Fighting Falcons. Two AIM-9 Sidewinder air-to-air missiles hung from the Sniper Advanced Targeting Pods beneath their wings as they screamed down the runway and climbed into the darkness. The Falcons' avionics swiftly acquired the Gulfstream's transponder signal and began tracking it as they accelerated to Mach 1.5 in pursuit.

"This is Flying Falcon five-zero-niner," the lead F-16 pilot said, his eyes riveted to the heads-up display on his canopy. "Tracking target and closing. Please advise."

"Copy that," the Joint Andrews fire control officer replied. "You are authorized to acquire and lock on target."

Chapter Fifty-Seven

In the House Chamber, the president was midway into his speech, extolling America's global stature: "The United States of America is the most powerful nation on Earth. Surveys show our standing around the world is higher than when I was elected to this office. People of the world do not look to Beijing or Moscow to lead—they look to us.

"I know this is a dangerous time. But that's not because of diminished American strength or some looming superpower. We're threatened less by evil empires and more by failing states. Russia is pouring resources to prop up Ukraine and Syria—states they see slipping away from their orbit. Both al-Qaeda and ISIL pose a threat because terrorists who place no value on human life, including their own, can do a lot of damage."

In Amtrak Control, the red line on the tracking screen was moving like the beam of a laser toward the heart of the District. As Grabowski had calculated, it took approximately fifteen miles and as many minutes for the mile-long train with its nine thousand tons of toxic cargo to reach notch 8. The indicator read: SPEED: 92 MPH. "Push is coming to shove, here," he said, his voice taut with concern. "That train's six, seven miles from the E Street Bridge and the sharp curve before the tunnel. At that speed we're seven, eight minutes from derailment. Running the—"

"And disaster!" Farrell exclaimed.

"Running the numbers in my head," Grabowski charged on, "with the load that train's pulling, even in emergency-braking mode, it'll take half that time to come to a full stop or slow down enough so that it *doesn't* derail."

"And if you're wrong, and the F-16s don't make it? We've got, what? Less than four minutes before it's into that curve?!"

"Five, if we're lucky."

Grabowski, Farrell, and Katkov hurried to Pash's workstation, where Carlsen, Caitlin, and tech team members were working with him to counter Lana's cyberattack.

"You've got less than five minutes to shut Nichols down," Grabowski said.

"Fifty wouldn't be enough," Pash retorted.

"What?!" Farrell exclaimed.

"She's using a rootkit webcrawler to control the operating system," Pash explained. "It's a virus that self-replicates faster than I can delete it!"

"So it's never deleted and Nichols never loses control!" Caitlin added.

Katkov looked confused. "This cyber war. Might I ask where it's taking place?"

"In those servers," Grabowski replied, indicating the rows of sleek metal cabinets behind them. "It's move/countermove between his computer and hers, and they're the battlefield."

Katkov's eyes widened with insight. "My God, I suspect we're overthinking again. I don't know much about computers and servers, but I know things that run on electricity stop working when they're unplugged."

"The servers can't just be *unplugged*. That'd red-board the whole system. We'd be shutting down the onboard electronics of every train between here and—"

"But if the servers are down, Nichols is out of business. Yes?"

"Yes, but without ESR and PTC it'll be up to the engineer to stop the train. You still with me, Al?" Grabowski barked into his pipe-stem mic.

"I'm hanging in!" the engineer shouted over the screeching alerter.

"Get ready to go to dynamic braking!" Grabowski ordered as he and Katkov dashed between the rows of servers to a wall of equipment racks. Each was labeled by sector and the computer program it controlled. An electronic box labeled "Emergency Shut Down" was prominently positioned at the top of each rack.

"Which sectors are we targeting?" Katkov asked, frantic with uncertainty.

"Locomotive electronics are five, six, and seven. ESR and PTC are eight, nine, and ten," Grabowski replied as he and Katkov started throwing switches. "Hit the brakes, Al!" Grabowski shouted into his pipe-stem. "Hit 'em now!"

CSXT 5415's engineer entered the emergency braking code on his keyboard, then thumbed the emergency braking button. "I just did! Nothing's happening!" he shouted over the alerter's deafening screech.

"What?!" Grabowski exclaimed. "You sure you entered the code correctly?!"

"Positive! I'd be looking at a re-enter prompt if I hadn't!"

"What's wrong?!" Katkov asked, his eyes wide with alarm.

"The servers haven't shut down!" Grabowski replied. "The backup power must've kicked in!" He ran through the canyons of servers to another wall of equipment racks labeled "Emergency Generators" and threw every circuit breaker to the Off position. "Al?! Al, try it again now!"

The engineer repeated the keyboard procedure and thumbed the emergency braking button again. The sudden deceleration slammed him forward into the dash as the hurtling train shuddered and screeched in protest. "I have control! Emergency brakes engaged! Dynamic brake five! Six! Seven! Dynamic brake eight!" he went on calling out the stages over the ear-piercing shriek of steel grinding against steel that came from the more than 550 brake blocks—four per carriage, eight per tanker car, sixteen per each of the two locomotives at the head of the train—that had slammed hard against the train's wheels, sending showers of sparks and streams of smoke into the darkness.

In the infinite blackness above the Atlantic, the pilot of the lead F-16 was monitoring the heads-up display on his canopy. An "X" appeared in the center of the blue, data-filled targeting diagram that was tracking the Gulfstream. "This is Flying Falcon five-zero-niner," the pilot said. "I have a lock on target. Request permission to fire."

"Permission granted," the fire control officer at Joint Andrews replied.

In the Amtrak Computer Control Center, the alphanumeric indicators read: CSXT 5415. SPEED: 70-65-60. As the train's speed continued to decrease, Farrell realized there was no longer any need to take out the Gulfstream and made a call. "Abort the mission! Abort!" he barked when the fire control officer at Andrews responded. "Call off those F-16s!"

In the lead F-16, the pilot lifted his thumb from the firing button on his joystick and coolly reported, "Missile away."

"I don't know if you heard that, sir," the fire control officer said to Farrell. "But the pilot just reported missile away."

The heat-seeking AIM-9 Sidewinder came to life as it dropped from the pod beneath the F-16's wing and pulled its fiery trail through the darkness.

In Computer Control, Pash was standing at his workstation, eyes riveted to the panoramic screen that showed the train racing into the heart of the District when his cell phone rang. Lana's face filled the screen.

"I beat you Pash! I beat you! I won!" Lana exclaimed when he answered.

Pash shuddered and was about to reply when Lana screamed and her image was vaporized by a blinding orange flash.

Having homed in on the heat signature of the engine beneath the Gulfstream's right wing, the Sidewinder had flown dead-center into its exhaust manifold, and exploded in a spectacular fireball, turning the aircraft into massive chunks of flaming debris that arced through the darkness and plummeted toward the waters of the Atlantic below.

"Target engaged and destroyed," the pilot reported.

"Damn, damn, dammit!" Farrell muttered through clenched teeth.

"It's not over yet!" Grabowski exclaimed, pointing to the red line on the tracking screen that indicated the train was still moving. The alphanumeric indicators read: SPEED: 45 MPH—POSTED LIMIT: 20 MPH as the train raced across the E Street Bridge. The wheels of the locomotive and the sixty-five chlorine-filled tankers in its wake were fighting to stay on the rails as it leaned hard into the curve and roared into the Virginia Avenue Tunnel. More than thirty tank cars had vanished into the blackened shaft before the train ground to a bone-jarring stop.

In Computer Control, the hum of the servers that were still operating filled the pin-drop silence that followed. Everyone from Katkov, Scotto, Farrell and Ruben to Grabowski, Pash, Carlsen, and Caitlin, and on down to the lowliest Amtrak comp-tech was too exhausted from the lack of sleep and the hours of unrelenting pressure to react. Indeed, they were all beyond cheering or applauding and just sagged collectively in a combination of shell-shocked relief and wary disbelief.

On the TV monitor overhead, the president was wrapping up his speech, his staccato cadence building to a stem-winding crescendo: "I can promise that a little over a year from now, when I no longer hold this office, I'll be right there with you as a citizen, inspired by those voices of fairness and vision, or grit and good humor and kindness that have helped America travel so far . . . That's the America I know. That's the country we love. Clear-eyed. Bighearted. Optimistic that unarmed truth and unconditional love will have the final word. That's what makes me so hopeful about our future . . . And that's why I stand here confident as I have ever been that the State of our Union is strong!"

"Wait till he finds out the State of our Union was a heartbeat away from chaos and total destruction," Grabowski said, breaking the silence.

Farrell winced. His brows rose and fell. "Yeah, she almost pulled it off," he said, segueing into an angry growl. "Damn, I wanted her. I wanted 'em all. I wanted to bust their asses, prosecute the hell out of them and lock 'em up . . ."

"In solitary for a hundred fucking years," Ruben added.

"They *are* in solitary . . ." Katkov corrected with a pregnant pause. "For all eternity. We should take heart in the knowledge that Grusha and Agent Jones were their last victims, and that we brought their killers to justice."

"Yeah!" Scotto exclaimed with a fist pump. "Buried the scheming bastards at sea."

"Indeed, as a famous Russian writer once said," Katkov intoned, sounding profoundly philosophical, "'*Sem'ya, kotoraya shpionit vmeste umirayet vmeste*'."

"What the hell does that mean?" Farrell asked.

"The family that spies together, dies together," Katkov replied, deadpan.

"Come on," Farrell scoffed. "I read 'em all: Tolstoy, Dostoyevsky, Solzhenitsyn, Pushkin, Pasternak . . . no way it was one of them."

"You're quite right," Katkov said with an amused grin. "The famous Russian writer who said that . . . was me."

Epilogue

After the dust cleared, Katkov spent a few days in the District attending to personal affairs. He met with Joel Pollack, founder of Big Planet Comics, who had been evaluating Katkov's collection from the computer file his assistant, Nick, had downloaded. Katkov had had each comic graded, upon acquisition, by the Certified Guarantee Company, one of the best in the field, and had included the assigned grades with each listing. Pollack, confident of the collection's quality, made Katkov a high six-figure offer: twenty-five percent now, the balance upon receipt of the collection and visual confirmation of condition. Elated upon leaving the meeting, Katkov took a moment to call Vera with the good news, then, check in hand, he opened an account with an investment bank in the District, informed them another substantial deposit would be made in due course, and arranged for income to be disbursed to him as necessary.

The night before he was scheduled to return to Moscow, Scotto and Ruben gave him a send-off bash at Le Diplomate. Farrell, Carlsen, Grabowski, Caitlin, and Ruben's wife, Julie, were there. Pash, forced to return to New York to deal with the international bureaucratic complexities regarding the disposition of his wife's and parents' remains, and of the latter's estate, wasn't able to attend.

The skies were clear at Dulles International the next morning when Katkov's flight departed, and thanks to the unseasonably warm winter, cherry trees were just starting to bud throughout the District and in Baron Cameron Park just across Lake Anne from Casa Diaz, where Ruben and Julie were strolling.

"That roll-aboard suitcase full of cash brought the house down, didn't it?"

Ruben nodded, savoring it. "Yeah, set the whole endgame in motion."

"But you didn't get to lock her up, did you?"

"Can't win 'em all," Ruben said with shrug. "Look at them," he went on, gesturing to Amelia and Rafa, who had run on ahead with the dog. "That's what really matters, isn't it?"

Julie nodded and broke into a remorseful smile. "Yeah, I'm sorry about the other day, Ruben. I mean . . . I've . . . I've just been in denial," she said defensively. "I know going back home is unrealistic. Rafa . . . Amelia. They're great kids, and they're game, and incredibly adaptable, but their sense of adventure has its limits."

"Yeah, a week in Bogotá with your family and they were climbing the walls."

"They were like . . . like Eskimos in the desert," Julie said with a laugh. "This is all they know. Their friends, books, music, movies, their geeky gadgets, their rooms, they're all here—their lives are *here*."

"Yeah, they sure love their cyber caves, don't they?" Ruben prompted with a laugh. "They're dyed-in-the wool pain-in-the-ass American kids."

"So are we, Ruben," Julie said, her voice breaking slightly.

"Tell me about it. I was kind of getting into it a little with Rafa the other day. He looked me square in the eye and said, 'If you guys are serious about this Bogotá thing . . . Well, you know that rebellious teenage phase you think I skipped? Get ready.'"

The sun was burning off a morning haze when Katkov's flight landed at Sheremetyevo. Vera and Mika were waving like crazy as he emerged from Passport Control, pulling his bag. They ran into his arms, bear-hugging him until he couldn't breathe, then headed for the taxi line outside the terminal.

Chunks of ice were bobbing in the Moskva, which was flowing with ferocity when the taxi reached the city and made its way through central Moscow to Katkov's apartment. Vera and Mika watched in astonishment as he dropped his bags in the foyer, dashed to the bookcase, and unlocked the door to the hidden room where he kept his comic-book collection. "Yes!" he exclaimed upon opening it, his eyes wide with delight. "Yes, yes, yes, it's all here!" he went on, relieved that the collection was not only there but arranged, alphabetically, box by box, shelf by shelf as it had been before the FSB confiscated it. In the weeks that followed, he arranged for them to be properly packaged and shipped to Big Planet Comics, then turned his attention to more important matters.

Shafts of brilliant sunlight were streaming through the windowed domes of the Choral Synagogue as he walked Mika down the aisle. Alexa, Slava, Vitaly, *Novaya Gazeta* staffers, family members, friends, and even Chief

Investigator Churkin, resplendent in his favorite linen suit, filled the pews. Sasha and his best man stood on one side of the rabbi, and Michela and Vera, her maid of honor, stood on the other.

Once pronounced man and wife, Mika and Sasha led the way into the synagogue's event hall for the reception. The best man wasted no time roasting and toasting the groom, and the happy couple were soon sailing across the dance floor, and Katkov and Vera were among the other couples who joined them. After a few turns about the floor, Mika initiated a change of partners, and as Sasha and Vera whirled off in one direction, and she and Katkov in another, she put her head close to his and whispered, "I know, Nikasha. I know."

"You know what?" Katkov asked, sounding amused.

"That the father of the bride gave her away today . . ."

Katkov looked astonished, pleased, and puzzled all at the same time. "But how? Grusha told *me* just before . . . before . . ." He let it trail off and sighed. "She was going to tell *you* over dinner that night."

"Well, I've been going through her things," Mika explained. "And came across a box of old documents. A few had to do with . . . with the Bolshoi."

"Dmitri's physical . . ." Katkov said knowingly.

Mika nodded, leaned back from him, and smiled. "Yes, and in that moment, Dyadya Nikasha became Papa Nikasha."

"And maybe one day Dedushka Nikasha?" Katkov prompted with a mischievous grin.

"Dedushka?" Sasha said, overhearing as he tapped Nikolai on the shoulder, breaking in. "Mika? Is there something you haven't told me?" he teased, taking his bride in his arms.

"Triplets! I'm having triplets," Mika joked as they danced off, leaving Katkov alone in the middle of the floor. He was standing there lost in his thoughts when Churkin joined him. "I'd ask you to dance, but it seems our partnership went bust."

"What does that mean?" Katkov asked with laugh.

"That kryptonite turned out to be fairy dust," Churkin replied, taking Katkov aside. "I couldn't use it to compromise a file clerk, let alone Bortnikov."

"I know. It looked like the K was scheming to take over an American railroad—an international scandal if it got out. I thought you could use it to leverage him."

"That would have been nice," Churkin replied wistfully. "What happened?"

"Turned out to be a ploy, part of an SVA op to take out the entire U.S. government and population of Washington, DC, with a trainload of lethal chlorine."

"Not so nice," Churkin said with a facetious chuckle. "So, let's see . . ." he went on, as if making a calculation, "between that debacle and my Herculean effort to rescue your pension plan, you owe me a couple, maybe more."

"Don't hold your breath, Sergei," Katkov said, leaving no doubt he meant it. "My pen's run dry. I'm retiring. Vera and I are going to travel. See the world. Matter of fact, we just did an online rental for an *appartamento* in *bella Venezia,* as she calls it."

"Come on, Katkov," Churkin scolded. "That's just another pile of fairy dust and you know it. You're going to die at your keyboard, typing furiously, in yet another futile attempt to make Russia a better place."

"That's exactly what I told Grusha when she started talking about kvelling over her grandchildren."

"Decided, maybe, she was onto something?"

Katkov nodded sadly.

"Yeah, well," Churkin said with a sly smile, "good luck."

"Thanks, same to you," Katkov said with a cagey grin. He slipped a flash drive from a pocket and offered it to Churkin. "This might help."

Churkin's eyes narrowed. "What the hell is that?"

"A gift from Grusha."

"Grusha?"

Katkov nodded. "There's enough kryptonite in her files to keep Bortnikov and his Rottweilers off your back for long time. Double-click on 'Wonder Woman.'"

Churkin's eyes widened with delight. "She was, wasn't she?"

Katkov smiled in reflection. "One of these days, she's going to come swooping down into the Kremlin with her Lasso of Truth and Bracelets of Submission and bring Putin to his knees."

In Villa Ruchey in Sochi overlooking the Black Sea, Vladimir Putin was circling the conference-room table like an angry panther. Lavrov, Bortnikov, and other staff members sat, cringing in anticipation, staring blankly at the cable-news broadcasts on the TV monitors.

"Not only did the code-red, priority-one op fail! Not only did we fail to destabilize and destroy the American government," Putin exclaimed, his voice rising in anger with each phrase. "We also lost three of our most effective sleeper agents!"

"Yes, sir," Lavrov said. "Svetlana Nikolshevskaya was one of the best, if not *the* best cyber warrior in SVA, FSB, and GRU combined. She was a rare—"

"I don't need to be reminded of that!" Putin snapped

"If I may, sir," Bortnikov said timorously. "I'm forced to disagree with my esteemed colleague. We have many equally skilled cyber warriors, code writers, and hackers in our employ, and though we failed to *destroy* the United States government, it might be to even greater advantage to use those assets to *gain control* of it instead."

"Control of it?" Putin snapped. "I've been working on that for decades!"

"Really, Alexie," Lavrov chided as he got to his feet, letting his chest fill. "Either you're holding some sort of trump card the rest of us are unaware of, or—"

"Perfect choice of words!" Bortnikov interrupted. "You see, I was thinking—"

"Enough thinking, dammit!" Putin erupted. "Get to the fucking point!"

"Well, sir, keeping those cyber assets that I mentioned in mind"—Bortnikov paused and glanced toward one of the TV monitors, where Donald Trump, who had become a serious contender for the Republican nomination, was holding a raucous campaign rally—"how would you like to decide who becomes the next president of the United States?"

About the Author

Greg Dinallo, a New York Times Notable Author, has published six novels: *Rockets' Red Glare*, *Purpose of Evasion*, *Final Answers*, *Touched by Fire*, *Red Ink*, *The German Suitcase*, and *Bridge of Lies*, Dinallo's latest novel. He has also written and produced many dramatic programs and movies for television. He lives in Greenwich Village, New York.

GREG DINALLO

FROM OPEN ROAD MEDIA

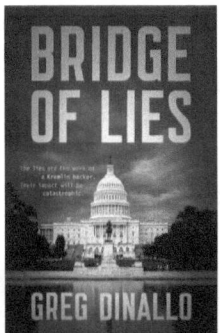

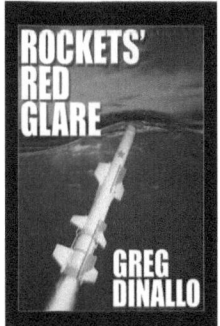

Find a full list of our authors and
titles at www.openroadmedia.com

FOLLOW US
@OpenRoadMedia

EARLY BIRD BOOKS

FRESH DEALS, DELIVERED DAILY

Love to read?
Love great sales?

Get fantastic deals on
bestselling ebooks delivered
to your inbox every day!

Sign up today at
earlybirdbooks.com/book

www.ingramcontent.com/pod-product-compliance
Lightning Source LLC
Chambersburg PA
CBHW060423030726
47495CB00003B/705